*Another feast for fans of
America's favorite small town*

"In *A New Song*, Karon anoints us
with her healing oil and, along the way,
comforts and entertains us."

—*The Charlotte Observer*

PENGUIN BOOKS

A NEW SONG

Jan Karon writes "to give readers an extended family, and to applaud the extraordinary beauty of ordinary lives." She is the author of eight Mitford novels, *At Home in Mitford; A Light in the Window; These High, Green Hills; Out to Canaan; A New Song; A Common Life; In This Mountain;* and *Shepherds Abiding*, all available from Penguin. She is also the author of *Patches of Godlight: Father Tim's Favorite Quotes; The Mitford Snowmen: A Christmas Story; Esther's Gift;* and *The Trellis and the Seed.* Her children's books include *Miss Fannie's Hat* and *Jeremy: The Tale of an Honest Bunny.* Coming from Viking in fall 2005 is *Light from Heaven*, the ninth novel in the Mitford Years Series.

Now you can visit Mitford online at
www.mitfordbooks.com

Enjoy the latest news from the little town with the big heart including a complete archive of the *More from Mitford* newsletters, the Mitford Years Readers Guide, and much more.

The Mitford Years

A New Song

JAN KARON

PENGUIN BOOKS

PENGUIN BOOKS
Published by the Penguin Group
Penguin Group (USA) Inc., 375 Hudson Street, New York, New York 10014, U.S.A.
Penguin Group (Canada), 10 Alcorn Avenue, Toronto,
Ontario, Canada M4V 3B2 (a division of Pearson Penguin Canada Inc.)
Penguin Books Ltd, 80 Strand, London WC2R 0RL, England
Penguin Ireland, 25 St Stephen's Green, Dublin 2,
Ireland (a division of Penguin Books Ltd)
Penguin Group (Australia), 250 Camberwell Road, Camberwell,
Victoria 3124, Australia (a division of Pearson Australia Group Pty Ltd)
Penguin Books India Pvt Ltd, 11 Community Centre,
Panchsheel Park, New Delhi – 110 017, India
Penguin Group (NZ), Cnr Airborne and Rosedale Roads,
Albany, Auckland, New Zealand (a division of Pearson New Zealand Ltd)
Penguin Books (South Africa) (Pty) Ltd, 24 Sturdee Avenue,
Rosebank, Johannesburg 2196, South Africa

Penguin Books Ltd, Registered Offices: 80 Strand, London WC2R 0RL, England

First published in the United States of America by Viking Penguin,
a member of Penguin Putnam Inc., 1999
Published in Penguin Books 2000
This edition published in 2005

1 3 5 7 9 10 8 6 4 2

Copyright © Jan Karon, 1999
Illustrations copyright © Penguin Putnam Inc., 1999
All rights reserved

Illustrations by Donna Kae Nelson

Grateful acknowledgment is made for permission to reprint excerpts from the following copyright works: "If Once You Have Slept on an Island" from *Taxis and Toadstools* by Rachel Field. Copyright © 1926 by The Century Company. Used by permission of Random House Children's Books, a division of Random House Inc. "God's Way" by Kao Chung-Ming, appearing in *Your Will Be Done,* Youth Desk of Christian Conference of Asia, 1986. By permission of the author.

PUBLISHER'S NOTE
This is a work of fiction. Names, characters, places, and incidents either are the product of the author's imagination or are used fictitiously, and any resemblance to actual persons, living or dead, business establishments, events, or locales is entirely coincidental.

THE LIBRARY OF CONGRESS HAS CATALOGED
THE HARDCOVER EDITION AS FOLLOWS:
Karon, Jan, date
A New Song / Jan Karon.
p.   cm.
ISBN 0-670-87810-3 (hc.)
ISBN 0 14 30.3507 X (pbk.)
1. Mitford (N.C.: Imaginary place)—Fiction.   2. City and town life—Fiction.
3. Clergy—North Carolina—Fiction.   4. Christian fiction, American.
5. Domestic fiction, American.   I. Title.
PS3561.A678N49   1999
813'.054—dc21   98-55141

Printed in the United States of America
Set in Times Roman
Designed by Francesca Belanger

In memory of my aunt,
Helen Coyner Cloer,
who, when I was ten years old,
typed my first manuscript.
October 4, 1917–October 12, 1998
". . . . we shall be like Him . . ."

1 John 3:2

Sing unto the Lord a new song, and His praise from the end of the earth, ye that go down to the sea, and all that is therein, the isles and the inhabitants thereof.

Isaiah 42:10, KJV

Acknowledgments

Gentle Reader,

In the Mitford books, there are nearly as many acknowledgments as there are characters in the story. That's because I try to thank absolutely everyone who helps make the story more authentic. Sometimes I toss in a name out of sheer sentiment, like that of my sixth-grade teacher, Etta Phillips, who comes to my book signings and looks as youthful as ever. Many readers enjoy these acknowledgments because they occasionally find the name of an old school chum, friend, or family member.

Sometimes, they even find themselves.

Warm thanks to:

Brother Francis Andrews, BSG; Rev. Roy M. King; Flyin' George Ronan; John Ed McConnell; Ralph Emery; Dr. Carl Hurley; Loyal Jones and Billy Edd Wheeler; Bonnie Setzer; Mary Richardson; Fr. John Mangrum; Fr. Jeffrey Scott Miller; Dr. George Grant; Austin Gragg; Roger David Craig; Frank Gilbert and his Mustang convertible; the Mitford Appreciation Society; Gwynne Crosley; Rev. Gale Cooper; Sue Yates; Dr. David Ludwig; Dan Blair; Linda Foster; Will Lankenau; William McDonald Parker; Blowing Rock police chief, Owen

Tolbert; Officer Dennis Swanson; Bishop Christopher Fitz-Simons Allison; James F. Carlisle, Sr.; Betsy Barnes; Rayburn and Sheila Farmer; Fr. Scott Oxford; Bishop William C. Frey; Bishop Keith Ackerman; Rev. Stephen J. Hines; Larry Powell; Barry Hubert; Derald West; Sandy McNabb; Donna Kae Nelson for her oustanding cover illustrations for the Mitford series; Captain Weyland Baum, early keeper of the Currituck Light; Billy McCaskill; Major John Coffindaffer; "Bee" Baum; Drs. Melanie and Greg Hawthorne; John L. Beard; Greg and Kathy Fishel; Frank LePore; Garry Oliver; my first-grade teacher, Mrs. Downs; my fifth-grade teacher, Mrs. Sherrill; Dr. Michael C. Ain; Captain Mike Clarkin of *Fishin' Frenzy*; First Mate Matthew Winchester; Dr. Sue P. Frye; Ross and Linda Dodington; Fr. Richard B. Bass; Colonel Ron and Cathey Fallows; Murray Whisnant; Robert Williams; Chris Williams; Michael Freeland; Rabbi David and Barbara Kline; Officer Kris Merithew; Bruce Luke; Johnny Lentz; Judith Burns; Wonderland Books; Tom Enterline; J.W.D.; Loretta Cornejo; Tex Harrison; Jerry Gregg; Officer Tracy Toler; Jeff Cobb; Walter Green; and Anita Chappell.

Special thanks to:
Dr. Bunky Davant, medical counsel to Mitford and Whitecap; Tony DiSanti, legal counsel to Mitford; Grace Episcopal Church, the lovely architectural model for St. John's in the Grove; Fr. Charles Gill, rector of St. Andrews by the Sea; Fr. James Harris, friend and helper; Judy Bistany South, for her warm encouragement over the years; my valued assistant, Laura Watts; Captain Horace Whitfield, master of the *Elizabeth II*; hardworking booksellers everywhere; and, as always, my devoted readers.

Contents

xii　　　　　　　*Contents*

A New Song

CHAPTER ONE

Angel of Light

Dappled by its movement among the branches of a Japanese cherry, the afternoon light entered the study unhindered by draperies or shades.

It spilled through the long bank of windows behind the newly slipcovered sofa, warming the oak floor and quickening the air with the scent of freshly milled wood.

Under the spell of the June light, a certain luster and radiance appeared to emerge from every surface.

The tall chest, once belonging to Father Tim's clergyman great-grandfather, had undergone a kind of rebirth. Beneath a sheen of lemon oil, the dense grain of old walnut, long invisible in the dark rectory hallway next door, became sharply defined. Even the awkward inscription of the letter M, carved by a pocketknife, could now be discovered near one of the original drawer pulls.

But it was the movement and play of the light, beyond its searching incandescence, that caused Father Tim to anticipate its daily arrival as others might look for a sunrise or sunset.

He came eagerly to this large, new room, as if long deprived of light or air, still incredulous that such a bright space might exist, and especially that it might exist for his own pursuits since retiring six months ago from Lord's Chapel.

As the rector of Mitford's Episcopal parish, he had lived next door in the former rectory for sixteen years. Now he was a rector no more, yet he owned the rectory; it had been bought and paid for with cash from his mother's estate, and he and Cynthia were living in the little yellow house.

Of course—he kept forgetting—this house wasn't so little anymore; he and his visionary wife had added 1,270 square feet to its diminutive proportions.

Only one thing remained constant. The house was still yellow, though freshly painted with Cynthia's longtime favorite, Wild Forsythia, and trimmed with a glossy coat of the dark green Highland Hemlock.

"Cheers!" said his wife, appearing in jeans and a denim shirt, toting glasses of lemonade on a tray. They had recently made it a ritual to meet here every afternoon, for what they called the Changing of the Light.

He chuckled. "We mustn't tell anyone what we do for fun."

"You can count on it! Besides, who'd ever believe that we sit around watching the light change?" She set the tray on the table, next to a packet of mail.

"We could do worse."

They thumped onto the sofa, which had been carted through the hedge from the rectory.

"One more week," he said, disbelieving.

"Ugh. Heaven help us!" She put her head back and closed her eyes. "How daunting to move to a place we've never seen . . . for an unknown length of time . . . behind a priest who's got them used to the guitar!"

He took her hand, laughing. "If anyone can do it, you can. How many cartons of books are we shipping down there, anyway?"

"Fourteen, so far."

"And not a shelf to put them on."

"We're mad as hatters!" she said with feeling. During the past week, his wife had worked like a Trojan to close up the yellow house, do most of the packing, and leave their financial affairs in order. He, on the other hand, had been allowed to troop around town saying his goodbyes, sipping tea like a country squire and trying to keep his mitts off the cookies and cakes that were proffered at every turn.

He had even dropped into Happy Endings Bookstore and bought two new books to take to Whitecap, a fact that he would never, even on penalty of death, reveal to Cynthia Kavanagh.

She looked at him and smiled. "I've prayed to see you sit and relax like this, without rushing to beat out a thousand fires. Just think how the refreshment of the last few weeks will help you, dearest, when we do the interim on the island. Who knows, after all, what lies ahead and what strength you may need?"

He gulped his lemonade. Who knew, indeed?

"The jig, however, is definitely up," she said, meaning it. "Next week . . ."

"I know. Change the furnace filter next door, weed the

perennial beds, fix the basement step, pack my clothes . . . I've got the entire, unexpurgated list written down."

"Have your suit pressed," she said, "buy two knit shirts—nothing with an alligator, I fervently hope—and find the bicycle pump for Dooley."

"Right!" He was actually looking forward to the adrenaline of their last week in Mitford.

"By the way," she said, "I've been thinking. Instead of loading the car in bits and pieces, just pile everything by the garage door. That way, I can check it twice, and we'll load at the last minute."

"But it would be simpler to—"

"Trust me," she said, smiling.

Barnabas would occupy the rear seat, with Violet's cage on the floor, left side. They'd load the right side with linens and towels, the trunk would be filled to the max, and they'd lash on top whatever remained.

"Oh, yes, Timothy, one more thing . . . stay out of the bookstore!"

She peered at him with that no-nonsense gleam in her sapphire eyes, a gleam that, for all its supposed authority, stirred a fire in him. As a man with a decidedly old-shoe nature, he had looked forward to the old-shoe stage of their marriage. So far, however, it hadn't arrived. His blond and sensible wife had an unpredictable streak that kept the issues of life from settling into humdrum patterns.

"Anything wonderful in the mail?" she asked.

"I don't know, I just fetched it in. Why don't you have a look?"

His wife's fascination with mail was greater even than his own, which was considerable. William James, in his opinion, had hit the nail on the head. "As long as there are postmen," James declared, "life will have zest."

"Oh, look! Lovely! A letter from Whitecap, and it's to *me!*"

He watched her rip open the envelope.

"My goodness, listen to this. . . .

" '*Dear Mrs. Kavanagh, We are looking forward with great enthusiasm to your interim stay in our small island parish, and trust that all is going smoothly as you prepare to join us at the end of June.*

" '*Our ECW has been very busy readying Dove Cottage for your stay at Whitecap, and all you need to bring is bed linens for the two bedrooms, as we discussed, and any towels and pillows which will make you feel at home.*

" '*We have supplied the kitchen cupboards with new pots, and several of us have lent things of our own, so that you and Father Kavanagh may come without much disruption to your household in Mitford. Sam has fixed the electric can opener, but I hear you are a fine cook and probably won't need it, ha ha.*

" '*Oh, yes. Marjorie Lamb and I have done a bit of work in the cottage gardens, which were looking woefully forlorn after years of neglect. We found a dear old-fashioned rose, which I hear your husband enjoys, and liberated it from the brambles. It is now climbing up your trellis instead of running into the street! We expect the hydrangeas and crepe myrtle to be in full glory for your arrival, though the magnolias in the churchyard will, alas, be out of bloom.*

" '*Complete directions are enclosed, which Marjorie's husband, Leonard, assures me should take you from Mitford straight to the door of Dove Cottage without a snare. (Leonard once traveled on the road selling plumbing supplies.)*

" '*Please notice the red arrow I have drawn on the*

map. You must be very careful at this point to watch for the street sign, as it is hidden by a dreadful hedge which the property owner refuses to trim. I have thought of trimming it myself, but Sam says that would be meddling.

" 'We hope you will not object to a rather gregarious greeting committee, who are bent on giving you a parish-wide luau the day following your arrival. I believe I have talked them out of wearing grass skirts, but that embarrassing notion could possibly break forth again.

" 'When Father Morgan joined us several years ago, he, too, came in the summer and was expecting a nice holiday at the beach. I'm sure you've been warned that summer is our busiest time, what with the tourists who swell our little church to bursting and push us to two services! We all take our rest in the winter when one must hunker down and live off the nuts we've gathered!

" 'Bishop Harvey was thrilled to learn from Bishop Cullen how greatly you and Father Kavanagh were appreciated by your parish in Mitford! We shall all do our utmost to make you feel as welcome as the flowers in May, as my dear mother used to say.

" 'Goodness! I hope you'll forgive the length of this letter! Since childhood, I have loved the feel of a pen flowing over paper, and often get carried away.

" 'We wish you and Father Timothy safe travel.

" 'Yours sincerely,

" 'Marion Fieldwalker, vestry member of St. John's in the Grove, and Pres. Episcopal Church Women

" 'PS. I am the librarian of Whitecap Island Community Library (35 years) and do pray you might be willing to give a reading this fall from one of your famous Violet books. Your little books stay checked out,

*and I believe every child on the island has read them at
least twice!' "*

His wife flushed with approval. "There! How uplifting! Marion sounds lovely! And just think, dearest—
trellises and old roses!"

"Not to mention new saucepans," he said, admiring
the effort of his future parishioners.

She drank from her perspiring glass and continued to
sort through the pile. "Timothy, look at his handwriting.
He's finally stopped printing and gone to cursive!"

"Let me see. . . ."

Definitely a new look in the handwriting department, and a distinct credit to Dooley Barlowe's Virginia
prep schooling. Miss Sadie's big bucks, forked over annually, albeit posthumously, were continuing to put spit
and polish on the red-haired mountain boy who'd come
to live with him at the rectory five years ago.

" *'Hey,' "* he read aloud from Dooley's letter, " *'I
have thought about it a lot and I would like to stay in
Mitford and work for Avis this summer and make money
to get a car and play softball with the Reds.*

" *'I don't want to go to the beach.*

" *'Don't be mad or upset or anything. I can live in
the basement with Harley like you said, and we will be
fine. Puny could maybe come and do the laundry or we
could do stuff ourselves and eat in Wesley or at the Grill
or Harley could cook.*

" *'I will come down to that island for either Thanksgiving or Christmas like we talked about.*

" *'Thanks for letting me go home from school with
Jimmy Duncan, I am having a great time, he drives a
Wrangler. His mom drives a Range Rover and his dad
has a BMW 850. That's what I would like to have. A
Wrangler, I mean. I'll get home before you leave, Mr.*

Duncan is driving me on his way to a big meeting. Say hey to Barnabas and Violet. Thanks for the money. Love, Dooley.' "

"Oh, well," said his wife, looking disappointed. "I'm sure he wanted to be close to his friends. . . ."

"Right. And his brother and sister. . . ."

She sighed. "Pretty much what we expected."

He felt disappointed himself that the boy wouldn't be coming to Whitecap for the summer, but they'd given him a choice and the choice had been made. Besides, he learned a couple of years ago not to let Dooley Barlowe's summer pursuits wreck his own enjoyment of that fleeting season.

It was the business about cars that concerned him. . . . Dooley had turned sixteen last February, and would hit Mitford in less than three days, packing a bona fide driver's license.

"Knock, knock!" Emma Newland blew down the hall and into the study. "Don't get up," she said, commandeering the room. "You'll never believe this!"

His former part-time church secretary, who had retired when he retired, had clearly been unable to let go of her old job. She made it her business to visit twice a week and help out for a couple of hours, whether he needed it or not.

"I do it for th' Lord," she had stated flatly, refusing any thanks. Though Cynthia usually fled the room when she arrived, he rather looked forward to Emma's visits, and to the link she represented to Lord's Chapel, which was now under the leadership of its own interim priest.

Emma stood with her hands on her hips and peered over her glasses. "Y'all won't believe what I found on th' Internet. Three guesses!"

"Excuse me!" said Cynthia, bolting from the sofa.

"I'll just bring you a lemonade, Emma, and get back to work. I've *gobs* of books to pack."

"Guess!" Emma insisted, playing a game that he found both mindless and desperately aggravating.

"A recipe for mixing your own house paint?"

"Oh, *please*," she said, looking disgusted. "You're not trying."

"The complete works of Fulgentius of Ruspe!"

"Who?"

"I give up," he said, meaning it.

"I found another Mitford! It's in England, and it has a church as old as mud, not to mention a castle!" She looked triumphant, as if she'd just squelched an invasion of Moors.

"Really? Terrific! I suppose it's where those writing Mitfords came from—"

"No connection. They were from th' Cotswolds, this place is up north somewhere. I had a stack of stuff I printed out, but Snickers sat on th' whole bloomin' mess after playin' in the creek, and I have to print it out again."

"Aha."

"OK, guess what else!"

"Dadgummit, Emma. You know I hate this."

She said what she always said. "It's good for you, keeps your brain active."

As far as she was concerned, he'd gone soft in the head since retiring six months ago.

"Just tell me and get it over with."

"Oh, come on! Try at least one guess. Here's a clue. It's about the election in November."

"Esther's stepping down and Andrew Gregory's going to run."

She frowned. "How'd you know that?"

"I haven't gone deaf and blind, for Pete's sake. I do get around."

"I suppose you also know," said Emma, hoping he didn't, "that the restaurant at Fernbank is openin' the night before you leave."

"Right. We've been invited."

She thumped into the slipcovered wing chair and peered at him as if he were a beetle on a pin. Though she'd certainly never say such a thing, she believed he was existing in a kind of purgatory between the inarguable heaven of Lord's Chapel and the hell of a strange parish in a strange place where the temperature was a hundred and five in the shade.

"Will you have a secretary down there?" she asked, suspicious.

"I don't think so. Small parish, you know."

"How small can it be?"

"Oh, fifty, sixty people."

"I thought Bishop Cullen was your *friend*," she sniffed. She'd never say so, but in her heart of hearts, she had hoped her boss of sixteen years would be given a big church in a big city, and make a comeback for himself. As it was, he trotted up the hill to Hope House and the hospital every livelong morning, appearing so cheerful about the whole thing that she recognized it at once as a cover-up.

Cynthia returned with a glass of lemonade and a plate of shortbread, which she put on the table next to Emma. "I'll be in the studio if anyone needs me. With all the books we're taking, we may sink the island!"

"A regular Atlantis," said Father Tim.

"Speakin' of books," Emma said to his wife, "are you doin' a new one?"

"Not if I can help it!"

He laughed as Cynthia trotted down the hall. "She usually can't help it." He expected a new children's book to break forth from his energetic wife any day now. Indeed, didn't she have a history of starting one when life was upside down and backward?

Emma munched on a piece of shortbread, showering crumbs in her lap. "Do you have those letters ready for me to do on th' computer?"

"Not quite. I wasn't expecting you 'til in the morning."

"I'm coming in th' morning, I just wanted to run by and tell you all th' late-breakin' news. But," she said, arching one eyebrow, "I haven't told you everything, I saved th' best 'til last."

His dog wandered into the study and crashed at his master's feet, panting.

"If you say you already know this, I'll never tell you another thing as long as I live. On my way here, I saw Mule Skinner, he said he's finally rented your house."

She drew herself up, pleased, and gulped the lemonade.

"Terrific! Great timing!" He might have done a jig.

"He said there hadn't been time to call you, he'll call you tonight, but it's not a family with kids like Cynthia wanted."

"Oh, well . . ." He was thrilled that someone had finally stepped forward to occupy the rectory. He and Harley had worked hard over the last few months to make it a strong rental property, putting new vinyl flooring in the kitchen, replacing the stair runners, installing a new toilet in the master bath and a new threshold at the front door . . . the list had been endless. And costly.

"It's a woman."

"I can't imagine what one person would want with all that house to rattle around in."

"How quickly you forget! *You* certainly rattled around in there for a hundred years."

"True. Well. I'll get the whole story from Mule."

"He said she didn't mind a bit that Harley would be livin' in the basement, she just wanted to know if he plays loud rock music."

Emma rattled the ice in her glass, gulped the last draught, and got up to leave. "Before I forget, you won't believe what else I found on th' Internet—church bulletins! You ought to read some of th' foolishness they put out there for God an' everybody to see."

She fished a piece of paper from her handbag. " 'Next Sunday,' " she read, " 'a special collection will be taken to defray the cost of a new carpet. All those wishin' to do somethin' on the new carpet will come forward and do so.' "

He hooted with laughter.

"How 'bout this number: 'Don't let worry kill you, let th' church help.' "

He threw his head back and laughed some more. Emma's life in cyberspace definitely had an upside.

"By th' way, are you takin' Barnabas down there?" She enunciated "down there" as if it were a region beneath the crust of the earth.

"We are."

"I don't know how you could do that to an animal. Look at all that fur, enough to stuff a mattress."

Barnabas yawned hugely and thumped his tail on the floor.

"You won't even be able to *see* those horrible sandspurs that will jump in there by th' hundreds, not to mention *lodge in his paws.*"

Emma waited for an argument, a rationale—something.

Did he have no conscience? "And th' *heat* down there, you'll have to shave 'im bald."

Father Tim strolled across the room to walk her to the door. "Thanks for coming, Emma. Tell Harold hello. I'll see you in the morning."

His unofficial secretary stumped down the hallway and he followed.

He was holding the front door open and biting his tongue when she turned and looked at him. Her eyes were suddenly red and filled with tears.

"I'll miss you!" she blurted.

"You *will?*"

She hurried down the front steps, sniffing, searching her bag for a Hardee's napkin she knew was in there someplace.

He felt stricken. "Emma! We'll . . . we'll have jelly doughnuts in the morning!"

"*I'll* have jelly doughnuts, *you'll* have dry toast! We don't want to ship you down there in a coma!"

She got in her car at the curb, slammed the door, gunned the motor, and roared up Wisteria Lane.

For one fleeting moment, he'd completely forgotten his blasted diabetes.

$\sim$

"I'm out of here," he said, kissing his wife.

"Get him to leave something for the island breezes to flow through, darling. Don't let him cut it all off."

"You always say that."

"Yes, well, you come home looking like a skinned rabbit. I don't know what Joe Ivey *does* to you."

Considering what Fancy Skinner had done to him time and time again, Joe Ivey could do anything he wanted.

"Leavin' us, are you?" Joe ran a comb through the hair over Father Tim's left ear and snipped.

"Afraid so."

"Leavin' us in th' lurch is more like it."

"Now, Joe. Did I preach to you when you went off to Graceland and left me high and dry?"

Joe cackled. "Thank God I come to m' senses and quit that fool job. An' in th' nick of time, too. I'm finally about t' clean up what Fancy Skinner done to people's heads around here, which in your case looked like she lowered your ears a foot an' a half."

"My wife says don't cut it too short."

"If I listened to what wives say, I'd of been out of business forty years ago. Do you know how hot it gits down there?"

If he'd been asked that once, he'd been asked it a thousand times. There was hardly anything mountain people despised more than a "hot" place.

"I'm an old Mississippi boy, you know."

"An' th' mosquitoes . . . !" Joe whistled. "Man alive!"

"Right there," he said, as Joe started working around his collar. "Just clean it up a little right there, don't cut it—"

Joe proceeded to cut it. Oh, well. Joe Ivey had always done exactly as he pleased with Father Tim's hair, just like Fancy Skinner. What was the matter with people who serviced hair, anyway? He had never, in all his years, been able to figure it out.

"I hear it's a ten-hour trot t' get there," said Joe, clearly fixated on the inconvenience of it all.

"Closer to twelve, if you stop for gas and lunch."

"You could go t' New York City in less'n that. Prob'ly run up an back."

"There's a thought."

Joe trimmed around his customer's right ear. "I'm gettin' t' where I'd like t' talk . . ."—Joe cleared his throat—"about what happened up at Graceland."

"Aha."

"I ain't told this to a soul, not even Winnie."

There was a long pause.

Father Tim waited, inhaling the fragrance from Sweet Stuff Bakery, just beyond the thin wall. Joe's sister, Winnie, and her husband, Thomas, were baking baklava, and he was starting to salivate.

"You couldn't ever mention this to anybody," said Joe. "You'd have to swear on a stack of Bibles."

"I can't do that, but I give you my word."

Joe let his breath out in a long sigh. "Well, sir, there towards th' end, I got to where I thought Elvis might be . . ."

"Might be what?"

"You know. *Alive.*"

"No!"

"I ain't proud t' admit it. Thing is, I was gettin' in th' brandy pretty heavy when I went up there. My sister's husband, he was laid off and things was pretty tight. Plus, their house ain't exactly th' Biltmore Estate when it comes to room, so ever' once in a while, I'd ride around after supper t' give Vern and my sister a little time to theirselves."

"That was thoughtful."

"I took to lookin' for Elvis ever'where I went, 'specially at th' barbecue place, they all said he was a fool for barbecue. My sister, when she heard I was lookin' to sight Elvis, she started pourin' my brandy down th' toilet. A man can't hardly live with somebody as pours 'is brandy down th' toilet."

"That would create tension, all right." Heaven knows, he'd tried for years to get Joe to quit sucking down alcohol, but Joe had told him to mind his own business. Something, however, had happened in Memphis that sent his barber home dry as a bone.

"Then one night I was drivin' around, I said to myself, I said, Joe, Elvis wouldn't be cruisin' through a drive-in pickin' up a chopped pork with hot sauce, he'd *send* somebody. So I said, if *I* was Elvis, where would I be at?

"Seem like somethin' told me to go back to Graceland, it was about eleven o'clock at night, so I drove on over there and parked across th' street with my lights off. I hate to tell you, but I had a pint in the glove department, and I was takin' a little pull now and again."

Joe took a bottle off the cabinet and held it above his customer's head. "You want Sea Breeze?"

"Is the Pope a Catholic?"

"First thing you know, I seen somethin' at th' top of the yard. There's this big yard, you know, that spreads out behind th' gate an all. It was somethin' white, and it . . ."—Joe cleared his throat—"it was movin' around."

"Aha."

Joe blasted his scalp with Sea Breeze and vigorously rubbed it in. "You ain't goin' to believe this."

"Try me."

Joe's hands stopped massaging his head. In the mirror, Father Tim could see his barber's chin quivering.

"It was Elvis . . . in a white suit."

"Come on!"

"Mowin' 'is yard."

"No way!"

"I said you wouldn't believe it."

"Why would he mow his yard when he could pay somebody else to do it? And why would he do it in a suit, much less a *white* suit? And why would he do it at *night!*"

Joe's eyes were misty. He shook his head, marveling. "I never have figured it out."

"Well, well." What could he say?

"I set there watchin'. He'd mow a strip one way, then mow a strip th' other way."

"Gas or push?"

"Push."

"How could he see?" Father Tim asked, mildly impatient.

"There was this . . . *glow* all around him."

"Aha."

"Then, first thing you know . . ."—Joe's voice grew hushed—"he th'owed up 'is hand and waved at me."

Father Tim was speechless.

"Here I'd been lookin' to see 'im for I don't know how long, and it scared me s' bad when I finally done it, I slung th' bottle in th' bushes and quit drinkin' on th' spot."

His barber drew a deep breath and stood tall. "I ain't touched a drop since, and ain't wanted to."

Father Tim was convinced this was the gospel truth. Still, he had a question.

"So, Joe, what's that, ah . . . bottle sitting over there by the hair tonic?"

"I keep that for my customers. You don't want a little snort, do you?"

"I pass. But tell me this . . . any regrets about coming back to Mitford?"

"Not ary one, as my daddy used to say. It's been a

year, now, since I hauled out of Memphis and come home to Mitford, and my old trade has flocked back like a drove of guineas. Winnie gave me this nice room to set my chair in, and th' Lord's give me back my health."

Joe took the cape from his customer's shoulders and shook it out. "Yessir, you're lookin' at a happy man."

"And so are you!" said Father Tim. "So are you!"

After all, didn't he have a new haircut, a new parish, and a whole new life just waiting to begin?

He couldn't help himself.

As the bells at Lord's Chapel pealed three o'clock, he turned into Happy Endings Bookstore as if on automatic pilot. He had five whole minutes to kill before jumping in the car and roaring off to Wesley for a bicycle pump, since Dooley's had turned up missing.

"Just looking," he told Hope Winchester. Hope's ginger-colored cat, Margaret, peered at him suspiciously as he raced through General Fiction, hung a right at Philosophy, and skidded left into Religion, where the enterprising Hope had recently installed a shelf of rare books.

He knew for a fact that the only bookstore on Whitecap Island was in the rear of a bait and tackle shop. They would never in a hundred years have Arthur Quiller-Couch's *On the Art of Reading,* which he had eyed for a full week. It was now or never.

His hand shot out to the hard-to-find Quiller-Couch volume, but was instantly drawn back. No, a thousand times no. If his wife knew he was buying more books to schlepp to Whitecap, he'd be dead meat.

He sighed.

"Better to take it now than call long-distance and have me ship it down there for three dollars."

Hope appeared next to him, looking wise in new tortoiseshell glasses.

No doubt about it, Hope had his number.

He raked the book off the shelf, and snatched Jonathan Edwards's *The Freedom of the Will* from another. He noted that his forehead broke out in a light sweat.

Oh, well, while he was at it . . .

He grabbed a copy of Lewis's *Great Divorce,* which had wandered from his own shelves, never to be seen again, and went at a trot to the cash register.

"I'm sure you're excited about your party!" Hope said, ringing the sale. Margaret jumped onto the counter and glowered at him. Why did cats hate his guts? What had he ever done to cats? Didn't he buy his wife's cat only the finest, most ridiculously priced chicken niblets in a fancy tinfoil container?

"Party? What party?"

"Why, the party Uncle Billy and Miss Rose are giving you and Cynthia!"

"I don't know anything about a party." Had someone told him and he'd forgotten?

"It's the biggest thing in the world to them. They've never given a party in their whole lives, but they want to do this because they hold you in the most edacious regard."

"Well!" He was nearly speechless. "When is it supposed to be?"

"Tomorrow night, of course." She looked at him oddly.

Tomorrow night they were working a list as long as his arm, not to mention shopping for groceries to feed

Dooley Barlowe a welcome-home dinner of steak, fries, and chocolate pie.

He mopped his forehead with a handkerchief. He'd be glad to leave town and get his life in order again.

"I'll look into it," he muttered, shelling out cash for the forbidden books. "And if you don't mind, that is, if you happen to see Cynthia, you might not mention that, ah . . ."

Hope Winchester smiled. She would never say a word to the priest's wife about his buying more books. Just as she certainly wouldn't mention to him that Cynthia had dashed in only this morning to buy copies of Celia Thaxter's *My Island Garden,* and the hardback of *Ira Sleeps Over.*

⁓

He knocked on the screen door of the small, life-estate apartment in the rear of the town museum.

"Uncle Billy! Miss Rose! Anybody home?"

He couldn't imagine the old couple giving a party; his mind was perfectly boggled by the notion. Rose Watson had been diagnosed as schizophrenic decades ago, and although on daily medication, her mood swings were fierce and unpredictable. To make matters worse for her long-suffering husband, she was quickly going deaf as a stone, but refused to wear hearing aids. "There's aids enough in this world," she said menacingly.

He put his nose against the screen and saw Uncle Billy sleeping in a chair next to an electric fan, his cane between his legs. Father Tim hated to wake him, but what was he to do? He knocked again.

Uncle Billy opened his eyes and looked around the kitchen, startled.

"It's me, Uncle Billy!"

"Lord if hit ain't th' preacher!" The old man grinned toward the door, his gold tooth gleaming. "Rose!" he shouted. "Hit's th' preacher!"

"He's not supposed to be here 'til tomorrow!" Miss Rose bellowed from the worn armchair by the refrigerator.

Uncle Billy grabbed his cane and slowly pulled himself to a standing position. "If I set too long, m' knees lock up, don't you know. But I'm a-comin'."

"Tell him he's a day early!" commanded Miss Rose.

"Don't you mind Rose a bit. You're welcome any time of th' day or night." Uncle Billy opened the screen and he stepped into the kitchen. The Watsons had cooked cabbage for lunch, no two ways about it.

"Uncle Billy, I hear you're giving . . . well, someone said you're giving Cynthia and me . . . a *party?*"

The old man looked vastly pleased. "Got a whole flock of people comin' to see you! Got three new jokes t' tell, you're goin' t' like 'em, and Rose is makin' banana puddin'."

Father Tim scratched his head, feeling foolish.

"Y' see, th' church give you 'uns a nice, big party an' all, but hit seemed mighty official, hit was anybody an' ever'body, kind of a free-for-all. I said, 'Rose, we ought t' give th' preacher an' 'is missus a little send-off with 'is *friends!*'" The old man leaned on his cane, grinning triumphantly. "So we're a-doin' it, and glad t' be a-doin' it!"

"Well, now—"

"Hit's goin' to be in th' museum part of th' house, so we can play th' jukebox, don't you know."

"Why, that's wonderful, it really is, but—"

"An' me an Rose took a good bath in th' *tub!*"

He had seen the time when Uncle Billy and Miss

Rose could empty two or three pews around their own. . . .

Miss Rose, in a chenille robe and unlaced saddle oxfords, stood up from her chair and looked him dead in the eye. He instantly wished for the protection of his wife.

"I hope you didn't come expecting to eat a day in advance," she snapped.

"Oh, law," said her mortified husband. "Now, Rose—"

She turned to Uncle Billy. "I haven't even *made* the banana pudding yet, so how can we feed him?"

"Oh, I didn't come to eat. I just came to find out—"

"You march home," said Miss Rose, "and come back tomorrow at the right time."

Uncle Billy put his hands over his eyes, as if to deny the terrible scene taking place in front of him.

"And what time might that *be?*" shouted Father Tim.

"Six-thirty sharp!" said the old woman, looking considerably vexed.

His wife went pale,

He felt like putting his hands over his own eyes, as Uncle Billy had done. "I'm sorry," he said. "I didn't know how to say no. Uncle Billy is so excited. . . . They've never given a party before."

"Why in heaven's name didn't they let us *know?*"

"I think they invited everybody else and forgot to invite us."

"Lord have *mercy!*" said his overworked wife, conveniently quoting the prayer book.

They had collapsed on the study sofa for the Changing of the Light, having gone nonstop since five-thirty that morning. He had made the lemonade on this occasion, and served it with two slices of bread, each curled hastily around a filling of Puny's homemade pimiento cheese.

"I can't even *think* about a party," she said, stuffing the bread and cheese into her mouth. "My blood sugar has dropped through the soles of my tennis shoes."

Ah, the peace of this room, he thought, unbuttoning his shirt. And here they were, leaving it. They built it, and now they were leaving it. Such was life in a collar.

"Timothy, are you really excited about going to Whitecap?"

"It comes and goes in waves. One moment, I'm excited—"

"And the next, you're scared to death?"

"Well . . ."

"Me, too," she confessed. "I hate to leave Mitford. I thought it would be fun, invigorating, a great adventure." She lay down, putting her head on one of the faded needlepoint pillows that had also made it through the hedge. "But now . . ." Her voice trailed off.

"We're pretty worn out, Kavanagh. This is a stressful thing we're doing, pulling up stakes. I've hardly been out of Mitford in sixteen years. But we'll get there and it will be terrific, wait and see. You'll love it. The freedom of an island . . ."

"The wind in our hair . . ."

"Gulls wheeling above us . . ."

"The smell of salt air . . ."

It was a litany they'd recited antiphonally over the last couple of months. It always seemed to console them.

He pulled her feet into his lap. "How about a nap? We've got a tight schedule ahead."

"Tonight," she said, "Puny helps us clean out all the cabinets. . . . Dooley comes tomorrow evening just before the Watson party, and will have supper with his mother. Then a day of shopping with our threadbare boy and moving him in with Harley, followed by your meeting with the new tenant, and Dooley's steak dinner. Then, of course, there's the grand opening at Lucera on Thursday night after we finish packing the car, and on Friday morning we're off. I don't think," she said, breathless, "that we'll have time to celebrate your birthday."

His birthday! Blast! This year, he would be sixty-six, and just think—in four short years, he would be seventy. And then eighty. And then . . . dead, he supposed. Oh, well.

"Don't be depressed," she scolded. "And for heaven's sake, dearest, relax. You're sitting there like a statue in a park."

"Right," he said, guzzling the lemonade.

He had noted over the last few days that the late June light reached its pinnacle when it fell upon the brass angel. Because of the exterior overhang of the room, the direct light moved no higher than the mantel, where the angel stood firm on its heavy base of green marble.

He had found the angel in the attic at Fernbank, Miss Sadie's rambling house at the top of the hill, now owned by Andrew and Anna Gregory. Only months before she died in her ninetieth year, Sadie Baxter had written a letter about the disposition of her family home and its contents. One thing she asked him to do was take something for his own, anything he liked.

As Cynthia rambled through Fernbank seeking her portion of the legacy, he had found the angel in a box, a box with a faded French postmark. Though the attic was filled with a bountiful assortment of inarguable treasures, he had known as surely as if someone had engraved his name upon it that the angel in a box belonged to him.

The light moved now to the angel, to its outspread wings and supplicating hands. It shone, also, on the vase of pink flowering almond next to the old books, and the small silhouette of his mother, which Cynthia had reframed and hung above the mantel.

As long as he could remember, he'd been afraid to sit still, to listen, to wait. As a priest, he'd been glad of every needy soul to tend to; every potluck supper to sit to; even of every illness to run to—thankful for the fray and haste. He'd been frightened of any tendency to sit and let his mind wander like a goat untethered from a chain, free to crop any grass it pleased.

He was beginning to realize, however, that he was less and less afraid to do what appeared to be nothing.

In the end, he wasn't really afraid of moving to Whitecap, either; he'd given his wife the wrong notion. He had prayed that God would send him wherever He pleased, and when his bishop presented the idea of Whitecap, he knew it wasn't his bishop's bright idea at all, but God's. He had learned years ago to read God's answer to any troubling decision by looking to his heart, his spirit, for an imprimatur of peace. That peace had come; otherwise, he would not go.

He inhaled the freshness of the breeze that stole through the open window, and the fragrance of oak and cherry that pervaded the room like incense.

Then, lulled by the sight of his dozing wife, he put his head back and closed his eyes, and slept.

CHAPTER TWO

Social Graces

Rose Watson set out what most people would call an outrageous assortment of cracked, chipped, and broken china, including mismatched cups and saucers that teetered atop a tower of salad plates anchored on a turkey platter.

After standing back and gazing at the curious pile with some satisfaction, she decided to flank the arrangement with a medley of soup bowls.

The large plastic container of banana pudding sat on the electric range, bristling with two serving spoons jabbed into its yellow center. For napkins, Uncle Billy supplied a roll of paper towels, which he stood on one end next to the pudding.

"Don't set paper on a *stove!*" Miss Rose snatched the roll and moved it like a pawn on a chessboard to the kitchen table.

"What about spoons?" shouted her husband. He was

fairly benumbed with the idea of having a swarm of people descend on their living quarters, though it had been his notion in the first place.

"Pull out the drawer! They can help themselves."

He did as he was told, thinking that his wife sometimes had a good idea, and wasn't half as crazy as most people thought. Mean-spirited, maybe, but that was her disease.

He had tried to read about schizophrenia in the Mitford library, one of the few times he had ever stepped foot in the place. He had looked for the oldest volunteer he could find, thinking she would be the boss, and asked her to lead him to a volume on a disease whose name he could not spell. He had then taken the book to a table and sat and asked the Lord to give him some kind of wisdom about what was so terribly, horribly wrong with his wife, but he couldn't understand anything the book had said, nothing.

"That's good thinkin'!" he shouted.

"You say somethin's *stinkin'?*" She turned and looked at him.

"Dadgummit, Rose, I said—"

"It might be your upper lip, Bill Watson." She suddenly burst into laughter.

There it was! The laughter he heard so seldom, had almost forgotten, rushing out like a bird freed from a cage, the laughter of the girl he'd known all those years ago. . . .

He stood, stunned and happy, tears springing to his eyes as suddenly as her laughter had come.

~<del>❍</del>~

Father Tim found the china assortment fascinating. He could spot several pieces of French Haviland in a pattern his grandmother had owned, and not a few pieces of Sevres.

At least he thought it was Sevres. He picked up a bread-and-butter plate and peered discreetly at the bottom. Meissen. What did he know?

He certainly didn't know what to do about the banana pudding. Everyone except themselves had been asked to bring a covered dish, so there was plenty to choose from. Miss Rose, however, stood like a sentinel by the stove, making sure that all comers had a hefty dose of what had taken her a full afternoon to create.

All those cracks in the china, he thought, all those chips and chinks . . . weren't they a known hideout for germs, a breeding ground? And hadn't he sat by the hospital bed of a woman who had put her feet under Rose Watson's table and barely lived to tell about it?

He could remember the story plainly. "Lord knows, I hadn't hardly got home before my stomach started rumblin' and carryin' on, you never heard such a racket. Well, Preacher, I hate to tell you such a thing, but you've heard it all, anyhow—five minutes later, I was settin' on th' toilet, throwin' up on my shoes."

He had not forgotten the mental image of that good lady throwing up on her shoes. He certainly hadn't forgotten her dark warning never to eat a bite or drink a drop at Rose Watson's house.

"Fill y'r plates and march into th' front room!" Their host's gold tooth gleamed. "Some's already in there, waitin' for th' blessin'."

Cynthia served herself from the pudding bowl as if she hadn't eaten a bite since Rogation Sunday.

"Fall to, darling," she said, happy as a child.

Oh, the everlasting gusto of his spouse! He sighed, peering around for the ham biscuits.

He found that everyone was oddly excited about being in a place as prominent as the town museum. It was a little awkward, however, given that not a single chair could be found, and they all had to mill around with their plates in their hands, setting their tea glasses on windowsills and stair steps.

The jukebox boomed out what he thought was "Chattanooga Shoeshine Boy," and laid a steady rhythm into the bare floorboards.

He and Cynthia made a quick tour of the exhibits, which he'd never, for some reason, taken time to study.

There was a copy of Willard Porter's deed to what had been the Mitford Pharmacy and was now Happy Endings Bookstore. There was also a handwritten list of pharmaceuticals that Willard had invented and patented, including Rose Cough Syrup, named for his then-ten-year-old sister, and their hostess for the evening.

There was the framed certificate declaring the Wurl-itzer to be a gift to the town from the owner of the Main Street Grill, where it was unplugged on June 26, 1951. It had been fully restored to mint condition, thanks to the generosity of Mayor Esther Cunningham.

He examined the daguerreotype of Coot Hendrick's great-great-grandfather sitting in a straight-back chair with a rifle across his knees.

It had been Coot's bearded ancestor, Hezikiah, who settled Mitford, riding horseback up the mountain along an Indian trading path, with his new English bride, Mary Jane, clinging on behind. According to legend, his wife was so homesick that Mr. Hendrick had the gen-erosity of spirit to give the town her maiden name of Mitford, instead of Hendricksville or Hendricksburg, which a man might have preferred to call a place settled by dint of his own hard labors.

" 'At's my great-*great*-granpaw," said Coot Hendrick, coming alongside the preacher and his wife. He'd been waiting to catch someone looking at that picture. For years, it had knocked around in a drawer at his mama's house, and he'd hardly paid any attention to it at all. Then somebody wanted it for the town museum and it had taken on a whole new luster.

"He looks fearless!" said Cynthia.

"Had twelve young 'uns!" Coot grinned from ear to ear, which was not a pretty sight, given his dental condition. "Stubs!" Mule Skinner had said, marveling at how he'd seen people's teeth fall out, but never wear down in such a way.

"Six lived, six died, all buried over yonder on Miz Mallory's ridge. Her house sets right next to where him and my great-great-granmaw built their little cabin."

"Well!" said Father Tim.

"Hit was a fine place to sight Yankees from," said Coot.

"I'll bet so."

"There probably weren't many Yankees prowling around up here," said Cynthia, who'd read that, barely a hundred and fifty years ago, an Anglican bishop had called the area "wild and uninhabitable."

"You'd be surprised," said Coot, tucking his thumbs in the straps of his overalls. "They say my great-great-granpaw shot five and give ever' one of 'em a solemn burial."

"I didn't know there were any battles fought around Mitford," said Cynthia, who appeared deeply interested in this new wrinkle of local history.

"They won't. Th' Yankees was runaways from their regiment."

Spying Esther and Gene Bolick making a beeline in

their direction, they excused themselves and met the Bolicks halfway.

"We just hate this!" said Esther. Overcome, she grabbed his hand and kissed it, then, mortified at such behavior, dropped it like a hot potato. "Gene and I have run th' gambit of emotions, and we still just hate to see y'all go!"

"We hate to go," he said simply.

"I baked you a two-layer orange marmalade and froze it. You can carry it down there in your cooler." There was nothing else she could do to keep her former priest in Mitford where she was certain he belonged— she had prayed, she had lost, she had cried, and in the end, she had baked.

Her husband, Gene, sighed and looked glum.

This, thought Father Tim, is precisely where a going-away party turns into a blasted wake unless somebody puts on a funny hat or slides down the banister, *something.* . . .

He turned to his wife, who shrugged and smiled and sought greener pastures.

"Gene's not been feelin' too good," said Esther.

"What is it?" asked Father Tim.

"Don't know exactly," Gene said, as Miss Rose strode up. "But I talked to Hoppy and went and got th' shots."

"Got the *trots!*" shouted Miss Rose. Everyone peered at them.

Gene flushed. "No, ma'am. The *shots.*"

"Bill had the trots last week," she said, frowning. "It could be something going around." Their hostess, who was monitoring everyone's plate to see whether her pudding had gotten its rightful reception, moved on to the next circle of guests.

"We reckon you know how hot it gets down there," said Gene.

"Honey, *hot*'s not th' word for it!" Fancy Skinner appeared in her signature outfit of pink Capri pants, V-neck sweater, and spike-heel shoes. "You will be boiled, steamed, roasted, baked, and fried."

"Not to mention sautéed," said Avis Packard, who owned the grocery store on Main Street, and liked to cook.

Fancy popped her sugarless gum. "Then there's stewed and broiled."

"*Please,*" said Father Tim.

"Barbecued!" contributed Gene, feeling pleased with himself. "You forgot barbecued."

Fancy, who was the owner of Mitford's only unisex salon, hooted with laughter.

"Did you consider maybe goin' to *Vermont!*" Gene wondered if their former rector had thought through this island business.

"Because if you think your hair's curlin' around your ears *now*," said Fancy, "wait'll all that humidity hits it, we're talkin' a Shirley Temple-Little Richard combo. That's why I liked to keep your hair *flat* around your ears when *I* was doin' it, now it's these chipmunk *pooches* again." Fancy reached out to forcibly slick his vagrant pooches down with her fingers, but restrained herself.

He looked anxiously around the room for Cynthia, who was laughing with the mayor and Hope Winchester.

❦

Omer Cunningham trotted in from the kitchen with a plate piled to overflowing, wearing his usual piano-key grin. Father Tim vowed he'd never seen so many big white teeth as the mayor's brother-in-law had in his head. It was enough for a regular Debussy concerto.

"Lord, at th' traffic I've run into today!"

"On Main Street?"

"I mean air traffic," said the proud owner of a rag-wing taildragger. "I been buzzin' th' gorge. You never seen th' like of deer that's rootin' around in there. Seems like ever'body and his brother was flyin' today."

Father Tim had instant and vivid recall of his times in the ragwing with Omer. Once to Virginia to hear Dooley in a concert, with his stomach lagging some distance behind the plane. Then again when they flew over Edith Mallory's sprawling house on the ridge above Mitford, trying to see what kind of dirty deal was behind the last mayoral race.

"I spotted a Piper Cherokee, a Cessna 182, and a Beechcraft Bonanza."

"Kind of like bird-watching."

"That Bonanza costs half a million smackers. You don't see many of those."

"I'll bet you don't."

"Listen, now," said Omer, ripping the meat off a drumstick with his teeth, "you let me know if I can ever buzz down to where you're at to help you out or any-thing. My little ragwing is yours any time of th' day or night, you hear?"

"Thank you, Omer, that's mighty thoughtful!"

Omer's chewing seemed unusually efficient. "I've flew over them little islands where you're goin' any number of times. Landed on many a beach. If you stay out of th' bad thunderstorms they have down there, it's as calm an' peaceful as you'd ever want t' see."

Omer picked up a ham biscuit and eyed it. "I don't like ham in a cathead biscuit," he said. "Have to dig too far for th' ham."

It was his fault. He was the one who casually mentioned it to Mule Skinner.

In nothing flat, the word of Dooley Barlowe's driver's license had replaced the party buzz about Avis Packard's decision to buy a panel truck for grocery delivery, and the huge addition to Edith Mallory's already enormous house.

Did he imagine it, or were they all peering at him as if to inquire when he was trotting out a car to go with Dooley's license?

Absolutely not. He had no intention of buying a car for a sixteen-year-old boy, then running off and leaving him to his own devices. Fortunately, Dooley had agreed to ride his red bicycle this summer, but he knew the notion of a car was definitely in the boy's mind. After all, didn't everybody's father in that fancy school toss around snappy convertibles and upscale four-wheel drives like so much confetti?

While it was obvious that Dooley couldn't earn enough money for a car by bagging groceries, Father Tim thought a summer of trying would hardly damage the boy's character.

In truth, there was an even more serious concern than Dooley's automobile hormones. And that was the fact he'd have nearly ten weeks to come and go as he pleased. Harley Welch would make a dependable, principled guardian, but Dooley could outwit Harley.

He muddled his spoon in the banana pudding.

As if reading Father Tim's mind, Mule said, "We'll all watch after 'im."

"Right," said Gene, "we'll keep an eye on 'im."

Adele Hogan, Mitford's only female police officer and nearly-new wife of the newspaper editor, caught up with him at the jukebox, as her husband snapped pictures for Monday's edition of the *Muse*.

"Just wanted you to know," said Adele, "we've got cars cruisin' around the clock. We'll keep our eyes open for your little guy while you're gone."

The truth was, there'd be a veritable woof of men to look after the boy, not to mention a fine warp of women, including Puny, and Dooley's mother, and now Adele.

"Thank you!" he said, meaning it.

Adele stood with her thumbs tucked into her belt, appearing for a moment to be hired security. She had come straight from the station in her uniform, wearing a Glock nine-millimeter on her hip. The sight of Adele, who was the new hotshot coach of the Mitford Reds and also the grandmother of three, never failed to astonish and impress him.

"Don't worry about a thing," said Adele.

He was almost inclined not to.

"Right!" agreed Avis. "I'm th' only one that'll drive my delivery truck, except for Lew Boyd's cousin, who's fillin' in on Saturdays. Anyway, I'm goin' to work your boy's butt off this summer. He won't have time to get in trouble." In a spontaneous burst of camaraderie, Avis slapped him on the shoulder.

The mayor barged up and slapped him on the other shoulder. He nearly pitched into the Wurlitzer, which was now playing "One Mint Julep."

"Run out on us, then," said Esther Cunningham. "See if I care."

"You don't need me anymore. After praying you into office eight times in a row, you're hanging it up and going off with Ray in the RV."

Esther narrowed her eyes and peered at him. "I guess you know about th' hurricanes they get down there."

"I do."

"And th' heat . . ."

Would they *never* hush . . . ?

A muscle twitched in the mayor's jaw. "We'll miss you."

"We'll miss you back," he said, putting his arm around his old friend's well-cushioned shoulders. He hated this goodbye business. He'd rather be home yanking a tooth out by a string on a doorknob, anything. "Are you laying off the sausage biscuits?"

"Curiosity killed the cat," she said.

⌐∽

Esther cupped her hands to her mouth and shouted, "Somebody unplug th' box!"

Omer squatted by the Wurlitzer, which couldn't be shut off manually, and pulled the plug.

"Must be Uncle Billy's joke," said Gene Bolick, getting up from the stair step where he was sitting with Mule.

Mule sighed. "I hope it's not that deal about th' gas stove! I've heard that more times than Carter has liver pills."

"Here's one for you," said Gene. "What's a Presbyterian?"

"Beats me."

"A Methodist with a drinkin' problem who can't afford to be Episcopalian."

Mule scratched his head. He had never understood jokes about Episcopalians.

"Come on, everybody!" yelled the mayor, her voice echoing in the vaulted room. "Joke time!"

Uncle Billy stood as straight as he was able, holding on to his cane and looking soberly at the little throng, who gave forth a murmur of coughing and throat-clearing.

"Wellsir!" he exclaimed, by way of introduction. "A farmer was haulin' manure, don't you know, an' 'is truck broke down in front of a mental institution. One of th' patients, he leaned over th' fence, said, 'What're you goin' t' do with y'r manure?'

"Farmer said, 'I'm goin' t' put it on m' strawberries.'

"Feller said, 'We might be crazy, but we put whipped cream on our'n.'"

Uncle Billy grinned at the cackle of laughter he heard.

"Keep goin'!" someone said.

"Wellsir, this old feller an 'is wife was settin' on th' porch, an' she said, 'Guess what I'd like t' have?'

"He said, 'What's that?'

"She said, 'A great big bowl of vaniller ice cream with choc'late sauce and nuts on top!'

"He says, 'Boys howdy, that'd be good. I'll go down to th' store and git us some.'

"Wife said, 'Now, that's vaniller ice cream with choc'late sauce and nuts. Better write it down.'

"He said, 'Don't need t' write it down, I can remember.'

"Little while later, he come back. Had two ham san'wiches. Give one t' her. She looked at that san'wich, lifted th' top off, said, 'You mulehead, I told you t' write it down, I wanted mustard on mine!'"

Loving the sound of laughter in the cavernous room, Uncle Billy nodded to the left, then to the right.

"One more," he said, trembling a little from the excitement of the evening.

"Hit it!" crowed the mayor, hoping to remember the punch line to the vanilla ice-cream story.

"Wellsir, this census taker, he went to a house an' knocked, don't you know. A woman come out, 'e said, 'How many children you got, an' what're their ages?'

"She said, 'Let's see, there's th' twins Sally and Billy, they're eighteen. And th' twins Seth an' Beth, they're sixteen. And th' twins Penny an' Jenny, they're fourteen—'

"Feller said, 'Hold on! Did you git twins ever' time?'

"Woman said, 'Law, no, they was hundreds of times we didn't git nothin'.' "

The old man heard the sound of applause overtaking the laughter, and leaned forward slightly, cupping his hand to his left ear to better take it in. The applause was giving him courage, somehow, to keep on in life, to get out of bed in the mornings and see what was what.

$\backsim$

Uncle Billy and Miss Rose looked considerably exhausted from their social endeavors; the old man's hands trembled as they stood on the cool front porch.

"I'd like to pray for you," said Father Tim.

"We'd be beholden to you, Preacher, if you would," said Uncle Billy, "but seems like we ought t' pray f'r you, don't you know."

Hardly anyone ever did that, he thought, moved by the gesture. "I'd thank you for doing it."

Cynthia slipped into the circle and they joined hands.

"Now, Lord . . ."—the old man drew a deep breath—"I ain't used t' doin' this out loud an all, but I felt You call me t' do it, an' I'm expectin You t' help me, don't you know.

"Lord Jesus, I'm askin' You t' watch over th' preacher an 'is missus. Don't let 'em git drownded down there, or come up ag'in meanness of any kind. You tell 'em whichaway to go when they need it."

Uncle Billy paused. "An' I 'preciate it. F'r Christ's sake, a-men!"

"Amen!"

Father Tim clasped his arms around his old friend. "Uncle Billy—"

"I hope they give you plenty of fried chicken down there!" squawked Miss Rose. She'd always heard preachers liked fried chicken.

He didn't know how many more goodbyes he could bear.

—⸙—

It wasn't that he and Cynthia hadn't wanted to go to Whitecap to see and be seen. They had carefully planned to go for five days in March, but the weather had turned foul, with lashing rains and high winds that persisted for days along the eastern shoreline.

He had then tried to set a date for April, but most of the Whitecap vestry, who were key players in any approval process, would be away for one reason or another.

"Don't sweat it," Stuart Cullen had said in a phone call. Stuart was not only his current bishop, but a close friend since seminary days. "They know all about you. They're thrilled you'll do the interim. Bishop Harvey agrees it's a match made in heaven, so don't worry about getting down there for the usual preview."

"It's a little on the pig-in-a-poke side, if you ask me."

Stuart laughed. "Believe me, Timothy, they need exactly what you've got to offer. Besides, if you don't like each other, Bill Harvey and I will give you your money back."

"How about telling me the downside of this parish? All Bill Harvey talks about is the church being so attractive, it ends up on postcards."

"Right," agreed Stuart. "He also vows he hears the nickering of wild ponies through the open windows of the nave, though I don't think Whitecap has wild ponies these days."

"What I'd rather know is, who's likely to stab the interim in the back? And who's plotting to run off with the choir director?"

He was joking, of course, but equally serious. He wanted to know what was what in Whitecap, and nobody was telling him.

"Ah, well, Timothy, there isn't a choir director." His bishop sounded strained.

"Really? Why not?"

"Well . . ."

"Stuart!"

"Because the choir director ran off with the organist."

"Is this a joke?"

"I wish."

"Surely you can come up with something slicker than that. Good heavens, man, we had a jewel thief living in the attic at Lord's Chapel, not to mention a parishioner who tried to buy the last mayoral election. Tell me something I can get my teeth into."

"Sorry. But I've just given you the plain, unvarnished truth."

There was a long silence. "What else do I need to know?"

The bishop told him. In fact, he told him a great deal more than he needed to know.

～⊛～

He stepped into the downstairs bathroom and took his glucometer kit from the medicine cabinet. With all the hoopla going on, and the radical changes in his diet, he figured he should check his sugar more often.

Once or twice, he'd felt so low he could have crawled under a snake's belly wearing a top hat. Other times, his adrenaline was pumping like an oil derrick.

He shot the lance into the tip of his left forefinger and spilled the drop of blood onto a test strip. Then he slid the strip into the glucometer and waited for the readout. 130.

Excellent. He didn't need any bad news from his body. Not now, not ever.

"Thank you, Lord," he murmured, zipping the case shut.

He and Dooley loped across Baxter Park with Barnabas on the red leash, then turned left and headed up Old Church Lane.

They ran side by side until the hospital turnoff, where Dooley suddenly looked at him, grinned, and shot forward like a hare.

As he watched the boy pull away toward the crest of the steep hill, he saw at once the reason for his greater speed. Dooley Barlowe's legs were six feet long.

He huffed behind, regretting the way he'd let his running schedule go. Oh, well. Whitecap would be another matter entirely. All that fresh salt air and ocean breeze, and a clean, wide beach that went on for miles . . .

He would even walk to his office, conveniently located in the basement of the church, only two blocks from Dove Cottage. Nor was he the only one whose physical fitness would take an upturn. Cynthia was sending her old blue Schwinn down with their household shipment, and would leave her Mazda in Mitford. For an island only eleven miles long and four miles wide, who needed a car? Even many of the locals were said to navigate on two-wheelers.

"Better watch your step down there," Omer had advised. "Them bicycles'll mow you down, they ride 'em ever' whichaway."

"Wait up!" he shouted to Dooley.

Dooley turned around, laughing, and for a crisp, quick moment, he saw the way the sun glinted on the boy's red hair, and the look in his blue eyes. It was a look of triumph, of exultation, a look he had never, even once, seen before on Dooley Barlowe's face.

He didn't know whether to whoop, which he felt like doing, or weep, which he dismissed at once. Instead, he lunged ahead, closing the gap between them, and threw his arm around the boy's shoulder and told him what must be spoken now, immediately, and not a moment later.

"I love you, buddy," he said, panting and laughing at once. "Blast if I don't."

~⊖~

They sat on the cool stone wall, looking into the valley, into the Land of Counterpane. There beyond the trees was the church spire, and over there, the tiniest glint of railroad tracks . . . and just there, the pond next to the apple orchard where he knew ducks were swimming. Above it all, ranging along the other side of the valley, the high, green hills outlined themselves against a blue and cloudless sky. It was his favorite view in the whole of the earth, he thought.

"There's something I'd like you to know," he told Dooley. "I believe we'll find Sammy and Kenny."

Father Tim had gone into the Creek with Lace Turner and retrieved Dooley's younger brother, Poobaw. Later, he'd driven to Florida on little more than a hunch, and located Dooley's little sister, Jessie. Now two of the five Barlowe children were still missing. Their mother, Pauline, recovering from years of hard drinking, had no idea where they might be. As far as he could discover, there were no clues, no trail, no nothing. But he had hope—the kind that comes from a higher place than reason or common sense.

"Will you believe that with me?" he asked Dooley.

A muscle moved in Dooley's jaw. "You did pretty good with Poo and Jessie."

Barnabas crashed into the grass at Dooley's feet.

"I believe we're closer to deciding on some colleges to start thinking about."

"Yep. Maybe Cornell."

"You've got a while before you have to make any decisions."

"Maybe University of Georgia."

"Maybe. Their specialty is large animals; that's what interests you. Anyway, that's all down the road. For now, just check things out, think about it, pray about it."

"Right."

"We're mighty proud of you, son. You'll make a fine vet. You've come—we've all come—a long way together."

There was an awkward silence between them.

"What's on your mind?" asked Father Tim.

"Nothing."

"Let's talk about it."

Dooley turned to him, glad for the invitation. "It looks like you could let me borrow the money and I'll pay you back. Working six days a week at five dollars an hour, I'll have sixteen hundred dollars. Plus I figure three yards a week at an average of twenty apiece, I'm countin' it seven hundred bucks because some people will give me a tip. Last year, I saved five hundred, so that's two thousand eight hundred."

He had the sudden sense of being squeezed between a rock and a hard place. . . .

"Nearly three thousand," said Dooley, enunciating clearly. "I could prob'ly make it an even three if I cleaned out people's attics and basements."

Aha. He hadn't counted on three thousand bucks being a factor in the car equation. He gazed out to the view, unseeing.

"This just isn't the summer for it. We can't be here, and that's a very crucial factor. Besides, you know we agreed you'd have a car next summer. If we're still at Whitecap, you'll come there, and everything will be fine." He looked at Dooley. "Call me hard if you like, but it's not going to happen."

Dooley turned away and said something under his breath.

"Tell you what we'll do. Cynthia and I will match everything you make this summer." It was a rash decision, but why not? He still had more than sixty thousand dollars of his mother's money, and was a homeowner with no mortgage. It was the right thing to do.

Dooley stared straight ahead, kicking the stone wall with his heels.

If Dooley Barlowe only knew what he knew—that Sadie Baxter had left the boy a cool million-and-a-quarter bucks in her will, to be his when he turned twenty-one. He knew that part of Miss Sadie's letter by heart: *I am depending on you never to mention this to him until he is old enough to bear it with dignity.*

"Look. We gave you a choice between staying in

Mitford and a summer at the beach. That's a pretty important liberty. We didn't force you to do anything you didn't want to do. Give us credit for that. The car is a different matter. We're not going to be around to—"

"Harley's going to be around all the time, he's going to let me drive his truck, what's the difference if I have my own car?"

Well, blast it, what *was* the difference? "But only once a week, as you well know, with a curfew of eleven o'clock."

Father Tim stood up, agitated. He never dreamed he'd be raising a teenager. When he was Dooley's age in Holly Springs, Mississippi, nobody he knew had a car when they were sixteen. Today, boys were given cars as casually as they were handed a burger through a fast-food window. And in fact, a vast number of them ended up decorating the grille of an eighteen-wheeler, not critically injured, but dead. He was too old to have a teenager, too old to figure this out the way other people, other parents, seemed to do.

"Look," he said, pacing alongside the stone wall, "we talked about this before, starting a few months ago. You were perfectly fine with no car this summer; we agreed on it. You even asked me to hunt down your bicycle pump so you could put air in the tires."

He knew exactly what had happened. It was that dadblamed Wrangler. "Is Tommy getting a car this summer?"

"No. He's working to raise money so he can have one next year. He's only saved eight hundred dollars."

This was definitely an encouragement. "So, look here. Harley was going to mow our two yards once a week, but why don't I give you the job? I'll pay twenty bucks a shot for both houses."

"If Buster Austin did it, he'd charge fifteen apiece, that's thirty. I'll do both for twenty-five."

"Deal!"

He looked at the boy he loved, the boy he'd do anything for.

Almost.

⟲

It rained throughout the night, a slow, pattering rain that spoke more eloquently of summer to him than any sunshine. He listened through the open bedroom window until well after midnight, sleepless but not discontented. They would make it through all this upheaval, all this tearing up and nailing down, and life would go on.

He found his wife's light, whiffling snore a kind of anchor in a sea of change.

⟲

Bolting down Main Street the next morning at seven o'clock, he saw Evie Adams in her rain-soaked yard, dressed in a terry robe and armed with a salt shaker.

"Forty-two!" she shouted in greeting.

He knew she meant snail casualties. Evie had been at war with snails ever since they gnawed her entire stand of blue hostas down to nubs. Some years had passed since this unusually aggressive assault, but Evie had not forgotten. He pumped his fist into the air in a salute of brotherhood.

After all, he had hostas, too. . . .

⟲

"If I have to say goodbye to you one more time, I'll puke," said Mule.

Actually, Mule was moved nearly to bawling that his

old buddy had come by the Grill at all. Father Tim could have been loading his car, or turning off the water at the street, or changing his address at the post office—whatever people did who were leaving for God knows how long.

"Livermush straight up," Father Tim told Percy as he slid into the booth. "And make it a double."

"Livermush? You ain't ordered livermush in ten, maybe twelve years."

"Right. But that's what I'm having." He grinned at the dumb-founded Percy. "And make it snappy."

It was reckless to eat livermush, especially a double order, but he was feeling reckless.

Percy set his mouth in a fine line as he cut two slices from the loaf of livermush. He did not approve of long-term Grill customers moving elsewhere. Number one, the Father had been coming to the Grill for sixteen, seventeen years; he was established. To just up and run off, flinging his lunch and breakfast trade to total strangers, was . . . he couldn't even find a word for what it was.

Number two, why anybody would want to leave Mitford in the first place was beyond him. He had personally left it only twice—when Velma was pregnant and they went to see cousins in Avery County, and when he and Velma went on that bloomin' cruise to Hawaii, which his children had sent them on whether he wanted to go or not.

But worse than the Father leaving Mitford, he was leaving it for a location that had once *broken off from the mainland,* for Pete's sake, and could not be trusted as ground you'd want under your feet. So here was somebody he'd thought to be sensible and wise, clearly proving himself to be otherwise.

As he laid two thick slices on the sizzling grill, Percy

shook his head. Every time he thought he'd gained a little understanding of human nature, something like this came up and he had to start over.

J. C. Hogan thumped into the booth. "Man!" he said, mopping his face with a rumpled handkerchief. "It's hot as a depot stove today. I hope you know how hot it gets *down there.*"

Father Tim put his hands over his ears and shut his eyes.

"Lookit," said J.C. He tossed the *Muse,* still smelling of ink, on the table. "You made today's front page."

"What for?"

Mule snatched the eight-page edition to his side of the table and adjusted his glasses. "Let me read it. Let's see. Here we go." The realtor cleared his throat and read aloud.

" *'Around Town by Vanita Bentley . . .'*

"Blah, blah, blah, OK, here's th' meat of it. *'Father Kavanagh treated everybody as if equal in intelligence and accomplishment, making his real church the homes, sidewalks and businesses of Mitford. . . .*

" *'Whether we had faith or not, he loved us all.' "*

Father Tim felt his face grow hot. "Give me that," he said, snatching the newspaper.

"What's the matter?" said J.C. "Don't you like it?"

He didn't know if he liked it. What he knew was that it sounded like . . . an obituary.

❧

He was hunkering down now, trying to cover all the bases.

Thanks be to God, it was nearly over, they were nearly on their way. He'd been going at this thing of leaving as if it were life or death, when in fact it was more like a year to sixteen months, and then he'd be back in Mitford, with half the population not realizing he'd left.

He screeched into Louella's room at Hope House, breathing hard. Miss Sadie's will had provided her life-long companion with Room Number One, which was the finest room in the entire place.

Louella plucked the remote from her capacious lap and muted *All My Children.*

"You look like you been yanked up by th' roots!" she said, concerned.

"Ah . . . ," he replied, unable to muster anything else.

"An' it yo' *birthday!*" she scolded.

"It is?"

"You sixty-six today!"

"Louella, do I remind you of your age?"

"Honey," she said, looking smug, "you don' know my age."

He'd been coming to see Louella every day since Miss Sadie died. Sometimes they played checkers, but more often they sang hymns. The thought of leaving her made him feel like a common criminal. . . .

"How's your knee?" he asked, kissing her warm, chocolate-colored cheek. "How's your bladder infection? Have you started the potting class yet?"

"Set down on yo' stool," she said. He always sat on her footstool, which made him feel nine years old. A feeling, by the way, he rather liked.

"Now," she said, beaming, "we ain' goan talk about knees an bladders, an' far as pottin' classes goes, I decided I ain't messin' wit' no clay. What I'm wantin' to do is *sing,* and ain't hardly anybody roun' here can carry a tune in a bucket."

"I'll go a round or two with you," he said, feeling better at once.

"I take th' first verse, you take th' second, an' we'll chime in together on number three."

Louella closed her eyes and raised her hands and began to lift her rich, mezzo voice in song. She rocked a little in her chair.

"The King of love my shepherd is,
Whose goodness faileth never;
I nothing lack if I am his,
And he is mine forever."

He waited two beats and picked up the second verse, not caring if they heard him all the way to the monument.

"Where streams of living water flow,
My ransomed soul he leadeth;
And where the verdant pastures grow,
With food celestial feedeth."

Two nurses stuck their heads in the door, grinning, as he joined his voice with Louella's on the third verse.

"Perverse and foolish oft I strayed,
But yet in love he sought me,
And on his shoulder gently laid,
And home, rejoicing, brought me."

They were silent for a moment. "Now," said Louella, "that feels better, don't it?"

He nodded, sensing the tears lurking in him, some kind of sorrow that he'd noticed for a week or more.

"You pushin' too hard," she said.

"You have to push, Louella." Out there in the world, he wanted to say, it was all about push.

"Maybe you done stepped aroun' th' Lord an' tryin' to lead th' way."

He stood up and looked out the window, into the green valley he called the Land of Counterpane. Maybe she was right.

Louella didn't often get out of her chair these days, but now she rose and stood by him, and put her hand on his shoulder.

"You know I pray for you and Miss Cynthia every mornin' an' every night, and I ain' goin' to stop. Anytime you get in a tight place down yonder, you just think, Louella's prayin' for me, and go on 'bout your business."

As he left Room Number One, he found himself humming. He couldn't remember doing that in a very long time.

"Where streams of living water flow, my ransomed soul he leadeth. . . ."

Maybe the real issue wasn't how Louella would manage without him, but how would he manage without Louella?

———— ✦ ————

He cantered down the hall and found Pauline finishing up in the dining room.

"Pauline?"

"Father!"

He gave her a hug. "What do you hear from Buck?

"He'll be home the fifteenth of October."

"And we'll roar in on the twenty-fifth, after which I'll personally see to it that you become Mrs. Buck Leeper."

She smiled and looked at her hands. He'd never seen her more beautiful. In fact, the miracle of watching

Pauline Barlowe become whole wasn't unlike watching the slow unfolding of the petals on his Souvenir de la Malmaison.

"That is what you want, isn't it?"

"More'n anything. Yes, sir, I do."

"You've waited, and I admire that. How's his job in Alaska?"

"Real good. He says he'll bring it in on time."

"He always does," he said, feeling proud with her. "And Jessie and Poo? How're they feeling about all that's ahead?"

"Excited." She hesitated, then dared to use a word she had never trusted in her life. "Happy!"

He nodded, pleased. "Dooley will be in safe hands with Harley, and I know he'll be coming around to your place often. You might want to . . ." *Watch over him*, he wanted to say.

"I will," she replied, knowing.

He was halfway along the hall when she called after him. "Father!"

He turned around. "Yes?"

"We hate to see you go."

"I'll be back before you know I'm gone."

She smiled and waved, and he saw Dooley in her for a fleeting moment, something about the way she held her head, and the thrust of her chin. . . .

—∽—

"Law, help!" said Puny, looking exhausted. "I'll be glad to see y'all *go!*"

There! The truth from somebody, at last.

"You never seen th' like of mess Dooley'd squirreled away in his room that we had to drag to th' basement. Harley said if we kept on haulin' stuff down there, he'd have to go to livin' out of his truck." The freckled Puny hooted with laughter.

"Where are my grandbabies?" he wondered. Puny sometimes fetched the twins from church school a little early. Sissy and Sassy even kept a stash of toys at the yellow house, consisting of a red wagon, several dolls, stuffed monkeys, crayons, and other paraphernalia.

"They're dead asleep in th' front room, Miz Hart said they fussed all day."

"Uh-oh."

"But they'll be glad to see their granpaw." Puny smiled hugely. The poor soul standing in front of her would never have had the joy of grandchildren if it hadn't been for her generosity. She'd given him her babies as free-handed as you please, and he'd taken to them like a duck to water. The truth was, Sissy was crazy about her granpaw and often kissed a framed picture of him that Puny had proudly placed in her home.

He patted his pocket. "I'm ready when they are."

"You'll make their little teeth fall out with that candy."

"Once a week, two small pieces? I hardly think so. Besides," he said, "they're going to fall out, anyway."

She shook her head, tsking, happy that someone she loved also loved her twin three-year-olds. It would be different around here with the Father gone, and Cynthia, who was always so bright and helpful. . . .

Every last scrap of Dooley's tack had made it to Harley's basement apartment, and Father Tim had helped Dooley clean his room at the rectory, top to bottom. In addition, all the books for Whitecap were packed, sealed, and ready for the shipper to pick up tomorrow.

Before he dragged himself upstairs to take a shower, he'd just lie down and put his head on the arm of the sofa, but only for a moment, of course.

If there was ever a birthday when he had no time or energy to read St. Paul's letters to Timothy, this was it. Ever since seminary, he'd made a point of reading the letters on, or adjacent to, the date of his nativity. Perhaps his yearly pondering of these Scriptures was one way of taking stock.

" 'To Timothy, my dearly beloved son,' " he murmured, quoting at random from the familiar Second Epistle. " 'Grace, mercy, and peace, from God the Father and Christ Jesus our Lord . . . watch thou in all things, endure afflictions, do the work of an evangelist, make full proof of thy ministry.' "

He was sinking into the sofa. " 'The cloke that I left at Troas with Carpus,' " he whispered—this was a favorite part—" 'when thou comest, bring with thee, and the books, but especially the parchments—' "

"Timothy!"

It was his wife, calling from the front hall.

"Can you come here a moment?"

He forced himself off the sofa and trotted along the hall, obedient as any pup.

"You rang?" he asked, rubbing his eyes.

She smiled. "Walk out to the porch with me."

"Why?" he asked, peevish.

"Why not?" she said, taking his hand. It occurred to him that she looked unusually . . . expectant, somehow, on the verge of something.

When they stepped to the porch, he noticed it at once. A slick-looking red convertible was parked at the curb, with the top down. Hardly anybody ever parked in front of their house. . . .

"I wonder who *that* belongs to."

"I'm looking at him," said Cynthia.

His wife was lit up like a Christmas tree.

"What do you mean you're—"

"Happy birthday, dearest!" She was suddenly kissing his face—both cheeks, his nose, his mouth.

"But you can't possibly—"

"It's *yours!* To you from me, for our trip to Whitecap, for zooming around like feckless youths in the rain, in the sunshine, in the *snow,* what the heck!"

"But . . ."

Without meaning to, exactly, he sat down hard on the top step.

She laughed and sat with him. "What do you think?"

He stared at it, aghast, unable to think. "But," he said lamely, "it's red."

"So? Red is good!"

"But I'm a priest!"

"All the better!" she crowed. "Now, darling, don't get stuffy on me."

He saw that he might easily wound her to the very depths.

"But the Buick . . ."

"What about it?"

"It's . . . it's still perfectly *good.*"

She raised one eyebrow.

He suddenly had another thought, this one worse than the others.

"The new priest rolling into town like a rock star . . . what will people think?"

"I never mind what people think—ever! We didn't sleep together 'til we were married, and yet, imagine how the tongues wagged when we were seen sneaking back and forth through the hedge."

"I never sneaked," he said, indignant.

"Timothy. How quickly you forget."

But surely she hadn't *bought* it. "It's a rental! Right?"

"Darling, remember me? I'm Cynthia, I don't do rentals. It's yours. Here's the key." She shoved it into his hand.

She was tired of fooling around, he could tell. He started to stand up, but sat again, weak-kneed.

"I can't believe it," he said, feeling contrite. "Please forgive me. God knows, I thank you. But I mean, the *expense* . . ." Why couldn't he quit babbling about the negatives? What did these things cost, anyway? It was horrifying to contemplate. . . .

She patted him on the knee. "It's not nice to talk about the cost of a gift. Besides, if you really must know, it's three years old and the radio isn't working."

"It looks brand-new!"

"Yet bought with old money. Royalties from *Violet Goes to the Country* and *Violet Goes to School,* tucked into a money market fund long ago. I've worked very hard, Timothy, and been conservative as a church mouse—I wanted to do this."

He was ashamed to ask what make it was. He'd never been able to identify cars, unlike Tommy Noles, who knew Packards from Oldsmobiles and Fords from Chevrolets. Actually, a Studebaker was the only car he'd ever been able to guess, dead-on.

Maybe a Jaguar. . . .

"It's a Mustang GT," said his wife, looking mischievous.

He put his arm around her and drew her close and nuzzled his face into her hair. "You astound me, you have always astounded me, I need to sit here and just look at it for a minute. Thank you for being patient." He felt wild laughter rising in him, as he'd felt the tears earlier. What kind of roller coaster was he on, anyway?

"I don't deserve it," he said. There. He'd finally gotten down to the bottom line.

She lifted her hand to his cheek. "Deserve? Since when is love about deserving?"

"Right," he said. He felt his heart beginning to hammer at the sight of it sitting there so coolly parked at the curb, as if it owned the house and the people in it.

He realized he'd come within a hair of hurting her by persisting in his fogy ways. No, he'd never have believed he'd be driving a red convertible, not in a million years, but he knew it was absolutely crucial that he begin believing it—at once.

He felt the grin spreading across his face, and didn't think he could stop the laughter that was lurking in him.

"Wait'll Dooley sees this!" he said, as they trotted toward the curb.

CHAPTER THREE

Going, Going, Gone

"Timothy!"

His wife was calling him constantly these days. From the top of the stairs, from the depths of the basement, from the far reaches of the new garage.

It was Timothy here, Timothy there, Timothy everywhere.

"Yes?" he bellowed from the study.

"Do we really need this cast-iron Dutch oven?" she yelled from the hallway, where the items to be packed in the car were being severely thinned.

"How else can I make a pork roast?" he shouted.

"I don't think people at the beach *eat* pork roast!" she shouted back.

He hated shouting.

Cynthia appeared in the study, her hair in a bandanna, wearing shorts and a T-shirt. She might have been a twelfth-grade student from Mitford School. Why was his wife looking increasingly younger as he grew increasingly older? It wasn't fair.

"I think," she said, wiping perspiration from her face, "that beach people eat ocean perch or broiled tuna or . . ." She shrugged. "You know."

He took the heavy pot from her, feeling grumpy. "Leave it," he said, toting it to the kitchen.

"And do you really think," she hooted from the study, "that we need those Wellington boots you garden in?"

He stepped back to the study. "What did you say?"

"Those huge green boots. Those Wellingtons."

"What about them?"

"I mean, there's no mud at the beach!"

He sighed.

"Besides, we can't lash anything on top of the car . . ."—she grinned, bouncing on the balls of her feet like a kid—"because we'll have the top *down*."

"Axe the boots."

"And the Coleman stove. Why would we need a Coleman *stove*? We won't be camping out, you know."

If he didn't watch her every minute, they would be roaring down the highway with nothing but a change of underwear and a box of watercolors. Besides, he had thought of maybe cooking out one night on the beach, under the stars, with a blanket. . . .

He blushed, just thinking about it.

"We're taking the stove," he said.

He made a quick sweep of the rectory, looking once more in the kitchen drawers, feeling along the top shelves of the study bookcases, peering into the medicine cabinets.

Clean as a whistle.

Their tenant was moving in tomorrow with what she called "light furnishings," a grand piano, and a cat, and he didn't want any of his jumble lying around to welcome her. Ever since he moved in behind Father Bellwether in Alabama, he was careful to clean up any rectory he was vacating.

Father Bellwether had left behind a 1956 Ford on blocks, several leaf bags filled with old shirts and sweaters, a set of mangled golf clubs, three room-size rugs chewed by dogs, an assortment of cooking gear, several doors without knobs, a vast collection of paperback mysteries, and other litter that couldn't be completely identified. Determined not to whine to the vestry who had called him, Father Tim remembered using a shovel and a hired truck to clean the place out while the movers huffed his own things in.

His footsteps echoed along the hallway to the basement door. He opened it and called down the stairs.

"Harley, are you there?"

Lace Turner appeared at the bottom of the steps, her blond hair in French braids.

"Harley's taking a test," she said.

He thought that each time he saw the fifteen-year-old Lace Turner, she had grown more beautiful, more confident. The hard look he'd once seen on her face had softened.

"But you can come down," she said. "He's almost through."

"What's the test on?" he inquired, trotting to meet her in the basement hallway.

"History. It's his favorite subject."

"Hit ain't no such of a thing!" Harley called from the parlor.

Harley was sitting on the sofa with a sheaf of papers

in his lap, using a hardcover book as a writing surface. A fan moved slowly left, then right, on a table next to the sofa.

"It was your favorite last week," she said patiently, as they came into the room.

"Rev'rend, she's got me studyin' Lewis 'n' Clark, how they explored th' Missouri River and found half a dadblame nation. . . ."

"Sounds interesting."

"Oh, hit's in'erestin', all right, but this question she's wrote down here is how many falls is in th' Great Falls of th' Missouri. They won't a soul ever ask me that, I don't *need* t' know it, hit won't *pay* t' know it—"

"Harley . . . ," said Lace, looking stern.

"Two falls!" said Harley.

"No. We talked about it yesterday."

"Six!"

Lace shook her head. "Think about it," she advised. "You don't like to think, Harley."

"Didn't I make eighty-nine on my numbers test you give me?" Harley grinned, displaying pink gums perfectly lacking in teeth.

"Yes, and you can make a hundred on this one if you'll just think back to what you read yesterday."

Father Tim quietly hunkered into a chair.

"I don't give a katy how many falls make up th' Great Falls. I quit, by jing." Harley laid his pencil on the arm of the sofa and put his papers to one side. "I'm goin' to pour th' rev'rend a glass of tea. You can mark up m' score on what I done."

Harley marched to the kitchen, looking as determined as his instructor. He turned at the kitchen door. "An' say some of y'r big words for th' rev'rend."

Lace gazed at Father Tim, her amber eyes luminous

and intense. "He's learned an awful lot," she said, defending her practice of coming regularly to educate the man who protected her as she was growing up. It had been Harley who often fed Lace, and hid her from a violent, abusive father. To Lace, it was no small matter that Harley had sometimes risked his life for her well-being.

Lace was now living with Hoppy and Olivia Harper, and adoption procedures were under way. Father Tim considered that her privileged life with the Harpers might have turned the girl's affinities in other directions. But, no. Lace visited Harley often, frequently cooked to encourage his finicky appetite, and protected him fiercely. As for her desire that Harley become a learned man, the Education of Harley Welch was entering its third year.

Lace picked up the test papers and examined them. Her eyes glanced quickly over the pages, and she alternately sighed or nodded.

Father Tim gazed at her, profoundly moved. When he had first met Lace Turner, she was living in the dirt under her ramschackle house on the Creek, foraging for food like a dog. Her transformation was a miracle he'd been privileged to witness with his own eyes.

"Ninety," she pronounced, making a mark with the pencil.

"Why, that's terrific!"

"He spelled the Willamette River correctly."

"Good! I hope you'll give him a couple of extra points for that."

Lace smiled one of her rare smiles. He was dazzled, and no help for it.

"Ninety-two, then!" she said, looking pleased.

"So, how many falls?" he asked.

"Five."

"Aha."

"I'm sorry you're leaving," she said.

"Thank you, Lace. Of course, we won't be gone forever, it's an interim situation."

"What's a interim situation?" asked Harley, coming in with two glasses of tea. "This 'uns your'n," he said to Father Tim, "no sugar."

"It means a time between," said Lace.

"Between what?" Harley wondered.

"Between what I've been doing and what I'm going to do later," said Father Tim, laughing.

Lace held up the test paper. "Harley, you made ninety-two on your test."

Harley's eyes widened. "How'd I git two odd points in there?"

"You spelled Willamette right."

"I got it wrote on m' hand. Naw, I'm jis' kiddin', I ain't." He handed her the tea. "Here's your'n."

"*Yours,*" she said. "And thank you."

Harley grinned. "She's like th' *po*'lice, on you at ever' turn." Harley's days in liquor hauling, not to mention car racing, had taught him about police. "Boys, she can go like whiz readin' a book, says words you never heerd of. Did you say one of them big words for th' rev'rend?"

"Omnipresent," said Lace quietly.

"What'n th' nation does that mean?"

"Everywhere at one time."

"That describes my wife's mama near perfect. She had eyes in th' back of 'er head. That woman was a chicken hawk if I ever seen one. Say another'n."

She flushed and lowered her eyes. "No, Harley."

"Look what I done f'r *you.*"

"You didn't do it for me, you did it for you."

Harley nodded, sober. "Jis tell th' rev'rend one more, an I'll not ask ag'in."

"Mussitation."

"Aha."

Lace hurriedly drank the tea, then collected her books. "It's nice to see you, sir. Harley, eat your supper tonight, and thank you for a good job on your test."

"Thank you f'r teachin' me."

"Well done, Lace!" Father Tim called, as she left by the door to the driveway.

Harley glowed with unashamed pride. "Ain't she somethin'? I've knowed 'er since she was knee-high to a duck. She agg'avates me near t' death, but I think th' world of that young 'un."

Father Tim wished his dictionary weren't packed, as he didn't have a clue as to the meaning of "mussitation."

He sat with Harley next to the fan that turned left, then right.

"Lord, at th' rust they've got down there," sighed Harley, shaking his head. "I don't know but what I'd park your new ride in th' garage and drive th' Buick."

"I don't think so."

In the escalating temperature of an official heat wave, the two men spoke as if in a dream. Harley leaned toward Father Tim, to better catch the stream of air on the left; Father Tim leaned closer to Harley to catch the right stream.

Both had their elbows on their knees, their heads nearly touching, gazing at the floor.

"Think you can keep up with our boy?"

"Rev'rend, don't you worry 'bout a thing. Y'r boy'll

be workin', I'll be watchin,' an' th' Lord 'n' Master'll be in charge of th' whole deal."

"I don't know, Harley. . . ."

"Well, if *you* don't, who does?"

"Seems like I can trust Him with everything but a teenager."

"That's what you got t' trust 'im with th' most, if you ask me."

Father Tim felt a trickle of sweat between his shoulder blades.

"Don't let Dooley forget to take the livermush to his granpaw."

"Nossir."

"Every other week is how Russell likes to get it."

Harley nodded. "I'll git them hornets' nests off th' garage come Friday."

"Good. I thank you."

"I ain't goin' t' rake y'r leaves b'fore winter, if you don't mind, hit'll be good f'r th' grass."

"Fine."

"I'll mulch 'em so they'll rot easy. An' I'll mulch up around y'r plants come October."

"And the roses . . ."

"I'll prune 'em back, jis' like you said."

"I wrote the numbers down by your phone in the kitchen; I gave you the church office and home. Call us any time of the day or night, I don't care how late it is or how early."

"I'll do it. And I'll have Cynthia's little scooter runnin' like a top when you come home f'r the' weddin'. In case she gits wore out ridin' that bicycle, she can drive it back."

"Good. But don't soup it up."

"Ain't nothin' t' soup in a Mazda."

He remembered that Harley had once fiddled around with his Buick so it ran like a scalded dog; he had shot by the local police chief in a blur—twice. Not good.

They sat quiet for a time, Father Tim cupping his chin in his hands.

"And don't let Dooley play loud music down here, or we'll run our tenant off."

Harley sighed. "Lord knows I ain't a miracle worker."

⟡

He went out into the night, damp with perspiration, leaving his wife sleeping like a child.

Ten to eleven. No moon. Only a humid darkness that sharply revealed its stars as he looked up.

They weren't used to heat like this in the mountains. Mitford was legendary for its cool summers, which brought flatlanders racing up the slopes every May through October, exulting in the town's leafy shade and gentle breezes.

He walked with Barnabas around the backyard of the yellow house, stopping by the maple and hearing the stream of urine hiss into the grass.

The path through the hedge, he saw in the light from the study windows, had nearly grown over. Harley usually came around to the front door these days, and it had been three years or more since he courted his next-door neighbor.

He smiled, remembering the quote from Chesterton: "We make our friends, we make our enemies, but God makes our next-door neighbor."

Once, the depth of their feeling for one another might easily have been judged by the smooth wear on the path through the rhododendrons. Now the branches on either side of the weed-covered path had nearly grown together; one would have to duck to dash through.

As he stepped under the tulip poplar, he felt a sudden coolness, as if a barrier had been formed around the tree, forbidding the day's heat to collect beneath its limbs.

He thumped onto the sparse grass under the poplar, and Barnabas lay at his feet, panting.

Another party tomorrow night. He was weary of parties, of the endless goodbyes that stretched behind him since last December's retirement party in the parish hall. He remembered feeling his head grow light as a feather, and could not imagine the occasion to be any thing but an odd and disturbing dream. Then he found himself gone from Lord's Chapel, the parish that had both succored and tormented him, and made him happier than ever before in his life.

Retiring had been precisely what he wanted to do, and yet, when he did it, it had felt awkward and unreal, as it must feel to walk for the first time with a wooden leg.

He rubbed his dog's ear; it might have been a piece of velvet, or a child's blanket that gave forth consolation, as he stared across the hedge at the rectory's double chimneys rising in silhouette against the light of the street lamp.

It seemed an eternity since he'd lived there, quite another person than the one sitting here in the damp night grass.

For many years in that house, he had made it a practice to do what he'd learned in seminary, and that was spend an hour in study for every minute of his sermon. More than twenty hours he had faithfully spent; then fifteen, and later, starting a couple of years ago, ten. Where had the quiet center of his life gone? It seemed he was racing faster and faster around the tree, turning into butter.

On the other hand, wasn't his life now richer and deeper and more solid than ever before? Yes! Absolutely yes. He would not turn back for anything.

God had, indeed, put Cynthia Coppersmith right next door, and given her to him. But marriage, with all its delight and aggravation, seemed to swell like a dry sponge dipped into water, and occupy the largest, most fervent part of his life. Surely that was why some priests never took a spouse, and remained married to their calling.

Barnabas rolled on his side and smacked his lips, happy for the cool night air under the tree.

He loved Cynthia Kavanagh; she'd become the very life of his heart, and no, he would never turn back from her laughter and tears and winsome ways. But tonight, looking at the chimneys against the glow of the streetlight, he mourned that time of utter freedom, when nobody expected him home or cared whether he arrived, when he could sit with a book in his lap, snoring in the wing chair, a fire turning to embers on the hearth. . . .

He raised his hand to the rectory in a type of salute, and nodded to himself and closed his eyes, as the bells of Lord's Chapel began their last peal of the day.

Bong . . .

"Lord," he said aloud, as if He were there beneath the tree, "Your will be done in our lives."

Bong . . .

"Guard me from self-righteousness, and from any looking to myself in this journey."

Bong . . .

"I believe Whitecap is where You want us, and we know that You have riches for us there."

Bong . . .

"Prepare our hearts for this parish, and theirs to receive us."

Bong . . .

"Thank You for the blessing of my wife, and Dooley; for this place and this time, and yes, Lord, even for this change. . . ."

Bong . . .

Bong . . .

The bells pealed twice before he acknowledged and named the fear in his heart.

"Forgive this fear in me which I haven't confessed to You until now."

Bong . . .

"You tell us that You do not give us the spirit of fear, but of power, and of love, and of a sound mind."

Bong . . .

"Gracious God . . ." He paused.

"I surrender myself to You completely . . . again."

Bong . . .

He took a deep breath and held it, then let it out slowly, and realized he felt the peace, the peace that didn't always come, but came now.

Bong . . .

❧

The tenant was a surprise, somehow. A small woman in her late forties, overweight and mild-mannered, she appeared to try to shrink into herself, in order to occupy less space. He supposed her accent to be French, but wasn't very good at nailing that sort of thing.

They met in the late afternoon in the rectory parlor,

now furnished sparingly with her own sofa and two chairs, and a Baldwin grand piano by the window.

The cherry pie he had brought from Sweet Stuff Bakery had been placed on the table in front of the sofa where she sat, her feet scarcely touching the floor. After a day of moving into a strange house in a strange town, he thought she might have been utterly exhausted; to the contrary, she looked as fresh as if she'd risen from a long nap.

". . . very interested in old homes, Father," she was saying.

"Well, you'll certainly be living in one. The rectory was built in 1884, and wasn't dramatically altered until a bishop lived here in the fifties. He closed the fireplace in the kitchen and rebuilt the fireplace in the study—a definite comfort during our long winters. I hope you don't mind long winters."

"Oh, no. We have those in Boston with dismaying frequency."

"Mr. Skinner has shown you around—the attic, the basement?"

"Top to bottom."

"You know you may call him at any time. He'll be looking after everything for us—and for you."

"Thank you, Father, and again, thank you for allowing me to lease for such a short time. It's always good to test the waters, *n'est-ce pas?*"

"Of course."

"Mr. Skinner mentioned that you and Miss Sadie Baxter were dear friends."

"Yes, Miss Sadie meant the world to me. Did you know her?"

"Oh, no. I saw her lovely old home from Main Street and inquired about it. I'm sure she must have left you some very beautiful things."

"I might have taken anything I liked, but I took almost nothing, really. My wife found some needlepoint chair covers she's thrilled with, and so . . ."

He raised his hands, palms up, and smiled. At that moment, a large cat leaped into his lap from out of nowhere, its collar bell jingling.

"Holy smoke!" he exclaimed.

"That's Barbizon," said Hélène Pringle, unperturbed.

He sat frozen as a mullet. Barbizon had taken over his lap entirely, and was licking his white paws for a fare-thee-well. The odor of tinned fish rose in a noxious vapor to his nostrils.

His tenant peered at him. "Barbizon's no bother, I hope."

"Oh, no. Not a bit. Cats don't usually like me."

"Barbizon likes all sorts of people other cats care nothing for."

"I see."

"He was named for my mother's birthplace in France, just south of Paris. I spent my childhood there."

"Well, well."

"Do you speak French, Father?"

"Pathetically."

"I imagine Mr. Skinner told you I'll be giving piano lessons. . . ."

"That's wonderful!" he said. "We need more music in Mitford."

"He's checking to see if I might hang out a sign."

"Aha."

"Only a very small sign, of course."

"Not too small, I hope. We want people to see it!"

" 'Hélène Pringle, Lessons for the Piano, Inquire Within.' " She recited the language of her sign with some wistfulness, he thought.

"Excellent!" He glanced at his watch discreetly, and tried to rise from the chair, thinking the longhaired creature with yellow eyes would pop off to the floor. But no, it clung on with its claws, for which reason Father Tim regained his seat with a strained smile. "I must go. We've a great many things to settle at the last minute, you understand."

Hélène Pringle nodded. "*Parfaitement!* No one could understand better."

"Well, then . . ." He tried to detach the cat from his lap by picking it up, but a single claw was entrenched in his fly. Blast.

"Naughty fellow!" scolded Hélène Pringle, who rose from the sofa and came to him and took the cat, which relaxed its claws at once. He saw, then, the weariness in his tenant's eyes, in her pinched face.

She set the great animal down and it disappeared beneath the Chippendale sofa. "Cats don't like moving, you know."

He sighed agreeably. "Who does?"

"I wish you well on your journey, Father."

"And I wish you well on yours, Miss Pringle. May God bless you, and give you many happy hours here."

"Happy hours . . . ," she said, her voice trailing away.

"Oh, I nearly forgot. The key!" Harley had opened the house for their tenant and the movers.

He placed the key in her hand, and found himself staring at it, lying in her palm. She looked at it, also, and for the briefest moment, something passed between them. He could never have said what, exactly, but he would wonder at the feeling for a long time to come.

⚬

He hesitated to put the top down for the haul up the hill to Lucera, thinking it would only agitate Dooley's car lust.

"Put it down, darling!" urged his wife. "That's what it's for!"

Oh, well. It *was* a warm June night, and Dooley would just have to grow up and take it like a man. . . .

"Hey, let me drive," Dooley said as they walked to the car he'd been ogling all day. Father Tim thought their charge looked like something out of a magazine in his school blazer, a tie, and tan pants.

"You look great, like something out of a magazine," said Father Tim, rushing around to the driver's side.

"Let me drive," repeated Dooley, staying focused. "It's just up the hill."

Cynthia took her husband's arm and steered him to the passenger side. "Why not let him drive, Timothy? It's just up the hill. But I can't sit in the back, it'll ruin my hair."

Two against one.

———⊖———

What was left of his own hair was flying forty ways from Sunday as they roared up Fernbank's driveway and saw lights blazing from every window in the grand house. He was still combing when they went up the steps and through the open front door.

He blinked. Then he blinked again.

"Wow!" said Cynthia.

"Man!" exclaimed Dooley.

Father Tim remembered flushing Miss Sadie's toilets more than once with rainwater that had leaked from this very ceiling into soup pots and a turkey roaster.

"No way," Dooley muttered, shaking his head in disbelief.

Fernbank's cavernous entry hall had become . . . what? Miraculously warm. Smaller, somehow. Intimate. He fairly shivered with excitement. Was this a dream?

And the music—by jove, it was opera, it was Puccini, he couldn't believe his ears. The last time he'd heard opera was months ago, through the static of his car radio.

"Garlic!" rhapsodized his wife, inhaling deeply.

Along the walls in wooden bins were fresh tomatoes and crusty loaves of bread, bundles of fragrant herbs and great bunches of grapes, yellow globes of cheese and bottles of olive oil. The contents of the bottles gleamed like molten gold in the candlelight.

"Timothy, look! The walls!"

Good grief, there were some of those walls his wife had created in the rectory kitchen a couple of years ago—pockmarked, smoky, primitive—not Miss Sadie's walls at all. Miss Sadie would be in a huff over this, and no two ways about it.

"Father! Cynthia! Dooley! Welcome!"

It was the hospitable Andrew Gregory, coming through the door of the dining room in a pale linen suit.

He felt positively heady with the rush of aromas and sounds, and the sight of Mitford's favorite antiques dealer transformed into a tanned and happy maître d'.

Mule and Fancy dropped by the table where the Kavanaghs and Dooley were seated with the Harpers and Lace Turner.

"How do you say th' name of this place?" Fancy asked in a whisper. "I can't remember for shoot!"

"Lu-*chair*-ah!" crowed Cynthia, glad to be of help.

Fancy stared around the room, disbelieving. "There's people here I never laid eyes on before."

Mule sighed. "This is gonna be a deep-pocket deal," he muttered, following Fancy to their corner table.

Father Tim was fairly smitten with his dinner companions, it all seemed so lively and . . . *fun,* a thing he was always seeking to understand and claim for his own.

Olivia hadn't aged an iota since he married her to the town doctor a few years ago; he remembered dancing at their reception in the ballroom, across the hall from this very table. Her dark hair was pulled into French braids, such as she eagerly wove each day for Lace, and her violet eyes still pierced his heart with appealing candor.

Hoppy grinned at his wife and took her hand. "Where *are* we, anyway?"

"Certainly not in Mitford!" she said, laughing.

"I think we're . . . in a dream," said Lace, so softly that only he and perhaps Dooley could hear.

Enthralled, that was the word. They were all enthralled.

The large dining room, where he'd once eaten cornbread and beans with Miss Sadie and Louella, was crowded with people from Wesley and Holding, with the occasional familiar face thrown in, as it were, for good measure.

There was Hope Winchester waving across the room, and a couple of tables away were the mayor and Ray with at least two of their attractive, deluxe-size daughters, sitting where Miss Sadie's Georgian highboy used to stand, and over in the far corner . . .

His heart pumped wildly, taking his breath away.

Edith Mallory. Just as he spotted her, she looked up and gazed directly into his eyes.

He turned away quickly. Any contact at all with his former parishioner was akin to a sting from a scorpion. He had foolishly believed she would somehow drop out of sight, and he'd never be forced to lay eyes on her again. She'd been a thorn in his flesh for years—seeking to manipulate and seduce him, trying to buy the last mayoral race, treating the villagers like pond scum. . . .

Cynthia peered at him. "What is it, dearest? You're white as a sheet."

"Starving," he mumbled, grabbing a chunk of bread.

<hr />

A couple of years ago, Lace Turner had helped Dooley save Barnabas from bleeding to death when hit by a car. When minutes counted, Dooley and Lace had pitched in to get the job done, and a bond formed between them where only enmity had existed.

But time and distance had strained that bond, and they were now two new and different people.

Father Tim hadn't missed Dooley's fervent appraisal of Lace Turner as she studied her hand-printed menu. He found it more telling, however, that Dooley feigned indifference each time Lace spoke, which wasn't often. Further, he observed, the boy who was known for his appetite picked at his food, laughed nervously, eternally twisted the knot in his tie, and knocked over his water glass.

No doubt about it, Dooley Barlowe was interested in more than cars.

<hr />

They had feasted on risotto and scallopini, on lamb shank and fresh mussels, on chicken roasted with rose-mary from the Fernbank gardens, and on Anna Gregory's freshly made pasta stuffed with ricotta and bathed in a sultry marinara from local greenhouse tomatoes; they had ordered gallons of sparkling water, Coke, and a bottle of Chianti from Lucera, and had all placed their order for Tony's tiramisu.

Hoppy Harper sat back and looked fondly at Lace, who was seated next to him and across from Dooley. "Lace, why don't you tell everyone your good news?"

Lace gazed around the table slowly, half shyly.

Father Tim observed that Dooley pretended to be more interested in drumming his fingers on the table than hearing what Lace had to say.

"I'm going away to school in September."

The fingers stopped drumming.

"Lovely!" said Cynthia. "Where?"

"Virginia. Mrs. Hemingway's." Fresh color stole into the girl's tanned cheeks.

"Oh, man," said Dooley, rolling his eyes. "Gross."

Father Tim bristled. "I beg your pardon?"

"Mrs. Hemingway has geeky girls."

Father Tim could have shaken the boy until his teeth rattled. "Apologize for that at once."

Dooley colored furiously, undecided about whether to stick up for what he had just said, or do as he was told.

He stuck up for what he had just said. "They hardly ever get invited to our school for parties, they're so . . . *smart.*" He said the last word with derision.

"Lace has just told us good news," Father Tim said quietly. "You have just shown us bad behavior. I ask once more that you apologize to Lace."

Dooley tried to raise his eyes to his dinner partner, but could not. "Sorry," he said, meditating on his water glass.

Hoppy slipped his arm around Lace's shoulders. "Dooley's right, actually. The girls at Mrs. Hemingway's are very smart, indeed. Gifted, as well. Lace and several of her classmates will spend next summer in Tuscany, studying classical literature and watercolor—on scholarships. We're very proud of Lace."

Father Tim saw on the girl's face the kind of look he'd seen when he caught her stealing Miss Sadie's ferns—the softness had disappeared, the hardness had returned.

Lace sat straight as a ramrod in the chair, staring over the head of the miserable and hapless wretch opposite her.

Dooley Barlowe had stepped in it, big-time.

⎯⎯⎯⎯⎯⎯⎯⎯⎯⎯

While Cynthia trotted off with Dooley to bring the car around, Father Tim went in search of Andrew, seeking the whereabouts of their check.

Andrew Gregory still looked as fresh and unwrinkled as if he'd sauntered through the park, not opened a restaurant and catered to the whims of more than fifty people. He was the only man Father Tim knew who didn't wrinkle linen.

His mind couldn't avoid a momentary flashback to Andrew's earnest courtship of Cynthia. He'd watched their comings and goings from his bedroom window at the rectory, feeling miserable, to say the least. He remembered once thinking of the tall, slender Andrew as a cedar of Lebanon, and of himself, a lowly country parson, as mere scrub pine.

But who had won fair maid?

"I've had quite a visit with your new tenant," Andrew said. "She stayed in Wesley the last few days, waiting for the movers, and came several times to the shop. Very inquisitive about Fernbank, it seems. Wanted to know what was sold out of the house, and so on. Said she had a great interest in old homes."

"Yes, she mentioned that to me."

"She asked me to name the pieces I bought from you, and was eager to learn whether anything was left in the attic. I told her no, it had all been cleaned out and given away. She asked whether relatives had taken anything, and I said I didn't really know."

"Curious."

"I thought so," said Andrew. "And by the way, your money doesn't spend here."

Andrew's wife joined them from the kitchen, looking flushed and happy.

"Put away, put back," said Anna, indicating his wallet. He thought Andrew's Italian bride of two years, who had come from the village of Lucera, bore a breathtaking resemblance to Sophia Loren.

"But . . ."

"It's our gift to you, our farewell present," Andrew insisted.

"Well, then. Thank you. Thank you so much! You've made a great contribution to Mitford, Miss Sadie would be proud to see Fernbank filled with light and laughter. Anna, Andrew—'til we meet again."

"*Ciao!*" cried Anna, throwing her arms around him and kissing both his cheeks. He loved Italians. "Go with God!"

"Father!" It was Tony, Anna's younger brother and Lucera's chef, running from the kitchen in his white hat and splattered apron. "*Grazie al cielo!* I thought I'd missed you!"

Tony embraced him vigorously, kissed both cheeks, then stood back and gripped his shoulders. Father Tim didn't know when he'd seen a handsomer fellow in Mitford. *"Ciao!"* said Tony, his dark eyes bright with feeling. "God be with you!"

"And also with you, my friend."

"Ciao!" they shouted from the car to Andrew and Anna, who came out to the porch as they drove away from Fernbank, away from the grand old house with the grand new life.

$\backsim$

He was driving on the Parkway with the top down, when he looked in the rearview mirror and saw his Buick pulling up behind him.

Who was the driver? It was Dooley, with Barnabas sitting in the seat beside him, looking straight ahead.

Dooley was grinning from ear to ear; he could see him distinctly. Yet, when he looked again, the car was gone, vanished.

He woke up, peering into the darkness.

Two a.m., according to the clock by their bed. He sighed.

"Are you awake?" asked Cynthia.

"I had a dream."

"About what?"

"Dooley. He was driving my Buick."

"Oh. I can't sleep, I can never sleep before a long trip." She sighed, and he reached over and patted her shoulder.

"Maybe I could give Dooley the Buick next year. He could pay something for it, two or three thousand. . . ."

"Umm," she said.

Suddenly he had a brilliant idea. Not everybody

could wake in the middle of the night and think so cleverly.

"Tell you what. Why don't I give *you* the Buick, and you let Dooley pay you a few thousand for the Mazda. I think he'd like your car better. It's newer, has more . . . youthful styling."

"Not on your life," she said. "I may be a preacher's wife, but I did *not* take a vow of poverty."

"Cynthia, the Buick drives like a dream."

"Dream on," she said. His wife was stubborn as a mule.

"It never needs any work."

"It is fourteen years old, the paint is faded, and there's rust on the right fender. The upholstery on the driver's side is smithereens, a church fan works better than the air conditioner, and it reeks of mildew."

He sighed. "Other than that, Mrs. Lincoln, how did you like the play?"

She giggled.

He rolled over to her and they assumed their easy spoon position, which someone had called "the staple consolation of the marriage bed." She felt warm and easy in his arms.

"Listen," he said.

"To what?"

"I heard something just then. Music, I think."

They lay very still. The lightest notes from a piano floated through the window.

"A piano," he said.

"Chopin," she murmured.

Moments later, he heard her whiffling snore, found it calming, and fell asleep.

Hammer and tong.

That's how they were going at it in the yellow house.

The plan was to get on the road by eight o'clock, which was when Dooley reported to The Local.

Excited about the idea that had come to him in the dream, Father Tim asked Dooley to help tote the last of the cargo to the curb, where Violet was already in her cage on the rear floor of the Mustang.

The top was down, the day was bright and promising, and Barnabas had been walked around the monument at a trot.

"Ah!" Father Tim inhaled the summer morning air, then turned to Dooley, grinning.

"You're pretty happy," said Dooley.

"I'm happy to tell you that next summer, with only a modest outlay of funds on your part, Cynthia and I would like to make you the proud owner of . . . the Buick."

Dooley looked stunned.

"I ain't drivin' that thing!" he said, reverting to local vernacular and obviously highly insulted.

They were standing on the sidewalk as the Lord's Chapel bells chimed eight.

Puny and the twins were first in line, and he was up to bat.

"Say bye-bye to Granpaw," urged Puny.

"Bye-bye, Ba," said Sissy. She reached out to him, nearly sprawling out of Puny's arms.

He plucked her from her mother and held her, kissing her forehead. "God be with you, Sissy."

Her green eyes brimmed with tears. "Come back, Ba."

He set her down on chubby legs, wondering how he could go through with this. . . .

He hoisted the plump, sober Sassy, who was chewing a piece of toast, and kissed the damp tousle of red hair. "God's blessings, Sassy." Barnabas, who was sitting patiently on the sidewalk, licked Sissy's face.

Puny was openly bawling. Blast. He took it like a man and gave her a hug, feeling her great steadfastness, smelling the starch in her blouse, loving her goodness to him over the years. "You're always in our prayers," he told her, hoarse with feeling.

Puny wiped her nose with the hem of her apron. "We'll miss you."

"We'll be back before you know it."

Puny and the children fled into the yellow house, as Cynthia stood on tiptoe and gave Dooley a hug. "Take care of yourself, you big lug."

"I will."

"And write. Or call. A lot!"

"I will."

Father Tim clasped the boy to him, then stood back and gazed at him intently. "I'm counting on you to help Harley hold things together around here."

"Yes, sir. I will."

"We love you."

"I love you back." Dooley said it fair and square, looking them in the eye. Then he turned and ran to his red bicycle, leaped on it, and pedaled toward Main Street. Before he reached the corner, he stopped, looked back, and waved. " 'Bye, Cynthia, 'bye, Dad!"

They waved as Dooley disappeared around the rhododendron bush.

Father Tim jingled the keys in his hand. "Harley, reckon you can sell the Buick for me?"

Harley looked skeptical, scratched his head, and gazed at the sidewalk.

"Would you . . . like to drive it while I'm gone?"

"Rev'rend, I 'preciate th' offer, but I'll stick to m' truck."

"Aha." Clearly, he had a vehicle he couldn't even give away, much less sell.

"Well, Harley . . ." He put his arm around the shoulders of the small, frail man who was now holding down the fort.

"Rev'rend, Cynthia . . . th' Lord go with you." Harley's chin trembled, and he wiped his eyes with his sleeve.

" 'Bye, Harley," said Cynthia. "We love you."

Father Tim opened the passenger door and put the seat forward. "Come on, fellow, get in."

Barnabas leaped onto the leather seat, sniffed Violet's cage, and lay down, looking doleful.

"Don't even think about crying," he told his wife as they climbed in the car.

"The wind in our hair . . . ," she said, laughing through the tears.

He started the engine. "The cry of gulls wheeling above us . . ."

"The smell of salt air!"

He turned around in a driveway at the end of Wisteria Lane. Man alive, he liked the way this thing handled, and the seat . . . the seat felt like an easy chair.

They waved to Harley, who was rooted to the spot and waving back.

After hooking a right on Main Street, he drove slowly, as if they were a parade car. J. C. Hogan was just trotting into the Grill.

Father Tim hammered down on the horn and J.C. looked up, dumbstruck, as they waved.

Then he stepped on the gas and whipped around the monument, consciously avoiding a glance in the rearview mirror.

CHAPTER FOUR

The Smell of Salt Air

He was loving this.

"You're loving this!" crowed his wife.

He couldn't remember ever having such a sense of perfect freedom; he felt light as air, quick as mercury, transparent as glass.

And hot as blazes.

He looked into the rearview mirror. Barnabas, currently sitting up with his head riveted into the scorching wind, was attracting the attention of all westbound traffic.

"You must stop and get a hat!" his wife declared over the roar of an eighteen-wheeler. "Your head is turning pink!"

"Lunch and a hat, coming up," he said, reluctant to delay their journey, even if it was into the unknown.

They were barreling toward Williamston, through open tobacco country.

"Flat," said Cynthia, peering at the landscape.

"Hard to have an ocean where it isn't flat."

"Hot," she said, reduced to telegraphic speech.

"Don't say we weren't warned. Want to put the top up?"

"Not yet, I'm trying to get the look of an island native." His wife was wearing shorts and a tank top, sunglasses and a Mitford Reds ball cap. All exposed areas were slathered with oil, and she was frying.

"I think we need to get Barnabas under cover before long. We'll put it up at Williamston."

Whoosh. A tractor-trailer nearly sucked them out of the car. He reached up and clamped his new hat to his head.

"Did Miss Pringle say why she left Boston to live in Mitford?"

"No. Didn't say."

"And you didn't ask?"

"Never thought to."

"Why on earth would she pick Mitford? And for only six months! Can you imagine hauling a piano from Boston for only six months? Does she have friends or relatives in Mitford?"

"I don't think so, but I'm not sure."

"Darling, how can you ever *know* things about people if you don't ask?"

As a priest, he usually managed to find out more than he wanted to know, though hardly ever through asking.

She sat thinking, with Violet asleep at her feet on the floorboard.

"Remember that chicken salad we had for lunch?" she inquired.

"Only vaguely."

"It's becoming a distant memory to me, too. I'm starved. Actually, during the entire lunch, I was dreaming of something finer."

"Oh?"

"Esther's cake."

"Aha."

"In the cooler. . . ."

"Umm."

"I've been thinking how moist it is, how cold and sweet, how velveteen its texture. . . ."

"That's Esther's cake, all right."

"And those discreet little morsels of bittersweet rind that burst in your mouth like. . . . like sunshine!"

"You're a regular Cowper of cake."

"Don't you think we should have some?" she asked.

"Now you're talking."

"Did you bring your pocketknife?"

"Always," he said, producing it from his pocket.

She got on her knees in her seat and foraged around on the floorboard in back, cranking off the cooler top and fetching out the foil-wrapped mound.

"Oh, lovely. Nice and cold on my legs. Well, now. How shall we do this?" she asked, peeling back layers of foil. "This is the cake that nearly sent you to heaven in your prime. You probably shouldn't have a whole slice."

"If you recall," he said, "it was *two* slices that nearly sent me packing. I'll have one slice, and would appreciate not being able to see through it."

She carefully carved a small piece and put it on a napkin from the glove compartment. "Don't keel over on me," she said, meaning it.

Driving to the beach in a red convertible, eating Esther's cake—how many men wouldn't crave to be in his shoes? The sweetness and delicacy of the vanishing morsel in his hands were literally intoxicating. *Priest Found Drunk on Layer Cake* . . .

"Darling, you talked in your sleep last night."

"Uh-oh."

"You said 'slick' several times; you were very restless."

"Slick?"

"Yes, and once I think you said 'Tommy.' "

"Aha!" The dream flooded back to him instantly. His boyhood friend, Tommy Noles, and that miserable experience that earned him his nickname, a nickname he'd never mentioned to his wife. . . .

"Who is Tommy?" she queried.

"Tommy Noles, my old friend from Holly Springs."

"The one who always knew the make and model of cars."

"Right."

"What were you dreaming?"

As usual, his inquisitive wife wanted to know everything. Should he tell her?

"Well, let's see. I was dreaming about . . . well, about the time when . . ."

"When what?"

Weren't couples supposed to tell each other their fondest wishes, their deepest secrets, their blackest fears? He'd never thought much of that scheme, but so far, it had worked. In fact, he'd found that for every one of his deepest secrets, Cynthia Kavanagh would pour forth two or three of her own; it was like winning at slots.

". . . when I got my nickname."

"Are you blushing or is that the sun?"

"The sun," he said.

"What about when you got your nickname? I never knew you had one."

Tommy Noles had lived right up the road, next to his attorney father's gentleman's farm. Mr. Noles was a history teacher and a packrat. He hauled every imaginable oddity to his seven acres, and parked it around the property as if it were outdoor sculpture. A rusting haymow, an antique tractor, a gas tank from a service station, a prairie schooner, a large advertising sign for tobacco . . .

Mr. Noles mowed around these objects regularly and with great respect, but neglected to trim the grass that grew directly against them, so that each was sheathed in a colorful nest of sedge and wildflowers, which, as a boy, the young Tim had found enhancing.

His father found none of it enhancing, his father who idolized perfection above all else, and no son of his would be allowed to play with Tommy Noles.

But he had, in fact, played with Tommy Noles, wading in the creek, building a fort in the woods, constructing a tree house, fishing for crappie, searching for arrowheads in the fields.

Tommy Noles had wanted to be a fighter pilot in a terrible war, and he, Timothy Kavanagh, wanted to be a boxer or an animal trainer or, oddly enough, a bookbinder, for hadn't he been outrageously smitten with the smell and the look of his grandfather's books?

He remembered training Tommy's dog, Jeff, to catch sticks in midair, and to roll over and play dead. It had been deeply satisfying to finagle another living creature into doing anything at all, and he longed for a dog of his own, but his father wouldn't allow it. Dogs had fleas, dogs scratched, dogs defecated.

He grew uneasy thinking about how it had happened.

Tommy Noles, urged by the others and unbeknownst to him, had put dog poop just inside the double doors of the schoolhouse, two piles of it.

Bust in through those doors, runnin', Tommy said to him, *and we'll give you a nickel.*

Why? he asked. The teachers were in a meeting in the gym, and he smelled trouble brewing.

Just because, just for nothin', just run up th' steps, bust through th' doors, and run down th' hall all th' way to th' water fountain, and we'll give you a In'ian head nickel.

He still didn't know why he did it, he didn't remember wanting the money especially, perhaps he did it because he was the scrawny one, the geek, the one who loved to read and write and think and ponder words and meanings.

Without caring, he just did it; he burst through the doors running, and hit the piles and skidded down the hall as if he'd connected with a patch of crankcase oil. Just outside Miss McNolty's classroom, he lost his balance and crashed to the floor.

He heard the boys screaming with laughter at the front door as he got up, stinking, and tried to scrape the slimy stuff off his shoes. It was slick as grease. . . .

He walked toward them, his heart thundering. He had never picked a fight or been in one; he would have run first, not looking back.

But this was different. His friend had betrayed him.

They watched him coming toward them and backed down the steps.

Hey, Slick! somebody yelled. Three boys who were laughing and holding their noses suddenly turned and ran to the oak tree, where they stopped and peered from behind it. Lee Adderholt and Tommy Noles stood fast near the bottom of the steps, looking awed, mesmerized.

What had they seen on his face? He would never know.

I . . . I'm sorry, Tim, Tommy said.

He felt something building in himself, something . . . towering. He seemed to be suddenly six feet tall, and growing.

I really am! wailed Tommy.

He never remembered what happened, exactly, he just knew that he plowed into Tommy Noles without fear, without trembling, and beat the living crap out of him.

Then he was sitting in the principal's office—thank God it was Mr. Lewis, who was too tenderhearted to whip anybody. Mr. Lewis had looked at him for what seemed a long time, with what appeared to be kindness in his face, but the young Kavanagh couldn't be sure.

He knew, sitting there, that he had liked beating the tar out of Tommy Noles. But most of all, he had liked making him *cry* in front of the people who had hooted and laughed, holding their noses.

Your father will never hear this from me, Mr. Lewis said. *But if anyone tells him and he asks, I will, of course, be required to . . .*

For the first time in his life, he had been glad, thrilled, that everyone he knew, his classmates and friends, were terrified of his father, and wouldn't dare speak to him, much less reveal the dark transgression of his son brawling in a fistfight.

What happened, Timothy? asked his mother.

He dropped his head. He had never lied to his mother.

I beat up Tommy Noles.

She studied him. *I'm sure he asked for it,* she said, simply.

Yes, ma'am.

But don't ever do this again.

No, ma'am.

He hadn't ever done it again; he hadn't needed to. It had been the fight of his life, the Grand Inquisition. In his rage, he had taken on the very world with his two hands, and somehow, oddly, won.

The scrawny kid with the scrawny arms and the penchant for reading large books and making straight A's had been suffused with a new aura. They gave him a wide berth when they called him Slick, for they had seen his rage, and witnessed his consuming power, and hadn't understood it and never would. He was Timothy Kavanagh, not to be messed with.

Period.

He grinned, pulling around an RV from Texas. After that incident, Tommy Noles had become the best friend he had in the world, even if he had failed to hand over the nickel. Sometimes, when he had nothing else to do, he'd calculate what Tommy would owe him today, given fifty-six years of accumulated interest on a nickel.

"I'm growing older," said his eager wife, "just waiting to hear your nickname."

"Slick," he said, looking straight ahead.

He wasn't surprised that she nearly doubled over with laughter. "Slick! *Slick?*" Clearly, that was the funniest thing she'd ever heard in her life.

"Slick! That's *too* wonderful! I can't *believe* it!"

Ha, ha, ha, on and on. He would nip this in the bud. "So what was *your* nickname, Kavanagh?"

She stopped laughing.

Bingo, he thought.

"Must you know?"

"Cynthia, Cynthia . . . need you ask?"

"You won't laugh?"

"Laugh? I'll kill myself laughing. So tell me."

She sighed deeply and tucked a strand of blond hair under the ball cap. "Tubs."

"Tubs?" Marriage was a wonderful thing. It produced all sorts of ways to get even with somebody without necessarily going to jail. But seeing the look on her face, he couldn't laugh.

"Tubby to begin, then shortened to Tubs. Fatter than fat, that was me."

He couldn't imagine it.

"You couldn't even imagine," she said. "When I was ten years old . . . do you remember those photographers who traveled around with a pony?"

He remembered.

"One took my picture and I waited for weeks for it to come in the mail. When we opened the envelope, I couldn't believe my eyes, nor could anyone else. They all said I was . . . they said I was bigger than the pony."

"No."

"Oh, yes, they raved about it 'til kingdom come, Tubs this and Tubs that. My mother and father loved having their picture taken, so they'd dashed in the house and come out looking like Ginger Rogers and Fred Astaire. I, on the other hand, had been popped onto that sulking pony in a hideous dress, looking precisely like W. C. Fields."

She peered at him. "If you ever mention that hideous name to a soul, I'll murder you."

"If you ever mention mine, same back."

"Deal," she said, shaking his hand.

"Deal," he said, seeing a sign that said *Williamston, 10 miles.*

⌁

He was looking at his watch when a raindrop hit the crystal face.

Two-thirty, they should be there around six-thirty or seven o'clock, with plenty of daylight to unload the car and check out their new home.

The suddenness of the downpour was shocking. Without warning, a sheet of wind-driven rain was upon them, thundering out of darkened skies. He veered off the road and careened to a stop, the engine running. Dear God, he knew how to put the top *down* on this thing, but Dooley had been the one who put it up. He fumbled with the button on the console, but nothing happened.

"Timothy!" His wife was drenched, sopping.

"What do we do?" he shouted.

"I don't know!" The wind carried her voice away.

He lunged to the right and felt in the glove compartment for the owner's manual, as Barnabas, quaking with fear, leaped into Cynthia's lap, which was already occupied by Violet.

"Back! Go back!" She was almost wholly concealed by his mass of streaming fur. Barnabas went back.

The force of the rain was unbelievable. It thudded against their skin and heads like so many small mallets. He shoved the manual under the dashboard on Cynthia's side, his glasses running with rain. Index, page 391, not under "Top," not under . . . there it was. "Convertible," page 213. He managed to see the words *Engage the parking brake* before the book absorbed water like a sponge and the instructions ran together in a blur.

He pulled the brake, then pressed the button repeatedly, to no avail. *Dear God, help.* . . .

"The boot!" Cynthia cried.

He leaped out, dangerously close to the highway on which cars were still racing, and fumbled to remove the side edges of the boot clip from under the side belt moldings. It took an eternity, and they were drowning.

Back in the car, he pressed the button, and the top began rising. They were taking on water like a bottomless canoe.

The top rose midway and, like a sail on a boat, was instantly filled with wind and driving rain. The top appeared to freeze in midair.

"We'll have to do it manually!" he shouted above the roar. "Get out!"

Help us, Lord, he prayed, as they hauled the thing over, straining against the terrible force of the wind, then brought it down and opened the doors and sloshed into the brimming seats. They turned the levers and secured the top, and sat back, panting, daunted now by the deafening thunder on the roof.

"The towels!" she shouted. "In the back!"

He strained around and reached behind her seat and found the wrapped bundle of a dozen terry towels, which had been cunningly advertised as "thirsty." They were sodden.

Violet howled in Cynthia's lap.

"If we wring them out, we can mop our seats!"

They wrung the water onto the floorboard at their feet, afraid to open the windows, and swabbed the leather seats. It sounded as if the pounding rain would tear through the canvas and swamp them utterly.

Then the lightning began, cracking over their heads.

Barnabas returned to the front in a single leap, and landed in Father Tim's lap, trembling.

The windows were fogged completely, his glasses were useless. He took them off and put them in his shirt pocket. As he held on to his dog, all he could see from their red submarine were the stabbing streaks of lightning.

—◦—

The rain that began so violently at two-thirty stopped at three o'clock, then returned around three-thirty to pummel the car with renewed energy, as lightning cracked around them with a vengeance.

Sitting on the shoulder since the last downpour began, they briefly considered trying to get back on the highway and drive to a service station, a bridge, anything, but visibility was zero.

Pouring sweat in the tropical humidity of the car, they found the air-conditioning was no relief. Its extreme efficiency made them feel frozen as cods in their wet clothing.

If only they were driving the Buick, he thought. The feeble air-conditioning his wife had so freely lambasted would be exactly right for their circumstances. In fact, his Buick would be the perfect security against a storm that threatened to rip a frivolous rag from over their heads and fling it into some outlying tobacco field.

The temperature in the car was easily ninety degrees. He remembered paying ten pounds for an hour's worth of this very misery in an English hotel sauna, without, of course, the disagreeable odor of steaming dog and cat fur.

"When life gives you lemons . . . ," he muttered darkly.

". . . make lemonade," said his wife, stroking her drenched cat.

"Four o'clock," he said, pulling onto the highway. "We've lost nearly two hours. That means we'll get into Whitecap around dark."

"Ah, well, dearest, not to worry. This can't go on forever."

He hoped such weather would at least put a crimp in the ridiculous notion of wearing grass skirts tomorrow night.

⟨∽⟩

The aftermath of the storm was not a pretty sight. Apparently, they'd missed the worst of it.

Here and there, billboards were blown down, a metal sign lying in the middle of the highway advertised night crawlers and boiled peanuts, and most crops stood partially immersed.

"Our baptism into a new life," he said, looking at the dazzling light breaking over the fields.

⟨∽⟩

At a little after seven o'clock, the rain returned and the wind with it. No lightning this time, but a heavy, insistent pounding over their heads that clearly meant business.

He stopped and did a glucometer check to make sure he wasn't in a nonketotic hyperglycemic coma, thanks to Esther's cake, and was fairly pleased with the reading.

"What do you think?" he asked, parked by the

pump at an Amoco station. "Should we look for supper or keep moving?" When he was tired, he still referred to the evening meal as "supper," as he had in childhood.

"It's a wasteland out there. Where would we find supper unless we catch it off a bank?"

"Now, now, Kavanagh. You were thinking wild asparagus with spring lamb, while I was thinking hot dogs all the way."

"I don't know, darling, I feel we should get there and settle in. After all, we have to make the bed when we arrive, and here we are, hours away, and I'm already dying to be *in* one!"

"No supper, then?"

"Maybe a pack of Nabs or some peanuts while we're here. I mean, look what you've got to drive through for who knows how long."

The Mustang shuddered in a violent crosswind.

"You're right," he said, getting out of the car.

He trudged into the neon light of the service station, feeling like a garden slug in his still-damp clothes.

⟲

"This is endless, she said as they crept through the several blinkers of a business district that they presumed to be Roper—or was it Scuppernong? The blinkers danced wildly in the wind, on electric wires strung above the street.

It seemed the wind and rain would hit them for twenty or thirty minutes, slack off or let up altogether, then hit them again with another wallop.

Violet snored in Cynthia's lap, Barnabas snored on the backseat.

Father Tim hunkered over the wheel, staring down the oncoming lights. "Marry a preacher, Kavanagh, and life ceases to be boring."

"I'd give an arm and a leg for a boring life," she said grimly, then suddenly laughed. "But only for five minutes!"

There was a long silence as he navigated through the downpour.

"Dearest, what exactly did you *say* to God in your discussions about what to do in retirement?"

"I said I was willing to go anywhere He sent me."

"Do you recall if He said anything back?"

"He said, 'That's what I like to hear.' Not in an audible voice, of course. He put it on my heart."

"Aha," she said, quoting her husband.

"Look," he said, "there's a sign for Columbia. Do we go on to Columbia, or make a turn somewhere?"

"On to Columbia," she said, squinting at the map.

His wife had never professed to be much of a navigator; he hoped they didn't end up in Morehead City.

When they reached the bridge to Whitecap, the wind and rain had stopped; there was an innocent peace in the air.

A sign stood at the entrance to the bridge, which had been closed off with a heavy chain and a soldierly row of orange cones.

BRIDGE OUT
FERRY 2 Blocks
& Left **$10**
No Ferry
After 10 P.M.

"Good heavens," said his wife, "isn't it after ten o'clock?"

"Five 'til," he said, backing up. He made the turn and hammered down on the accelerator.

"That's *one* block . . . ," she said.

Going this fast on wet pavement didn't exactly demonstrate the wisdom of the ages. "This is two," he counted.

"Now turn left here. I'm praying they'll be open."

He turned left. Nothing but yawning darkness. Then, a dim light a few yards ahead, swinging.

They inched along, not knowing what lay in their path. A sign propped against a sawhorse revealed itself in the glare of the headlights.

Ferry to Whitecap
Have Your $ Ready

A lantern bobbed from the corner of what appeared to be a small building perched at the edge of the water.

He'd read somewhere about blowing your horn for a ferry, and gave it a long blast.

"Lord, is this a joke?" his wife inquired aloud of her Maker.

A light went on in the building and a man came out, wearing a cap, an undershirt, and buttoning his pants.

Father Tim eased the window down a few inches.

"Done closed."

"Two minutes," said Father Tim, pointing to his watch. "Two whole minutes before ten. You've got to take us across." He nearly said, *I'm clergy,* but stopped himself.

"You live across?"

"We're moving to Whitecap."

"Don't know as you'd want to go across tonight," said the man, still buttoning. " 'Lectricity's off. Black as a witch's liver."

Father Tim turned to Cynthia. "What do you think?"

"Where would we stay over here?"

"Have t' turn back fourteen miles."

Cynthia looked at her husband. "We're going across!"

"Twenty dollars," said the man, unsmiling.

"Done," said Whitecap's new priest.

───────⟨∘⟩───────

Leaving the tropical confines of the car and clinging to the rail of the ferry, they looked across the black water, and up to clouds racing over the face of the moon. They were leaving the vast continent behind, and going to what looked like mere flotsam on the breast of the sea.

The ferry rocked and labored along its passage, belching oily fumes. Yet, quite apart from the noxious smell, Cynthia detected something finer, "There it is, Timothy! The smell of salt air!"

"Gulls wheeling above us," he muttered lamely, noting that a few gulls followed the ferry, even in the dead of night.

She leaned against his shoulder, and he put his arm around her and took off her cap and nuzzled her hair. She was his rock in an ocean of change, no pun intended.

"Look at the stars coming out, my dearest. The sky is as fresh and new as the fourth day of Creation. It's going to be wonderful, Timothy, our new life. We're going to feel freer, somehow, I promise."

That was a very nice speech, he noted, as only his wife could make.

"Absolutely!" he said, trying to mean it.

Their car had been unchained from its moorings, and the ramp to Whitecap cranked down. The ferry pilot stood by the ramp, a cigarette in his mouth, holding the gas lantern and signaling them off.

"Would you look at our map?" Father Tim leaned out the window. "We're trying to get . . . here." He pointed to the location of Dove Cottage, marked by a red arrow. "Since we're not approaching from the bridge . . ."

The lantern was lifted to light the hand-drawn map. "No problem," said the pilot, leaving the cigarette in place. "I've been around in there a few times. Go off th' ramp, take a left, drive about a mile and a half, turn right on Tern Avenue, go straight for about a mile, then take a left on Hastings. Looks like your place is on th' corner . . . right there."

"Left off the ramp, a mile and a half . . ." Father Tim repeated the litany. "Any idea when the power might be restored?"

"By mornin', most likely. Worst out was three days, back in '89. What line of business you in?"

"New priest at St. John's in the Grove."

The pilot took a heavy drag on his cigarette and pitched it over the rail. Then he reached in his pants pocket, withdrew a ten-dollar bill, and handed it through the window.

"Oh, but—"

"Godspeed," said the ferry pilot, walking away.

A waxing moon drifted above them as they drove along the narrow road.

"They all look alike," Cynthia said, peering at the darkened houses. "White, with picket fences. Some on stilts. Goodness, do you think all these people are really sleeping?"

"I saw something that looked like candles in one window."

"Did we bring candles?"

"What do you think?"

"I think we brought candles! I'm thrilled to be married to such a predictable stick-in-the-mud. I hope you brought extra blades for my razor."

"If I didn't, which I did, you could find them at a store. Whitecap isn't the Australian Outback."

"You know one reason I love you?" she asked.

"I haven't the foggiest."

"Because," she said, "you're steady. So very steady."

A former bishop had once said something like that, calling him a "plow horse." The bishop made it clear, however, that it was the racehorse that clambered to the top of the church ladder and made a fine stall for himself.

Barnabas thrust his head out the window, sniffing. New smells were everywhere, there was nothing known or expected about the smells in these parts.

"Hastings Avenue should be coming up," he said. "There! Do you hear it?"

"The ocean! Yes! Oh, stop—just for a moment."

He slowed to a stop, and realized the great roar was out there somewhere, that just over the high dunes was a beach, and, lying beyond, a vast rink of platinum shimmering under the moon.

" 'Listen!' " he whispered, quoting Wordsworth. " 'The Mighty Being is awake, and doth with His eternal motion make, a sound like thunder, everlastingly.' "

"Lovely!" she breathed.

They moved on slowly, as if already obeying some island impulse, some new metabolism. With only the moon, stars, and headlights to illumine their way in the endless darkness, they might have been the last creatures on earth.

"Let's put the top down!" crowed Cynthia.

"Fat chance," he said, turning off Tern.

∽

He walked back to the car with the flashlight.

"I don't see the half-hidden street sign Marion Fieldwalker talked about. . . ."

"I can't understand it," she said, studying the map under the map light. "We turned right on Tern, we went left on Hastings to the corner. This must be it."

"The overgrown hedges are definitely there."

"Maybe the sign blew away in the storm. Should we . . . retrace our steps and try again, or do you think . . . ?"

It had all become a blasted nuisance as far as he was concerned. And he would never say so to his wife, but it was spooky out here, stumbling around on some godforsaken jut of land in the pitch-dark, miles from home and reeling from what had become a fifteen-hour trip with nothing but a pack of blasted peanuts to . . .

"We did exactly as the map said. I don't think trying to do it all over again would help us. Why don't we investigate?"

He helped her out of the car and shone the flashlight onto the porch. It was an older beach cottage, with a line of rocking chairs turned upside down to keep the wind from blowing them into the yard. A derelict shutter leaned against the shingled wall.

"Gosh," she said, otherwise speechless.

"I don't see a rosebush climbing up anything," He'd been looking forward to that rosebush.

"Maybe the storm . . . ," she suggested.

". . . blew it down," he said.

They went up the creaking steps to the door.

"Look, Timothy, up there."

A sign hung lopsided above the door, dangling from a single nail.

OVE

OTTAGE

"Oh, my," she said quietly.

Surely this wasn't . . . surely not, he thought.

"They said it would be unlocked," whispered his wife. "Should we . . . try the door?"

The door swung open easily. He was afraid to look. "Aha."

The furnishings sat oddly jumbled in the large, paneled room. A slipcovered sofa faced away from two club chairs, card tables blocked the entrance to what appeared to be a dining room, a faded Persian carpet covered one side of the floor, but was rolled up on the other.

They went in carefully, as if walking on eggs.

Cynthia hugged herself and stared around in disbelief. "How could this *possibly* . . . ?"

He passed the light across one of the tables and saw a half-assembled jigsaw image of the Grand Canyon.

"Look at that lovely old fireplace," she said. "Marion never mentioned a fireplace. . . ."

"Mildew," he said. "Do you smell it?"

"Yes, but how odd. Marion said they'd worked like

slaves to clean everything up. Timothy, this can't be Dove Cottage."

"It's certainly where her map led us, and the sign above the door said . . ." He sighed, dumbfounded.

"Let's try a lamp. Maybe the power's back on." It wasn't.

Barnabas sniffed the rugs and the sofa, with special interest in an unseen trail that led to the hallway. They followed him, numb with disappointment and fatigue.

In the kitchen, the refrigerator door stood ajar, as did several cabinet doors.

"Ugh!" she said. "I can't believe they'd do this to us. Surely they didn't think we were coming next week. Remember we originally told them it would be next week. Maybe somehow they got confused and the cleaning hasn't been done, yet. . . ." Her voice trailed off.

She was trying, but he wasn't buying. He wouldn't live in this dump if they sent the cleaning crew from the Ritz-Carlton in Paris, France. Just wait 'til he got hold of the senior warden. He'd had a round or two with senior wardens in his time; he was no babe in the woods when it came to what's what with senior wardens. . . .

"The phone, there must be a phone around here. We can call the Fieldwalkers, shine the light around."

They found a wall phone on the other side of the cabinets, but the line was dead.

"The bedrooms," she said, desperate.

At the end of the hallway, which was covered by a Persian runner, they found a cavernous bedroom, and surveyed it with the flashlight. Closet doors standing agape . . . windows open . . . curtains blowing . . . the bed made, but sopping wet.

"This can't be right, they wouldn't *do* this to us." He

could tell his wife was teetering on the edge of hysteria. "Wait 'til I get my hands on that fine bishop of yours who would send you out to some . . . uninhabited wasteland, after the years of faithful service you've given him.

"That . . . that vainglorious *dog!*"

"Nothing personal," he told Barnabas, who was sniffing the closets.

———❧———

Because they hadn't known what else to do at nearly midnight on a strange, dark island with no lights and no phone, they made the double bed in the guest room and got in it, Barnabas on the floor on one side and Violet in her open crate on the other, where his inconsolable wife sighed and fumed herself to sleep as he lay staring at the pale circle cast by the flashlight onto the ceiling, muttering words and thinking thoughts he never dreamed he would say or think, and feeling distinctly waterlogged even in a perfectly dry pair of pajamas from his bureau in Mitford, thanks be to God for small favors.

CHAPTER FIVE

A Patch of Blue

He sat up in bed, dazed.

Where in heaven's name . . . ?

Barnabas barked wildly, and someone was knocking on a door. As the room came into focus, he remembered the predicament they were in, and counted it odd that one should wake to, rather than from, a nightmare.

He glanced at his watch—seven o'clock—and bolted into the hallway without robe or slippers. He padded through the dark, paneled living room and opened the door, feeling anger rise in him again.

"Father? Father Kavanagh?"

"Yes!" he snapped, buttoning his pajama top.

"Sam Fieldwalker, sir, your senior warden." The tall, gentle-looking man appeared deeply puzzled.

"Sam . . ." He shook hands as Barnabas sniffed the stranger's shoes.

"We saw your car out front, and . . . well, you see, we waited for you and Mrs. Kavanagh 'til eleven o'clock last night—"

"Waited? Where?"

"In your cottage. Over there." He pointed off the porch.

"You mean . . . this isn't our cottage?"

"Well, no. I'm terribly sorry, I don't know how . . . it must have been the storm and no lights to see by . . ."

"The wrong cottage!" shouted his wife, peering around the hall door in her nightgown. "Thank heaven!"

Sam let Barnabas sniff his hand. "There you are, old fellow, smelling our little Bitsy. My gracious, Father, you all have a dog and a half there!"

"But that sign . . . ," said Cynthia, "that sign above the door . . ."

Sam glanced up, adjusting his glasses. "Oh, my goodness. Of course. Well, you see, this is one of the old *Love* Cottages. . . ."

Cynthia looked fierce. "It certainly doesn't live up to its name!"

"It's owned by the Redmon Love family, who started coming here in the forties. Gracious sakes, Father, Mrs. Kavanagh, I can't begin to tell you how *sorry* . . ."

Father Tim thought Sam Fieldwalker might burst into tears.

"Oh, no, please," he said. "I don't know how we could have thought for a moment . . . well, you see, it was dark as pitch, and we couldn't find the street sign in the hedge, the one Marion told us to look for. . . ."

"Ah, now I'm getting a clear picture!" Sam brightened considerably. "You turned into Love's old driveway, which is wide enough to look like a street—property wasn't so dear in the forties—and, of course, there's a shabby hedge bordering their property, as well. Oh, my, I'm sure Marion never thought of that."

"No harm done! We're glad the mystery is solved. But do the Loves always leave their house unlocked?"

"Hardly anyone on Whitecap locks their doors. And, of course, the Love children and their kids come and go during the summer, though not so much anymore."

"Aha." The sunlight was dazzling, his glasses were by the bed, and he was squinting like a monk at vespers.

"Let me help you move your things, Father. Marion's waiting at Dove Cottage to show you around and cook your breakfast. She's baking biscuits. . . ."

He felt covered with shame. How could he have mistrusted this kind person, believing even for a moment that this was the right cottage? *Lord, forgive me.*

". . . and," Sam continued, looking earnest, "she's found some nice, fresh perch, if . . . if that's all right."

At that moment, Father Tim heard his stomach rumble, and, at the thought of Marion Fieldwalker's fresh perch and biscuits, felt close to tears himself.

—◉—

Marion met them on the porch of Dove Cottage, a tall, large-boned woman in an apron, with a pleasant face and snow white hair like her husband.

"In case you'd taken the ferry," said Marion, "we waited 'til eleven. Then, when you didn't come, we thought the storm had held you up and you'd stayed somewhere for the night."

"When we found the bridge was out, we thought it too far to turn back for a place to sleep," Cynthia said.

"And we nearly missed the ferry!" exclaimed Father Tim, oddly enjoying the account of their travail. "We made it with two minutes to spare."

"Oh, my poor souls! That bridge goes out if you hold your mouth wrong. You know the state bigwigs don't pay much attention to little specks of islands like they pay to big cities. Well, we're thrilled you're here, and I hope you like perch."

"We *love* perch!" they exclaimed in unison.

" 'Where two or more are gathered together in one accord . . .' " quoted the senior warden, laughing. Sam liked both the looks and the spirit of this pair.

In truth, he was vastly relieved that his prayers had been answered, and, as far as he could see, St. John's hadn't been delivered two pigs in a poke.

"Before we go inside," said Marion, "take a look at your rose."

"Ah!" said Cynthia.

They rushed to the trellis and buried their noses in the mass of blooms. "Lovely!" murmured his wife.

"It was running toward the street when we found it, and terribly trampled by the men who worked on the floors. But we loved it along and fed it, and came and watered it every day, and *now* . . ."

"What is it, do you think?"

"I have no idea. Marjorie Lamb and I searched our catalogs and rose books, but we can't identify it to save our lives."

"I believe I know exactly what it is," he said, adjusting his glasses and inspecting the petal formation.

"You *do?*"

"Yes. It's the Marion Climber."

"Oh, Father! Go on!"

"It is, I'd recognize it anywhere."

"The Marion Climber!" crowed Cynthia. "I never thought I'd live to see one. They're rare, you know."

"Oh, you two!" said Marion, flushed with delight.

❧

"What do you think about your kitchen?" asked Sam.

Father Tim was a tad embarrassed to see tears brimming in his wife's eyes. "It's too beautiful for words!" she said.

"We couldn't like it better!"

If last night had been a nightmare, this was a dream come true. The sun streamed through a sparkling bay window and splashed across the broad window seat. Bare hardwood floors shone under a fresh coat of wax.

"One of our parishioners bought this cottage a few months ago and had it completely redone," said Sam. "Otis Bragg— you'll meet him tonight—Otis and his wife offered it to the parish for the new interim."

"You see just there?" Marion pointed out the window. "That patch of blue between the dunes? That's the ocean!" She proclaimed this as if the ocean belonged to her personally, and she was thrilled to share it.

"Come and have your breakfast," said Sam, holding the chair for Cynthia.

On a round table laid with a neat cloth, they saw a blue vase of watermelon-colored crepe myrtle, and the result of Marion Fieldwalker's labors:

Fried perch, crisp and hot, on a platter. A pot of coffee, strong and fragrant. A pitcher of fresh orange juice. Cantaloupe, cut into thick, ripe slices. Biscuits mounded in a basket next to a golden round of cheese and a saucer of butter, with a school of jellies and preserves on the side.

"Homemade fig preserve," said Marion, pointing to the jam pots. "Raspberry jelly. Blueberry jam. And orange marmalade."

"Dearest, do you think it possible that yesterday in that brutal storm we somehow died, and are now in heaven?"

"Not only possible, but very likely!"

He'd faced it time and again in his years as a priest—how do you pour out a heart full of thanksgiving in a way that even dimly expresses your joy?

He reached for the hands of the Fieldwalkers and bowed his head.

"Father, You're so good. So good to bring us out of the storm into the light of this blessed new day, and into the company of these blessed new friends.

"Touch, Lord, the hands and heart and spirit of Marion, who prepared this food for us when she might have done something more important.

"Bless this good man for looking out for us, and waiting up for us, and gathering the workers who labored to make this a bright and shining home.

"Lord, we could be here all morning only thanking You, but we intend to press forward and enjoy the pleasures of this glorious feast which You have, by Your grace, put before us. We thank You again for Your goodness and mercy, and for tending to the needs of those less fortunate, in Jesus' name."

"Amen!"

Marion Fieldwalker smiled at him, her eyes shining. "Father, when you were talking to the Lord about me doing this instead of something more important, I think you should know . . . there was nothing more important!"

Their hostess passed the platter of fried perch to Cynthia, as Sam passed the hot biscuits to his new priest.

Oh, the ineffable holiness of small things, he thought, crossing himself.

◦—◦

Marion insisted on cleaning up the kitchen while they sat around the table, idle as jackdaws.

"You're welcome at the library anytime," she said, pouring everyone a last cup of coffee, "as long as it's Monday, Wednesday, or Saturday from nine 'til four!"

"We'll drop in next week," said Father Tim. "And that reminds me, how's the bookstore? I hear you have a small bookstore on the island."

Marion laughed. "It's mostly used paperbacks of Ernie's favorite author, Louis L'Amour!"

"Ernie doesn't sell anything he hasn't read first and totally approved." Sam's eyes twinkled. "I hope you like westerns."

"We've got fourteen boxes of books arriving on Monday," Cynthia announced. "We can open our own bookstore!"

"By the way," said Sam, "Ernie also offers a notary service and UPS pickup, and rents canes and crutches on the side."

"Diversified!"

"Actually, you'll pass Ernie's every morning as you walk to church. It's right up the road."

"Sounds like the place to be."

"Ernie has his quarters on one side of the building, Mona has hers on the other. In fact, they've got a yellow line painted down the center of the hall between their enterprises, and neither one steps over it except to conduct business."

"Aha."

Sam stirred cream into his coffee, chuckling. "Ernie likes to say that yellow line saved their marriage."

Marion looked at the kitchen clock. "Oh, my! We'd better show you how your coffers are stocked, and get a move on!"

She took off her apron and tucked it in her handbag, then opened the refrigerator door as if raising a curtain on a stage.

"Half a low-fat ham, a baked chicken, and three loaves of Ralph Gaskell's good whole wheat . . . Lovey Hackett's bread-and-butter pickles, she's very proud of her pickles, it's her great aunt's recipe . . . then, there's juice and eggs and butter, to get you started, the eggs are free-range from Marshall and Penny Duncan—he's Sam's junior warden.

"And last but not least . . ."—Marion indicated a large container on the bottom shelf—"Marjorie Lamb's apple spice cake. It's won an award at our little fair every year for ten years!"

Father Tim groaned inwardly. The endless temptations of the mortal flesh . . .

"What a generous parish you are, and God bless you for it!"

"We've always tried to spoil our priests," said Marion, smiling. "But not all of them deserved it."

Sam blinked his blue eyes. "Now, Marion, good gracious . . ."

"Just being frank," Marion said pleasantly.

"Dearest, I think we should be frank, too."

"In, ah, what way?" inquired Father Tim.

"About your diabetes. My husband likes to think that St. Paul's controversial thorn was, without doubt, diabetes."

"Oh, dear!" said Marion. "That means . . ."

"What that generally means is, I can't eat all the cakes and pies and so on that most folks like to feed a priest."

"But I can!" crowed his wife.

"It helps to get the word out early," he said, feeling foolish. "Cuts down on hurt feelings when . . ."

Sam nodded sympathetically. "Oh, we understand, Father, and we'll pass it on. Well, we ought to be pushing off, Marion. We've kept these good people far too long."

"Everybody's having a fit to get a look at you," Marion said proudly. "We hope you'll rest up this afternoon, and we'll come for you at six. It looks like we've got lovely weather on our side for the luau."

"Is the, ah, grass skirt deal still on?" asked Father Tim.

Marion laughed. "We nixed that. We didn't want to run you off before you get started!"

"Well done! And how do we get to St. John's? I'm longing to have a look."

"Good gracious alive!" said Sam, digging in his pockets. "I nearly forgot, I've got a key here for you."

He fetched out the key and handed it over. "Go out to the front gate, take a left, and two blocks straight ahead. You can't miss it. Oh, and Father, there are a couple of envelopes on the table in your sitting room. From two of our . . . most outspoken parishioners. They wanted to get to you before anyone else does . . ."—Sam cleared his throat—"if you understand."

"Oh, I do," he said.

"If I were you, Father," Marion warned, "I'd visit the church and take a nice nap before you go reading those letters. To put it plainly, they're all about bickering. We hate to tell you, but our little church has been bickering about everything from the prayer book to the pew bulletins for months on end. I've heard enough bickering to last a lifetime!"

They walked out to the porch, into the shimmering light. For mountain people accustomed to trees, it seemed the world had become nothing but a vast blue sky, across which cumulus clouds sailed with sovereign dignity.

"Thank you a thousand times for all you've done for us," Cynthia said.

"It's our privilege and delight. You know, we White-cappers aren't much on hugging, but I think you could both use one!"

Sam and Marion hugged them and they hugged back, grateful.

The senior warden looked fondly at his new priest. "We'll help you all we can, Father, you can count on it."

He had the feeling that he would, indeed, be counting on it.

$\backsim$

His wife notwithstanding, he had eagerly obeyed only a few people in his life—his mother, most of his bishops, Miss Sadie, and Louella. He thought Marion Fieldwalker might be a very good one to mind, so he lay down with Cynthia and took a nap, feeling the warmth of the sun through the large window, loving the clean smell of the softly worn matelassé spread, and thanking God.

$\backsim$

Setting off to his new church with his good dog made him feel reborn. But he wouldn't go another step before he toured the garden, enclosed by a picket fence with rear and front gates leading to the streets.

Along the pickets to the right of the porch, a stout grove of cannas and a stand of oleander . . .

By the front gate, roses gone out of bloom, but doing nicely, and on the fence, trumpet vine. Several trees of some sort, enough for a good bit of shade, and over there, a profusion of lacecap hydrangea . . .

He walked around to the side of the house, where petunias and verbena encircled a sundial, and trotted to the backyard. An oval herb garden, enclosed by smaller pickets, a bird feeder hanging by the back steps. . . .

He made a quick calculation regarding the grass. Twenty minutes, max, with the push mower Sam had sharpened, oiled, and left in the storage shed.

A light breeze stole off the water, and the purity of the storm-cleansed air was tonic, invigorating. He thought he heard someone whistling as he went out the rear gate, and was amazed to find it was himself.

Zip-a-dee-doo-dah, zip-a-dee-ay . . .

They cantered along the narrow lane, spying the much-talked-about street sign at the corner of the high fence. The fence was thickly massed with flowering vines and overhung by trees he couldn't identify. It was wonderful to see things he couldn't identify—why hadn't he been more of a traveler in his life, why had he clung to Mitford like moss to a log, denying himself the singular pleasures of the unfamiliar?

He had the odd sense he was being watched. He stopped in the middle of the street and looked around. Not a bicycle, not a car, not a soul, only a gull swooping above them. They might have been dropped into Eden, as lone as Adam.

⟍⟋

Ernie's and Mona's, he discovered, sat close to the street, with a dozen or so vehicles parallel-parked in front. Cars and pickups lined the side of the road.

Mona's Café
Three Square Meals
Six Days A Week
Closed Sunday

Ernie's Books, Bait & Tackle
Six 'Til Six
NO SUNDAYS

Twelve-thirty, according to his watch, and more than five whole hours of freedom lying ahead. Hallelujah!

He tied the red leash to a bench, and Barnabas crawled under it, panting.

As the screen door slapped behind him, he saw the painted yellow line running from front to back of the center hallway. A sign on an easel displayed two arrows—one pointed left to Mona's, one pointed right to Ernie's.

He read the handwritten message posted next to the café's screen door:

Don't even think about cussing in here.

Should he follow the seductive aromas wafting from Mona's kitchen, or buy a *Whitecap Reader* and see what was what?

He hooked a right, where the bait and tackle shop had posted its own message by the door:

A fishing rod is a stick with a hook at one end
and a fool at the other.
—Samuel Johnson

"What can I do for you?" A large, genial-looking man in a ball cap sat behind the cash register.

"Looking for a copy of the *Whitecap Reader,*" Father Tim said, taking change from his pocket.

"We prob'ly got one around here somewhere. You wouldn't want to pay good money today since a new one comes out Monday. Roanoke, we got a paper over there?"

Roanoke looked up, squinting. "Junior's got it, he took it to th' toilet with 'im."

"That's OK," said Father Tim. "I'll pay for one. How much?"

"Fifty cents. You can get it out of the rack at th' door."

He doled out two quarters.

"We thank you. This your first time on Whitecap?"

"My wife and I just moved here."

"Well, now!" The man extended a large hand across the counter. "Ernie Fulcher. I run this joint."

"Tim Kavanagh."

"What business're you in?"

"New priest at St. John's."

"I never set eyes on th' old one," said Ernie. "I think Roanoke ran into 'im a time or two."

Roanoke nodded, unsmiling. He thought Roanoke's weathered, wrinkled face resembled an apple that had lain too long in the sun.

"Well, thanks. See you again."

"Right. Stop in anytime. You fish?"

"Not much."

"Need any shrimp, finger mullet, squid, blood-worms, chum . . . let me know."

"I'll do it."

"Plus we're th' UPS station for th' whole island, not to mention we rent crutches—"

"Good, good."

"And loan out jigsaws, no charge."

"I'd like to look at your books sometime."

Ernie jerked his thumb toward a room with a hand-printed sign over the open door: *Books, Books and More Books.* "I got a deal on right now—buy five, get one free."

"Aha."

"Can't beat that."

"Probably not. Well, see you around."

He was unhooking the leash from the bench leg as two men walked out of Mona's, smelling of fried fish.

"What kind of dog is that?" one asked, popping a toothpick in his mouth.

"Big," said his friend.

$\sim$

He loved it at once.

St. John's in the Grove sat on a hummock in a bosk of live oaks that cast a cool, impenetrable shade over the churchyard and dappled the green front doors.

The original St. John's had been destroyed by fire during the Revolutionary War, and rebuilt in the late nineteenth century in Carpenter Gothic style. Sam Fieldwalker said the Love family purchased the contiguous property in the forties and gave it to St. John's, so the small building sat on a tract of thirty-five acres of virgin maritime forest, bordered on the cemetery side by the Atlantic.

Father Tim stood at the foot of the steps inhaling the new smells of his new church, set like a gem into the heart of his new parish. St. John's winsome charm and grace made him feel right at home, expectant as a child.

He crossed himself and prayed, aloud, spontaneous in his thanksgiving.

"Thank You, Lord! What a blessing . . . and what a

challenge. Give me patience, Father, for all that lies ahead, and especially I ask for Your healing grace in the body of St. John's."

He walked up the steps and inserted the key into the lock. It turned smoothly, which was a credit to the junior warden. Then he put his hand on the knob and opened the door.

Though heavy, it swung open easily. He liked a well-oiled church door—no creaking and groaning for him, thank you.

The fragrance of St. John's spoke to him at once. Old wood and lemon oil . . . the living breath of last Sunday's flowers still sitting on the altar . . . years of incense and beeswax.

To his right, a flight of narrow, uncovered stairs to the choir loft and organ. To his left, an open registry on a stand with a ballpoint pen attached by a string. He turned to the first entry in the thick book, its pages rustling like dry leaves. *Myra and Lewis Phillips, Bluefield, Kentucky, July 20, 1975 . . . we love your little church!!*

He looked above the stand to the framed sign, patiently hand-lettered and illumined with fading watercolors.

Let the peace of this place surround you as you sit or kneel quietly. Let the hurry and worry of your life fall away. You are God's child. He loves you and cares for you, and is here with you now and always. Speak to Him thoughtfully, give yourself time for Him to bring things to mind.

Oh, the balm, he thought, of a cool, quiet church full of years.

He walked into the center aisle, which revealed bare

heart-of-pine floorboards. They were more than a hand-breadth wide, and creaked pleasantly under his tread. Creaking doors, no, he thought, but floorboards are another matter. He'd never lived in a house in which at least two or three floorboards didn't give forth a companionable creak.

On either side of the broad aisle, eight long oak pews seating . . . three, four, five, six, seven, eight, and four short pews seating four. Here and there, a cushion lay crumpled in a pew, reserving that site as someone's rightful, possibly long-term, territory.

His eye followed the aisle to the sanctuary, where a cross made of ship's timbers hung beneath an impressive stained glass.

In the dimly illumined glass, the figure of Christ stood alone with His hands outstretched to whoever might walk this aisle. Behind Him, a cerulean sea. Above, an azure sky and a white gull. The simplicity and earnestness of the image took his breath away.

" 'Come unto me . . .' " he read aloud from the familiar Scripture etched on the window in Old English script, " 'all ye that labor and are heavy laden, and I will give you rest.' "

These were his first spoken words in his new church, words that Paul Tillich had chosen from all of Scripture to best express his personal understanding of his faith.

Suddenly feeling the weariness under the joy, he slipped into a pew on the gospel side and sank to his knees, giving thanks.

$\backsim$

Barnabas strained ahead, his nose to the ground; St. John's new priest-in-charge allowed himself to be pulled hither and yon, as free as a leaf caught in a breeze.

They walked around the church and out to the cemetery, where he pondered the headstones and gazed beyond the copse of yaupon to yet another distant patch of blue. He cupped his hand to his ear and listened, hoping to hear the sweetly distant roar, but heard only a gull instead.

Shading his eyes, he turned and searched toward the Sound, across the open breast of the hummock and into the trees, wondering whether the wild ponies were mythic or actually out there. He hoped they were out there.

Before he and Barnabas headed home, he stood for a moment by the grave site of the Redmon Love family, which was guarded by an iron fence and a tall, elaborately formed angel clothed in lichen. Redmon, his wife, Mary, and a son, Nathan, were the only occupants.

Next to the Love plot was a grave headed by a simple, engraved tablet, which he stopped to read.

A loved one from us has gone,
A voice we love is stilled.
A place is vacant in our home,
Which never will be filled.

Estelle Woodhouse, 1898–1987

He took a deep breath and stroked the head of his good dog who sat contentedly at his feet.

All will be well and very well, he thought. He felt it surely.

Dear Father Kavanagh:

I have been baptized, confirmed, and married at St. John's.

I have served on the Altar Guild, sung in the choir, and

taught Sunday School (except for the years I was away on the mainland, getting my schooling).

I have ushered, been secretary and treasurer of the ECW for five terms, read the propers each Sunday for seven years, and in 1975, headed the fund-raising drive for the complete restoration of our organ.

The only thing I haven't done in the Episcopal Church is attend my own funeral.

My point is that I know what I am talking about, and what I am talking about is all those people who refuse to do the things of the church with respect and dignity, wishing only to satisfy their whims and confuse our young people.

Would you agree, Father, that you do not list cars for sale in the pew bulletins? Would you agree that you do not switch back and forth from the 1928 prayer book to the 1979, willy-nilly and harum-scarum, on whatever notion happens to strike? Would you agree that holy communion is a time best savored and appreciated in quietude, rather than with the blare and clamor of every odd instrument conceivable, including the harmonica?

I earnestly hope and pray that Father Morgan's favorite instrument, the guitar, will not be making any surprise appearances during your term as interim.

It grieves me that you should come into such a jumble as we've created at St. John's, but Bishop Harvey guarantees that you are without a doubt the one to save us from ourselves.

I fervently hope you will not allow such behavior to continue, and will remind one and all in no uncertain terms how the venerable traditions of the church are to be properly maintained.

Respectfully yours,
Jean Ballenger

He couldn't help but chuckle. If that was the worst squabbling he'd face as interim, he'd be a happy man.

His wife could be heard puttering about in bare feet, humming snatches of tunes, and boiling water to make iced tea. He sat back in his chair and sighed, deciding that he liked this room very much.

Two club chairs, slipcovered in striped duckcloth, flanked a painted green table topped by a reading lamp.

An old parson's table stood against the facing wall, beneath framed watercolors of a country lane, a lake bordered by trees in autumn foliage, ducks on a pond, a small blue and red boat on the open sea, and an elderly man and woman at prayer over an evening meal. An oddly pleasing combination, he thought, nodding approval.

Their books would arrive on Monday, and he would go foraging for bricks and lumber straightaway. By Tuesday evening, if all went well, they would have bookcases in their sitting room, along the now-barren end wall.

The only doubt he entertained about the room was a print of the Roman Colosseum, which had faded, over-all, to pale green.

He felt the weariness of recent days in his very bones. Thanks be to God, he wouldn't be preaching in the morning; however, on the following Sunday, it would be fish or cut bait.

He eyed the other letter, propped against the base of the lamp.

Dear Father,

Avery Plummer is a harlot.
Look up the true meaning of this word if you don't already know it which you probably do. Several months ago, she ran off with another woman's husband and God

have mercy on the children in this mess, much less the church that helped them do it.

You ask how a church could help anybody commit a sin, and I say the church helps by seeing what is going on and turning its head the other way when certain steps might be taken that would solve the matter once and for all. Read Matthew 18 if you don't already know it which you probably do.

Somebody said that Jeffrey Tolson, our former choir director and the scoundrel that cares for nothing but himself, wants to come back to St. John's because it is where he grew up, and this is to let you know that if he ever sets foot in our narthex again my husband and I will be gone and so will a lot of other people. <u>What this means is that more than half the annual church budget will walk straight out the door and never look back.</u>

We are looking forward to meeting you at the luau at our home this evening.

Regards to you and Mrs. Kavanagh and I hope you have a successful time in Whitecap.

Yours truly,
Marlene Bragg

———— ∾ ————

"Here's what you do," said Otis Bragg, waving his fork as he spoke. "If a hurricane's gonna hit, everybody shows up at th' church basement. Built like a oil tanker down there. Everybody in th' parish knows about it, we even got a little stash of canned goods and coffee."

"Thinking ahead," said Father Tim.

"We don't have coffee down there anymore," said Marjorie Lamb. "We ran out for the bishop's brunch last spring and had to use it."

Otis grinned. "Have t' bring your own, then." Otis Bragg was short, thickset, and balding, with a fondness for Cuban cigars. Father Tim noticed he didn't light the cigars, he chewed them.

They were sitting at picnic tables in the Braggs' backyard, behind a rambling house that looked more like a resort hotel than a residence. The water in the kidney-shaped pool danced and glinted in the sunlight.

Cynthia furrowed her brow. "Has a hurricane ever hit Whitecap?"

"You better believe it," said Otis. "*Whop,* got one in '72, *blam,* got a big 'un in '84."

"How bad?" she asked.

"Bad. Dumped my gravel trucks upside down, tore the roof off of my storage buildin's."

Leonard Lamb looked thoughtful. "I believe it was Hurricane Herman that took your roof off, but it was Darlene that set Sam Fieldwalker's RV in his neighbor's yard and creamed half the village."

"Nobody on Whitecap's had any kids named Herman or Darlene in a real long time," said Otis. "By th' way, I hear th' Love cottage over by where you're stayin' has a good basement; same thing at Redmon Love's old place. Hard to dig a good basement around here, but that part of the island's on a ridge just like St. John's. You have t' have a ridge to dig a basement."

Father Tim peered at his wife and knew it was definitely time to change the subject. "Do we get home mail delivery, by any chance?"

Otis helped his plate to more coleslaw and another slab of fresh barbecue. "You mountain people have it soft, Father, we have t' haul to th' post office over by QuikPik." Otis dumped hot sauce on the barbecue. "Th' mail usually comes in about two o'clock, just watch for th' sign they stick in th' window, says 'Mail In.' Course, if th' bridge is out, th' ferry runs it over."

"Is the bridge fixed yet?"

"Prob'ly, don't usually take long. It's one thing or another 'til a man could puke, either the rain causes a short, or the roadbed and bridge expand in th' heat, or the relay switch goes out. I remember th' good old days when my business didn't depend on anybody's bridge, we made our livin' right here."

"What's your business?"

"Commercial haulin'—gravel, sand, crushed oyster shell, you name it. Plus we offer ready-mix cement for all your concrete needs—be it residential or commercial."

"Aha!"

"Today, you've got a Bragg's on Whitecap and Manteo, not to mention five locations on th' mainland."

"Cornered the market!"

"You got it!" said Otis, flushing with pride.

—❧—

Marlene Bragg was an intense woman with long, fuchsia nails, a serious tan, and a great mane of blond hair with dark roots.

"We're real glad to have you and your wife—and you brought your cool weather with you!"

Father Tim smiled at their hostess, who had just toured him through her home. "Actually," he said, "I believe I did feel a mountain breeze this morning!"

"It's usually awful hot this time of year."

"I've heard that," he said.

"But I know you'll love it on Whitecap, just like we do."

"Have you been on Whitecap long?"

"Seventeen years, we're from Morehead City. My

husband has worked very hard, Father, to make a name for himself in this area." She pursed her mouth. "He's been mighty generous with the diocese, not to mention St. John's."

"I'm sure."

She smiled. "We'd like to keep it that way."

"I'm sure," he said. Too bad he'd just said that.

Jean Ballenger was a small woman with bangs that appeared plastered to her forehead. At the dessert table, she looked deeply into his eyes and pressed his hand.

"Thank you for your wise consideration of all the matters contained in my letter," she said.

"You're welcome," he replied.

"Who in the world is *this?*" asked Father Tim. A child who appeared to be around three years old was making a beeline toward him with no adult in hot pursuit.

"This is Jonathan Tolson!" said Marjorie Lamb, beaming.

Jonathan fell against Father Tim's legs and clasped them tight, gazing up as if they were old acquaintances.

He squatted and took the youngster's hands in his. "Hey, buddyroe!"

The blond toddler sucked his lower lip and gazed steadily at Father Tim with blue, inquisitive eyes. Then he turned and raced back the way he'd come.

"He just wanted to tell you hello," piped Marjorie, looking pleased as punch.

The message light on their answering machine was blinking.

"Hey," said Dooley. "I hate answerin' machines. I hope you got there OK. I mowed a yard after work and got fifteen dollars. Avis's truck is cool, it came today."

"Well . . ." Deep sigh. "Harley got the hornet nests down." Long pause. "I miss ol' Barnabas. Talk to you later. 'Bye."

Click. Beep.

"I heard there was a terrible storm down there," said Emma. "I hope it didn't blow you in a ditch. You hadn't hardly left town 'til Gene Bolick keeled over and they had to carry him to th' hospital. I called Esther and th' doctor said he's keepin' him awhile for tests."

Crackling sounds, as if Emma had her hand in a potato chip bag.

"I hear that young interim at Lord's Chapel has been passin' out *song sheets,* they're not even usin' a *book,* plus they say two or three people lifted up their hands while they were singin', I bet I can guess who." She snorted. "I hear your old choir director's lower lip is stuck out so far he could trip over it."

Emma crunched down on a couple of chips.

"I saw that woman tenant of yours the other day, she was scurryin' along like a mouse, oh, an' I saw Dooley at Avis's, he looks even better than when you're here, so don't worry about a thing."

Chewing and swallowing, followed by slurping through a straw.

"Snickers has ear mites, I hope Barnabas is doin' fine in all those sandspurs, I hope to th' Lord you'll check his paws on a regular basis."

Emma was running her straw around the bottom of the cup and sucking with great expectation, but not finding much. He turned the volume down on the answering machine.

"Oh, by th' way, Harold got a real raise, the first one in a hundred years, I wish th' post office would get its act together. Well, got to run, this is costin' a war pension."

Click. Beep.

"Timothy! Bill Harvey here. How do you like the pounding surf? I know you're going to love every minute with the fine people at St. John's. You'll be just what the doctor ordered. All they're looking for is Rite Two, a sermon that doesn't rock the boat, and a little trek across the bridge to Cap'n Willie's Sunday brunch.

"I'll be there on the eighth to plug you in. Barbara's not coming—the grandkids are here from Connecticut— she sends her regrets. I'll bunk in with Otis Bragg and Marlene, as usual.

"Well, listen, call me if you need me, you hear? And be sure and eat plenty of spot and pompano, they're probably running pretty good right now. But I wouldn't eat anything *fried* if I were you; broiled is how I like it, better for the heart. Oh, be sure and do right by Otis, now. He and Marlene are mighty generous donors, wouldn't want to lose *them,* ha ha. Well! Felicitations to your beautiful bride! See you on the eighth."

Click. Beep.

❧

"Let's go find the beach," he said, after returning Dooley's call.

"Now?"

"It's only ten o'clock."

"Nearly everyone in Mitford is sound asleep," said his wife.

"This isn't Mitford." He put his arms around her and drew her close and nuzzled her hair.

"But I'm already in my nightgown."

"Wear it. Nobody's looking."

"And barefoot."

"Perfect," he said.

Pamlico Sound

Whitecap Island

Atlantic Ocean

CHAPTER SIX

The Long Shining

Whitecap Island loosely duplicated the shape of a Christmas stocking with a toe full of nuts and candy.

In the toe, Otis Bragg had stationed an extensive system of gravel, rock, and crushed oyster shell inventories, custom cement facilities, and sprawling hangars of grading and construction equipment.

In the heel, the lighthouse stood comfortably surrounded by a hedge of yaupons, an abandoned corral for wild ponies, and a small museum. The remainder of the island was chiefly comprised of high dunes, white beaches, canals and marshes, maritime forest, and a small village of homes, shops, inns, and restaurants, woven together by narrow lanes. The acreage on which St. John's in the Grove sat was located in the top of the stocking.

Increasingly, Whitecap attracted tourists from as far away as Canada and California, swelling the ranks of island churches every summer. While many churches on the mainland cranked down, the churches on Whitecap cranked up, both in numbers and activities.

Even so, a carefree sense of remoteness insinuated itself almost everywhere.

Sandy lanes wound under the heavy shade of live oaks, past summer cottages with picket fences and pleasantly unkempt yards.

Egrets could be seen standing in the marshes, as poised as garden statuary, their black eyes searching the reedy places from which alligators slithered onto banks and sunned themselves.

Early on, St. John's new interim learned that island culture made Mitford look like a beehive of cosmopolitan activity. Time seemed to pass more slowly on Whitecap, and then, even with a calendar, a watch, a phone, and a fax machine, the days began to blend into one another like watercolors. Wednesday might as easily have been Tuesday or Thursday, had it not been distinguished by the midweek celebration of Holy Eucharist.

Sam Fieldwalker chuckled. "This sort of thing soon passes," he said. "You're still in the honeymoon phase."

Father Tim laughed with his affable senior warden. "It all seems like a holiday, somehow, a vacation!"

"You've been going pretty hard, Father, I wouldn't call your first few weeks here a vacation. Truth is, I recommend you take a day off."

Sam looked at his watch. "Good gracious! Got to run by the *Reader* and hand in a story on the Fall Fair, then go across with Marion to the eye doctor and take my fax machine to be fixed. Hope I can get back in time for the planning meeting on the fair."

Even on a small, peaceful island, thought the new priest-in-charge, everybody was going at a trot.

"By the way," said Sam, "glad to hear you're working with Reverend Harmon. The Baptists sure do their part to make the fair the biggest event on the island. We raise a lot of money for needy people."

He went with Sam to the office door that led to the churchyard. "Speaking of needy people," said Father Tim, "I've been counseling Janette Tolson."

"Glad to hear it. When Jeff walked out, Janette didn't feel she could go to Father Morgan, because he was friendly with Jeff. She's gone through the worst of this thing with no priest to turn to."

"She's suffering badly, as you know."

"This has come against us all in a hard way. Not to mention how the choir has fallen into disarray."

Recently, their best tenor had stepped forward to direct the choir and, profoundly disliking such a wrinkle, the lead soprano had quit in disgust and was now teaching Sunday School.

"It'll come right." It was what his mother always said of a rotten situation. "The first thing we need to do is stop thinking of it as a performance choir, and be pleased with how well they lead the congregational singing."

Sam nodded. "Good point."

"You know we're auditioning an organist next week."

"I dislike the thought of a paid organist at St. John's. The Lord has always provided us with somebody in the congregation."

"It may be for the best, Sam. No ties to the church, no axe to grind . . . that's how we handled it at Lord's Chapel for the last few years, and it worked."

"Well, brother . . ."—Sam shook his hand—"hold down the fort while we're across. Oh, my goodness! I forgot the banana bread. I'll just run out to the car. Marion wouldn't be pleased if I come home with it still sliding around in the backseat."

Early on, Father Tim had learned that Marion Fieldwalker was right—the parish really did like to spoil their priests.

He and Cynthia had been treated to brunch at Cap'n Willie's every Sunday, and to dinner at Mona's Café with the Lambs and Fieldwalkers.

They'd received a bushel of hard crabs and clams from the Braggs, and were regularly inundated with bread still warm from parishioners' ovens, not to mention sacks of snap beans and tomatoes.

For performing a baptism, he'd been given a free-range chicken and a pound of butter from the Duncans' little farm, while a wedding ceremony he conducted under the oaks had swelled the Dove Cottage larders with a honey-baked ham.

Thank goodness he was running three days a week, and Cynthia was riding her Schwinn from the post office to the dry cleaner's to the grocery store. She might have been a tanned schoolgirl, wheeling along with carrot tops poking from the grocery sack in her bike basket.

The light on the answering machine blinked as he came in from a meeting with Stanley Harmon at Whitecap Baptist.

"Hey, this is Puny, how y'all doin'? Ever'thing's goin' jis' great up here, hope it's th' same with you. Th' girls wanted to say hey . . . Sissy, come back this minute, come back and say hey to Miss Cynthia and Ba!"

Sounds of small feet storming up the hall, amid shrieks and laughter.

"And there goes Sassy, oh, mercy! Hold on, y'all, 'scuse me . . ."

Sounds of Puny chasing the girls into another room of her small house. "No, no! Put that down! Ba and Miss Cynthia are waitin' for you to say hey! Oh, Lord help, I can't believe this, come out from under there, Sissy!

"All right, then, I'll let *Sassy* say hey. What a good girl your *sister* is! Come here, Sassy."

Clattering noises along the hallway to the phone.

"Here, now say *hey* to Ba and Miss Cynthia."

Heavy breathing.

"You *wanted* to say hey, you *cried* to say hey . . . now say *hey!*" spluttered a frustrated Puny.

"Kitty?" said Sassy.

"Sassy, honey, stay right there and talk to Ba while I get Sissy! *Sissy!* I see what you're doin', get your hands out of th' toilet this minute!"

Bawling from the bathroom. Heavy breathing on the phone. Puny's footsteps hurrying along the hall.

"Did you say hey yet?"

"Dog!" said Sassy.

"Here, f'r pity's sake, give me th' phone. Well, y'all . . ."

Loud wailing. "Want to say hey! Want to say hey!"

"Not 'til you say somethin' else first," commanded Puny.

"*Ple-e-ease!!!*"

"All right, here's the phone, say hey and get it over with!"

Deep breath. "Hey, Ba!" Giggling.

"Now go find your cookie! Ba, I mean, Father, I saw your tenant yesterday, she was standin' on 'er tiptoes lookin' in your study window on th' hedge side. I guess

I scared her half t' death. I wadn't supposed to go to your house yesterday, but I needed to take in your mail an' all. She said she was lookin' for her cat that run off, and just took a little peek in your window to see how nice it was, said she didn't think y'all'd mind. Well, anyway, Joe Joe says t' tell you hey, and Winnie at Sweet Stuff—

"Sissy, put th' mop down *this minute!* Oh, *law . . .*"
Click. Beep.

The next message was clearly from a dog, who was barking furiously.

"Hush *up!*" shouted Emma. "Go get your sock!

"I guess you know your phone call meant th' world to poor Esther. I've never seen her like this, practically wringin' her hands, and she's not th' hand-wringin' type, but they still can't find out what's wrong with Gene. They're goin' to run more tests on Monday, you ought to see 'im, he looks bad to me, I hope you're prayin' is all I can say.

"Snickers! Get away from there! Snickers is tryin' to eat th' meatloaf I just made! Oh, shoot, hold on a minute. . . ."

Growling, huffing, rattling of pots and pans.

"I had to set it on the counter, plus check my beans, I'm havin' string beans and . . . *go get your sock and lie down* . . . mashed potatoes with I Can't Believe It's Not Butter.

"Listen to this. Who just jumped in th' mayor's race against Andrew Gregory? You will *not* believe it. Three guesses! Call me and tell me who you think it is, OK? You will keel over.

"By th' way, I heard it's not even hot where y'all are, they say it's strange th' way th' weather's so cool at th' beaches this year. Oh, I just remembered you got a big box of somethin' from Florida at th' post office, I think somebody sent you grapefruit, do you want me to ship it down there or haul it home with me? Harold loves grapefruit, it would save payin' postage all th' way to that island you're on.

"Speakin' of Harold, here he comes, he does *not* like me talkin' on long-distance."

Click. Beep.

"Father? Otis Bragg here. Wanted to send you a little present by one of my boys. You like bourbon? Scotch? You name it. How 'bout a little Wild Turkey? Somebody said you like sherry, but I must've heard wrong.

"Call my secretary on th' mainland, two-eight-two-four, and let 'er know, OK?"

Click. Beep.

"Hmmm," said his wife, puzzling over who had jumped into Mitford's mayoral race.

"Lew Boyd!" he said. "That's who I'd guess. Either Lew or Mule Skinner. Mule's mentioned doing it for years."

Cynthia furrowed her brow. "Would *you* like to see Fancy Skinner as first lady of Mitford?"

"It might add a certain . . ." He was at a loss for words.

"I don't know, I don't have a clue," said his wife, who was usually up for guessing games.

"What do you think about . . . no, no way . . . let's see . . ."

"Or maybe . . . ," said Cynthia, pondering deeply.

"Then again . . . but I don't think so."

"Oh, poop! If you don't call Emma back, I will!"

They raced into the sitting room and took their chairs. He dialed Emma's number.

"Who?" he inquired, when she answered the phone.

"Is this an owl?" asked Emma.

"I guess Lew Boyd!"

"Two more guesses."

He hated that she always made him do three guesses.

"Mule Skinner!"

"Wrong."

"J. C. Hogan!" shouted Cynthia, in a burst of supernatural insight.

"Is it J.C.?" asked Father Tim.

"Are you sittin' down?" inquired his erstwhile secretary.

"We are. Get on with it."

"Coot Hendrick!"

"Coot Hendrick?"

"He says his great-grandaddy founded th' whole town, and it's time he did something that carries on th' family tradition."

"I'll be darned."

"I personally couldn't vote for anybody who has stubs for teeth, but he says he's goin' to work hard to win."

"It's just as well we aren't there. I don't think I could go through another mayor's race," he said, still not fully over the last one.

⟋◦⟍

While he cooked dinner, his wife sat in the kitchen window seat, looking out but not seeing. She was busy twisting a strand of hair around one finger and humming.

He didn't have to be as wise as Solomon to know

that every time she got that glazed-over look and twisted her hair and hummed, something was up.

The fresh croaker sizzled in the skillet. "Cynthia?"

No reply. Still humming.

Blast. She definitely had that conjuring-up-a-book look. All of which meant she would soon stop riding her bicycle and lash herself to the drawing board for months on end, getting a crick in her neck and feeling grumpy. When people did what they profess to absolutely love, why didn't they smile and laugh and be carefree and upbeat?

Salt, pepper, a spritz of lemon . . .

Another book would mean this whole beach experience, which might have been relaxing for his overworked wife, would, in fact, be just another nose-to-the-grindstone deal. . . .

"Timothy," she said, "I've been thinking."

He sighed and flipped the croaker, without breaking it apart. He was getting good at this.

"You know how lovely everyone's been to us," she said.

"They have."

"How they've loved us. . . ."

"Right."

"We must do something that loves them back."

"Aha."

She turned to face him, looking fierce. "But *not* a Primrose Tea!" His wife had worked her fingers to the very bone doing two enormous and successful Primrose Teas in Mitford.

"I don't think there's a primrose within two hundred miles of here."

"Absolutely, *positively* not a Primrose Tea!" she said.

"I *hear* you, Kavanagh!"

"It's killing, you know."

"No Primrose Tea."

"Anyway, I'm not sure beach people *drink* tea. Hot tea, I mean, to go with things like scones or shortbread."

"I never thought much about it."

"It seems beach people would be more interested in . . . something *cold,* like lemonade, or a lovely punch with an ice ring of lime sherbet . . . and maybe lots of fresh fruit in a vast, icy watermelon carved with its own handle, to which we could attach a bouquet of flowers from our little garden. . . ."

"There you go!" Out of the pan, onto the plate, and done to perfection.

"And a beautiful cake, three or four layers with white icing—and wedding cookies, don't you think? Except they're so messy, all that powdered sugar falling on your shoes . . ."

"My mouth is watering." He spooned new potatoes onto the dinner plates, cheek by jowl with the fish. Now a dollop of butter, a sprinkle of fresh parsley . . .

"I think we should have everyone here, not at the parish hall," she said. "Parishioners like seeing how their priest lives."

"I'll help. You can count on me."

. . . and a dash of paprika, for color. He felt like a heel for thinking his wife was plotting to write a new book and get a crick in her neck when she was, in fact, intent on doing something exceedingly generous for others. Thank goodness he hadn't opened his big mouth and put his foot in it.

"And I'll probably try something wonderful with peaches, too, I don't know what yet, maybe tarts, very small like this." She made a circle with her thumb and forefinger. "I hear the peaches are lovely this year!"

"Dinner is served," he announced, setting the plates on the table. "Come and get it."

She stared at the plates with surprise. "You *angel!*" She apparently hadn't noticed he was making dinner. "Croaker! And new potatoes and fresh asparagus! Oh, Timothy, I'm so glad you can cook."

"I'm even gladder that you can cook. You have kitchen duty for the next four evenings, I hope you recall."

"Four? Why four?"

"Meetings," he said. "Choir practice. The Whitecap Fair Planning Commission. The vestry . . ."

"Umm," she said.

"Umm what?"

"Well, dearest, I've been thinking that maybe . . ."

"Yes?"

"It's so beautiful here, and so liberating, even Violet loves it, have you noticed?"

"I have."

She looked at him in that way he could never resist, with her head tilted slightly to one side and her sapphire eyes gleaming. "I thought I might begin right away . . . working on a new book."

"Let's bow in prayer," he said.

He dialed a number he easily remembered by heart.

"Esther? Is that you?" Esther Bolick didn't sound like herself.

"What's *left* of me."

His heart ached for his old friends; worse, he felt guilty that he wasn't there to go the mile with them.

"How's Gene?"

"Not good." He heard Esther sigh. He couldn't bear

it when Esther sighed; Esther was not a sigher, she was a doer.

"We're praying," he said, "and believing Gene's going to be well and strong again. Now tell me about you, Esther, how're *you* doing?"

"I went yesterday to pick out my casket."

"You *what?*"

"It had to be done sometime. All this with Gene reminded me."

"Do you think this is the right time, I mean . . . ?"

"When Louise Parker went to Wesley to pick hers out, Reverend Sprouse went with her."

"Aha."

"There was nobody to go with me."

He felt very uncomfortable. It was the guilt again. "What about your interim? Couldn't he go?"

"Father Hayden? Lord *help!* He's so wet behind the ears, he's still on strained peas and applesauce!"

Father Hayden was forty-five if he was a day. "So what did you pick?" Might as well be upbeat about it.

"Do you know it costs four thousand dollars to get buried in Mitford? Can you believe it? I was goin' to be cremated, but there's nothin' to look at in a jar. I remember when we buried Mama, it was a *comfort* to see her in th' casket."

"Closure," he said.

"So I picked somethin' with a nice iv'ry satin lining. I always looked good in iv'ry."

"I seem to recall that." He honestly did.

"Then you think you're through with th' whole mess, and what happens?"

"What?" He was interested.

"They want to sell you a *liner!* Some bloomin' metal

thing you drop th' casket down in, to keep it protected from *dirt*." Esther snorted.

Miss Sadie had been very upset about liners, he remembered.

"Anyway, so I got th' dadblame thing, and now it's all taken care of and if I kick before Gene, everything's done, he can put his feet up! I even filled th' freezer in case I go first."

He didn't like this at all. Clearly, Esther was in denial about Gene's uncertain future; to avoid thinking of his, she was concentrating on her own.

"Lasagna, chicken divan, squash casserole—"

"Esther . . ."

"There's only one problem," said his former parishioner.

"What's that?"

"I can't decide what to be buried in. Mama had her outfit hangin' in th' closet, ready to go, even panty hose. Course, it hung there so long, th' dress rotted off th' hanger and we had to dive in and come up with another outfit at th' last minute."

"Umhmm."

"So yesterday, Hessie came over and helped me go through th' closet. I laid out my royal blue suit, do you remember my royal blue suit?"

"I think so." He really did think so.

"But Hessie says it's too plain. So I laid out my pink dress with the chiffon sleeves. Do you remember my pink dress with the chiffon sleeves?"

"Ah . . . let's see . . ."

"I wore it to Fancy and Mule's anniversary party in their basement. It's Gene's favorite."

"Right." He felt like dropping onto the floor prostrate, and giving up the ghost.

"Well, that's what we finally decided on. But after Hessie left, it hit me—what if I die in th' winter?"

He hesitated. "I don't understand."

Esther sighed heavily, "Pink is a *summer* color!"

He gave her what was his only word of wisdom in the entire conversation.

"I recommend you surrender all this to the Lord, Esther. He'll be glad to take care of everything when the time comes."

She kissed him goodbye, one of those lingering kisses that he feared might come to a grinding halt when her book began. Seizing the moment, he kissed her back.

"Darling," she said, brushing his face with the tips of her fingers, "I think you need to take a day off."

"Why? We just got here!"

"We just got here six weeks ago, and you've been working nonstop. I mean, racing across to the hospital twice a week, and teaching adult Sunday School, and setting up the men's fall prayer breakfast, and working with Reverend Harmon . . ."

"But it all seems like a vacation, somehow."

"Trust me. You need to take a day off." She kissed him again, drawing him close in that protective way she sometimes had of making him feel both a man and a child.

He sighed. "I can't do it today."

"Rats!"

"But maybe tomorrow. . . ."

"I'll count on it, dearest."

Headed for St. John's, he ran down the steps of the cottage with Barnabas on the red leash.

Another glorious day! If they ever had to pay a price for the ambrosial weather they continually enjoyed, he shuddered to think how steep the cost might be.

Taking out his pocketknife, he stopped at their bed of cosmos and cut several stems for his office bookshelf.

Glory! He gazed at the cumulus clouds scudding overhead, and took a deep breath. The flowers, the everlasting gulls, the patch of blue beyond the dunes—it hit a man in the solar plexus, between the eyes, in the soul.

It was vastly different, this place, from the protected feeling he had in the mountains. There, summer was one long green embrace. Here, it was one long shining, and the sense of endless freedom.

Barnabas suddenly growled, then barked.

Father Tim glanced around for a stray dog or someone walking by. Nothing.

He quickly snipped two more blooms and put the small bouquet in his shirt pocket.

Trotting through the gate and into the narrow lane, he had the strange sense that someone was watching him. He turned to see if Cynthia might be standing on the porch, but she was not.

⊜

His parishioners had given him an earful about the uncaring, self-centered, musically gifted choir director who had abandoned his wife and children for St. John's married organist. Speaking of Jeffrey Tolson, a parishioner had quoted John Ruskin: "When a man's wrapped up in himself, he makes a pretty small package."

He had frequently prayed for Jeffrey Tolson, but was unable to dismiss the hardness of heart he often felt when doing it. And, though he'd never laid eyes on St. John's former choir director, he knew precisely who it was when the tall, blond Scandinavian walked into the church office from the side door.

"Jeffrey Tolson," said his caller. He stood by the desk, arms crossed.

He couldn't help but notice that his caller wore leather clogs, and a full-sleeved white shirt in the manner of eighteenth-century poets.

"Jeffrey." *Lord, give me the words, the wisdom, the heart for this, Your will be done. . . .*

"I won't take much of your time."

He wanted to say, *My time is yours,* but could not. It was what he always liked to say to parishioners, no matter what the time constraints.

Jeffrey Tolson removed his billfold from a rear pocket. "I'm back in Whitecap for a few days. I wanted Janette to have this." He withdrew a hundred-dollar bill and handed it to Father Tim.

"You can't give it to her yourself?"

"She's in no mood to deal with me."

He looked at the money and had a fleeting vision of punching Jeffrey Tolson in the nose—squarely, no holds barred. Gone eight months and this was the only offering?

"I'll see that she gets it."

"I know you think hard of me, most people do. But Janette was no angel to live with. Moody, depressed, demanding. I'm a sensitive man, Father. It was like living with a wet blanket."

"How was it living with those children of yours?"

Jeffrey Tolson's face was suddenly hard. "Don't preach to me."

"Far from it, Mr. Tolson."

His heart was pounding, his mouth dry as he stood facing the man who had brought hurt and anger into the midst of St. John's.

Jeffrey Tolson turned and stomped from the office. He jerked open the door to the outside steps, then slammed it behind him.

He awoke to find Barnabas standing by the bed, his black nose barely an inch from his face.

"Don't let him kid you, Timothy, I've already taken him out to the garden."

He rolled over and put his arm around his wife.

A day off! He'd have to swallow down the guilt before he could get up and enjoy it.

"Timothy . . ." He knew that tone of voice; she could read him like a book.

"Umm?"

"I hear your wheels turning already, clickety-clack! You're going over all the things you should be doing today at church."

"Right. You see, we're working with Marion and her staff to organize and catalog St. John's library, which means—"

"I'm hoping you'll rent a bike and go riding with me today."

Barnabas licked him on the ear and wagged his tail, urgent. His dog was never completely satisfied with Cynthia's idea of a morning constitutional.

"But first," she said, "I think you should walk down to Ernie's after morning prayer and look over his books. You've been wanting to do it ever since we came."

"Ernie's . . . I don't know."

"It's six-thirty. You could have breakfast at Mona's and maybe read the paper like you used to do at the Grill . . ."

He *had* missed that sort of thing.

". . . then, meet me back here at nine and we'll go to Mike's Bikes and—"

"I thought I'd make your breakfast," he said.

"You're always looking for something to do for someone." She stroked his cheek. "It might be good if you spent a little time doing . . . whatever it is that men do."

What did men do? He'd never figured it out.

He yawned. "The next thing I know, you'll be packing me off for a day of deep-sea fishing."

She looked at him and burst into laughter. "How did you guess? I can't *believe* it! I just bought you a ticket on Captain Willie's charter boat!"

CHAPTER SEVEN

A Little Night Music

At seven a.m., the day was already sultry; forecasts were for ninety-nine degrees by noon.

He broke a sweat before he reached Mona's, where he found Ernie paying for a sausage biscuit and a cup of coffee at his wife's cash register.

"I'm only allowed over th' yellow line as a payin' customer," said the genial proprietor from next door. "Get your order and come over to my side— chew th' fat awhile."

"Well . . . ," he said, pleased to be asked, "don't mind if I do."

"That'll be two bucks." Mona extended her hand to her husband, who shelled out the tab, mostly in change.

"I'll have what he's having," said Father Tim.

The red-haired Mona had a no-nonsense look behind a pair of glasses with brightly painted frames. "So you're hangin' with the guys this mornin'?"

He nodded, feeling suddenly shy and excited about having someone to hang with.

"They get too rough for you," said Mona, "come on back to where it's civilized."

"Right," he said.

"This yellow line . . . ," said Father Tim, stepping over it, "it must be a real conversation piece."

"Thing was, Mona kept nosin' around my side sayin' old books wouldn't pay th' light bill. Then I'd go over to her side raisin' Cain because she hadn't hiked her prices in four years. We nearly ended up in divorce court."

"Aha."

"We had to learn to mind our own business, you might say. Thing is, I've come to believe all married people ought t' have a yellow line of some kind or another."

Ernie held the screen door open to Books, Bait & Tackle.

"Welcome to where th' elite meet to eat. Boys, watch your language, Preacher Kavanagh's goin' to join us this mornin'."

"Tim," said the preacher, nodding to the assembly. "Call me Tim."

Ernie set his bag on one of the scarred tables by the drink machines. "You remember Roanoke, he don't much like preachers. But he's harmless."

Roanoke nodded curtly and poured a packet of sugar into a Styrofoam cup.

"That's Roger Templeton over there, an' his dog, Lucas. Lucas is blind. Roger's his Seein' Eye human."

"Tim, nice to meet you," said Roger, who was holding what appeared to be a block of wood in his lap. Roger was a tall, slender man, probably in his sixties, with a pleasant face. The filmy eyes of his brown Labrador appeared to rest on the newcomer with some interest.

"Set your sack down," said Ernie, "and pull up a chair. It's not fancy, but it's all we got. Junior, come out here and meet Preacher Kavanagh."

A sandy-haired, bearded young man came through the door of the book room. He wiped his hand on his work pants and extended it with solemn courtesy.

"How you do, sir, glad to meet you."

"Glad to meet you, Junior."

"Junior's off work today, he hauls for Otis Bragg. You know Otis, I reckon."

"Oh, yes. Otis is a member at St. John's."

Roanoke snorted.

Ernie launched into his sausage biscuit with considerable gusto. "Well, boys, we got a lot of work to do to get Junior's ad in before th' deadline. Tim, we're glad you're here, because you're an educated man and know how to put things. Course, Roger's pretty educated hisself. He was runnin' a billion-dollar corporation before him and his wife retired to Whitecap."

Roger smiled as he deftly used a pencil to make marks on the block of wood. "Half a billion."

"Don't sound as good to say half a billion." Ernie gulped his coffee. "Junior, you got your notepad?"

"Right here," said Junior. He removed a ballpoint pen and notepad from his shirt pocket, which was machine-embroidered with the name *Junior Bryson*.

"What's your ad about?" asked Father Tim.

Junior looked at Ernie.

"*You* tell 'im." Ernie said to Junior.

"Well, sir, I'm tryin' to find a wife." Junior's face colored.

"Aha."

"So, me an' Roanoke an' Ernie an' Roger come up with this idea to advertise."

"That's been known to work," said Father Tim, unwrapping his sausage biscuit.

"We recommended advertising off the island," said Roger.

"Right," said Ernie. "Everybody on Whitecap knows Junior, and he knows everybody."

"Does that mean there aren't any candidates on Whitecap?"

"Not to speak of," said Ernie. "Besides, our advice is, get a woman you have to go *across* to see, makes it more . . . more . . ."

"Romantic," said Roger.

Junior beamed and nodded.

"If I was you," said Roanoke, "I'd run me a big ad with a border around it." He drew a cigarette from a pack of Marlboros in his shirt pocket.

"That'd cost more," said Ernie.

Roanoke struck a match. "Might be worth more."

"Read what you have so far," said Roger.

"White male, thirty-six, five foot eleven an' a half . . ."

Roanoke sipped his coffee. "I'd say six foot."

"Right," said Ernie. "Sounds better."

"That'd be a lie," said Junior.

"Put a lift in your shoes," said Roanoke.

"I ain't goin' to lie. Five foot eleven an' a half with kep' beard—"

Ernie shook his head. "I wouldn't mention a beard. Some women don't like face hair a tall."

"Might as well git things out in th' open," said Junior.

"Keep readin'," said Roanoke.

"Five foot eleven an' a half with kep' beard, likes country music, fishin', and Scrabble, drives late-model Bronco."

Roanoke leaned forward. "What'd you say Scrabble for? You ought t' say poker or gin rummy."

Ernie frowned. "It's th' Bronco I wouldn't say anything about. I'd say more like a . . . like a . . ."

"A Mustang convertible!" suggested Roanoke, unsmiling. "Maybe you could borry the preacher's car."

"Yessir," said Junior, grinning. "I've seen your car around, it's a real sharp ride."

"Thank you."

"We got to hurry up," said Ernie, checking his watch. "If this is goin' to run in th' *Diplomat,* Junior's got t' call it across in thirty minutes."

"Read it again," said Roanoke. He wadded up his biscuit wrapper and lobbed it into a box beside the Pepsi machine.

Junior cleared his throat and ran a hand through his thinning hair. "White male, thirty-six, five foot eleven an' a half with kep' beard, likes country music, fishin', and Scrabble, drives late-model Bronco . . . plus, I'm addin' this . . . lookin' for serious relationship, send photo."

"I wouldn't put nothin' in there about a serious relationship," said Roanoke. "That'll scare 'em off."

Junior gazed helplessly at his advisors. Then he zeroed in on Father Tim. "What do *you* think, sir?"

In truth, he'd hardly been thinking at all. "Well . . ."

Junior's pen was poised above the notepad.

"Actually, I like your idea about getting things out in the open."

Junior nodded, looking relieved. "Well, good! It's wrote, then."

❧

The sweat was trickling down his back as he made a quick sweep through the book room, finding a ragged copy of Conrad Richter's *The Trees*. He knew he'd never read it again, but he recalled his early fondness for it with such reverence that he couldn't resist. Especially not for fifty cents.

He found a cat asleep in one of the numerous book-filled boxes stationed around the room, and nearly leaped out of his running shorts when it sprang up and hissed at him.

"That's Elmo th' Book Cat," said Ernie, standing in the doorway. "He's older'n dirt. That's his sleepin' box, it's full of Zane Grey paperbacks. You ever read Zane Grey?"

"Tried," he said, his eyes roving the shelves. "Couldn't."

"Ever read Louis L'Amour?"

"Never have."

"That's my main man. Listen to this." Ernie grabbed a book off the shelf, thumbed through the pages, and adjusted his glasses.

" 'We are, finally, all wanderers in search of knowledge. Most of us hold the dream of becoming something better than we are, something larger, richer, in some way more important to the world and ourselves. Too often, the way taken is the wrong way, with too much emphasis on what we want to have, rather than what we wish to become.' "

Ernie looked up. "A world of truth in that."

Father Tim nodded. "I'll say."

"This is his autobiography. Looky here." Ernie

turned to the back of the book and displayed a long list. "That's some of th' books he read. He read thousands of books and kep' account of every one. Plus he traveled and wandered all over th' world an', with no education to speak of, turned around an' wrote hundreds of books his own self."

Ernie scratched his head. "I guess if I could, I'd just read books and not strike a lick at a snake."

"Sounds good to me!"

The proprietor took a paperback off the shelf. "Here you go, I'm givin' this to you. Take it an read it, and tell me what you think."

"I'll do it.

"To my way of thinkin', *Last of the Breed* was L'Amour's best book, and if it don't keep you on th' edge of your pew, nothin' will."

"I thank you, Ernie. Thank you!"

"I take you for a big reader, yourself."

"I guess you could say Wordsworth is my main man."

"Wordsworth, Wordsworth . . . ," said Ernie, trying to place the name.

"I'll bring you something, see what you think."

"Good deal," said Ernie, looking pleased.

At the cash register, Father Tim fetched a dollar and change out of his shorts pocket for the Richter book and the eight-page *Whitecap Reader*.

"Seen your neighbor yet?" asked Ernie. "Guess I ought to say heard 'im, is more like it."

"What neighbor is that?"

"Th' one behind th' hedge."

"Didn't know there was one behind the hedge."

"You didn't?" Ernie looked incredulous.

"Should I have?"

"Seems like somebody would've told you."

He waited for Ernie to elaborate, but he didn't. "Maybe you could tell me."

"Well . . . it's what's left of th' Love family, is what it is."

He thought Ernie looked pained, as if regretting that he'd introduced the subject.

"Aha."

"See, there was a whole clan of Loves at one time. Redmon Love, th' grandaddy, bought that big trac' of land up th' road where you are, built him a fine home in there and put a wall around it. Then planted a hedge both sides of th' wall. It's grown up like a jungle th' last twenty years or so."

Father Tim looked at his watch. If he was going to ride bikes this morning, not to mention walk his dog, he'd better get a move on.

"Th' Love house was th' finest thing on any of these islands, a real mansion, but you can't see it's back there 'less you're lookin' for it."

"I'll be darned."

"Mr. Redmon had somebody come in from upstate New York and make him a tropical garden, had palm trees and monkeys an' I don't know what all."

"Monkeys?"

"Well, there ain't any monkeys in there now, but used to be. I used to hear 'em when I was a kid." Ernie paused and gave a loud rendition of what, it might be supposed, was the call of a monkey.

"Like that," said Ernie.

Father Tim nodded, impressed.

"Used to be macaws in there, too, an' some said elephants, but I never went for that."

"Pretty far-fetched," agreed Father Tim, rolling up his newspaper and putting it under his arm.

"Anyway, th' whole clan built around th' mansion. You're livin' up from th' place his second grandson used 'til, oh, I don't know, maybe two or three years ago, then they pretty much stopped comin'."

"Right. So who lives behind the wall?"

Ernie looked at him soberly. "I wouldn't say nothin' to your wife."

"Really?"

"No use to make 'er worry."

"Who?"

The screen door slammed behind two fisherman. While one examined sinkers and knives, the other ordered bait.

"We need a half pound of shrimp, a dozen bloodworms, and a pound of squid. Better make that a pound and a half."

"Catch you later, Tim," said Ernie. "Come again anytime, you hear?"

⟳

He dropped by St. John's to see how the organization of the church library was developing. Marion Fieldwalker and her volunteers were cataloging, dusting, shelving, and generally making sense of books that had been stacked in a room off the narthex since the time of the early prophets. He cheered them on and made a pot of coffee as his contribution to the effort.

There was no reason at all, of course, for his wife to know he'd taken this little detour. . . .

He was zooming by his desk as the phone rang.

"Hello?"

"Hey!" said Dooley.

"Hey, yourself, buddy! What's going on?"

"The Reds whipped th' poop out of th' Blues last night!"

"Hallelujah! Tell me everything!" He thumped into his groaning swivel chair and leaned back.

"You should of seen ol' Mule, he come t' bat four times with runners on base, got a base hit ever' time!"

Ah, it was music to his ears when Dooley lapsed into the old vernacular.

"I scored four runs on 'is hits. We whipped 'em by seven runs."

"Man alive!" he said, rejoicing with his boy. "Well done!"

"Waxin' th' Blues was great, we cleaned their plows. You should of been there."

He should have, it was true. "Good crowd?"

"Ever'body, nearly. Ol' Coot Hendrick, he was there shakin' hands like he was President of the United States. Ol' Mayor Cunningham, she throwed out th' first ball."

"How are Poo and Jessie and your mom?"

"Great. I had supper with 'em Saturday. Poo's gettin' really tall, Jessie's quit suckin' her thumb."

"Have you seen Lace?"

Silence. "A couple of times."

"Really? You took her to a movie?"

"Are you kidding? She hardly looks at me. Anyway, she's not allowed to go out with guys 'til next year. She's still fifteen."

"Aha." He noted that Dooley's speech had returned to the prep school mode.

"But I saw her with some friends a couple of times, like when I took Jenny to a movie."

He rubbed his chin and frowned. That wouldn't have been his agenda for Dooley's summer, but who was he to judge? Jenny was their pretty, soft-spoken neighbor who'd regularly come looking for Dooley, knocking on the back door year after year, summer after summer. What if his own neighbor, his very wife, had not come knocking on the rectory door?

"Is Lace still tutoring Harley?"

"She comes when I'm working, she gave him A-plus on something. I don't know what it was, but he was pretty excited, I think it was math."

"Are you ready to go back to school?"

"I don't want to go back."

"If you're going to be a vet, you have to go to school," he said, stating the obvious.

"Yeah, right. So I'm goin' back, but I'd rather stay home."

"You've got eight days, make the most of it. As we discussed, the Barnhardts will swing by with Joseph to return you to academe."

"Where?"

"By the way, Harley says you're doing great with your curfew."

"He said he'd whip my tail if I messed up." Dooley cackled. The thought of the thin, toothless Harley whipping him was clearly a great amusement.

"What are you guys eating these days?"

"Harley made pizza last night, it was great."

"With everything?" He loved the details.

"No anchovies, no onions, tons of sausage and cheese. He could get a franchise."

"How's our tenant?"

"She asked me twice if I'd show her your house, said she wanted to see what y'all did, the addition and all. I said maybe when you come in October, you'd show it to her. Why would she care anything about the addition? She's not going to do one."

"I have no idea."

"Anyway, I think Lace is taking lessons over there before she goes off to school, she leaves in a week. She'll hate that school."

"Please. Keep your opinions on that school to yourself."

"I promise you those girls are weird. They write and draw and read and wear totally weird clothes like lace-up shoes and glasses with wire rims. I mean, they can't even dance, they step all over you."

"How's your bank account?"

"Huge."

"How huge?"

"I made six hundred dollars so far."

"I owe you six to match it, that makes twelve, what's the total?"

"With what I saved last year, that makes seventeen hundred, even."

"You can buy a sharp little ride for what you'll have by the end of summer."

"I don't want an old car, I told you over and over."

"We'll both be old as the hills if we wait 'til you earn enough for a new one."

Dooley sighed.

"Look," he said, feeling guilty, repressed, and prehistoric. "Cynthia and I will kick in another five hundred, that brings you up to twenty-two hundred."

"Thanks! Hey, really! Thanks, Dad."

"You're welcome. Now stay out of trouble."

"I'm stayin' out."

"Good. Well done. If we're still here, you're going to love this place next summer."

"Why?"

"Sand. Water. Girls. Shrimp and hush puppies. I don't know, good stuff."

"And I'll have a car."

"You'll have a car. Right."

"Look, I've got to go."

"Tell Harley hello."

"I miss ol' Barnabas. Tell Cynthia hey, is she OK?"

"She misses you, she looks great, she has a tan and a half."

"Well, I got to go."

"Love you, buddy."

"Love you back."

He sat for a moment at the desk, nodding to himself and smiling. He was proud of that boy. Though there was only about sixty thousand left of the inheritance from his mother, he should have kicked in an extra hundred.

Hot. Hotter than hot.

He walked into Dove Cottage, thankful for the fan whirring in the living room, and was greeted by his dog bounding down the hallway, pursued by a youngster.

"Look who's here!" he said.

"Jon'than!" said Jonathan Tolson.

Cynthia appeared from the kitchen. "Jonathan's come to spend the day with us. I didn't think you'd mind having company. We can go bike riding Saturday."

"Right!"

"Your dog," said Jonathan, hugging Barnabas around the neck. "My dog."

"Right. Any dog of mine is a dog of yours." He squatted down and met the blue-eyed gaze of their blond-haired visitor.

"I went to visit Jonathan's mommy this morning and she wasn't feeling well, so . . ." Cynthia lifted her palms, smiling.

"So, we'll have an adventure," said Father Tim. "We'll take a walk on the beach, then we'll go eat hotdogs, and ice cream after. How's that?"

"Not hotdogs," said Jonathan, wrinkling his nose.

"Pizza, then! Or french fries. I'm easy."

Jonathan nodded eagerly, his curls bobbing. "French fries."

"You're lots more fun with kids around," announced his wife.

"Your big dog can go?" asked Jonathan.

"Absolutely. He loves ice cream."

Cynthia took her husband's hand and pulled him along the hall to the kitchen.

"Janette's terribly depressed," she said in a low voice. "She doesn't want to get out of bed. I went to check on her this morning—I'm not sure Jonathan had been fed recently. He just devoured a whole plate of cheese and crackers, thank heaven I had milk. . . ."

"What about the other children?"

"Gone across to cousins. She said they didn't have room for Jonathan. Apparently, Janette hasn't been working for some time. She takes in sewing, you know."

"Dear Lord," he murmured. He'd recommended medical help for Janette Tolson, but she refused, assuring him she'd be fine. He'd seen the emptiness in her gaze, heard it in her voice, and knew she was in trouble.

"I'll be back," he said, kissing his wife.

⊖

"The children . . . ," he said, sitting by Janette's bed.

"I don't . . . care," she whispered.

He remembered Miss Sadie talking about her love for Willard Porter, about caring so much for so long that all caring was at last exhausted.

"God cares. He's with you in this."

She turned her head slowly and looked at him, disbelieving.

He put his right palm on her damp forehead. He remembered his mother's cool hand on his forehead when he was sick, and how much that simple gesture had counted to him.

"I promise," he told her.

She closed her eyes and the tears seeped from under her lashes.

The average view of the Christian life, Oswald Chambers had said, is that it means deliverance from trouble. Father Tim agreed with Chambers that, in fact, it means deliverance *in* trouble. That alone and nothing more, and nothing more required. But the child of God had to face the strain before the strength could be provided. Janette Tolson could not face the strain.

"Let me pray for you," he said.

He kept his palm against her forehead, and with his other hand, held hers.

⊖

"I *not* stay," said Jonathan, frowning.

"We'll have pancakes for breakfast," he implored. It was a lame strategy, but the best he could do.

Jonathan shook his head and stomped one foot. "*No!* I want to go *home.*"

"In the shape of ducks!"

"*No.*"

"Babette and Jason are having fun with cousins. Don't you want to spend the night and have fun with Barnabas?"

They couldn't take him home; his mother was in no condition to look after him. He had called Jean Ballenger, who, eager to please her new priest, had agreed to spend the night with Janette. Tomorrow, following the counsel of Hoppy Harper, he would talk with Janette's own doctor, whom she had avoided for months, and take Janette across to the hospital. He dreaded the prospect.

He looked to his wife, who, of all people, should be able to come up with something to entice a three-year-old.

"I don't know how to get little boys to spend the night in a strange house," she said.

Jonathan's eyes were filling with tears.

Hand shadows! He suddenly recalled a family friend in Holly Springs who had kept him engrossed for hours with a kerosene lamp, a bare wall, and two dexterous hands.

"Turn off the lights in the study," he said, feeling desperate.

"Whatever for?"

"Trust me."

"I want to go *home!*" said Jonathan, meaning it.

"Light the big candle in the hurricane globe," he said. Scalpel, sutures . . . "Put it on the table between our chairs."

Cynthia looked at him as if he'd lost his mind and hurried off to the study.

"Movies!" he said to Jonathan. "Picture show!" He thought he could make a dog. At least a pig. He was certain he could make an eagle; he'd made one on his study wall in Mitford only months ago.

"Popcorn?" asked the boy.

"Now you're talking! Cynthia!" he shouted. "Popcorn, and plenty of butter!"

Cynthia appeared from the study.

"Turn off the lights, light the candle, popcorn with plenty of butter . . . where's the division of labor so popular in modern marriage?"

"My dear, I am the *entertainment,* I can't do it all, this takes teamwork!"

"My mommy, my mommy makes popcorn!" said Jonathan, running behind Cynthia to the kitchen.

─◦─

Lying awake after midnight, he felt the humidity weighing upon them like a blanket. He also felt what he'd dismissed for weeks:

He was homesick.

He was homesick for Mitford and his boy and Harley, for all the countless components that made his mountain village home.

Whitecap had its charms, of course. There was a great deal to be said for the smaller parish, not to mention the general ease induced by sunshine, salt air, and surf. In times past, hadn't doctors prescribed the seashore as a cure-all for nearly anything that ailed?

But he wasn't ailing, and he didn't need curing.

He believed he was making progress in putting the parish into less quarrelsome order. Several rifts had been healed, and he had ignored the petty issues that, he wasn't surprised, were fading away for want of being nursed.

Better still, he saw his wife finding some repose and freedom of spirit after years of toiling like a Trojan. Yes, she'd begun the new book, but overall, he saw her rested, tanned, and vibrant, and flourishing like a kid at summer camp.

Last and certainly not least, St. John's had fallen in love with Cynthia Kavanagh and freely said as much. She stood with him in the churchyard every Sunday after services, giving and receiving handshakes and hugs, and serving in several parish trenches, including the nursery, like paid help.

"But I love doing it!" she'd said only last week, when he thanked her again.

"What don't you love?" he asked.

"Fading eyesight, creeping forgetfulness, and . . . and calendars with no room to enter all the day's events!"

His wife could derail a train of thought in a heartbeat, jump to another track, and run on it with all engines smoking.

Hot.

He drew the sheet off, eased out of bed, and walked down the hall, floorboards creaking.

In the living room, Barnabas left his blanket in the corner and stretched, then came and stood with him at the screen door, looking into the moon-silvered night.

He unlatched the screen and stepped onto the porch. The full moon cast its image on the distant patch of water.

The sight of two moons, voluptuous and shimmering between two sleeping cottages, caused him to shiver in the heat.

What a different world, this immense expanse of sand and shelf that had heaved itself up from the deeps. . . .

He sat on the top step and gazed at the vast dome above, at what James Joyce had called "the heaventree of stars, hung with humid nightblue fruit."

Great beauty was something he had to work up to, he had to take it in slowly, not gulping, but sipping. He put his hands over his eyes and saw the stars dancing behind his hands, another double image in this deep and silent night.

In Mitford, he'd felt tethered; tethered to Lord's Chapel, tethered to the rectory, tethered to the little yellow house. Here, he felt as if he were falling into space, tethered only to God.

He got up and walked down the steps to the garden, restless and excited, like a child who wakes in the night, filled with fervent dreams.

Barnabas lifted his leg against a favorite spot at the picket fence.

If he could, he'd call home and talk with Dooley again. He'd talk even longer than he'd done today, then ask Dooley to pass the phone to Harley. Next, he'd call Esther and check on Gene, even though they'd spoken on Wednesday, and after that, he might ring Louella and they would sing a hymn, right on the phone. . . .

Truth be known, he'd like nothing better than to call Miss Sadie and hear the bright voice that had always made him listen up and step more smartly.

"Miss Sadie," he said aloud to his still-favorite parishioner, "this is a toll-free call. I hope you like it up there and aren't getting in trouble for bossing the angels around. . . ."

He saw the shooting star plummet toward the silhouette of an oceanfront cottage and vanish.

Then he heard the music.

He turned, thinking that somehow a radio had come on in the house.

But the music wasn't coming from the house.

It was Karg-Elert's "Now Thank We All Our God," and it was coming from . . . across the street.

He stood, frozen and alert.

Someone was playing their stereo full blast. It was an extraordinary rendition of one of his sworn favorites for the organ—mighty, dramatic, charged with power.

He walked to the picket fence and looked across the street at the high-grown, moonlit hedge.

Though distant, he could hear each note clearly and, perhaps because the piece was familiar, he was free to hear beneath the notes the terrible urgency of the music behind the wall, under the full and looming moon.

$\backsim$

He crept back to bed, thinking of Hélène Pringle and the faint piano music that had floated out on Mitford's night air.

He shivered in the breeze that came suddenly from the water and blew through their open windows.

$\backsim$

Sometime before dawn, he felt the bed move near his feet and thought it was Barnabas.

It was Jonathan Tolson. The boy crept toward the head of the bed, silent, and found a place between them. Father Tim heard him sigh and then, in a moment, heard the boys rhythmic breathing and smelled his damp, tousled hair.

He prayed for Janette and for today's mission before he drifted again to sleep.

$\backsim$

On the way to St. John's, he stopped by Mona's for a coffee to go, and ducked into the bait and tackle shop.

"Here's th' latest," said Ernie. "Th' *Democrat* hit th' street last night, Junior's already had an answer to his ad."

"*And?*" This was pretty exciting stuff, looking for a wife.

"And it was a guy."

"Aha."

"Wanted to know if Junior'd be interested in sellin' his Bronco."

"That's *it?*"

Ernie shook his head, looking gloomy. "I think we need to doctor that ad."

"Maybe so. By the way, you were going to tell me who lives behind the wall."

"Oh, yeah. Right. Well, that's Morris Love that lives back there."

"Morris Love." He searched Ernie's face. "Tell me more."

"Well, Morris is, you know . . ." Ernie pointed to his head and made a circle with his forefinger.

"Like the rest of us," said Father Tim, looking on the positive side.

"Nothin' to worry about. Morris keeps to hisself, never leaves th' place, except he's bad to holler at people sometimes. Kind of hides behind th' wall and hollers crazy stuff. But tell your missus not to worry, he's harmless."

"Why doesn't he leave the place?"

"Don't want anybody to look at 'im."

"Why's that?"

"Well, see, he's got this . . . handicap. There's a woman takes care of him, comes every day or so, does his cookin' an all, an' th' organ tuner, he comes in his panel truck from Virginia. Not enough traffic in and out of there to keep th' grass off th' driveway."

"Well, well."

"See, there was a big organ put in there by his grandaddy, they say it was world-class in its time, and ol' Morris, he can play th' hair off that thing, but I ain't heard much about him playin' lately. We all take Morris for granted. Most people don't hardly remember he's in there."

"I'll be darned."

"But don't you worry about a thing. He's harmless, just a little mean streak like 'is grandaddy, is all."

"Aha. So, here's the book I promised you."

"Holy smoke! I gave you a used paperback, and this sucker is *leather*."

"Take that and keep it, and I hope you like it."

"You got th' wrong end of th' stick, if you ask me, but I appreciate it." Ernie opened the book, squinted at a random page, and read aloud, slowly:

> *"On his morning rounds th' Master*
> *Goes to learn how all things fare;*
> *Searches pasture after pasture,*
> *Sheep and cattle eyes with care;*
> *And, for silence or for talk,*
> *He hath comrades in his walk;*
> *Four dogs, each pair of different breed,*
> *Distinguished two for scent, and two for speed.*
>
> *"See a hare before him started!*
> *—Off they fly in earnest chase;*

Every dog is eager-hearted,
All th' four are in th' race. . . ."

Ernie looked up, grinning. "Got a good bit of action to it."

As he left the tackle shop, he glanced in the front window, pleased to see the proprietor giving rapt attention to the little book of pastoral ruminations.

~~~~~~~

Janette Tolson wept all the way across the bridge to the hospital fourteen miles away. He sat with her through the admission to the psychiatric floor, explaining to the clerk there was no insurance, and giving his word the bill would be taken care of. How, he didn't know; that would be God's job. He waited until her doctor arrived and she was settled in a shared room.

Reluctantly, she let go of his hand as he left. "Jonathan . . ."

"Don't worry," he said.

~~~~~~~

He clung to Cynthia before leaving for the vestry meeting at St. John's.

Oh, the blessed softness of a wife in a hard world . . .

He kissed her, his hands at her waist. Even with all the bike riding, there was a pleasant little roll there.

He winked. "See you later, Tubs."

She jerked away from him, glaring.

No doubt about it, he thought as he raced for the door, he had stepped over his wife's yellow line.

CHAPTER EIGHT

The Spark in the Flax

The rain began in the night, drumming steadily on the red roof of Dove Cottage.

At six a.m., he tried to think of one good reason to spend a full day at the church office, but couldn't. Didn't clergy usually take two days every single week, and hadn't he taken only one since arriving? He would go in after lunch, that was the ticket.

"Wonderful, darling, you can help me feed Jonathan!" His wife had a positively wicked gleam in her eye.

"No! I don't like it!" Jonathan shook his head vigorously when a bowl of cereal was set before him.

Cynthia proffered buttered toast.

"No!" said Jonathan. "No toast!"

"What if we put jelly on it?" asked Father Tim.

"I've tried that," she said. "It doesn't work. We go through this every morning while you trot happily down the street, whistling." She sighed. "I don't know how to make children eat things they don't like."

"Hasn't he given you any clues?"

"I've tried oatmeal, Froot Loops, buttered grits, bacon, not to mention eggs scrambled and boiled. Nothing will do. He always ends up in tears with crackers and cheese."

"We could call someone," he said brightly, "and *ask* what he likes for breakfast."

"Who could we call?"

"Let's see. Jean Ballenger! She knows the family!" What a great solution. He was a regular Sherlock.

"I got to pee-pee," said Jonathan.

"You just pee-pee'd," said Cynthia, looking frazzled.

Jonathan tumbled from the chair and headed toward the bathroom at a trot.

"Your turn to go with him," said his wife. "And please put the seat down afterward."

"I have no idea!" exclaimed Jean when he rang her small cottage next to the library. "I never saw anyone eat anything while I was at the Tolsons'."

After the useless phone inquiry, Cynthia pulled him into the study. "I don't suppose Jean would like to keep Jonathan for a little while?"

"Jean Ballenger? I can't imagine such a thing!" Jean, a fastidious spinster with crocheted antimacassars on her armchairs, would hardly be up for tending a strong-willed three-year-old.

"What are we going to do?" asked Cynthia. "I think he's adorable, truly he is. But he's running me ragged. I'm too *old* for this!"

"I'll be here 'til one o'clock. Go to your drawing board, relax, everything is under control."

So why did she peer at him like that, with one eyebrow up and one down?

~~❧~~

"Eureka!" he shouted, running along the hall to her studio. "I've found it!"

"Found what?" she asked, not looking up from a watercolor of Violet under a yellow and blue beach umbrella.

"What he likes for breakfast!" He was positively triumphant; he might have located the very Grail.

"I'll never guess, so tell me." She couldn't help grinning at her husband, who looked as if he'd been run through a food processor.

"Guess!" he insisted, playing the mean trick Emma always played on him.

"M&M's?"

"Not even close. Two more."

"Reese's peanut butter cups! That would certainly be *my* preference for breakfast every morning!"

"Cynthia . . ."

"All right, I'm not trying. Here goes, and I'm quite serious this time." She looked out the window. She curled a strand of hair around one finger. She sighed.

"I don't have a clue," she said.

"Spaghetti."

"No."

"Yes!"

"Al dente, I presume."

"A little respect, please. I've just made an important discovery here."

"Yes, dear, and thank you. Plain or with marinara?"

"With butter. No fork, no spoon. Just dump it in a bowl and set it in front of him. Of course, you'll have to bathe him after it's all over."

"Bathe him?" There went that eyebrow again.

"All right, *I'll* bathe him. But just this once."

Why did children keep turning up on his doorstep? Not that he was complaining, but wasn't it odd that he'd lived a full six decades with hardly a youngster in his life except those he encountered in Sunday School? But then, look what it had gained him, after all—Dooley Barlowe. One of the greatest gifts, most of the time, that had ever "come down from the Father of lights," as St. James had put it.

In any case, this was a picnic compared to Father Traccy, who, with his good wife, had adopted fourteen children. Fourteen! It boggled the mind. And then there was Father Moultrie, who had passed into legend, though still living as far he knew. This good fellow had collected twenty-one children of various ages and backgrounds and had managed, so it was said, to keep the lot in good order, though the addition he built to his suburban home had literally fallen down one night after a communal pillow fight; thanks be to God no one was badly hurt.

"And darling . . . ," said his smiling wife as he turned to leave the room.

"Yes?"

"Thank you for mopping the floor under his chair when you've finished."

"No problem," he said, trying to mean it.

⟳

He looked out the study window at the incessant rain, then checked his watch.

A quarter 'til twelve.

Mule and J.C. would just be trooping into the rear booth.

He knew it was a busy time at the Grill, but he was missing those guys, and how much trouble could it be for Velma to call somebody to the phone?

He listened as the red phone on the wall beside the grill rang twice. Four times. Six. Seven . . .

He was ready to hang up when Velma answered.

"Velma, it's Tim Kavanagh!"

"Who?"

"Tim Kavanagh."

"What can I do for you, we've got a lunch trade here to take care of."

"Right. Could you, ah, call Mule to the phone? Or J.C.?"

"Hold on."

He heard the receiver being laid on top of the wall unit, then heard it fall, swinging on the cord and knocking against the wall, *blam . . . blam . . . blam.* He held his own receiver away from his ear.

The babble in the Grill sounded a continent away, all the clatter and uproar that had been so familiar for so long seemed so . . . distant. His heart sank.

"I don't serve grits after nine o'clock!" That was Percy.

Clink. Clank. Thunk.

"Dagummit!" Percy again. Must have dropped his spatula.

"Lord help! Lookit what th' President's done now." Sounded like Leonard Stanley, who always sat at the counter opposite the phone. "Oh, boy! *Un*believable."

"I don't read th' paper, makes my stomach wrench. Except for th' funnies, I've plumb quit." Coot Hendrick. "But I like those fliers that come with th' paper—you know, Wal-Mart, Ken's Auto Parts, discount coupons for Domino's Pizza, like that."

Whop. Sizzle.

"We ain't got a special today!" yelled Percy. "I'm over offerin' specials, have t' take it straight off th' menu!"

"So, what'd th' President do?"

"Trust me, you don't want to know. I wonder if there's any Alka-Seltzer in this place." *Rustle, crackle.* Leonard must have sprung for a big newspaper like the *Atlanta Constitution,* considering the racket it made as he turned the pages.

"Can you *believe* it?" He heard Velma stomp by the phone. "Th' front booth wants a 'BLT without lettuce or tomato!' I said right to 'is face, 'How can you have a BLT without *L* an' *T*?' an' he said, *'What?'* That's th' same fool ordered a cheeseburger th' other day an' asked me to hold th' *cheese.*"

"I'd take early retirement if I was you," said Coot.

It was clear that in the lunch-hour rush, Velma had forgotten his phone call.

He yelled into the mouthpiece. "Velma! Percy! *Hello!*"

He heard the front door open and slam, the hiss of a pop-top soda being opened.

"Hello! Somebody! *Anybody!*"

"What's this phone doin' hangin by th' cord?" asked Percy. "Must have got knocked off th' hook."

Click.

Jonathan poked a chubby finger at the television screen in the guest room. "I want to watch a movie," he said.

"Ah. A movie."

"In a box," said the three-year-old.

He looked at his watch. "In a box." Fifty-seven minutes to go.

"Peter Pan."

"Peter Pan. Right."

"You like Peter Pan?"

"Oh, yes. Very much!"

Jonathan poked his finger at Father Tim's leg. "So, let's watch it then!"

"We could tell a story. I could read to you, how's that?"

"Watch a movie in a box!"

In a box, in a box. He had a box left over from the books. He dashed to the back porch and hauled it in.

"I one time had a *Li'n King* movie," said Jonathan, "an' my daddy, my daddy, my daddy wouldn't let me watch it." Jonathan furrowed his brow.

He set the boy in the cardboard box and turned on the TV. Good grief! He couldn't believe his eyes, and in broad daylight, too. He surfed. Fifty minutes to go.

"Peter Pan!" yelled Jonathan. "In a *box!*"

He trucked to the studio. "For Pete's sake, Kavanagh, what is a movie in a box?"

"A video, dear. We don't have any."

"Why not?"

"We don't have a VCR."

"We don't even have a microwave," he said, perplexed.

He dashed back to the guest room and pulled Jonathan out of the box. "We're going for a walk."

"I don't want to walk!"

"In this life, my boy, you'll be forced to do many things you'd rather not do, so consider this a rehearsal."

He marched Jonathan into the kitchen and dragged Barnabas from under the table. He snapped the red leash on his dog's collar as the phone rang.

He glanced out the kitchen window as he snatched up the cordless from the window seat. Blast! They couldn't go for a walk, he'd forgotten it was raining cats and dogs.

"Hello!" he barked.

"Father? Is that *you?*"

"Esther!"

"You didn't sound like yourself," said Esther, who didn't sound like herself, either. "I've got to talk to you about Gene."

"Shoot!" he said, cantering down the hall after Jonathan, who was making a beeline for the front door.

"He's actin' so strange, I hardly know him. I'm tellin' you, he's just not my Gene, he could be some body named Hubert or Pete or Lord knows who, he's actin' so peculiar."

"What's he doing?" he asked, grabbing the boy before he dove off the porch.

He carried him back into the house under one arm. "Down!" yelled the boy, squirming and kicking.

"Who in the world is that?" asked Esther.

"That's Jonathan. Tell me what Gene's doing."

"He's counting things. He stares at me and says, 'Seven.' And I say, 'Seven what?' And he says, 'That's seven times you opened the cabinet door over the stove.' "

"Down!" said Jonathan, wriggling out of Father Tim's grasp.

"Aha. I'm listening, Esther, keep talking. You opened the cabinet door seven times . . ."

Jonathan had dropped to all fours and was drinking water from the dog bowl. He transferred the cordless to his left hand and removed the red leash from Barnabas's collar with his right. He snapped the leash to the boy's romper strap and looped the other end over the back of a kitchen chair.

"He looked at me last night, said, 'Eighteen.' I said, 'Eighteen what?' He said, 'Curlers.' We're goin' up to bed, he said, 'Fourteen.' Lord knows, my nerves are shot by this time, he'd been doin' it all day, I didn't even ask fourteen what, an' he said, 'Steps.' I can tell you right now I do not like it, he has been pullin' this dumb trick for months, but it's gettin' worse by th' minute.

"To tell th' gospel truth, I could knock him in th' head. Can you imagine livin' with somebody who walks around goin' '*Sixty-six!* That's sixty-six window panes.' Or, '*Nineteen!* That's nineteen knobs on th' cabinet doors.' The other day I thought, wonder why there's just nineteen knobs and not twenty, and th' first thing you know, I was countin' knobs *myself.*"

"I'll be darned."

"I'm on th' hall phone, but I can hear him, he's countin' squares in th' kitchen linoleum as we speak!"

"Oh, boy."

"For the umpteenth time!" Esther lowered her voice. "Father, do you reckon he's . . . crazy? It scares th' daylights out of me to even think a word like that."

"Does Hoppy know what's going on?"

"We had all those tests run, you'd think somethin' mental would show up in th' blood work."

"I feel you should talk to Hoppy. When are you seeing him again?"

"Two weeks."

"You may want to give him a ring."

"I can't, he's on vacation. You know he never took one for years, so I reckon he deserves it."

"Talk to his associate, talk to Dr. Wilson."

"Are you kiddin' me? He's green as tasselin' corn."

"I'd talk to Dr. Wilson, Esther."

Esther had started to cry and was trying to hide it. "Only one thing hasn't changed."

"What's that?"

Jonathan was dragging the chair across the kitchen, as Barnabas sat under the table, bewildered.

"He still pats me on the cheek and says, 'Goodnight, Dollface,' just like he's done for forty-two years."

"Horsie!" shouted Jonathan.

"I wish you were here," sobbed Esther.

"I wish I were, too," he said, meaning it.

─ｅ─

He put socks on the kitchen chair legs and let Jonathan pull the darned thing all over the house. Cynthia shut her door—in fact, it sounded like she locked it—and Barnabas hid in the corner of the study by the bookshelves. As for himself, he sat in the living room like a country squire, and perused the *Whitecap Reader*.

Some members of the Wadamo tribe of the Zambezi Valley in Zimbabwe are born with only two toes on each foot, which is an inherited trait. However, these people can walk as well as anyone with five toes on each foot.

This Space for Rent

Get Geared Up! Your One Stop Fishing Gear and Auto Supply Store, Whitecap Fishing Gear And Auto Parts

Custom Modular homes, Affordable Quality, Tozier Builders (across from Bragg's in the Toe)

Trivia: Which night precedes May Day? Which island separates the Canadian part of Niagara Falls from the American? Whose army were canned foods developed to feed?

SHEAR CREATIONS: Hairstyling for the entire family, fish sandwiches and pasta to go . . .

Laugh for the week: "I don't mind her being born again, but did she have to come back as herself?"

He sighed. The *Reader* was the only newspaper he'd ever seen that made the *Muse* look like the *Philadelphia Inquirer.*

He allowed the boy to exhaust himself until, on the dot of one, he went down for a nap without a whimper. "Hallelujah!" Father Tim whispered to his dog as he tiptoed from the guest room and closed the door.

∽

He got into his car at the rear gate and drew the dripping umbrella in with him. As he turned the key in the ignition, he noticed a panel truck parked at Morris Love's entrance. He adjusted his glasses.

L. L. Mansfield, Tuning for Fine Organs.

A driver got out of the truck and went to the iron gate, swung it open, came back to the truck, and drove through.

He sat for a moment, curious at the first sign of coming and going he'd seen across the road. He watched the driver trot back and lock the gate behind him.

Fort Knox! he thought, driving away.

∽

I tell thee what I would have thee do . . .

He sat in the church office, hearing rain peck the windowpanes like chickens after corn, and read from a sermon of Charles Spurgeon, delivered at Newington on March 9, 1873.

> *Go to Him without fear or trembling; ere yon sun goes down and ends this day of mercy, go and tell Him thou hast broken the Father's laws—tell Him that thou art lost, and thou needest to be saved; tell Him that He is a man, and appeal to His manly heart, and to His brotherly sympathies.*
> *Pour out thy broken heart at His feet: let thy soul flow over in His presence, and I tell thee He cannot cast thee away . . .*

He jotted in his sermon notebook: *Not that He <u>will</u> not turn a deaf ear, but that He <u>cannot.</u> Press this truth.* Spurgeon had put into a nutshell what he wanted to preach on Sunday to the body at St. John's.

> *. . . though thy prayer be feeble as the spark in the flax, He will not quench it; and though thy heart be bruised like a reed, He will not break it.*
> *May the Holy Spirit bless you with a desire to go to God through Jesus Christ; and encourage you to do so by showing that He is meek and lowly of heart, gentle, and tender, full of pity.*

Bottom line, he would tell his congregation what Nike had told the world:

Just do it.

He finished typing up the pew bulletin and rang the hospital. Janette was down the hall. "Tell her I'll be there tomorrow," he said to the nurse. "Tell her Jonathan's having a wonderful time."

He fished the umbrella from the stand by the down-stairs door and prepared to head into the downpour.

"Father Kavanagh, is that you?"

He spun around. "Good heavens!"

"I frightened you, Father, I'm sorry as can be!"

"Mercy!" he said, not knowing what else to say. A tall, thin, stooped woman in a dripping hat and raincoat stood before him, her glasses sliding off her wet nose.

"I came in through the front door and couldn't find a soul, so I helped myself to these stairs. I'm Ella Bridgewater, come to audition!"

He was addled. "But I thought tomorrow . . ."

"I wrote down today in my appointment book, Father, I am very precise about such things, and besides, I couldn't have done it tomorrow, for I'm going across to my niece. I always do that on Saturday, so I would never have—"

"Of course. My mistake, I'm sure." He was very precise about such things, as well. But why quibble?

"Well, Miss Bridgewater, glad to see you!" He took her wet hand and shook it heartily, noting that she appeared considerably older than her letter had stated.

She patted her chest. "I have the music under my coat!"

"Excellent. We'll just pop upstairs and have at it. Thanks for coming out in the deluge."

He followed her up the stairs to the sacristy. She was certainly agile, he thought.

"I've always loved this church, Father. I think I wrote in my letter to you that I played for yoked parishes for many years in these islands."

"Yes. Wonderful!"

"So I certainly know the churches in these parts, though I never stepped foot in St. John's 'til this day." She looked around the sanctuary and nave with some wonder.

"You don't mean it!"

"Not once. Too busy playing elsewhere!"

"I wish you could see it in the sunlight, the way the stained glass pours color into the nave."

Wiry gray curls sprung up as she removed her rain hat. "I believe I *will* see it in the sunlight!"

Mighty perky lady, he thought. And seventy if she was a day. Her letter, however, had said sixty-two, and added "in vibrant good health."

"There's the choir loft, as you can see. I believe you'll find our old Hammond in fine working order. Well, then, let me help you off with your coat, and you can pop up the stairs there. Would you like a cup of coffee? Or tea? Won't take but a moment."

"No, thank you, Father, I'm ready to get on with it. I've been practicing like all get-out for days—you know they say if you fail to prepare, you prepare to fail."

"Perfect line for a wayside pulpit!"

"That's where I got it," she said, with a burst of laughter. "Well, here goes."

She walked briskly up the aisle, clutching her manila envelope, and made short work of the stairs to the loft.

There was a moment's rustling in the loft and, he thought, a mite of hard breathing.

"Great day in the morning!" she shouted down. "This organ is old as Methuselah."

"Manufactured the year of my fourth birthday!"

"Which was a good year, I'm sure. Now . . ."—he heard her clear her throat and heave a sigh—"sit and close your eyes. I'll give you a prelude and fugue, followed by a hymn. Then you're allowed to make one personal request."

"Thank you, Miss Bridgewater." He was glad he didn't mind being told what to do by women; he'd never lacked for direction in that department.

"My, my," he heard her say. "Oh, yes." She fiddled with the stops, pressed the pedals, hummed a little. "Well, then!"

The old organ nearly blasted him out of the pew. Aha! It was Bach's Little Prelude and Fugue in C Major, and she was giving it everything she had. This woman had eaten her Wheaties, and no doubt about it.

At the end, she called in a loud voice, "How was that, Father?"

"Why . . . play on!" he said. Very perky.

"For All the Saints" boomed up to the rafters. Ah. Good to have the organ going in this place, a benediction.

He listened carefully, unable to restrain himself from whispering the words under his breath.

" 'For all the saints, who from their labors rest, who thee by faith before the world confessed, thy Name O Jesus, be forever blessed. Alleluia, alleluia . . .' "

Not especially thrilling, as the rendition of it certainly could be, but better than he might have expected, to tell the truth. He patted his foot and attended each note, keeping an open mind to the very end.

Agreeably workmanlike, he concluded.

"How was that?" she trumpeted.

"Well done!"

"Thank you, Father, honesty is the best policy, and I don't mind saying that all my priests have liked my playing."

Rain blew against the windows, *peck, peck, peck.*

"Miss Bridgewater, is it time for my personal request?"

"It is, and I must say I'm filled with curiosity."

"What about 'Strengthen for Service, Lord'?" A communion hymn worth its salt and then some!

"Excellent, Father! Two-oh-one in the old hymnal, three-twelve in the new. Here we go."

He chuckled. He hadn't encountered such bravado since the last meeting of the youth group.

" 'Strengthen for service, Lord,' " he whispered as she played, " 'the hands that holy things have taken; let ears that how have heard thy songs, to clamor never waken . . .' " *To clamor never waken.* His favorite line.

He looked around the walls and up to the ceiling as if the music were painting the very timbers, bathing them, somehow, and making them stand more firmly.

He was drinking it all in as if starved, and then the audition was over.

He stood and faced the loft and clapped with some enthusiasm.

Huffing slightly and clutching her envelope, she was down the stairs, along the aisle, and standing by his pew in a trice. Her long nose and stooped shoulders gave her the appearance, he thought, of an Oriental crane.

"Well done!" he said again.

"Thank you, Father. I have a confession." She held her envelope like a shield against her chest, looking pained but confident.

"Shall we . . . go to the altar?" he asked.

"Don't trouble yourself, I'll just spit it out right here."

"Sit down," he said. He sat, himself, and scooted over.

She thumped into the oak pew. "I lied about my age."

"Oh?"

"I turned seventy-four last month. I didn't think you'd hire me if I told the truth, and I want you to know I'm sorry. As I was playing your request, the Lord convicted my heart and I asked Him to forgive me. Perhaps you'll do the same."

She looked exceedingly pained.

"Why, certainly, Miss Bridgewater. Of course. And may I say you don't look seventy-four."

She brightened considerably. "Why, thank you, Father. You see, I believe the Lord called me to St. John's. When I heard you had a need, I asked Him about it at once, and He said, 'Ella Jean'—the Lord always uses my middle name—'march over there and ask for that job, they need you.' "

"Aha."

"He doesn't speak to me in an audible voice."

"I understand."

"He puts it in my mind, you might say. As you well know, Father, you have to be quiet before the Lord and keep your trap shut for Him to get a word in edgewise, that's my experience."

"Miss Bridgewater—"

"Call me Ella," she said.

"Ella, if we can agree on your compensation, I think you may be just the ticket for St. John's."

Tears sprang to her eyes. "Do you really think so?"

"I do."

"But," she said, regaining her composure, "you'll have to run it by the vestry."

"Right. I intend to."

"When might that be?"

"Wednesday. I'll get back to you right after the meeting. Shouldn't be any problem. Do you have family?"

"I lived with my mother for many years, she went to heaven last March."

"I'm sorry to hear it. Or glad, as the case may be." Heaven! The ultimate place to escape the clamor . . .

"I'm an old maid," she said, bobbing her head and smiling. "But not the sort of dried-up old maid you see in cartoons."

"Oh?" A priest never knew what he might be told. He shifted uneasily on the pew.

"No, indeed. I fell head over heels in love when I was forty-seven, and truth be told, have never gotten over it. They say you came late to love, yourself."

"Late, yes," he said, smiling. "But not too late."

"Minor was a young explorer with Admiral Byrd, and spent his last years as a maker of hot-air balloons."

"You don't say!"

"Oh, yes. And I went up in one!" Her eyes were bright with feeling. "We sailed up the coast and across Virginia and landed in a cow pasture, where we picnicked on cheese and figs. It was the single grandest thing I ever did."

"I'm happy to hear it," he said. And he was.

Miss Bridgewater adjusted her glasses and peered at him. "And when would I begin if . . . if . . ."

"Sunday after next, I should think."

"Well!" she said, sitting back and beaming. "Well!"

⌇

The everlasting rain was still going strong at four-thirty, when he pulled into Ernie's for a gallon of milk.

Roger Templeton sat in the corner by a small pile of wood shavings, and looked up when he came in.

"Tim! Glad to see you! How's your weather?"

"You mean my own, apart from the elements? I'd

say . . . sunny!" Hadn't God just delivered an organist to St. John's?

He scratched Lucas behind the ears, then pulled up a chair next to Roger, peering into Roger's lap at what had been a block of wood. The rough form of a duck, though headless, had emerged, its right wing beginning to assume feathers.

"Amazing! May I have a look?"

"Help yourself," said Roger, pleased to be asked.

He took the duck and examined it closely. In principle, at least, this was how David had escaped from Michelangelo's block of marble.

"That's tupelo wood," said Roger. "I get it from up around Albemarle Sound. With tupelo, you can cut across the grain, with the grain, or against the grain."

"It's beautiful!" he said. How had Roger known the wood contained a duck just waiting to get out?

"That's a green-winged teal. It's not much to look at yet; I've rough-edged it with a band saw and now I'm carving in the feather groupings."

"How did you know you could do this?"

Roger took a knife from an old cigar box next to his chair. "I didn't. I'd never done anything with my hands."

"Except make money," said Ernie, walking in from the book room. He thumped down at the table.

"I used to go on hunting trips with my colleagues . . . Alaska, Canada, the eastern shore of Maryland around St. Michael's and Easton. I recall the day I dropped a green-winged teal into the river. When the Lab brought it to me, I saw for the first time the great beauty of it. My eyes were opened in a new way, and I wondered how I'd managed to . . . do what I'd been doing."

"Aha."

"Oh, I'm not preaching a sermon against hunting, Tim. Let a man hunt! I also have a special fondness for a boy learning to hunt. But I quit right there at the river, I said if God Almighty could make just one feather, not to mention a whole duck, as intricate and beautiful as that, who am I to bring it down?"

"He still fishes," said Ernie.

"Why did you start carving?"

Roger shrugged. "I wanted to see how close I could come to the real thing. I thought I'd try to make just one and then quit."

"I see."

"But I never seem to come very close to the real thing, so I keep trying."

Father Tim had never done much with his hands, either, except turn the pages of a book or plant a rosebush. "How long does it take to make one?"

"Oh, five or six weeks, sometimes longer."

"He works on 'is ducks in my place, exclusive," said Ernie, as if that lent a special distinction to Ernie's Books, Bait & Tackle.

"Do you also work at home?"

Roger colored slightly. "I paint at home, but my wife doesn't allow carving."

He'd heard of not being allowed to smoke cigars at home, but he'd never heard of a ban on duck carving.

"Roger, my wife has bought me a chair on Captain Willie's fishing boat. You ever go deep-sea fishing?"

"Does a hog love slop?" asked Ernie, who didn't care to be out of the loop in any conversation.

"Captain Willie has taken me out to the Gulf Stream many times."

"I don't mind telling you I'm no fisherman. I've never spent much time around water."

"That's no liability. Sport fishing is all about relaxing and having fun. It's an adventure."

An adventure! He'd always wanted to have an adventure, but wasn't good at figuring out how to get from A to B. Leave it to his wife to figure it out for him.

"I hear a lot about spending the day with your head over the side."

Roger and Ernie laughed. "Don't listen to that mess," said Ernie. "You stay sober the night before and get a good night's sleep and you'll be fine."

"And don't eat a greasy breakfast," said Roger. "Besides, if it's any comfort, statistics say only twelve percent get seasick."

He was encouraged.

"What'll we see out there?"

"Out in the Gulf," said Ernie, "you'll see your blue marlin, your white marlin, your sailfish, your dolphin—"

"There's wahoo," said Roger, "and yellow tuna—"

"Plus your black tuna and albacore tuna. . . ."

"Man. Big stuff!" He was feeling twelve years old.

Roger whittled. "You can see everything from a thousand-pound blue marlin to a two-pound mahimahi."

"No kidding? But what kind of fish can you actually *catch?*"

"Whatever God grants you that day," said Roger. "Of course, we always release marlin."

"Fair enough. What sort of boat would we go in?"

"Captain Willie runs a Carolina hull built over on Roanoke Island. About fifty-three feet long—"

"—an' eight hundred and fifty horsepower!" Ernie appeared to take personal pride in this fact. "What you might call a glorified speedboat."

"Eight hundred and fifty horsepower? Man!" He was losing his vocabulary, fast.

Roger adjusted his glasses and looked at Father Tim. "Just show up ready to have a good time. That's what I'd recommend."

"And be sure an' take a bucket of fried chicken," said Ernie.

❧

He cooked the requisite bowl of spaghetti while Jonathan sat in the window seat and colored a batch of Cynthia's hasty sketches. Something baking in the oven made his heart beat faster.

"Cassoulet!" said his creative wife. Though she'd never attempted such a thing, she had every confidence it would be sensational. "Fearless in the kitchen" was how she once described herself.

"It's all in the crust, the way the crust forms on top," she told him, allowing a peek into the oven. "I know it's too hot to have the oven going, but I couldn't resist."

"Where on earth did you find duck?"

"At the little market. It was lying right by the mahimahi. Isn't that wonderful?"

He certainly wouldn't mention it to Roger.

Jonathan had clambered down from the window seat. "Watch a movie!" he said, giving a tug on Father Tim's pants leg.

"Timothy, we've got to get a VCR. Could you possibly go across tomorrow, to whatever store carries these things? I don't think I can make it 'til Monday without in-house entertainment!"

"Do we just plug it in?" He'd never been on friendly terms with high technology, which was always accompanied by manuals printed in Croatian.

"Beats me," she said. "That's your job. I'm the stay-at-home mommy."

He put his arms around her and traced the line of her cheek with his nose. "Thank you for being the best deacon in the entire Anglican communion."

⎯⎯⎯⎯

Jonathan had wanted his mother tonight; his tears called up a few of Father Tim's very own.

He thought it must be agony to be small and helpless, with no mother, no father, no brother or sister to be found. He held Jonathan against his chest, over his heart, and let the boy sob until he exhausted his tears.

He walked with him through the house in a five-room circle, crooning snatches of hymns, small prayers and benedictions, fragments of stories about Pooh and Toad and that pesky rabbit, Peter. He didn't know what to do with a child who was crying out of bewilderment and loss, except to be with him in it.

⎯⎯⎯⎯

He covered the sleeping boy with a light blanket, praying silently. Then he closed the door and tiptoed down the hall and out to the porch where Cynthia sat waiting, a rain-drugged Violet slumbering in her lap.

Barnabas followed and sprawled at his feet.

What peace to retire into the cool August evening, after a dinner that might have been served in the Languedoc.

For the first time today, he liked the rain, it was friend and shelter to him, enclosing the porch with a gossamer veil.

They watched the distant patch of gray Atlantic turn to platinum in the lingering dusk.

"Weary, darling?" she asked, taking his hand.

"I am. Don't know why, though. Haven't done much today."

"You do more than you realize. Up at dawn, morning prayer, feed and bathe the boy, help the wife, write the pew bulletin, work on your sermon, hire an organist . . ."

He took her hand and kissed it. Of all the earthly consolations, he loved understanding best. Not sympathy, no, that could be deadly. But understanding. It was balm to him, and he had sucked it up like a toad, often denying it to her.

"Your book—how are you feeling about it?" he asked.

"I guess I don't know why I'm doing another book when I might have the lovely freedom to do nothing. I suppose I got excited about being in a new place, the way the light changes, and the coming and going of the tide. It spoke to me and I couldn't help myself." She smiled at him. "I think I make books because I don't know what else to do."

"You know how to make a ravishing cassoulet."

"Yes, but cassoulet has its limitations. Little books do not."

He nodded.

"Do you think we'll ever just loll about?" she asked.

"I don't think we're very good at lolling."

She put her head back and closed her eyes. "Thank God for this peace."

He heard it first, even through the loud whisper of rain. It was the organ music of their neighbor. He sat up, alert, and cupped his hand to his ear.

"What is it, Timothy?"

"It's Morris Love, in the house behind the wall. Listen."

They sat silent for long moments.

"Wondrous," she said quietly.

The rain seemed to abate out of respect for the music, and they began to hear the notes more clearly.

"Name that tune," she said.

"'Jesus My Joy.' A Bach chorale prelude." He couldn't help but hear the urgency—in truth, a kind of fury—underlying the music. He told her what he knew about Morris Love, leaving out the part about him shouting through the hedge.

"Is Mr. Love a concert organist?"

"Not unless you consider this a private concert for the Kavanaghs."

"What a lovely thought," she said, pleased.

～e～

When the phone rang, he fumbled for it. For a moment, he was at home in Mitford and expected to find it next to the bed. But blast, he was in Whitecap, and the phone was across the room.

It rang again; he bumped into the chair and tried to figure what time it was. The rain had stopped, and a stiff breeze blew through the windows.

As the phone continued to ring, he picked up his watch and glanced at the glowing dial. Twelve-forty. Not good. *Lord, have mercy. . . .*

"Hello!"

"I have a collect call from Harley Welch," said an operator. "Will you pay for the call?"

"Yes!"

"Rev'rend?"

"Harley?" His heart hammered.

"Rev'rend, I hate t' tell you this . . ."

CHAPTER NINE

Home Far Away

"They got Dooley in jail."

"*What?*"

"But he's all right, he ain't hurt or nothin'. . . ."

Cynthia sat up. "What is it, Timothy?"

He switched on the lamp. "Dooley."

"Dear God!" she said.

"Tell me, Harley." He once prayed he'd never live to hear what he was hearing now.

"Well, he was comin' home on time, goin' to be here right on th' nickel. . . ."

"And?" His mouth was dry, his stomach churning. *Christ, have mercy. . . .*

"An' he picked up Buster Austin standin' out on th' road. You remember Buster."

Indeed, he did. Buster had called yours truly a "nerd," for which Dooley had mopped the floor of the school cafeteria with him. The last run-in was when

Buster stole a pack of cigarettes and talked Dooley into smoking on school grounds. School principal Myra Hayes had nearly eaten one hapless priest alive for "allowing" such a thing to happen, and suspended Dooley for ten days.

"Buster said he needed a ride to git 'is clothes at somebody's house, would Dooley take 'im, an' Dooley said he would but make it snappy. Dooley set in th' truck while Buster took in a empty duffel bag and come out a good bit later. Seems like th' boys was goin' down th' road when two officers drove up behind 'em in a squad car. Pulled 'em over, hauled 'em off to th' station for breakin', enterin', an' larceny."

"Larceny?" This was a bad dream.

"You know that empty duffel bag Buster carried in? Hit was full when Buster come out of th' house. Had jewelry, a CD player, money, liquor, I don't know what all in there."

"No!"

"Police said th' house had a silent alarm on it, an' they was on th' boys before they got out of th' driveway good. But Dooley didn't do nothin'."

"I believe that."

"Nossir, he didn't, he was doin' th' drivin' is all, but the police says 'til they know better, he's locked up."

"What can I do?" His legs were turned to water; he sank into the chair by the lamp.

"If I was you, Rev'rend, I'd do what preachers do."

"Pray."

"That's right. I'm down at th' station, an' soon as I hear somethin', I'll call you. I know Dooley don't want you worried an' all. He would of called, but he's upset about worryin' you."

"How is he, Harley? Tell me straight."

"Well, he's scared. He's innocent, but hit's scary bein' th'owed in a cell like that an' locked up."

"Is Rodney there?"

"Last I heard, th' chief was puttin' on 'is britches an' bustin' over here."

"Thank God for you, Harley."

"Now, don't you worry, Rev'rend."

He hung up, trembling, feeling the immutable reality of six hundred miles between Mitford and his racing heart.

At one-thirty, he could bear it no longer and called the Mitford police station.

Rodney Underwood was questioning Dooley and Buster. No, they didn't know when the chief would be through, but he would call when he was.

Jonathan trotted in and clambered onto their bed. "I think I read somewhere that children aren't supposed to sleep with their parents," he said.

"We're not his parents," explained his wife.

Jonathan bounced down beside Cynthia, looking hopeful. "Watch a movie!"

Cynthia was not amused. "Jonathan, if you so much as utter the M word again, I will jump in the ocean!"

He nodded his head vigorously. "I can swim!"

"Good! Go to sleep."

He poked his chubby finger into Cynthia's arm. "You go to sleep, too."

Father Tim paced the floor, checking his watch.

"I'm hungry," said Jonathan.

"People don't eat during the night."

Jonathan held out both hands. "Give me candy, then?"

Cynthia leaned toward him, shaking her head. "If you weren't so utterly adorable . . ."

"You got bad breath," said Jonathan, wrinkling his nose.

"When I go to the library tomorrow," she told her husband, "I'll see if they have a book on what to do with children."

∽

The phone rang at two o'clock.

"Buster Austin's been askin' for trouble for years," said Rodney. "Now he's gone and stepped in it."

"What about Dooley?"

"Dooley says he rode Buster over to the house and sat in the truck, said he didn't have nothin' to do with it, but Buster says he did. Soon as th' paperwork's done, I'll drive th' boys over to Wesley and take 'em before th' magistrate."

"Good Lord, Rodney. What does that mean?"

"Th' magistrate's th' one signs th' arrest warrant, then I'll serve it. I'm goin' to tell 'im I think Dooley's innocent, he's never been in any trouble, and we'll see where we go from there. He'll set bond, and you'll have to talk to a bondsman if you want Dooley out of jail."

"Right. I know the bondsman in Wesley. Call me the minute you know something. What kind of bond do you think we're talking about?"

"Breakin' and enterin' and larceny is serious business. You might get off for twenty thousand, maybe ten. Th' Austins will probably post a property bond, Buster don't come from fancy circumstances."

He couldn't believe this was happening. It was a nightmare. It was also the ruination of his boy's summer, his last precious days at home. . . . He felt sick in his very gut.

"Where do we go from there?" he asked.

"Th' magistrate will set a court date, two weeks to thirty days away."

"Let me talk with Dooley, if I may." He felt like a Mack truck was sitting on his chest.

"Hey," said Dooley.

"Hey, yourself," he replied, drawing thin comfort from their old greeting.

"I didn't do it."

"I believe you."

"Buster Austin's still th' same lyin', cheatin' geek he always was. I should've known better. I picked 'im up 'cause I thought he was in trouble, I thought maybe his ol' car was broke down an' I was tryin' to help. I could kill 'im, maybe I will."

"I think you did the right thing."

"You do?"

"I do. It was someone you knew, you thought he needed help, and you stopped."

"So how come it turned out like this?" He could hear the barely controlled rage in the boy's voice.

"Sometimes we do good and it turns out badly. I don't know why. But it definitely doesn't mean we're to stop doing the right thing."

"Yeah, well, wait'll Lace an' ever'body hears about it."

"I thought you weren't seeing much of Lace."

"I don't care what she thinks, anyway, but what about ever'body else, like Avis? And what if it gets back to school? I mean, some of th' guys will think it's cool, but th' headmaster, he'll . . . he'll freak."

"If it comes up, tell the truth."

"I want to go home," said Dooley. He sounded exhausted. "I got to work tomorrow."

"Rodney will take you home as soon as the bail issue is settled."

"Did you know I'll have to go to court for this stupid mess?"

"Yes."

"I'll have to come home from school, but I ain't tellin' this to Mr. Fleming, no way. You can say I've got to have an operation or somethin'. Maybe on my kidneys or tonsils or . . . on my brain or spine."

"We'll cross that bridge when we get to it. I'm sorry this happened, I wish we were there. God bless you, everything's going to be fine. I'll call the bondsman as soon I hear back from Rodney, don't be afraid, we love you." He tried to cover all the bases, but his heart felt empty as a gourd.

Rodney called at three a.m.

He'd done everything he could to convince the magistrate that Dooley was a good kid with no previous offenses, emphasizing that his daddy was a clergyman. The magistrate said he was a preacher's kid himself, and based on that alone had a notion to set bail at forty thousand. Bottom line, the magistrate was releasing Dooley on a secured five-thousand-dollar bond, and Rodney was driving him home as soon as the bondsman could get over to the Wesley jail. Buster Austin's parents had refused to post bond, and Buster would not be going home.

He found Ray Porter's number in his black book, and woke him up.

"Ray, Tim Kavanagh. My boy's in the Wesley jail

and he's innocent. He's under a five-thousand-dollar se-cured bond. How fast can you get him out of there?"

"Let me jump in my clothes," said Ray. "I'll have him out in twenty, thirty minutes. Y'all still down at th' coast?"

"Afraid so. How shall I send the fee?"

"Put a check in the mail. You got my address?"

"I have it somewhere."

"Post office box six twenty-one."

"God bless you."

"I've got two boys," said Ray Porter, considering that sufficient empathy.

He was buttering Jonathan's breakfast spaghetti when the phone rang. His hand was on the receiver be-fore it rang again.

"Hello?"

"I hate to tell you this . . . ," said Emma.

"I already know," he said.

"How'd you know?"

"Harley called me last night."

"How'd he know?" she asked, sounding irritable.

"He was *there*."

"I don't know what you're talkin' about," she said, "but I'm talkin' about Gene Bolick havin' a brain tumor."

"*What?*"

"He keeled over again yesterday, they sent him down to Baptist Hospital and did a MRI scan. That's why he's been actin' so peculiar, it was that tumor pressin' on his brain."

"Dear Lord!"

"Here, I wrote down what it is, I have to spell it.

M-e-n-i-n-g-i-o-m-a. It's way down deep towards th' base of his brain."

"Is it operable?" He realized he was holding his breath.

"Let's see. Where'd I write that down? Here it is on my shoppin' list. No, they can't operate, it's too far down in there. The doctor said unless it gets bigger, leave it alone."

"Do you know anything else?"

"Nothing except I hear Esther's a basket case. Ray Cunningham drove 'em down to Baptist and called back to give th' report. I know it's none of my business, but . . ."

"But what?"

"Like I say, it's none of my business, but I think you ought to come home."

∽

Come home. Come home.

It went around in his head like a liturgical chant.

But how could he go home? As far as he could figure, there wasn't a soul who could take Jonathan in. Everybody was working, away for the summer, or too old to trot after a three-year-old. And there was Janette, who needed him, or so he believed, and Cynthia's parish tea coming up at Dove Cottage in three weeks, and the vestry meeting, and the Ella Bridgewater issue, and his responsibilities to the Whitecap Fair Planning Commission. . . .

"This is home!" he said aloud. But he couldn't force himself to believe it. *Bloom where you're planted,* he'd read on a plaque at Mona's. And wasn't he trying?

In truth, he was longing for Mitford. Longing to see his boy and encourage him and cheer him on and help him pack for school and tuck a few Kit Kats in his suitcase, and sit with Gene and Esther and pray about this terrible thing that had come against them. . . .

He wanted to lay his head on his pillow in the yellow house and walk Barnabas down Main Street and pop into the Grill and surprise everybody. He wanted to dash up to Fernbank and discover what new tricks Anna and Tony were doing with garlic, and visit Uncle Billy and Esther Cunningham, and see his rosebushes, some of which would be more fragrant and richly colored now than in June. . . .

Sleep-deprived and numb with exhaustion, he drove south to the Toe in heat that was ninety degrees and rising.

He didn't know what he expected, but Otis Bragg's office was definitely nothing to write home about. It was, in fact, smaller than his own office in the church basement, and covered with a film of dust from the gravel operation next door. An air conditioner hummed and rattled in the window.

"Well, now!" said Otis. He removed a large cigar butt from his mouth and spit into a wastebasket. "I'd say it's either money or politics that brings you runnin' to th' Toe."

"I didn't know money and politics were necessarily two separate entities."

Otis growled with laughter. "I like a priest with a sense of humor. Seems like the church is a callin' that turns a man sour if he don't watch out."

Father Tim sat down without being asked. "I have come about money."

A strange sadness crossed his parishioner's face. "That's what always sends clergy to my door."

He looked at the short, round man before him, and

was oddly moved. He would come back again when he didn't have his hand out; he'd come back just to visit, to say hello.

Otis leaned forward and squinted at him. "What can I do for you, Father? You look like you wrassled alligators half the night."

"There are plenty of alligators out there, only one of which has put Janette Tolson in the hospital with severe depression."

"We heard that. We hear you've got her boy."

"She's having a rough go of it. And there's no insurance in the family. I thought if you'd be willing, I'll see that St. John's matches what you feel led to give."

Otis rolled the cigar butt between his fingers.

"How do you figure St. John's to be dolin' out money for a thing like this?"

"Janette's one of the body, we're her church family. I figure we can put on a fund-raiser, even do something special at the fair—I don't know, but we'll match what you give."

"What if I gave, say, five thousand bucks? Think you could match that?" Otis clamped the cigar in his mouth, narrowing his eyes.

"Well." He was startled. He had expected some largesse, but . . .

"I don't know if we can raise five thousand. I suppose I was hoping for . . . I don't know, maybe a thousand, tops."

"Father, you goin' to rise in this world, you got to think big."

His bishop, Stuart Cullen, firmly held that philosophy; why couldn't he?

"Thanks, Otis. God bless you! Five thousand is more

than generous, it will go a long way in helping Janette's children recover their mother."

"I hope I don't ever run across th'—I'll watch my language, out of respect—th' son of a gun. I despised him from the minute I laid eyes on 'im." Otis spit furiously into the wastebasket. "Always struttin' around preenin' hisself, makin' th' choir sing those mid'eval hymns that go back a hundred years."

"Well, there's some good news, Otis. I think we've found our organist."

"Fine, fine, glad to hear it. You just keep up th' good work, you hear?" Otis punched a button on his phone. "Agnes, write th' preacher a check for five thousand, make it to St. John's." He pitched the unlit butt in the wastebasket and stood up. "Now you're in th' Toe, let me show you around my little operation."

Father Tim wanted to decline, but thought better of it. Maybe it wouldn't hurt to see the results of what it means to think big.

"Miz Tolson is not sleeping," said the nurse, clearly displeased. "She just likes to keep her eyes closed." He wanted nothing more than to crash and sleep, himself.

At the door of the room, the nurse whispered, "I hope you'll speak to her about cooperating. She's been acting like she swallows her pills, but we just found out she spits them in her pajama drawer!"

"I'll do my best," he said.

He sat quietly for a time, saying only, "I'm here, Janette." She had her back to him, and didn't move or acknowledge his presence.

His head fell forward twice as he dozed off, then recovered himself. He was here for a purpose, and he'd better get to it. "Janette?"

No answer. Well, then, he would speak to her as if she were listening; he would speak to her heart, her spirit, and let the chips fall where they may. He'd learned a few things about depression, his own as well as that of others. He'd learned that even when the soul seems fallow, there's a vulnerable spot that can be seeded. Whether the seed flourishes was God's job. "I have planted, Apollo's watered, but God gave the increase," St. Paul had written to Corinth.

He took the Book of Psalms from the bag.

"I brought you something. You may not be able to read it for a while, but keep it near. It's King David's songs—they're about joy and praise, loss and gain, about his battles with the mortal enemy, and his battles with depression.

"Let me read to you. . . ."

As a child, the most comforting thing he knew was being read to. He figured it worked for everybody.

" 'The Lord is my light and my salvation; whom shall I fear? The Lord is the strength of my life; of whom shall I be afraid?

" 'When the wicked, even mine enemies and my foes, came upon me to eat up my flesh, they stumbled and fell.

" 'Though an host should encamp against me, my heart shall not fear; though war should rise against me, in this will I be confident.' "

He sat silent for a moment.

"David had many foes, Janette, the human kind as well as the foes that have come against you: anger, bitterness, fear, maybe even resentment toward God.

"When I read the psalms, I read them as personal

prayers, naming the enemies that come against my own soul.

" 'For in the time of trouble," David says, "he will hide me in his pavilion: in the secret of his tabernacle shall he hide me: he shall set me upon a rock.'

"Let Him hide you, Janette, until you gain strength. He will set you upon a rock. Please know that."

He listened to her quiet, regular breathing. Maybe she really was asleep. He prayed silently for the seeds to fall on fertile ground.

"I've marked this psalm for you, the thirtieth. Hear this with your very soul, Janette. 'Weeping may endure for a night, but joy comes in the morning.' "

Without turning in the bed, she raised her hand slightly, and he stood, and held it.

He had gone deep into his pockets with the Wesley bondsman, but Dooley was at home with Harley, and that's what counted.

"People look at me different," said Dooley when they talked the following evening. "While I was baggin' their groceries, I could feel their eyes borin' a hole in me."

Dooley's vernacular always returned when he was angry, tired, or frustrated.

"Maybe. Maybe not. Even in a small town, word doesn't travel that fast. Just be yourself. You didn't do anything wrong and you have nothing to apologize for." Couldn't he say something wiser, more profound than that? "Keep smiling!" he said, sounding lame and feeling worse.

"Lace's mama just died," Dooley said.

"I'm sorry to hear it." Lace's mother, ill and failing for years, had never given loving support to her daughter, but had demanded it, instead, for herself. "Have you called Lace?"

"She hates my guts."

"Call her, send her a card, something. She's lost her mother and this will be a blow, no matter what the circumstances were. I'll do the same."

"I wish . . ." Dooley hesitated.

"Wish what?"

"I wish you an' Cynthia would come home. Well, I got to go."

Click.

"Man alive! What's *this?*"

"It's my new iced tea recipe," said his wife. "Do you like it?"

He raised his glass in a salute. "It's the best I ever tasted. I didn't know you could do this."

"I didn't, either. I never knew how to make good iced tea. So, with our parish party coming up, I asked the Lord to give me the perfect recipe."

"That's the spirit!"

"Do you honestly like it?"

"I never tasted better!" he exclaimed, stealing no thunder from his mother, whose tea represented the southern ideal—heavy on sugar, and blasted with the juice of fresh lemons.

"I woke up yesterday morning and was bursting with all these new ideas about tea. It was very exciting."

"Hmm," he said, gulping draughts of the cold, fruity liquid. "Tropical. Exotic." He swigged it down to the last drop. "Two thumbs up," he said. "But I'm not sure everybody would understand where the recipe came from."

She shrugged. "If He gave William Blake those drawings, why couldn't He give me a simple tea recipe?"

"Good point. What's in it?"

"I can't tell you."

"You can't tell me?"

"No, darling, I've decided to do something very southern—which is to possess at least one secret recipe." She looked pleased with herself.

"But you can tell *me*."

"Not on your life!"

"Why not? I'm your husband!"

"Some well-intentioned parishioner would yank it out of you just like that." She snapped her fingers.

"No!"

"Yes. And then I'd be in the same boat with poor Esther, whose once-secret orange marmalade cake recipe is circulating through Mitford like a virus."

"If that's the way you feel," he said, slightly miffed.

─⊖─

"Suicidal," the doctor had said, adding that he had no good idea when she'd be ready to come home.

Father Tim dialed Janette's cousin, long-distance. No, they really couldn't take Jonathan, it was all they could do to squeeze in Babette and Jason, they were sorry and hoped he understood, which he did.

─⊖─

He was definitely into the fray of Whitecap, with back-to-back meetings, hospital treks, home visitation, and a series of three talks to Busy Fingers, the needlework arm of the ECW. He was even pitching in once a week with Cynthia to help tour visitors through the church and grounds.

Because of the hither and yon-ness of it all, he usually took the Mustang. This morning, however, he was walking to church, leaving his dog behind to amuse Jonathan. He heard Jonathan's loud cries from the guest room; the boy definitely wanted his mother.

"I have story hour at the library this morning. It will take his mind off things." Cynthia nudged him down the steps. "He'll be fine, dear, just go!"

He went, not knowing what else to do.

As he passed through the gate into the street, he had the sense, once again, that someone was watching him. He shaded his eyes and peered toward the hedgebound, chest-high wall that surrounded his neighbor's house.

On impulse, he stepped closer to the hedge and called, "Mr. Love! Are you there?"

About two yards to his left, the foliage moved, shook slightly, and was still. What could he lose? If Morris Love was not there, then he was standing here talking to himself. If Morris Love was there, then he was merely being neighborly.

"If you're there, Mr. Love, I'd just like to say that we—my wife and I—enjoy your music very much."

"Out! Out!"

The sudden shout through the hedge was loud, hoarse, and furious.

Father Tim stepped back, startled.

"Out!" The command was repeated with even greater ferocity.

The voice sent chills up his spine. Yes, indeed, he'd done the wrong thing in trying to be neighborly.

He trotted quickly down the lane toward Ernie's, without looking back.

"Junior's got mail!" Ernie proudly announced.

"Off and running, then!" Father Tim sat down at the table with Junior.

"Lookit," said Junior, pushing a stack of letters his way. "You can read 'em if you want to."

He removed the lid from his coffee cup. "Anything promising?"

"See this one?" Junior pointed to the pink envelope that crowned the batch. "It's th' best, I'd read that."

"You sure you want me to read it?"

"Sure!" said Junior. "And I'll let you see her picture when you've read th' letter. You ain't goin' to believe it."

Ernie thumped down at the table, grinning. "Read it out loud. I'd like to hear that one again."

"Yes, sir," said Junior, "read it out loud, that's what I did."

"Here goes." He cleared his throat. " 'Dear—' "

The screen door slapped behind Roanoke. "How y'all?" he queried the general assembly.

"Fine," said Ernie. "Set down, th' preacher's readin' Junior's love letters."

Roanoke pulled up a chair and sat, taking the lid off his coffee. He had a cigarette stuck behind his ear. "I hope they ain't too mushy," he said.

Ernie punched Junior on the arm. "We're lookin' for mushy, right, Junior? Go ahead an' read, Tim."

" 'Dear Serious: I couldn't believe my eyes when I saw your ad. I truly love Scrabble and fishing better than anything! But I personally don't like a whole lot of country music except for Loretta Lynn. I have been looking for somebody to go fishing with and have played Scrabble since I was nine years old. It is my favorite. Are you a Christian? This is real important to*

me. If you are you ought to say so in your ad it could
help somebody decide whether to answer or not.

" 'If you are and if you are really serious like your
ad says you will have to meet my daddy before you can
take me out. I am not interested in dirty jokes or
cussing. Here's my picture. I am named for Ava Gard-
ner the movie star who was born in Smithfield the
same town as my mother who died four years ago with
cancer.

" 'Why am I writing a perfect stranger? My sister
said to do it especially as Daddy will meet you first. Before it goes that far though send me your picture to the
Box Number if you are interested. I am 29 and was married when I was 17 but my husband was killed driving a
tractor trailer which lost its brakes on a bad curve in
West Virginia. I have my own business and believe in
hard work.

" 'I also believe that honesty is the best policy.

" 'Sincerely yours,

" 'Ava Goodnight.' "

"Nice letter," said Father Tim. "Very neat handwriting."

"Now lookit," said Junior, taking a photograph out
of his shirt pocket.

Father Tim gazed at the photo of a young woman
with chestnut hair and a dazzling smile. "I'll be darned.
Beautiful!"

"Where's she live at?"

"Swanquarter," said Junior, seeming especially
proud of this fact.

"That'll be some mighty long distance courtin'."

Junior shrugged as Roanoke peered over Father
Tim's shoulder at the photograph. "Looks like you got
th' brass ring."

"I don't know. She has her own business an' all, plus she's really . . . nice-lookin'."

"*Good*-lookin' is what I'd say," said Ernie.

"Right. So she prob'ly wouldn't be interested in . . . you know . . . me, or anything."

"Wrong attitude!" said Ernie. "You were rarin' to go 'til you started gettin' feedback, now you want to crawl off an' quit."

"Well, not quit, exactly," said Junior, looking uneasy.

Roanoke blew on his coffee. "With women, you got t' fish or cut bait."

"Right," said Ernie. "Idn't that right, Tim?"

"That's right." Didn't he know? Hadn't he learned? He had cut bait 'til he nearly lost Cynthia Coppersmith for all eternity.

"Write her back," said Ernie. "You don't cuss too bad, and I never heard you tell a dirty joke, so you got that covered. Plus you're both dead set on bein' honest."

"*Are* you a Christian?" asked Roanoke, taking the cigarette from behind his ear. "Seem like that's pretty major in her opinion."

"Well . . ." Junior thought about it. "I guess. I mean, my mama went to church an' all, 'til she died, and I went pretty regular 'til a few years ago."

Roanoke lit his cigarette and inhaled deeply. "That don't necessarily cut it," he said. "I don't know much, but I do know that."

"Anyway," said Junior, "I don't have a picture."

"You got a camera?"

"Somewhere I got a camera I won at the fair."

"Bring it in tomorrow mornin' on your way to the Toe and I'll snap you one or two shots," said Ernie. "I got film over there, we'll use a roll of two-hundred if th' light's not good."

"Should I wear a tie?"

"I wouldn't do that. What you got on'll be fine."

"Maybe I should wear a cap." Junior smoothed his hair, which was thinning in front.

"Honesty is the best policy," said Ernie. "Don't wear a cap. But hold your stomach in an' all."

"I don't think I should wear what I got on, these are my work clothes."

Roanoke blew a smoke ring. "She said she believes in hard work."

Junior was looking increasingly frustrated. Suddenly he turned to Father Tim. "What do you think, sir?"

"Maybe . . . maybe a pair of jeans with a denim shirt and a jacket?"

Junior sighed. "I'll have to wash m' jeans and iron a shirt."

"So?" said Ernie. "Big deal. It ought to be worth a little effort, gettin' a letter like that from a nice girl. Just remember what some of those other letters said."

Junior blushed.

⚬

The light on his office answering machine was blinking.

Emma, as usual, did not stand on ceremony.

"Seems like things are fallin' apart up here since you left. I just heard Louella fell and broke her hip, just like Miss Sadie, and she's in th' hospital and Hoppy says it's a good thing she's well padded because it could have been worse. But if you ask me, practically every old person I hear about who breaks a hip . . . well, I don't want to say it, but you know what I mean—

"Snickers, stop that this minute! Hold on, he's chewin' Harold's church shoes." The phone clattered onto the countertop. General mumbling, barking, and door-slamming.

"By th' way, I been meanin' to tell you that Uncle Billy's havin' knee surgery. I think that's what he said, my phone has an awful lot of static since th' storm last week. . . ."

They said their prayers in the darkened room and held each other, talking in low voices lest Jonathan wake up and make his usual midnight invasion.

"I feel we need to run home to Mitford," he said.

"Run home to Mitford? Darling, you don't just *run home* when it's twelve hundred miles round trip and a hundred degrees in the shade. Dooley will be fine, I promise."

"It's not just Dooley. It's also Esther and Gene and Louella and Lace and . . ." He sighed. "I feel helpless."

"You want to help everybody and fix everything. But Timothy, you just can't."

"I've never been able to swallow that down."

"Remember the sign I have over my drawing board at home? 'Don't feel totally, personally, irrevocably responsible for everything. That's my job. Signed, God.' "

"Ummm."

She kissed his cheek. "I love you to pieces," she said.

"I love you to pieces back," he replied, smiling in the dark. He would be in a ditch without Cynthia Kavanagh.

"Listen," she whispered, "you run home to Mitford and I'll hold down the fort, OK? I've got at least two and a half tons of cookies to bake and freeze, not to mention a hundred miniature quiches and six loaves of bread with sun-dried tomatoes."

"You're doing it again, you're not letting anyone help with the party."

"Who can help? Marion is at the library practically every day, poor Jean Ballenger couldn't cook if her life depended on it, Marlene Bragg's fingernails are so long she can barely get ice out of a tray, and everyone else works."

"Who's doing flowers? I know you'll want them in all the rooms."

She sighed. "I'd give my French watercolors for a Hessie Mayhew in this parish. But alas, I suppose I'm doing them myself."

"I'll order flowers for you, have them delivered."

"How sweet, but no, I'll cut what's left in the garden and plunder Marion's little plot—you know I love that tousled look for flowers, nothing arranged. Anyway, darling, we're getting off the point. Run home to Mitford and see Dooley and make your rounds and come back to me."

"Are you sure?"

"Of course. Go to sleep."

She patted his cheek and turned on her side and he listened for her breathing to become regular, rhythmic. But it did not. He could feel her lying awake, just as he was doing.

"What is it, Kavanagh? Can't sleep?" He reached out and touched her shoulder.

"Cynthia?" Good heavens, she was crying.

He pulled her against him and she turned in his arms and wept quietly.

"My girl, my dearest love, what is it?"

"I'm homesick for Mitford, too, but I've tried and tried to be brave about it and not let you know. I see you wanting to go and take care of things, and, well, so do

I. I mean, I like it here, actually I love it here, but I miss Mitford, I miss our home."

"I understand."

"I'm so sorry you've caught me out, Timothy. I feel like a criminal, hiding this from you."

"Thank goodness it's hidden no more. You'll come with me, then, we'll leave first thing next Thursday morning. I'll get Father Jack to supply, I'm sure he'll do it, and we'll head back here on Sunday."

He might have gotten up and danced a jig.

"Best of all," he declared, "we'll have two days with Dooley before he goes off to school."

"Lovely!" she said, forgetting to whisper. "I can't wait to see the big lug. What a dreadful thing he's going through. Of course, we'll have to take Jonathan. . . ."

"Of course! They'll love him in Mitford."

"He can watch a movie, Dooley has a VCR!"

"Thank You, Lord!" he exclaimed, feeling a slow flush happiness.

"Yes, thank You, Lord!" she said, blowing her nose.

CHAPTER TEN

If Wishes Were Horses

He regretted being unable to introduce their new organist around on Sunday, but Sam and Marion said they'd do it for him.

He called Jack Ferguson.

"Happy to!" exclaimed the retired priest, who was fond of peppering his sermons with ecclesiastical jokes. "I'll just pop up with Earlene. Maybe you'll let us stay at your place Saturday night."

"Absolutely! We'll leave the keys under the potted geranium by the front door. You know where the church is . . ."

"Oh, yes, I've supplied St. John's several times, always a pleasure!"

". . . and I'll fax the directions to Dove Cottage."

"Super!" said Father Jack. "By the way, have you heard that Ron Cowper is leaving St. Michael's?"

"I'll be darned. I thought he was rooted in there like a turnip."

"One of the parish told him, said, 'Father Ron, I'm so sorry you're going, we never knew what sin was 'til you came.' "

He chuckled. "Jack, Jack."

"All true, Timothy. And did you hear about Bishop Harvey's big trip to Uganda?"

"Briefly, when he was here in July."

"At the end of a worship service, Bill had a notion to give the blessing in the language of the region. He picked up the printed sheet, made the sign of the cross, then very slowly and solemnly read in Luganda, 'Do not take away the service bulletin.' "

Father Tim laughed heartily. "Thank heaven you don't know anything to tell on me."

"Oh," said Father Jack, "I'll think of something."

There was a new spring in his step; he felt a fresh excitement both at home and at church.

"You're mighty perky," said a member of the Altar Guild, who was trimming candlewicks in the vesting room.

"Darling, you're positively glowing!" said his wife, who appeared to be unusually sunny herself.

"Hit'll be good t' clap eyes on you 'uns," said Harley. "I'll make us a pan of brownies."

"I'm really glad you're comin," said Dooley.

In the grand anticipation of it all, he made a long-distance "house call" to Uncle Billy.

"I'll be et f'r a tater if it ain't th' preacher!" exclaimed the old man, obviously delighted.

"Just checking on your knee, Uncle Billy."

"My knee? Hit's th' same as ever, ol' Arthur's got it, don't you know."

"I thought Emma said you were having knee surgery."

"Nossir, what I had was *tree* surgery."

"Aha. Well. Tell me about it."

"Hit was a big to-do, don't you know, th' town sent a crew t' doctor them old trees out back, they was rotted in some places and about t' fall over. Wellsir, they was there all day Wednesday, then come back again and was there all day Thursday, had a big crane an' all. Hit was like a tent meetin' th' way people turned out t' watch, we could of went t' sellin' corn dogs. Wish you'd been here."

"We'll be there late Thursday for a short visit. I'll get by and see you and Miss Rose on Saturday."

"Hit'll be a treat an' a half t' see you 'uns, I'll ask Rose t' whip up a banana puddin'."

"Don't go to any trouble," said Father Tim, meaning it. "In fact, don't even *think* about it!"

～⌒～

"We're going home, old buddy," he said to Barnabas as they loped toward Ernie's. "We're going to see Dooley, remember Dooley?"

Of course his dog remembered Dooley. Any dog with a penchant for Wordsworth, Cowper, and Keats was a smart dog.

Just four days and he'd be good as new, ready to pour himself back into St. John's and no need to run home again until October for Buck's and Pauline's wedding, which he'd cleared with his bishop early on.

He felt positively on holiday. He would put in five

hours at St. John's, and dash home to pack and take Cynthia and Jonathan out for an early dinner. Then, at six-thirty tomorrow morning, they were out of here.

⟨∘⟩

Janette's doctor reported only mild response to the medication. It would take time, he said, for her to feel any meaningful effects; meanwhile, they were monitoring her closely.

He called Janette's room. No answer. He thought he should have her approval to take Jonathan all the way to the other end of the state, but he dreaded the possibility of upsetting her. What if she felt bereft, knowing that her priest and children were all off the island? He recalled that even her doctor was leaving on Friday to play golf in Beaufort.

Marion agreed to go to the hospital after church on Sunday. He caught Jean Ballenger leaving a Busy Fingers class, and asked her to visit Janette on Thursday, Friday, and Saturday.

"Oh, yes!" she said. "I'll go. I enjoy the sick."

"Here," he said, taking out his wallet and giving her five dollars. "If you don't mind, please buy her some oranges, or . . ."

Jean took the bill. "Would you like them maybe in a basket with a little bow on the handle?"

"I'd be much obliged," he said.

"I could put in a pot of African violets for another five," she said, eyeing his wallet.

⟨∘⟩

He had celebrated Holy Eucharist with seven of the faithful remnant and four tourists from Canada, cleared his desk, returned his calls, thoroughly discussed Sunday's music with Ella Bridgewater by phone, and alerted the choir to be on their best behavior. He had also shown a couple from Delaware around the cemetery, typed the pew bulletin, emptied his wastebasket, and stamped the mail.

He was walking out the door when the phone rang.

"St. John's in the Grove!" he said. Then, feeling suddenly, inspired to elaborate, he quoted the psalmist. " 'This is the day the Lord has made!' "

There was a brief silence on the other end. "Timothy?" Sounded like Bill Harvey.

"Speaking."

"That was a very upbeat phone greeting." It was Bill Harvey, all right.

"I'm feeling upbeat, Bishop, how are you?"

"Wanting to have a little talk with you about something." Bill Harvey was not speaking in his let's-go-fishing voice; this was his high-church, gospel-side *vox populi.*

"Shoot!" He may as well walk straight into the wind, head down and hunkered over.

"It comes to my attention that you're making a little trip to Mitford."

"Why . . . yes." He cleared his throat. "Just four days."

"To attend, I believe, to the needs of several former parishioners . . ."

"Well . . . yes." He'd mentioned to one or two people why he was going away, but had said nothing about Dooley.

". . . and dismissing, I presume, your sworn duty to attend to the needs of your current parishioners?"

"I hadn't thought of it that way, Bishop." His stomach did a small turn.

"It's time you thought of it that way, Timothy. You know very well the policy of the church, and that is to be strictly hands-off the old parish while you go about the business of the new. Surely it doesn't escape your memory that Lord's Chapel has a priest of its own to attend these people."

"Certainly." He heard his voice come near to croaking. He didn't think it would help matters to say his boy had been in jail and might like a little cheering up before he went off to school.

Then again, the bishop was right, he wasn't supposed to meddle in the business of Mitford's new priest. But these people were his friends. . . .

"But they're my *friends*," he said, knowing it would avail him nothing.

"Of course they're your friends, you served them for sixteen years."

"It was my wish to . . . I only wished to—"

"If wishes were horses, Timothy, beggars would ride. Let us stick to the point. I believe you're going to Mitford in October to conduct a wedding."

"Yes."

"I strongly caution you against this current jaunt."

Suddenly out of breath, he thumped into his desk chair and stared unseeing at the wall.

───⊙───

His wife gave the entire episcopate a fine tongue-lashing, mincing no words, and got over the whole incident in a trice. While he enjoyed her stinging barbs, they did little to soothe his sense of injury. It was true that, in principle, Bill Harvey was right, but he'd found his tone of voice, his corporate indifference, rude beyond measure. He was accustomed to a bishop whose kindness extended throughout his diocese, with seeming affection for all his deacons and priests; indeed, he was proud to have in Stuart Cullen a bishop who actually wrote important letters "in his own hand," as St. Paul himself had been pleased to do.

"Blast!" he said, looking out the kitchen window. "Double blast!"

"That's right, darling, let it all out!" encouraged his wife, who was buttering Jonathan's spaghetti.

"Blast!" said Jonathan, smacking the table with both hands.

Why hadn't he kept his big mouth shut about going home? He felt like a traitor, a heel, disappointing everyone. And now he had to go back over all the ground he'd plowed, calling everyone and making excuses. . . .

"You need something . . . *vigorous* to do," she suggested.

"I'll take Barnabas and go running," he said testily.

"Isn't your fishing trip coming up soon?"

Fishing trip! The very last thing he wanted to do was go on a fishing trip. A fine spectacle he'd make, knowing almost nothing about a rod and reel, and even less about sliding around on the deck of a boat with an eight hundred and fifty horsepower engine throbbing under his tennis shoes. Didn't he make a fool of himself every Sunday morning of his life? Why do it all over again on a trip that was costing his wife a cool two hundred bucks, not including a bucket of chicken?

❧

Miss Rose answered the phone with a positive shout. *"Hello!"*

"Miss Rose? This is Father Tim."

"Are you here?"

"No, ma'am, I'm *here*," he shouted back. "You see, something's . . . *come up.*"

"What's that? *Bum luck?*"

"Well, yes, in a way. May I speak with Uncle Billy?"

She turned from the phone and squawked, "Bill! Bill Watson! It's our old preacher!"

He thought she might have put it another way.

There was a long silence.

"I'm sorry, son."

Dooley sighed. "I know. It's OK. Really."

"I'm going to try and have the court date set during the time I'm home for the wedding. You'll be home then, too, so I believe everything's going to work out just fine."

"Great," said Dooley, sounding relieved.

"Have fun these last days. How are Poo and Jessie?"

"Really good!"

He heard the sudden tenderness in the boy's voice.

"And your mother?"

"She's really good, too, she got a raise at Hope House."

"Glad news! You're always in our prayers, buddy. God cares about your needs."

"OK, 'bye." said Dooley. "Wait. That woman upstairs . . ."

"What about her?"

"She plays the dern piano mighty loud. Me'n Harley are thinkin' about knockin' on th' ceiling with a broom handle."

And he'd been worried about Dooley's music aggravating his tenant. "I wouldn't do that. Hang in there."

"I got Lace a card."

"Great! I did, too."

"It was hard as heck to pick out, there are millions of cards."

"True. What did it say?"

"Nothin'. It was blank."

"Aha."

"I just wrote in it, 'I'm sorry.' "

"Couldn't be better."

"I signed my whole name, in case she knows anybody else named Dooley."

"Probably not."

"Well, I got to go, Avis wants me to clean out th' butcher case. *Gross*. I told him I'll pick up anything but liver, he has to do that. I mean, you can feel liver all the way through those weird gloves we have to wear."

"Please!" he said, bilious at the thought.

It wrenched his heart to say goodbye. But what were hearts for, in the end? A little wrenching now and then was far, far better than no wrenching at all.

—❦—

He was trying to forgive Bill Harvey. In the scheme of things, the bishop's attitude was hardly worth his concern. Why couldn't he blow by it, forgive and forget? Of no small concern, however, was the hardness that would come in if he didn't forgive this slight. He was to drag it into the light and expose it before God and get it over with.

He dropped to his knees in the study and prayed silently. The early morning breeze pushed through open windows and puffed the curtains into the room.

There was a tap on his shoulder.

"What are you doin'?" asked Jonathan, standing next to him in rumpled blue pajamas.

He rose from his knees and picked the boy up. They thumped into the chair, Jonathan in his lap. "I was praying."

"Why?" Jonathan snuggled against him.

"That I might find God's grace to forgive someone."

"Why?"

"Because if I don't forgive this person, it will be unhealthy for me, and God won't think much of it, either."

He loved the chunky, vibrant feel of the boy on his lap, the warm, solid weight against his chest. Exactly the way God wants us to come to Him, he thought, his spirits suddenly brightening.

"I don't want p'sketti no more. No p'sketti."

"Good! Hallelujah! What do you want?"

Jonathan pondered this, then looked up at him. "I don't know."

"Well, if you don't, who does?"

Jonathan poked him in the chest with a chubby finger. "You find somethin'."

"Please."

"Please."

"Consider it done."

———✺———

He and Cynthia had been transplanted, that was all. He knew from years of digging around in the dirt and moving perennials from one corner of the yard to another what transplanting was about. First came the wilt, then the gradual settling in, then the growth spurt. That simple. What had Gertrude Jekyll said to the gardener squeamish about moving a plant or bush? "Hoick it!"

God had hoicked him and he'd better get over the wilt and get busy putting down roots.

He went out to the porch, whistling. Glorious day—

his fair wife sitting contentedly in a rocker, Jonathan rigged with a straw hat and playing in the garden with his dog, and an afternoon romp in the ocean on the family agenda.

He sat in one of the white rockers and kicked off his loafers. "Ahhhh!" he sighed.

"Timothy, you have that wilderness look again."

"What wilderness look?" he asked, as if he didn't know.

"That John the Baptist look."

He had been in denial about it for some time, now, until his hair had fanned out over his clerical collar like the tail of a turkey gobbler. He just didn't seem to have what it took to break in a new barber.

"I hear there's a little shop next to the post office, Linda's or Libbie's or Lola's . . . something like that."

"Aha." No, indeed. He'd cut it himself with an oyster knife before he'd put his head in the hands of another Fancy Skinner.

"I'll hold out for a barber, thank you," he said, feeling imperious.

He checked the answering machine when they came in from the grocery store.

"Father? It's me, Puny."

Puny didn't sound like herself.

"I don't know how to tell you this."

This was definitely his least favorite way for a phone call to begin.

"I just got to your house and realized I'd left th' door unlocked for four days!"

"Speak to Ba!" one of the twins pleaded.

"How in th' world I did a dumb thing like that, I

don't know, I'm jis' so sorry. But I've looked and looked, and nothin' seems missin', so I think it's all right, but I know how you count on me to take care of things, and I jis' hate lettin' you down on anything."

"It's OK!" he said aloud to the machine. He loved that girl like his own flesh. "Don't worry about it!"

"I know you sometimes don't lock your doors, but I always do because I'm responsible for things here, and I jis' hope that . . . anyway, we're real sorry you aren't comin', we all looked forward to it a lot, and I hope you'll not think hard of me for leavin' your door unlocked."

"Speak to Ba, speak to Ba!"

"Oh, for Pete's sake, Sissy, you'll wake up Sassy, *here!*"

"Ba! Come home, we got puppies. Come home, Ba!"

"Say 'bye, now. Tell 'im you love 'im."

"Love you, Ba."

"Tell 'im you love Miss Cynthia."

"Love Miss Cynthy."

"That was Sissy. Sassy's still asleep," said his industrious house help. "We've got an awful mess of puppies in th' garage, four little speckled things, I don't know what they are, oh, mercy, I'm prob'ly usin' up all your tape, now here's th' good news! Joe Joe's been promoted to lieutenant! That's right under th' chief. How d'you like that?"

He liked it very much indeed.

"We thought you was goin' home," said Roanoke.

"Change of plans. Where's Ernie this morning?"

"Him an' Roger's gone fishin'."

"Captain Willie?"

"Nope. Over to th' Sound."

"You're minding the store?"

"You got it," said Roanoke. Father Tim thought he'd never seen so many wrinkles in one face. Roanoke Clark, it might be said, looked like he'd been hung out to dry and left on the line.

He didn't exactly relish the idea of spending one-on-one time with a man who didn't like preachers. Then again, it was only six-thirty in the morning, and not a darned thing to do at the church office, since he'd already done it all for the trip to Mitford.

What the heck. He thumped down at a table, unwrapped his egg biscuit, and took the lid off his coffee.

"So . . . how's business?"

"We had a big run this mornin', it slacked off just before you come in."

He ate his biscuit while Roanoke read the paper and smoked.

"What about a good barber on the island? Know anybody?"

"Don't have an official barber on th' island. Have t' go across."

"Seems a waste of time to be running back and forth to the mainland just to get your hair trimmed."

Roanoke appeared to be talking to the newspaper he was holding in front of him. "Lola up by th' post office, she'll give you a trim. You won't need t' go back 'til Christmas."

"Who's Lola?"

"Lola sells fish san'wiches, cuts hair, you name it."

He shivered. "Is that where you get your hair cut?"

"Once every two months, whether I need it or not."

He examined Roanoke's haircut. No way.

"So, ah, where do Ernie and Roger get their hair cut?"

"I do it."

"You do it?"

"Keep my barber tools in th' book room over there." Roanoke indicated the book room with a wave of his hand.

"Aha."

"Six bucks a pop," said Roanoke, laying the paper on the table, "Six bucks and fifteen minutes, that's my motto."

"Did you . . . ever cut hair for a living?"

"I cut hair for truckers. When I was haulin' sheet metal, I had a stopover in Concord twice a month; I set up in th' back room of a barbecue joint. They rolled in there from New York City, Des Moines, Iowa, Los Alamos, California, you name it, they lined up from here to yonder." Roanoke looked proud of this fact, in stalling a fresh cigarette behind his ear.

"You might say I've cut hair from sea t' shinin' sea."

"I'll be darned." Now what was he going to do? His egg biscuit began to petrify in his stomach.

"You'll have t' set out here, since I got t' watch th' register, but I'll take care of it for you. I didn't want t' say nothin', but I wondered when you was goin' to get it off your collar. I thought maybe that was your religion."

Father Tim laughed uneasily and clapped his hip. He'd paid for his biscuit with pocket change; maybe he'd left his wallet at home. Sometimes he did. He hoped he did.

"You can pay me anytime. I run a little tab for Roger 'n' Ernie."

Oh, well, how bad could it be? He didn't recall that

Ernie or Roger looked too butchered; pretty normal, to tell the truth.

"Fine," he said. "Fifteen minutes?"

Roanoke dragged the battered stool from behind the cash register and set it by the front window.

"Couldn't we, ah, move the stool back a little?" He didn't want to be on display for every passing car and truck on the island.

"I need th' light," said Roanoke, squinting at his hair.

Though he'd spent considerable time at morning prayer in his study, he prayed again as he clambered onto the stool.

Roanoke brought a box from the book room, followed by Elmo the Book Cat. It was the first time he'd seen Elmo out in general society. The elderly, long-haired cat sat on the cement floor, flicked its tail, and stared at him, as Roanoke laid his barbering paraphernalia on the window seat.

"Here you go," said Roanoke, throwing a torn sheet around Father Tim's shoulders. The sheet smelled of fish. Maybe that was why the cat was staring at him.

"Back when I was drivin'," said Roanoke, leaning into his work, "I run thirty-seven states and two provinces of Canada. One time I was caught in a tornada, it blowed me over an embankment and totaled my truck, but I walked away without a scratch, which was th' closest I ever come to believin' in God."

Father Tim felt the scissors snipping away, saw the hair thump onto the cement. The cat watched, still flicking its tail.

"I hauled a lot of orange juice outa Florida in my time. If I was haulin' fresh, a load would run around fifty-five hundred gallons. Concentrate, that'd weigh in around forty-seven hundred." *Snip, snip.*

Barbering certainly loosened the tongue of the usually taciturn Roanoke; he'd turned into a regular jabbermouth. Come to think of it, Father Tim had noticed the same phenomenon in Fancy Skinner and Joe Ivey. Clearly, nonstop discourse was very closely related to messing with hair.

"I even hauled chocolate syrup outa Pennsylvania, a lot of chocolate comes outa Pennsylvania, but I never hauled poultry or anything livin', nossir, I wouldn't haul anything livin'."

"Good idea."

"I never got pulled but one time. Now, there's some drivers, they can be wild, they'll run their rigs hard as they can run 'em to git up th' next hill. Regulations say you cain't drive but ten hours a day, but cowboys, that's what we called 'em, they'll go up t' eighteen, twenty hours, drivin' illegal.

"Cowboys is only about two percent of th' drivers out there today, but they give th' rest of us a bad name, you know what I mean?"

"I do!"

Snip, thump. "I do a little roofin' now, a little house paintin', cut a little hair, a man can make a livin' if he's got ambition."

"I agree!"

"Got rid of my car, ride a bicycle now, it's amazin' how much money you can put back when you shuck a car."

"I'll bet."

"I was raised in a Christian home, but I fell away. See, my first wife run off with a travelin' preacher, I brought 'im home, give 'im a good, warm bed an' a hot meal, an' first thing you know, they hightailed it."

"Aha." So that was why Roanoke was never especially thrilled to see him; he'd been tarred with the same brush. He had a sudden, vivid recall of van Gogh's self-portrait in which he sported only one ear. *Please, Lord. . . .*

Elmo yawned and lay down, without removing his gaze from the customer on the stool.

"Now, you take me, I never run around on my second wife, an' they was plenty of chances to do it. Lot lizards is what we called 'em, they'll pester a man nearly to death. But I stayed true to my wife an' I'm glad I did, because you never know what you'll pick up on th' road an' bring home to innocent people."

"Right."

"I never did pills, neither, nossir, th' strongest thing I ever done when I was drivin' was Sun-drop, it'll knock your block off if you ain't used to much caffeine in your system. You want a Sun-drop, we got 'em in th' cooler."

"That's OK, I don't believe so. Maybe another time." Boy howdy, this was an education and a half.

Thump, thump, snip.

"But things is changed. It'd bring a tear to a glass eye to hear what a owner-operator pays these days to run a big rig."

"How much?"

"More'n sixty cent a mile. You have to be tough to make a livin' with truckin'."

"I'll bet so."

"I'm goin' to clean your neck up now. How's our time runnin'?"

Father Tim looked at his watch. "You've got a little under one minute."

"We're goin' to bring you in right on th' dot," said Roanoke, flipping the switch on his electric shaver.

Cynthia waved from the porch. Jonathan and Barnabas were waiting at the gate.

"Look at me!" said the boy, jumping up and down.

"I'm looking. That's a new shirt!"

"And new pants!"

He opened the gate. "Where did those snappy new clothes come from, buddyroe?"

"UPS!"

"Dearest, where's your hair?" called his wife from the porch.

"In a Dumpster behind Ernie's! What do you think?"

"I love it!" she said, sitting down on the top step. "We've got a surprise for you!"

His wife was herself wearing something new and boggling. Red shorts, which were plenty short, a strapless white top, and espadrilles.

He scratched behind his dog's ears and fairly bounded up the steps.

∿

His sermon was finished and walked through, thought for thought, precept upon precept. In the study, Jonathan had paced to the bookcase at his heels, then to the wall with the painting of the Roman Colosseum. Exhausted at last, Jonathan fell asleep on the rug, where Father Tim stepped over him without missing a beat.

The rest of the day lay ahead, shimmering like silk. They would swim in the ocean, they would go out to dinner in their new duds, and tomorrow they'd hear the organ raising its mighty voice to the timbers.

He felt as young as a curate, as bold as a lion.

∿

"Having a little boy is different," said his wife, drying her hair after their frolic in the ocean. "We're going out to dinner and it's only five-thirty."

"Like a bunch of farmhands," he agreed, pulling on his brand-new shorts and golf shirt. One thing he could say about golf, which he'd never played and never would, he sure liked the shirts.

"I sketched Jonathan today," she said.

"Aha!"

"For the new Violet book. I think he'll weave into it beautifully, just what I've been needing to . . . round it out, I think."

He heard someone knocking, and Barnabas flew at once to the door, his bark as throaty as the bass of St. John's organ.

He zipped his shorts and padded down the hall barefoot, stunned to see Father Jack and Earlene peering through the screen.

Good Lord! He'd completely forgotten to tell Jack Ferguson they weren't going home to Mitford!

Beet-red with embarrassment, he let the eager but surprised couple into the living room, and braced himself for the inept explanations he'd be forced to deliver, not only to the Fergusons but to his *wife*.

Dadgummit, now Father Jack would have a story to tell on him, which would spread through the diocese like fleas in August.

"Welcome to Dove Cottage," he said, trying to mean it.

They had gone to Mona's and eaten fried perch, hard crabs, broiled shrimp, yellowfin tuna fresh off the boat, hush puppies, french fries, and buckets of coleslaw. They had slathered on tartar sauce and downed quarts of tea as sweet as syrup, then staggered home in the heat with Jonathan drugged and half asleep on Father Tim's back.

As they walked, Cynthia did her part to deliver after-dinner entertainment, loudly reciting a poem by someone named Rachel Field.

> *"If once you have slept on an island*
> *You'll never be quite the same;*
> *You may look as you looked the day before*
> *And go by the same old name.*
> *You may bustle about the street or shop;*
> *You may sit at home and sew,*
> *But you'll see blue water and wheeling gulls*
> *Wherever your feet may go."*

"I declare!" said Earlene. "You're clever as anything to remember all that. I wonder if it's the truth."

"What?"

"That part about never being quite the same."

"I don't know," said Cynthia. "We'll have to wait and see."

They sat on the porch and watched the gathering sunset through the trellis, where the Marion Climber had put forth several new blooms.

"Now, Jack," he said, "don't go home and tell this story on me."

"I make no promises." Father Jack chuckled.

He gave a mock sigh. "Is there no balm in Gilead?"

"Not as long as Jack's around," said his wife.

He wondered if Jack had discussed his Mitford trip

with the bishop. Very likely they'd talked and Jack had mentioned it, a casual thing.

"Talked to the bishop lately?" he asked.

"Nope. Not a word. Saw him at the convention a while back. He's put on a good bit of weight."

"Who hasn't?" asked Father Tim, feeling relieved.

"I guess you heard what happened at Holy Cross over in Manteo."

"All I know about this diocese is what you tell me, Jack."

"More's the pity. Anyway, Bishop Harvey was making his annual visitation at Holy Cross, got there and saw about eight people sitting in the congregation. He was pretty hot about it, as you can imagine. He got vested, kept looking for somebody else to arrive, they didn't, so he asked Luke Castor, said, 'Father, didn't you tell them I was coming?'

"Luke said, 'No, but obviously they found out somehow.' "

"You have to take Jack with a grain of salt as big as your head," said Earlene.

The sunset delivered a great, slow wash of color above the beachfront cottages and turned the patch of blue to violet, then scarlet, then gold.

"Oh, the blessing of a porch," sighed Earlene. "When Jack and I walk out our front door, we just drop off in the yard like heathens."

"That's one way to put it," said her husband.

Earlene gave her hostess a profound look. "Don't let anybody talk you into a retirement home!"

"Never fear!" exclaimed Cynthia.

"It's not that bad, Earlene," said Father Jack. "You may not have a porch, but somebody else does the cooking three meals a day."

"You've got a point, dear," said Earlene, feeling better about lacking a porch. "And after supper in the dining room, some of us play gin rummy, or sometimes pinochle."

"Lovely!" said Cynthia.

Father Tim peered at his wife, thinking she was holding up gamely, though she appeared to be gripping the arms of her rocker with some force.

Earlene Ferguson did not care for silences in conversation, and was doing her level best to caulk every chink and crack, so he didn't know how long the music had been drifting across the street.

"Listen!" he said, during a chink.

"What's that?" asked Father Jack.

"Just listen." César Franck . . .

There was a brief silence on the porch.

"Goodness!" said Earlene. "Somebody's sure playing their radio loud. That's a problem we have at the retirement home, with so many being half deaf, plus, of course, our walls are thin as paper—"

"Hush, Earlene," said Father Jack.

—◦—

He'd never quite appreciated the wisdom of having a king-size bed until his wife introduced him to its luxuries on the second night of their marriage. As a bachelor, he'd spent several decades rolled into the middle of a sagging mattress like a hotdog in a bun.

Now, with the addition of a three-year-old in their lives, the chiefest virtues of a large bed were amply demonstrated. He looked in on Jonathan, who was sprawled across Cynthia's pillow, and went to the guest room and tapped on the door.

"Jack? We're going to step down to the beach for a few minutes."

Jack came to the door and cracked it. "How long have you been married?" he asked, grinning.

"Not too long," said Father Tim.

He unrolled the blanket and they spread it on the sand.

"Full moon, my dear, and no extra charge."

"Heaven," she breathed, kneeling on the blanket. "Heaven!"

"Didn't I tell you I'd give you the moon and stars?" He sat next to her and smelled the faintest scent of wisteria lifted to him on the breeze. He would go for months, used to her scent and immune to its seduction, then, suddenly, it was new to him again, compelling.

"How are you holding up being married to a parson?"

"I love being married to my parson."

"The Fergusons didn't throw you too badly?"

"Goodness, Timothy, what kind of wimp do you think I am? I don't know much, but I do know that the wife of a priest must be ready for anything."

"That's the spirit!"

She lay back on the blanket, and he lay beside her, loving her nearness, loving the sense that sometimes, if only for a moment, he couldn't tell where she left off and he began.

Lulled by the background roar and lap of the waves, he gazed up into the onyx bowl spangled with life and light, and took her hand. " 'Bright star,' " he quoted to her from Keats, " 'would I were steadfast as thou art . . .' "

"You've always thought me steadfast," she said, "but

I'm not, I'm not at all, Timothy. I'm sometimes like so much Silly Putty."

"You're always there for me, sending off for new clothes, taking in children, drumming up the parish tea, standing with me at the church door. I don't deserve this, you know, it scares me."

"You're all I have," she murmured, drawing him close, "and all I ever wanted. So stop being scared!"

"Yes," he said. "I'll try."

―⁊―

The windows and front doors were thrown open to a fickle breeze, the creaking ceiling fans circled at full throttle. Here and there, an occasional pew bulletin lifted on a draft of moving air and went sailing.

Peering loftward through a glass pane in the sacristy door, he couldn't help but notice that the soprano had returned to the fold and was cooling herself with a battery-operated fan. He also saw that every pew in St. John's was filled to bursting.

Air-conditioning! he thought, running his finger around his collar. Next year's budget, and no two ways about it.

Standing next to him in the tiny sacristy, Marshall Duncan pulled the bell rope eleven times.

. . . *bong* . . . *bong* . . .

On the heel of the eleventh bell, Ella Bridgewater, fully rehearsed and mildly fibrillating with excitement, hammered down on the opening hymn as if all creation depended on it.

Marshall opened the sacristy door and crossed himself reverently as the crucifer led the procession into the nave.

Glorious! His congregation was standing bolt up-right, and singing as lustily as any crowd of Baptists he'd ever seen or heard tell of.

> *"Lift high the cross*
> *the love of Christ proclaim . . ."*

He threw his head back and, with his flock, gave himself wholly to the utterance of joy on this morning of mornings.

> *". . . till all the world adore*
> *his sacred Name.*
> *Led on their way by*
> *this triumphant sign*
> *the hosts of God in*
> *conquering ranks combine."*

The organ music soared and swirled above their heads like a great incoming tide; surely he only imag-ined seeing the chandeliers tremble.

"Blessed be God," he proclaimed at the end of the mighty *Amen.* "Father, Son, and Holy Spirit!"

The eager congregational response made his scalp tingle. "And blessed be his kingdom, now and forever!"

He lifted his hands to heaven, and prayed.

"Almighty God, to You all hearts are open, all de-sires known, and from You no secrets are hid: Cleanse the thoughts of our hearts by the inspiration of Your Holy Spirit, that we may perfectly love You, and worthily magnify Your holy Name; through Christ our Lord."

"Amen!" they said as one.

He didn't sense it every time, no; if only he could.

But this morning, the Holy Spirit was moving in the music and among the people of St. John's; He was about the place in a way that left them dazzled and wondering, unable to ken the extravagant mystery of it.

For this moment, this blessed hour, heaven was breathing its perfume on their little handful in the church on the island in the vast blue sea, and they were honored and thankful and amazed.

CHAPTER ELEVEN

Worms to Butterflies

"Father?"

"Puny!"

"Th' most awful thing has happened, I don't know how to tell you. . . ."

He sank into the office chair. "Just tell me," he said, feeling suddenly weary.

"Your angel . . ." Weeping, nose blowing.

"My angel?"

"Th' one on th' mantel! I was runnin' th' dust rag downstairs, you know I run th' dust rag every time I come because of th' work goin' on in th' street, you knew they was relayin' pipes, didn't you?"

"No, I didn't know."

"Well, I was runnin' th' dust rag an' . . ." More nose blowing.

"It's all right. Whatever you're going to tell me is all right." She was dusting and the angel toppled off the mantel and fell to the floor and a wing broke off, or an arm. How bad could it be?

"Well, th' angel . . . it's not *there* anymore, it's gone!"

"Gone?"

"Today I was dustin' downstairs because I dusted upstairs last week, and when I come to th' mantel, I couldn't believe my eyes. It was jis' this empty place where it used to set!"

"Well, now . . ."

"I mean, th' other day when I called you about th' door bein' unlocked, I looked all around an' didn't see nothin' missin', I mean, I thought somethin' seemed different about your study, but I couldn't figure out what it was, I didn't notice anything bein' *gone*, so what I'm sayin' is, maybe it was gone last week, I don't know!"

"Have you talked with Harley? And Puny, stop crying, it's all right. Just sit down, take a deep breath, and tell me everything."

"I talked to Harley, he said he hadn't seen nothing' goin' on at your house, 'cept me goin' in an' out."

"Was anything else missing, anything moved around?"

"No, sir, an' I promise you I really looked, I've went over th' whole house with a fine-tooth comb, even th' closets, an' checked th' windows an' basement door, they're locked tight as a drum. I feel terrible about this, Father, I'll pay for th' angel, whatever it cost, me an' Joe will pay ever' cent."

"This is a mystery. I remember having a fifty-dollar bill and a credit card in my desk drawer. I wonder—"

"I'll go look!" she said.

Very odd, he mused.

"Your money and credit card's in th' drawer on th' left-hand side."

Odder than odd. "I wonder if Dooley would know anything."

"I don't think Dooley was in th' house a single time."

"I'll call him at school and ask. I don't know, Puny, I'm as baffled by this as you are."

"I'm real sorry."

"It's OK, I promise. We'll figure it out, don't worry. Just . . . lock up good when you leave."

He sat at his desk for some time, occasionally nodding his head, speaking half sentences aloud and, in general, feeling befuddled.

———❍———

Harley Welch sounded down and out.

"M'bunk mate's gone, and Lace has went off to school." He sighed deeply. "Hit's a graveyard around here."

"I believe it."

"Seem like I wadn't hardly ready f'r 'em to go off."

"We never are."

"You know, some of th' stuff Lace taught me, it's stickin'! I set here last night and wrote five pages of things that was goin' around in m' noggin."

"Great! Terrific! I'm proud of you!"

"I got to thinkin' about them great falls of th' Missouri, five of 'em, and how ol' Lewis an' Clark must've felt when they seen such a sight as that."

"Lace is a grand teacher. You're a genuine help and consolation to each other."

But Harley didn't sound consoled. "Both of 'em gone, an' not a soul t' set down an' eat a bite with, hit's jis' mope aroun' an' listen t' y'r head roar. . . ."

"Anytime you feel lonesome, walk up to the Grill, order the special, talk to people. It'll do you good." Heaven knows, that had saved his own sanity a time or two.

"I'm tearin' th' engine out of th' mayor's RV in th' mornin', I ain't got time t' lollygag."

"Puny says you haven't seen anybody around the house, nothing suspicious. . . ."

"Nossir. Course that door bein' unlocked an' all, an' that gang workin' on th' street . . ."

"Seems like they'd have taken something else, though. Well, listen, Harley, you hang in there. We'll be home in October. I'm going to hold you to that pan of brownies."

Harley cackled, sounding like himself again. "I practice on them brownies once ever' week, I'm about t' git it right."

They sat on the porch in the gathering twilight, and watched Jonathan play with a sand bucket and shovel in their end-of-summer garden. The Louis L'Amour paperback lay on the table beside him; Barnabas sprawled at their feet.

His wife knew absolutely nothing about the angel and was as dumbfounded as he. It was bizarre, it was unreal, it was—

"I'll get it," Cynthia said, when the phone rang.

She dashed inside and came back with the cordless.

"Those eggs you gave us last week are wonderful, the yolks are a lovely shade of yellow!"

Covering the mouthpiece, she whispered, "Penny Duncan."

"Oh, really?" She listened intently. "That's wonderful! How good of you, Penny, how thoughtful."

She gazed into the yard at Jonathan. "Oh, he's a handful, all right, but no, thank you so much, we love having him, we're all quite happy together. Yes, I'm sure, but thank you again, you're very dear, Penny. Really? I'd love it if you'd help at the tea. Could you possibly make an ice mold? What a good idea, yes, fresh peppermint would be perfect. Well, then—love to Marshall. See you in church!"

She laid the phone on the arm of the rocker and smiled at him.

"You had an offer for help with Jonathan and turned it down?"

"She has ten days of vacation and offered to keep him, but . . ." She shrugged.

"But what?"

"But I declined."

"Why?" he asked.

She shrugged again. "Because."

ϑ

"You won't believe this," said Dooley, calling from the hall phone in his dorm.

"Try me."

"Guess what girl's school our first dance is with."

"Mrs. Hemingway's." Who else?

"Can you believe it?"

He thought he discerned a kind of . . . what? Expectation, perhaps, under Dooley's evident disgust.

"I hope you'll ask Lace to dance."

"Not if she's wearing those weird shoes an' all."

"Come on, what do shoes have to do with anything?"

"Plenty," said Dooley, with feeling.

He had pulled whatever strings a clergyman can call

to hand, and the court date would fall the day after Buck's and Pauline's wedding, after which Harley would drive Dooley back to school. He gave Dooley the scoop.

"Great! Cool." The boy sounded relieved.

No, Dooley hadn't been in the yellow house, he didn't know anything about the angel, and had never once seen anybody go in or out except Puny.

"Give me a report on the dance," he said.

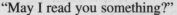

"May I read you something?"

"I like it when you read," Janette whispered. She sat with him in the cramped space of her semiprivate room, looking toward the wall.

> *"I asked the Lord*
> *for a bunch of fresh flowers*
> *but instead he gave me an ugly cactus*
> *with many thorns.*
> *I asked the Lord*
> *for some beautiful butterflies*
> *but instead he gave me*
> *many ugly and dreadful worms.*
> *I was threatened.*
> *I was disappointed.*
> *I mourned.*
> *But after many days,*
> *suddenly,*
> *I saw the cactus bloom*
> *with many beautiful flowers*
> *and those worms became*
> *beautiful butterflies*
> *flying in the wind.*
> *God's way is the best way."*

Earlier in the visit, he'd been encouraged to see light returning to her eyes, though it was a light that sparked, then waned, like a weak flame in damp wood.

Now she turned her head and looked at him and he searched for the flame, but it wasn't there.

"Someone named Chung-Ming Kao wrote this," he said. "From prison."

She closed her eyes, and he felt the despair of his own helplessness. In truth, he had no solutions to offer Janette Tolson, not even a burning homily.

In the end, all he had to offer was hope.

❧

"Father—Buck Leeper."

"Buck!" He rejoiced to hear Buck's rough baritone voice. As badly as the superintendent of the Hope House project had once treated him, he now remembered only that night in the rectory, the night Buck had knocked on his door, saying, "I'm ready to do whatever it takes."

What it took, in Buck's case, was a broken spirit and a willing heart. That Christmas Eve night, Buck Leeper prayed a simple prayer and asked Christ to be his Savior and Lord.

They had stood there by the fire, their arms around one another—two old boys from Mississippi, bawling like babies.

He sat forward in his office chair, doubly excited, given that he'd never had a phone call from Alaska.

"How are you, buddy?"

"Scared," said Buck.

"I know. I've been there."

"Yeah, but when you tied th' knot, it was your first time. I've been there three times and messed up."

Buck's three marriages had all ended tragically. His first wife had died of an undiagnosed blood disease, his second wife had committed suicide, and, twelve years ago, his third wife left with his foreman and sued for divorce.

"In those three marriages, you didn't know Him, you didn't have a clue who He really is. St. Paul says that when we give our lives to Christ, we become new creatures. 'If anyone is in Christ, he is a new creation; old things have passed away; behold, all things have become new.' "

There was a grateful silence at the other end.

"I'm praying for you and Pauline and the children. You'll need His grace on this side of the cross as much as you needed it on the other. Pray for His grace, Buck, to carry you and Pauline from strength to strength as you build this new life together."

He listened to static on the line as his friend in Alaska struggled to speak.

"Thanks," said Buck, standing in a phone booth in Juneau, and feeling that a D-8 Cat had just rolled off his chest.

Hoppy Harper called the church office to say that Louella's break was bad, though nothing like Miss Sadie's had been. Louella would be down for the count for a while, but the prognosis looked good.

Gene Bolick's medication was helping, he'd counted the stairs to bed only twice in five nights, and Esther seemed more like her old self. She had, in fact, brought an orange marmalade cake to Hoppy's office.

Hoppy went on to say that a new priest had been called to Lord's Chapel. The interim would finish up the end of October, and the new man, Father Talbot, would be installed on All Saints' Day. Both agreed the call had come pretty quickly; some parishes took up to two years to replace a priest.

He hoofed along the lane toward the Baptist church and the big meeting with the Fall Fair committee.

Thank God things were on the mend in Mitford. He had fish to fry in Whitecap—not the least of which was getting his act together for his wedding anniversary, only three days ahead.

"Father, it's . . . Pauline Barlowe."

"Pauline!"

"I've found something."

He understood at once; she had found some clue, some trail to Kenny and Sammy. He literally held his breath.

"I was gettin' ready to throw out an old pocketbook I hadn't carried in years, and for some reason I looked through it real good, and in th' linin' . . ."

"Yes?"

"In th' linin' I found this little piece of paper, it said . . . Ed Sikes."

"Ed Sikes?"

"Yes. I must have written it down after I gave Kenny . . ." She hesitated, unable to speak the thought. "Th' man that took 'im was named Ed Sikes, that's all I know. I was . . . I was drunk, and didn't ever know where he worked or lived or . . . anything."

He felt the pain under her confession, the pain that might never heal completely, though Pauline Barlowe had come to know the Healer.

"I'd give anything if you could . . ." She didn't finish.

"I know this man gave you alcohol, but was there any other reason you let Kenny go with him?"

"I don't know . . . he seemed nice, I guess. It seems like I thought he could probably treat Kenny better than I did."

"I'll look into this and let you know if anything turns up. What about Buck? How is he?"

"He just called us, he's doin' real good, he's comin' th' end of September. We're all . . . real excited."

"Dwell on that," he told Dooley's mother.

"Emma, remember when you helped find Jessie Barlowe?"

Emma liked being reminded of the role she played in bringing Dooley's little sister home to Mitford. Emma had gone on-line and nailed the whereabouts of the woman who'd bolted to Florida with Jessie.

On a hunch, he'd piled Cynthia and Pauline into the Buick and driven sixteen hours to Lakeland, Florida, where they miraculously recovered the five-year-old Jessie, now living with her mother and older brother, Poo.

"I'd like you to get on the Internet and look for Ed Sikes. S-i-k-e-s. That could be Edward, Edmund, Edwin—"

"Edisto, even! I had an uncle Edisto we called Ed."

"Whatever. Whatever you can think of."

"Is this about one of Dooley's brothers?" she asked.

"It is."

"I'll get right on it," said his erstwhile secretary, "and I'll pray. Sometimes I pray while I surf."

He slid the Mustang into the gravel area by the church as the heavens burst open in a deluge.

He raced down the basement steps with the *Mitford Muse* under his arm and, sopping wet, trotted to the men's room to dry himself off with paper towels.

"Is that you, Father?" Marion called from the sink at the end of the hall.

"It is! How are you, Marion?"

"Spry! I just made coffee, want a cup?"

"I do!"

A violent clap of thunder crashed overhead as he punched the play button on his office answering machine.

"Father Timothy? Cap'n Willie. We've got a bad storm warnin' for Thursday, and we're cancelin' th' trip. We're right in th' heart of hurricane season, so I guess it's no surprise. I'll make good on your trip anytime, just call to reschedule, four-oh-two-eight." There was an awkward pause. "Thank you for your business, and good fishin' to you."

Hotdog and Hallelujah!

He took the sodden newspaper apart and draped the three double sheets over Sunday School chairs to dry. Another clap of thunder rolled above them. It was comforting, he thought, to be snug in the basement of the old church, the smell of coffee wafting along the hallway, someone nearby to call to, the rain pelting the windows. . . .

Marion bustled in with a mug in either hand.

"There's sugar cookies left from Sunday School," she said, "but I don't suppose you can have any."

"Not a crumb."

Marion settled into the chair by his desk. "Ella

Bridgewater's all the talk," she said, nodding her approval. "You did a fine job rounding her up."

"I didn't do the rounding up. Ella was heaven-sent."

Marion smiled. "You and Cynthia were heaven-sent, is what Sam and I think."

He felt his face grow warm. "Now, Marion . . ."

"Well, it's true. How are you all doing, now that you've dug in? Are you happy in Whitecap?" Marion possessed one of his mother's most desirable characteristics—a frank simplicity that invited the truth.

"We are. There are good people at St. John's, we feel very blessed."

"We've got our downside, but I suppose we're no worse than the rest of the lot. You've helped us settle some of our petty squabbles."

"At least the pew bulletin is no longer running classifieds," he said, smiling.

Marion laughed. "And just think—that's where I found my carpet sweeper for nine dollars! In any case, I hope parenting isn't proving too much for you. Goodness, after our grandchildren used to leave, we were pooped for a month of Sundays. And that's when they were old enough to feed and dress themselves!"

"He's a handful, all right."

"Janette's not doing so well, is she? She hardly spoke on Sunday, bless her heart."

"The doctor says the downward spiral has been going on for a long time. The upward spiral takes time, too."

She blew on the steaming coffee. "Thank the Lord I never had trouble with depression. Complaining, that's been my thorn."

"I hadn't noticed," he said.

"I don't suppose most people confide their thorns. Saint Paul only said he had one. I wish he'd gone ahead and told us what it was!"

He laughed. "You'll never hear mine from me!" Self-righteousness, he thought, and no two ways about it.

He enjoyed Marion's company. There was a decided comfort to being in her presence.

"Did you know Janette sews like an angel?" she asked.

"I only know she takes in sewing."

"She sews every bit as well as Jeffrey Tolson sings," Marion said with feeling. "Made all our choir robes and banners, makes all her children's clothes, plus earns a living with it. I guess she'll have to depend on her calling for support 'til she takes him to court. *If* she takes him to court." Marion sipped her coffee, looking concerned. "I saw Jeffrey Tolson the other day."

"Aha."

"I think he's living on the island."

He shook his head. What could he say?

"He thinks this is his church, that it belongs to him because his father and grandfather were members here, as if half the congregation couldn't say the very same thing." She gave a mild shudder. "Oh, how I'd hate to see him come back. Some predict he'll try. It would put us through the wringer."

"Once through the wringer seems quite enough to me," he said, meeting her gaze.

"They say the business with Avery Plummer didn't work out, she left him and went to her mother in Goldsboro." Marion sighed. "I always felt sorry for Janette, being so plain and her husband so handsome. Some people, I won't say who, called her Church Mouse. The boy has his mother's sweet spirit, but looks the spit image of his father, don't you think?"

"I agree."

"Jeffrey always reminded me of an apple I took my sixth-grade teacher, Miss Fox. I'll never forget that apple. I was so proud of it, I polished it on my dress all the way to school; it was the prettiest thing in our orchard. I stood right by her desk and watched her bite into it. I thought she'd say, *Why, Marion Lewis, this is the best apple I ever tasted!* Well! When she bit into it, she had the oddest look on her face."

"Really?"

"Rotten inside! I was embarrassed to death, just mortified."

"Aha."

"We're all excited about the tea," she said, changing a sore subject. "I'm taking a day off from the library to help Cynthia, and Sam and I will loan you our nice canvas folding chairs for the garden. At the ECW meeting, we prayed for sunshine. I don't think that's too pushy, do you?"

" 'Come boldly to the throne of grace!' " he quoted from Hebrews.

"Well, no rest for the weary!" she exclaimed, rising from the chair. "I've got to clean up under the sink, you never saw such a mess of old vases, there's enough oasis under there to capsize a ship. Speaking of ship, when are you going on your big fishing trip with Cap'n Willie?"

"Postponed!"

"Oh, I'm sorry."

"Don't be," he said.

It was nagging him, reminding him of the time years ago when he'd found the lock broken on the church door. He'd found nothing stolen, nothing amiss, and he didn't report it. Then he'd discovered the burial urn filled with precious stones, sitting innocently on the shelf of the makeshift columbarium in the church closet. . . .

"Rodney? Tim Kavanagh, how's business?"

"Slow, thank th' Lord," said Mitford's police chief. "How you doin' down there at th' end of th' world?"

"Pretty well, thanks. Listen, Rodney—an odd thing . . . Puny Guthrie, Joe Joe's wife, you know she's our housekeeper . . ."

"Right."

"She tells me something is missing from our house next door to the old rectory. Just disappeared off the mantel."

"What's th' missin' item?"

"A bronze angel on a green marble base, probably about eighteen inches high, maybe twenty."

"What's th' value?"

"I don't know. But it's a fine piece, very fine. I'd estimate three thousand, at least. Old bronzes aren't cheap."

"What else is missin'?"

"Nothing. And nothing out of place. But Puny had left the door unlocked by mistake, and there's work being done on the street out front, so . . ."

"Any suspects?"

"No, and nobody was seen going in or out. No one even knew the door was unlocked."

"I don't know what we can do but file a report. No suspects, nothin' else missin', no vandalism. That don't leave much to go on. What we probably need to do is go down and take fingerprints."

He remembered that Rodney Underwood loved taking fingerprints.

"Wouldn't it cause an uproar to have your men crawling all over the house? Besides, this was maybe a week or so ago, and Puny dusts pretty faithfully, wouldn't that remove fingerprints?"

"Don't you worry about a thing, you let me take care of it! Now, how do we get in?"

Given the excitement in Rodney's voice, he might have handed the chief the keys to a Harley hog. "Talk to Puny," he said, half regretting he'd brought it up in the first place.

———⌒———

With the newspaper sufficiently dry, he reassembled it and carried it to his desk.

He was surprised to see the gated, well-secluded mountain lodge of Edith Mallory in a photograph. A white arrow pointed to a grove of trees next to Edith's rambling house.

Mallory Property Sight of Tension Over Town History

When the great-great-grandfather of Mitford native and mayoral candidate, Coot Hendrick, settled our town in 1853, he built a dog trot cabin on Lookout Ridge, and a small trading depot where Happy Endings Bookstore now stands.

Later, as the family of Hezikiah Hendrick grew, our town founder built a spring house, barn, and corncrib on his forty-acre ridge property.

The cabin and outbuildings are long gone, but the stone foundations remains, according to Dr. Lyle Carpenter of Wesley College in our neighboring township. There is also a family graveyard and the graves of five Union soldiers reputed to exist on the property.

"What we discovered on the ridge is a classic example of how our early mountain settlers lived," says Carpenter. "We wish to see this valuable site preserved, perhaps with an eventual replication of buildings, so that residents and visitors can understand and enjoy our mountain frontier heritage."

Dr. Carpenter reports that the Hendrick family dump sight, allegedly located only yards from where the cabin stood, may contain pottery shards, milk buckets, plow shares and other remnants of early highland life.

There is a rub, however. The Hendrick property is now owned by Mrs. Edith Mallory, whose 95-acre ridge-top estate, Clear Day, includes the old homesite. In fact, her house is reported to sit but forty-six feet from the south-facing foundation of the Hendrick cabin.

Mrs. Mallory currently has a town permit to construct an additional 3,000 square feet of residential space, which will intrude on part of the historic sight. She is reported to say she has no intention of halting construction, which is scheduled to begin in September, and has issued a no trespassing warning.

"This is a crucial moment in our local history," says Dr. Carpenter. "We must find a way to preserve this important property, which my colleagues and I have only recently discovered, thanks to the fine work of the Mitford town museum and its archives."

Coot Hendrick, the great-great-grandson of Mitford's founder, says he will fight for the old homeplace to be designated a historic sight.

Dr. Carpenter said that a walking path to the sight

from the town, and a nature trail identifying the abundant flora, would also be a fine idea.

The town council is appealing to the State Department of History and Archives for counsel in the matter.

Mrs. Mallory could not be reached for comment.

Edith Mallory, he thought, had the ominous persistence of leaking propane. Just when he thought she had vanished forever in Spain or Florida, she reappeared, and always with malice.

Surely there was some way she could come to terms with the town over this thing.

In the end, had she ever done anything for the benefit of Mitford? Never once, as far as he could remember. Her multimillion-dollar home sprawled along the ridge above the village, looking down on a community of souls who'd been through one tough scrape after another, yet she'd never been forthcoming, even to the library when it was struggling for its very existence.

And hadn't he been sent knocking on her door when the town museum was trying to pull itself together, and hadn't she made her usual seductive, albeit fruitless, overtures and sent him packing? The annual Bane and Blessing had long ago given up asking for contributions, not to mention the volunteer fire department.

Of course, she had given fifteen thousand to add beds to the Children's Hospital, his favorite charity. He'd quickly learned, however, that it was all part of a plan to get him into a bed of her own.

His very skin crawled at the thought of how she'd trapped him in that blasted Lincoln, forcing him to leap from the thing while it was still moving.

He folded the *Muse* and threw it in the wastebasket. As far as he was concerned, the only good news was that J. C. Hogan had evidently installed software with a spell check. Too bad there was no software out there for grammar.

In truth, he was tired of knowing what was going on in Mitford. He didn't want to hear another peep from that realm for a while.

He was going to do what Mona's sign said, and bloom where he was planted.

$$\sim\!\!\!\ominus\!\!\!\sim$$

Somehow, he'd managed to turn the ringer off and didn't hear the phone while he was washing his cup at the sink down the hall.

"I don't know why I keep missin' you," said Emma, when he punched the play button.

"I thought you'd want to know the scoop on Father Talbot, it's what everybody's talkin' about. I didn't lay eyes on him when he was here tryin' out, but Esther Bolick says he's good-lookin' as anything, and *tall*. *Very* tall. Oh, and thin, she thinks he exercises, maybe with weights. Esther Cunningham said he walked up the street to her office when he was here, said he just wanted to meet the mayor of such a fine town, wanted to shake her hand, wadn't that nice?

"He's comin' in November, is what they're sayin', has a wife that could be th' twin of Meg Ryan, and two kids, both on th' honor roll. Anyway, people are real excited about finally gettin' somebody permanent down at Lord's Chapel, and from a big church, too, I think it was Chicago. They say they saw him on a video and he preaches up a storm and is funny as heck, he had everybody rollin' in th' aisles.

"Let's see, what else . . . somebody, I forget who,

said he sings great an' has real white teeth an' looks terrific in . . . whatever it is, maybe his hassock."

Wears a halo, he thought, has wings . . .

"Oh, Lord, here comes Harold back, he must've forgotten his bag lunch."

Click. Beep.

✆

"Timothy?"

"Walter!" His only living cousin, as far as he knew, and lifelong best friend into the bargain. "It's been a coon's age."

"I thought I'd ring down to the boondocks while I'm waiting for a client to show up. How's the fishing?"

"I have no idea."

"Swimming? Doing any swimming?"

"Nope. No swimming."

"Clamming? Crabbing? Duck hunting? *Anything?*"

"Just the same old stick-in-the-mud you've always known me to be." Darn Walter, he was always looking for some big story, some action. So far, the most exciting thing he'd ever done was marry Cynthia Coppersmith. That was such a big one, it got him off the hook with Walter for a couple of years, but now his attorney cousin was at it again.

"Listen, Potato Head, I've got a new parish to take care of and a yard to mow. That's all the action I can handle right now. How's Katherine?"

"Mean as a snake, skinny as a rail."

"The usual, then!" They laughed easily together. They were both pretty fond of Walter's wide-open wife, her dazzling laughter and unstoppable generosity of spirit.

"And Cynthia?"

"Busy. Doing another book, reading at the library, tending a three-year-old."

"You've taken in another one?"

"Only briefly, his mother's in the hospital."

"How do you like your new parish?"

"I like it. Good people. We're happy here. When can you and Katherine come down? You haven't been my way in years, I was there last, you owe me."

"After you finish this interim, we'll drive down to Mitford for a week, how's that? Slog around in our bathrobes and eat you out of house and home."

"You can't scare me, pal."

"Speaking of scare," said Walter, "we had a little break-in the other night. They took our TVs and my Rolex. We're surprised it wasn't worse."

"We've just had an odd thing happen. Remember the angel I once mentioned, the one from Miss Sadie's attic? It disappeared off the mantel in Mitford. Nothing else was disturbed in the house, no sign of entry, nothing. Just gone, vanished. Very queer."

"Valuable?"

"Probably three thousand or so, maybe more. Bronze. On a heavy marble base. French, I think."

"Life has always been too mysterious to suit my tastes. Well, Cousin, here comes my erstwhile client. It's good to touch base. Love to Cynthia, love to Dooley—how is he?"

"Great!"

"Good. I've got a stock tip for you, so call me, you dog, and let's catch up."

"Consider it done," he said.

He'd written it everywhere but on his hand to make sure he didn't forget. No, indeed, forgetting birthdays and anniversaries did not cut it at his house—nor at any other house, as far as he could tell from his years in clergy counseling.

Headed for the town grocer with the windshield wipers on high, he mulled over the coming event.

They'd already gone to the beach and taken a blanket, but they hadn't gone to the beach and taken a blanket and a Coleman stove.

Just down the strand from the old Miller cottage with the red roof, he would set everything up in their favorite spot.

They would watch the sunset and he would grill fresh mahimahi and corn in the shuck.

He would cut a ripe, sweet melon—he didn't think it was too late in the season to find one—and pour a well-chilled champagne. He noted that he'd have to go across to find a decent label, but while he was there, maybe he could also find something to drink it from, since all they had in the cabinet were what appeared to be top-of-the-line jelly glasses.

For dessert, of course, he'd make her sworn favorite—poached pears—the very thing he'd served Cynthia Coppersmith the first time she came to dinner at the rectory.

All in all, pretty creative thinking for a country parson . . .

As for entertainment, they could search the night sky for Arcturus and Andromeda, maybe Pegasus. He'd bought a book at Ernie's that told very plainly how to find something other than the Big and Little Dippers, which, he'd been disappointed to learn, weren't even constellations.

He went over the list again.

Leonard and Marjorie Lamb had offered to babysit, and were scheduled to arrive at Dove Cottage at six-thirty. . . .

What had he forgotten?

He realized he was holding his breath, and exhaled. All bases covered. Consider the thing done!

Had it been four years ago when he'd raced through the sacristy into the nave of Lord's Chapel, trembling like a leaf in the wind, late for his wedding through no fault of his own, and spied his bride, also late and flushed from running, who appeared like a vision in the aisle?

If ever he'd known the definition of a waking dream, that had been it.

He remembered standing there, terrified that he'd burst into tears with half the congregation, and noted that he'd never seen so many handkerchiefs waving in the breeze. Under the swell of the organ music, there had been a veritable concerto of sniffing and nose-blowing by men and women alike.

And then, there she was, standing with him. He later admitted to his cousin, Walter, that the earth had moved at that moment. He felt it as surely as if the long-inactive fault running from somewhere in the Blue Ridge Mountains to Charleston, South Carolina, had suddenly heaved apart.

He remembered thinking, with a glad and expectant heart, I'm in for it now.

⟡

They were out of Jonathan's favorite milk at the gro-cer's, so back he schlepped to Ernie's, clobbered by rain.

"We had doubles developed," said Ernie, showing

him three-by-five glossies of Junior. "These are th' two that went off Friday, what do you think?"

In the first snapshot, Junior had a pained expression, as if he were sitting on a carpet tack. The other was of a red-eyed Junior standing like a statue in front of the drink boxes. He didn't believe Junior had gotten around to ironing his shirt, after all.

"What about these red eyes?" he asked, concerned for the outcome of the whole deal.

"I don't know what that is. Seems like Junior's camera wadn't too swift."

"Well . . ."

"It's been five or six days an' he hadn't heard back." This didn't look promising. . . .

"Tell me about Junior," he said. "He seems a good fellow. Any family?"

"Junior lost his mama when he was pretty young, and his daddy's not much account. Me an' Roger and Roanoke try to see after him, kind of help raise him."

"Doesn't seem like he'd need much raising at the age of thirty-six."

"Well, but th' thing is," said Ernie, lowering his voice, "Junior's not the sharpest knife in the drawer."

"Who is?"

"We'd like to see him settle down, get married, have a family. He's a hard worker, got money saved, has a little house, and there's not a bigger heart on Whitecap. Helps look after his next-door neighbor, she's blind as a bat. . . ."

"Good fellow!"

Ernie removed his glasses and squinted at Father Tim. "Roanoke told me he barbered you."

"Even my wife was pleased," he said, taking a gallon of milk from the cooler.

"We got a bad storm comin' Thursday."

"I hope it clears out by Friday evening."

Ernie opened the register and gave him change. "Big doin's on Friday?"

"Yep. Fourth anniversary."

"I got one comin' up here sometime, I can't recall when."

"Let it pass and you'll be stepping over something worse than a yellow line."

"You got a point," said Ernie. "By th' way, I'm readin' that Wadsworth book."

"How do you like it?"

"He sure does a lot of runnin' up hill an' down dale. Seems like he takes notice of every little thing, keeps his eyes an' ears peeled. . . ."

"Just like Louis L'Amour!"

"I wouldn't have thought of that," said Ernie, looking pleased.

He hauled the thing from the box.

"A VCR!" His wife was beaming.

He fetched something from a bag. "Not to mention . . ."

"Peter Pan!" she whooped. "Thanks be to God!"

He fetched something else from the bag.

"Babe! I've always wanted to see that."

"Now I've made two people happy," he said, feeling like a hero.

Jonathan flew ahead of them, running at sandpipers, shouting at gulls, squatting to examine a shell.

The sun had looked out an hour ago, and they agreed

they should take advantage of it. Barefoot and holding hands on the wide sweep of rain-soaked beach, he knew that what he'd told Marion and Walter was true—they were happy in Whitecap.

He stooped and picked up an old Frisbee and threw it for Barnabas, who loped along the sand in pursuit. Watching the boy and Barnabas tumble for the Frisbee, something came swimming back to him across time. He was nine years old in Pass Christian, Mississippi, and in love with a dog. He'd completely forgotten, and the sudden memory of that summer took his breath away.

"I can feel your wheels turning," declared his wife.

"Pass Christian," he said, as if in a dream. "We drove all the way from Holly Springs to the beach at Pass Christian, it's on the gulf near Gulfport and Biloxi. A wonderful place."

"Tell me everything!" she implored.

"It was the year my father decided I should invite a friend on our summer trek; he thought I was too studious, too much a loner. I wanted to take Tommy Noles, but . . ."

"But the Great Ogre refused."

"Oh, yes. He picked the friend I should take."

"Who was it?"

"Drew Merritt, the son of my father's colleague at his law office."

His wife never liked stories about his father. He should probably keep his mouth shut, but he wanted to talk, he wanted to let go of the constraints he felt he was eternally placing on his memories, on his feelings. If he couldn't talk freely here by the ocean, which lay perfectly open to the sun and the sky . . .

"Drew wasn't someone I wanted to spend two weeks with. He was selfish, short-tempered, demanding. I remember we took a jigsaw puzzle of the nation's Capitol . . . he insisted I do the cherry blossoms and he'd work on the Capitol building. Instead of piece by piece, we worked on it section by section. I didn't want to do cherry blossoms."

"But you did them," she said, "because you're nice."

"Nice has its advantages," he said.

She squeezed his hand. "I love you."

"I love you back."

"Finally, after we'd been there a few days, Drew found a crowd to hang with, and I started wandering off on my own. It was a safe place, of course, plenty of kids came and went, reporting in to parents during the course of an afternoon. We stayed at an old hotel, I wish I could remember the name. Anyway, one day I went down to the beach and met . . . a dog."

She smiled, loving even the simplest of his stories.

"It was a red setter, and he didn't seem to belong to anyone, though he was certainly no maverick. I remember his coat was long and silky, it shone when it blew in the wind. He was like something from heaven, we connected instantly. *Click*—just like that, he was mine and I was his."

"I wouldn't let Barnabas hear you talking this way."

He put his arm around her shoulder, laughing.

"No, Jonathan, don't touch it!" Cynthia cried. The heavy rain had helped the sea disgorge flotsam of great variety.

"We started meeting in the afternoons, I never saw him in the morning. I took a little red ball with me every day and threw it to him. He always brought it back." He was able to recall his sense of freedom, and the unutterable joy of having, at last, the dog that had long been forbidden at home.

"I named him . . . Mick," he said, suddenly uneasy with the confession of a time he'd never mentioned to anyone.

"Mick!" she said. "I love that name!"

"I remember the morning we left to go back to Holly Springs." More than five decades later, his heart could recall the grief of that morning.

"My father decided we should leave a day early, and I . . . hadn't said goodbye. I took a napkin full of biscuits down to the old house where we usually met, but of course he wasn't there, it was too early in the day, so I left the biscuits under the steps."

"I love that you did that."

"Ah, Kavanagh, what don't you love?"

"Husbands who can't talk about their feelings, sand in the bed, and maps that won't refold properly."

"Let's go fold into a rocker on our porch," he said.

"Yes, let's!" She turned and gazed at him, then put her hand to his cheek.

"I'd like to remember you just this way . . . every line of your dear face at this moment."

To his amazement, tears stood in her eyes, and she put her arms around him and kissed him with an odd tenderness.

Jonathan tugged at Cynthia's shorts.

"I got to poo-poo!" said the boy, looking urgent.

The tropical depression moved north from the Caribbean, hung a left toward the Outer Banks of North Carolina, migrated across Whitecap, and dumped six inches of rain inland to Smithfield. Not a hurricane, thanks be to God, but with severe high winds. On Friday morning, it seemed to relish pausing directly over Dove Cottage and unleashing itself for a full two hours.

He padded around the house in his robe the entire morning, working on his sermon, looking over the music for Sunday, scribbling in his quote notebook, reading whatever came to hand. As thunder rolled and wind howled, Barnabas and Violet hid themselves at various points under chairs and beds. Miraculously, Jonathan slept through much of it, while his wife worked at the end of the hall on her new book.

Oh, the ineffable peace of a house darkened by a storm, and the sound of rain at its windows. Though quite unknown to his Irish genealogy, he thought he must have a wide streak of Scot in him somewhere.

So what if his plans for the evening were dashed? Didn't all the world lie before them with, God willing, time to celebrate on the beach even without a special occasion?

He sat in his chair in the study and listened to the rain and wind and the beating of his heart.

Bottom line, wasn't life itself a special occasion?

$\backsim$

When the storm abated around six-thirty, they had their anniversary dinner in the kitchen.

Then the entire troop piled onto their bed, Barnabas and Violet at the foot, and Jonathan next to Cynthia, who was propped like a czarina against down pillows.

"And now," he announced, "a movie . . . *in a box!*"

He held the video box aloft for all to see.

"Peter Pan!" exulted Jonathan, clapping his hands.

He gave Cynthia a profound look. "You'll never know what you missed tonight."

"It's OK, darling," murmured his contented wife. "I love *Peter Pan!*"

They blew through *Peter Pan* and plugged in *Babe,* adrenaline up and pumping.

"I'm crazy about this movie!" crowed his wife. "But *ugh,* I despise that cat."

"Bad cat!" said Jonathan.

Actually, the cat reminded him of someone. Who was it?

Of course. That cat reminded him of Edith Mallory.

He awoke at two in the morning and listened for the rain. Silence. The storm had passed over, and the room was close and humid.

He went to the window and cranked it open.

The music came in with the sweet, cool breeze that whispered against his bare skin.

CHAPTER TWELVE

Over the Wall

Answering the loud knock, he looked through the screen door and saw Otis Bragg.

Otis was carrying what appeared to be a half bushel of shrimp in a lined basket. "Cain't have a party without shrimp!" Otis said, grinning. His unlit cigar appeared to be fresh for the occasion.

"Otis! What a surprise!" Surprise, indeed. His wife would not take kindly to cooking shrimp fifteen minutes before her big tea, and he wasn't excited about it, either.

"Already cooked, ready to trot. A man over on th' Sound does these for me, all we do is peel and eat. Where you want 'em set?"

"Thanks, Otis. This is mighty generous of you." He hastily cleared one end of the table they'd brought out to the porch and draped with a blue cloth.

"Marlene'll be comin' along in a minute or two with somethin' to dip 'em in." Otis wiped his forehead with a handkerchief. "Maybe I could get a little shooter at th' bar?"

"The bar? Oh, the *bar!* We don't have a bar. But there's tea!"

"Tea." Otis chewed the cigar reflectively.

"Or sherry."

"Sherry," said Otis with a blank stare.

"Good label. Spain, I think." He recalled that Otis had sent him a bottle of something expensive, but couldn't remember where it was. . . .

"Oh, well, what th' hey, I pass. Father Morgan always set out a little bourbon, gin, scotch . . . you know."

"Aha."

Otis squinted at him. "You raised Baptist?"

"I was, actually."

"Me, too," said Otis. "But I got over it."

"Let me get you a glass of tea. Wait 'til you taste it. You'll like it, you have my word." He certainly wouldn't mention where the recipe came from.

⌖

The soprano, no worse for wear from her brief career in Sunday School, shook hands vigorously. "Gorgeous day, Father!

"Glorious!" said Sam Fieldwalker. "Good gracious alive, what a day!"

"The best all summer!" crowed Marion, exchanging a hug with her priest.

Also receiving rave reviews were the flowers, the table, the refreshments, the hostess, and even the straggling garden in which he'd labored the livelong morning.

His dog's great size garnered a good share of cautious interest, and Jonathan, dressed in a new sailor suit, was busy eluding all prospects of being dandled on knees or pressed to bosoms.

Father Tim had to admit there was a magical air about Dove Cottage this afternoon; he felt as expansive as a country squire. His wife floated around in something lavender, leaving the scent of wisteria on the breeze and making the whole shebang look totally effortless. The truth was, she'd been up since five a.m., cutting flowers and baking final batches of lemon squares while he installed new lace panels in the living room.

"Lace *belongs* there," she told him. "It filters the morning light and makes patterns on the floor." He had nothing but respect for the miracles wrought via UPS.

Cynthia's workroom was of great interest to the parish children who showed up; eager tour groups processed through the minuscule space, once a large closet, pointing at walls adorned with drawings, book jackets, and—a particular favorite—rough sketches of Violet beneath a beach umbrella. The real Violet positioned herself atop the refrigerator, glowering at anyone who sought her celebrity.

Ella Bridgewater arrived, dressed entirely in black, and looking, he thought, even more like a crane adorning an Oriental screen. She was what his mother would have called "a sight for sore eyes," coming through the cottage gate with a bright rouge spot on either cheek.

Cynthia trotted their new organist around to various groups convened in the garden. "Penny, I don't believe you've met Ella Bridgewater. Ella, meet Penny Duncan. You'll have to see the lovely ice mold she made with fresh peppermint."

"Penny used to be a hippie!" said Jean Ballenger.

She proclaimed this as if announcing a former background in brokerage services or marketing. "She grows all their vegetables, raises chickens, and makes goat cheese!"

"Heavenly *days!*" Ella wagged her head in disbelief. "The cleverest thing I ever made was a cranberry rope for the Christmas tree!"

"Penny once made her own shoes," Jean continued, causing everyone to look at Penny's feet, which were shod in pumps for the occasion. "And," said Jean, ending on a triumphal note, "all her children say yes, ma'am!"

He moved away to join Leonard and Marjorie, who had thumped into two of Marion's folding chairs by the crepe myrtle and were busily shucking shrimp and tossing shells into the bushes.

If Violet knew what was going on out here . . .

"Seen anything of your neighbor?" asked Leonard.

"I've seen precisely nothing of my neighbor! But I certainly hear a good deal of him."

"We hope he doesn't make too much racket," said Marjorie.

"Racket! We enjoy it, actually. He's an outstanding musician."

Leonard dunked a shrimp into the sauce that appeared to be setting his lemon square afloat. "Some say he could have been a concert organist. I believe he was schooled at Juilliard. But he never liked the spotlight, as you can imagine. He's a real hermit. I haven't laid eyes on him in years."

"His grandaddy once got in Walter Winchell's column!" said Marjorie. "You remember Walter Winchell?"

"Oh, yes," said Father Tim, feeling suddenly antiquated. "What did he get in there for?"

"Going out with chorus girls in New York City!"

"Aha."

"Joan Crawford came to Whitecap to visit the Loves," Marjorie told him. "And Betty Grable, too, or let's see . . . maybe it was Irene Dunne!"

"It was Celeste Holm!" Jean Ballenger, who enjoyed moving from group to group, plunked into a chair.

"I never much cared for Celeste Holm, Father, did you?" asked Marjorie.

"I don't believe I remember Celeste Holm."

"You see," said Jean, "I told you Father Tim was younger than we thought."

He sucked in his stomach. "What age had you thought . . . exactly?"

"Marjorie said going on seventy."

Seventy!

"Why, Jean Ballenger! I said no such thing! I said with all your wonderful background and experience, Father, you *could* be going on seventy, but in the end, I guessed you to be sixty!"

"Thank you!" he said.

"Who else used to come down here and visit Redmon Love?" wondered Leonard.

Jean smoothed her bangs, which were going haywire in the humidity. "Somebody said Winston Churchill, but I never believed it for a minute. Mr. Churchill certainly had no time to be lollygagging around Whitecap, what with winning Nobel Prizes and putting out wars all over the place."

Leonard licked his thumb. "Well, anyway, we heard the family hid Morris whenever the bigwigs came around. They say Morris spent a lot of time in the attic as a boy. Redmon built him a room up there and put an organ in it, a small version of the big one downstairs.

Morris was never allowed to play his music when guests were in the house. I guess they didn't want anybody to know he existed."

"The terrible meanness of people!" said Jean, pursing her lips. "They ought to have been horsewhipped. But, 'Vengeance is mine, saith the Lord.' "

"Did his grandparents raise him, then?" asked Father Tim.

"Pretty much. His parents stayed in Europe most of the time. I went to school with Morris in the fifth or sixth grade, but the kids made it so tough on him, he never lasted to junior high. I'm sure they must have gotten him a tutor."

"What exactly . . . is his problem?"

"You mean you don't know?" asked Leonard.

"Not at all."

"Well, you see—"

"Father!" exclaimed Ella Bridgewater, joining the group. "As I've just said to your wife—your party is delightful, and this tea is *heavenly.*" She clinked the ice in her glass, looking appreciative.

"Well, thank you! As for the tea, I couldn't have said it better myself."

Marjorie squinted up at the new arrival. "Miss Bridgewater—"

"Call me Ella!"

"Ella, we hear you live on Dorchester Island." Marion, like the natives, pronounced it *Dorster.* "Lovely over there, quite remote."

"Remote isn't the word for it! I drive ten miles from my little coop by the sea, go over the causeway, come down Highway 20 for fifteen miles, take the bridge to Whitecap, and drive to St. John's at the north end. It's a trek and a half."

"And we thank you for doing it!" said Marjorie. "You nearly took the roof off Sunday. It's been ages since we heard our old organ give forth such a noise!"

"*A joyful noise,*" said their priest, wanting no misunderstanding.

—⊙—

"Do come to Dorchester, Father, and bring Cynthia. I'd like nothing better than to behold your faces at my door!"

For the first time, he noticed Ella's gold brooch—it was in the shape of a hot-air balloon.

"We'd like that. We haven't seen much of the area since we came."

"I know how busy your schedule must be with the summer people to shoehorn in, so just pop up whenever—except, of course, Wednesday, that's when I get my hair washed down at Edna's. Louise and I would love seeing you."

"Louise?"

"Louise is my canary. You should hear her sing, Father, you won't believe your ears!"

"I'm sure!"

"Louise is full of years, as they say in the Old Testament. But the older she gets, the sweeter her voice."

"Aha."

"I'll show you around little Dorchester, it's like going back in time. You'll see the oldest live oak on any of these islands, it's right by my house, and we'll visit Christ Chapel, it's hardly big enough to hold the three of us, it has the most glorious rose window above the altar! Then we'll walk over to the graveyard where Mother is resting. Did I tell you how we buried Mother?"

"I don't believe so."

"Holding the 1928 prayer book clasped to her heart."

"A fine way to go."

"You must come for lunch!" Ella's rouge spots appeared to brighten. "Are you fond of sea bass?"

"Fond is an understatement. One of my great favorites!"

"Miss Child taught me how to poach sea bass on TV. I miss Miss Child, don't you? I loved the way she dropped things on the floor and picked them up and went right on, a good lesson for us all, I think!"

"Indeed!"

Sam Fieldwalker joined them as St. John's organist drew herself up to her full height, which was impressive. "I'm a good hand at plum wine, into the bargain!"

He chuckled. "Yet another incentive to visit. Sam, Ella's asked us to Dorchester."

"Oh, my gracious, we love Dorchester. They do a good bit of fishing business up there. It's nice and quiet, without the tourism we get on Whitecap."

"I think you'll like my little house, Father, it's quite historic. Built in 1902 of timbers that washed up from shipwrecks. I like to say I live in a house that once sailed the sea!"

"When you go over to Miss Bridgewater's," Sam suggested, "that could be a good time to visit Cap'n Larkin. He's the old fellow I told you about who was a longtime member at St. John's. He lives with his twin brother now, on Dorchester."

"Their house is just a skip and a jump from mine," said Ella. "They keep an old pickup truck parked at the front door, that's where their dog sleeps."

"You could take him communion," said Sam. "That

would thrill him. Father Morgan never . . . got around to doing that."

"Consider it done! Of course, if we come anytime soon, Ella, you may have to entertain a three-year-old, as well. How would that be?"

Ella eyed Jonathan clattering across the porch tailed by two self-appointed Youth Group babysitters.

"I have a little garden plot fenced with pickets," she said. "We could stake him out there!"

⬦

He saw a group gathered to the right of the porch and walked over to see what was what. Cynthia stood by a lacecap hydrangea, holding Jonathan on her hip and peering into a variety of cameras. "Smile, Jonathan!" she urged.

"I declare," Jean Ballenger said, "that child looks enough like your wife to be her own! Do you see the resemblance?"

He did, actually. Two pairs of cornflower eyes. Two winning smiles. Two heads the color of ripe corn.

"I hope Janette can come home soon."

"It's going to be a while yet. It's . . . a hard thing." It hurt him to think about it. He could scarcely bear to witness deep depression; he had seen it in his father for years.

"Step over there," said Sam Fieldwalker, "and let's get one of you, too!"

Cynthia put her hand over her eyes and squinted in his direction. "Yes, dear, come and let them record your tan."

He hated photos of himself; in a picture in the new church album, he looked as if he'd been dug up by the roots.

Sheepishly, he put his arm around his wife, adjusted his glasses, and peered at the cameras.

"You better smile!" crowed Jonathan.

❦

"First to come, last to go!" Otis Bragg shook his host's hand with vigor. "Look here, they cleaned us out."

Father Tim peered into the depths of the empty shrimp basket. "A grand contribution, Otis. Thank you again and again."

"My pleasure!" he said. "Good to see th' parish turnin' out like this. It's what makes us family."

"I agree. Come back anytime, you and Marlene."

Like the rest of the common horde, his landlord and parishioner definitely had some traits that were unlikable. Yet he was growing to appreciate Otis; he had the odd feeling that if the chips were ever down, he could count on Otis Bragg.

"We ought to go on a little run with Cap'n Willie one of these days." Otis took the cigar from his mouth and eyed it fondly. "You do any fishin'?"

"I hardly know a hook from a sinker, but my good wife has bought me a chair on Captain Willie's boat, and looks like I'll be forced to go before it's over."

Otis pounded him on the back. "Do you good! Clergy has a tendency to think too much, you need a little fun in your life. Nothin' like a good, hard fight with a blue marlin to get a man's blood up!" Otis pounded him again. "Give me a call when you set a date, I'll try to go out with you."

"Well . . . ," he said, not knowing what else to say.

"I'll bring us a bucket of chicken," declared Otis, spitting shreds of Cuban tobacco into the border of cosmos.

⤳

While he took a cleanup shift in the kitchen, Cynthia carried Jonathan, now overtired and overwrought, through the house and out to the back stoop.

"Mommy! I want my mommy!" he sobbed.

Father Tim stood at the kitchen window and watched them approach the bird feeder in the backyard, his wife struggling to console and distract the weeping boy.

"I want Babette an' Jason!"

"There, Jonathan, it's all right. You'll see Mommy soon, and Babette and Jason, too, I promise. Oh, look at the bird on the fence, I wonder what it is. . . ."

He watched her holding the boy close, patting his back, and saw him lay his head on her shoulder. When she turned to look toward the house, he could see tears in her eyes, as well. His wife had a natural gift for "rejoicing with them that do rejoice and weeping with them that weep," as St. Paul commanded the Romans to do.

He lifted his hand and waved awkwardly as they passed from view.

Cynthia was growing attached to the boy, no doubt about it. She'd never been able to have children of her own; in fact, her former husband had spent most of his time, she said, "making babies with other women." The barrenness had been a deep hurt to her, a thorn.

He finished washing up as Cynthia carried Jonathan once more around the route they usually traveled when the boy was crying for family. He heard her murmuring softly to him, crooning bits of stories and songs.

This was torture for all alike, he thought, as Cynthia trudged up the porch steps, looking weary. Surely next week Babette and Jason would be back from visiting another set of family in Beaufort, and they could borrow them for an afternoon. . . .

He stood at the door as Cynthia eased the boy onto his bed and Barnabas leaped up and lay at his feet.

He watched her smooth Jonathan's damp blond hair from his forehead, and saw the infinite tenderness in her eyes.

"What a good boy," she whispered. Then she turned and patted Barnabas.

"And what a good dog!" she said.

Feeling an unexpected weariness of his own, he sat by the phone in the study and dialed Emma's number. "Found anything?"

"Oh, law, there's hundreds, maybe *thousands* of Ed Sikeses out there, it's like lookin' for Bob Jones or John Smith! There's two Ed Sikeses right over in Wesley, one Edmund an' one Edward, but Harold knows 'em both and says they couldn't possibly have run off with anybody's kid, one's a deacon at First Presbyterian and th' other one goes frog giggin' with Harold's brother.

"Plus, you don't even want to *know* how many different names Ed stands for."

"How many?"

"I looked it up on th' Internet and found thirteen— Edison, Eddrick, Edgar, Edwin, Eduardo, to name only a few. You know you can find anything you're lookin' for on th' Internet, you ought to be on th' Internet, it would help with your sermons, it seems like preachin' Sunday after Sunday, you'd be *desperately* lookin' for new material. . . ."

Emma Newland had been into the Little Debbies again, he knew sugar-induced hysteria when he heard it.

"So . . . ," he said, seeking an escape.

"So you'll have to come up with another gimmick this time," she announced.

He called Pauline.

"I forgot to tell you somethin'," she said. "He was from Oregon, or he maybe was goin' to Oregon."

"Excellent! Wonderful!"

"Father . . ."

"Yes?"

"I've been . . . I'm really scared about somethin'."

"What scares you?"

"Well . . . you see, I don't feel like I deserve . . . all this."

"All this what?"

She took a deep breath. "This . . . happiness. It don't seem right for me to have it."

"Grace isn't about deserving, Pauline. We can't earn God's grace, there's no way on earth we can earn it. Grace is free, and I believe as sure as I am sitting here that He brought the two of you together. Do you love Buck?"

"More'n anything. Just . . . more'n I can say. He's so good to me and th' children, he's . . . nobody sees it, but he's tenderhearted, you know."

"I know."

"I just pray everything's going to be all right. I've told the Lord I'll work real hard."

"You'll need to," he said. Why not speak the truth?

"Thank you, Father. It always helps when we talk. I feel better."

"Can you think of anything else? Anything else about Ed Sikes?"

"I've been prayin' to think of somethin' else, but there's only one other thing I remember. . . ."

"Yes?" He sat forward in the chair.

"He was losin' his hair in front."

Who isn't? he thought.

He rang Emma again.

"Oregon," he said. "Look up Ed Sikes in Oregon. We may be on to something."

"You should get your church to set you up on the Internet," she said, sounding grumpy. "Especially since they don't give you a secretary, it seems they could at least—"

"Emma, remember how you helped find Jessie? If it hadn't been for you, Dooley's little sister might still be missing."

"That's true!" she said, sounding brighter. "All right, I'll get to it soon as Harold and I go to Atlanta, we're goin' to borrow Avis Packard's RV, you know he never uses it, it just sits in his driveway losin' air in th' tires because he works all the time, he's th' only man I know who's more interested in rump roast than women.

"You and Cynthia ought to get an RV, it would do you good to throw your cares to the wind, after all, you *are* retired. When Harold retires from th' post office, we're goin' to do as we please and not kowtow to another living soul, he's got six years to go, then we might hit Hawaii or Alaska, maybe even Dollywood, have you ever listened to her sing, I mean really *listened?* She is very talented, I know you like Bach and Mozart, but you could at least *try* tunin' in to the real world once in a while, you have no idea what you might be missin'. . . ."

Roughly speaking, he figured the sugar content in a box of Little Debbie fudge rounds possessed the power to jolt the human system for a full eight hours, minimum.

❧

Why the angel?

He was beyond trying to figure out who had entered the yellow house, and wondered only why they would have taken the angel and nothing more.

If he'd been the thief, he would have stolen the books. Books, however, didn't seem to be a popular item with thieves. They liked silver, TV sets, and jewelry, yet none of those items had been touched.

Boggling. Each time he thought about it, he felt as if someone had removed the top of his head and poured in cooked oatmeal.

No word from Rodney, but he didn't want to call and stir that pot any more than he had already.

He looked at his watch. Six-fifteen, and the sun was setting. He didn't feel like running—maybe a long walk with Barnabas instead. If they'd held on to one of the babysitters, he might have talked his wife into coming along. . . .

He trotted down the steps in shorts and a golf shirt, amazed how all evidence of the merriment had vanished, that a lovely moment in the lives of forty-two people had become history—with scarcely a mark in the garden from the folding chairs.

He latched the gate behind him and hunkered into an easy lope, with Barnabas on the red leash. Maybe a trek past Ernie's, hang a left this side of St. John's, another left at the little gray house, and circle back by Morris Love's front gate.

Seventy, indeed, he thought, huffing up the lane.

❧

They were circling toward home when the fattest, sleekest squirrel he'd seen on Whitecap made a dash across the road. The leash was fairly torn from his hand as Barnabas leaped after the creature, leash flying.

"Barnabas!"

His dog was doing sixty miles an hour and barking like thunder as he raced toward Morris Love's rusted iron gate, and, in a flash, slithered under it.

"Barnabas! *Come!*"

Deaf as a doorknob, like any dog chasing a squirrel . . .

He huffed to the gate and examined it. Locked. Not to mention rusted. "Barnabas! Come *now!*"

He wiped the sweat from his eyes and saw his dog disappear into a thicket—no, a kind of loggia to the left of the house, which was barely visible through the trees. The furious barking continued unabated.

He whistled loudly. Dadgummit, his wife was a better whistler than he was. She could shake green apples from the tree.

More barking. More whistling.

What if Barnabas crossed the Love property, went under the fence on the other side, and into the street? He didn't keep his dog on a leash at all times for no good reason. Hadn't Barnabas been stolen by the vilest drug-dealing Creek scum, and kept staked and half starved for weeks on end?

Grasping the top of the wall with his hands, he gained a foothold against the rough surface and managed to heave himself up and over, landing beside the overgrown driveway with a thud.

He stood for a moment, still winded, and looked around.

He had entered another world.

Though he was mere inches beyond the gate, a few feet from the street, and only yards from Dove Cottage—he was no longer in Whitecap.

———◉———

It was a jungle in here, literally.

The grounds had the density of a rain forest, with trees and vegetation he'd never seen before, save for one enormous live oak, damaged by an old storm. He wouldn't be surprised to hear monkeys and macaws, the trumpet call of an elephant. . . .

He stood still, as if frozen to the spot. Cool in here, and quiet, strangely quiet. He heard his own hard breathing, and remembered his maverick dog.

"Barnabas!"

In reply, there was crashing through the underbrush to his left, and a revived fit of barking.

"Come! Come, old fella!"

Barnabas bolted into the driveway through a vine-entangled hedge, gave him an odd look, then turned and raced toward the house.

He ran, too, pounding along the weed-grown driveway, until the house came fully into view.

Spanish. Stucco. Tile roof. Moss growing in wide, lush patches on the walls of the loggia or portico; vines covering half the house; the smooth, worn roots of a huge tree gnarling up through a stone semicircle at the front door.

He looked at the windows, which returned only a blank and curtainless stare.

"Barnabas!" he hissed.

Dadgummit, there he came around the right side of the house, galloping like a horse after yet another squirrel, which was fleeing for its life through yet another iron gate on some kind of outbuilding that was nearly obscured by undergrowth.

Enough was enough, by heaven. The party was over.

He dashed after his dog as the squirrel ran through the partially open gate, and Barnabas followed, his long hair catching on the rusted iron and slamming the gate behind him.

As it clanged shut, Father Tim stood for a moment, swallowing down his anger.

It was some kind of ancient, stuccoed enclosure, an old dog run, perhaps, grown up with straggling shrubs and weeds. The squirrel was over the rear wall and gone from sight, leaving Barnabas stranded at the end of the run, barking with impotent fury.

Father Tim jiggled the gate, which appeared to have locked. He'd never seen such an odd contrivance to latch a gate; the rust didn't make it work any better, either. Blast! He hit the thing with the palm of his hand, smarting the flesh and drawing blood.

He could fairly throttle his dog, who now turned toward him with a look of sheepish regret. "Come," he said through clenched teeth.

Barnabas, clearly on the downside of his adrenaline rush, walked slowly toward the gate, head down.

His master punched the gate again, repeated the favorite expletive of his school buddy, Tommy Noles, then gave the blasted thing a stiff kick for good measure.

"Out!"

He heard the bellow as if it were projected on a loudspeaker.

"Out!"

His skin prickled. "Mr. Love," he shouted into thin air, "my dog is locked in your run, and I don't have a clue how to get him . . . *out.*"

"You're a fool to let him *in*," growled Morris Love.

Father Tim looked to an upstairs window where he thought the voice originated, but saw no one.

"I didn't let him in. He ran in on his own, chasing a squirrel!" He was fairly trembling with the frustration of this escapade, and suddenly angry at the man who refused to show himself, much less proffer a grain of human hospitality.

"Take the pin out," Morris Love yelled.

He slid the pin out. Whoever put this thing together ought to have his head examined. . . .

"Turn the latch to the right!"

He cranked it to the right. Nothing. Dead. Not to mention that something was eating his legs alive.

He was furious. He felt as if he could dismantle the gate with his bare hands, like Samson, and pitch it into the weeds. His blood pressure was probably halfway to the moon.

"It doesn't work!" he shouted, slapping at his bitten legs.

"It works, Father, it has always worked. *Don't push it when you turn it to the right!*"

Morris Love could wake the dead with that huge bellow, as if he were speaking through the pipes of his organ. Father Tim tried again, without pushing. The gate opened as easily as if it had just rolled off the assembly line.

He breathed a sigh of relief and wiped his forehead with the tail of his T-shirt. Blast, what a commotion.

His dog's tail was between his legs as they marched toward the house.

"Thank you!" he shouted to the open upstairs window. "We'll try not to trouble you again." Silence.

As they swung left into the driveway, he gave one of the gnarled roots an impatient kick.

"Goodbye and good riddance," he muttered under his breath.

❧

Now the duck possessed a portion of its other wing.

He handled it carefully, admiring the lifelike beauty of the emerging creature.

"Do you . . . sell these?" he asked Roger.

"Oh, yes. I haven't kept one for myself in a good while."

"What kind of money do they go for?" Four, maybe five hundred, he thought, and well worth it!

Rogers brown eyes sparkled, as they often did when he spoke of his craft. "I'll probably ask around fifteen hundred for this one."

With what he hoped wasn't obvious haste, he handed it back to Roger.

Ernie thumped into a chair at their table. "Junior's been turned down flat," he said, looking crestfallen.

"How? Who?"

"Ava. She won't go out with 'im, won't even let 'im meet 'er daddy."

"I hate to hear it."

"If you ask me," said Ernie, "it was those pictures that did 'im in. Junior's better lookin' than those pictures."

Roanoke took a cigarette from behind his ear. "His fish done wiggled off th' hook."

Ernie sighed. "We could take 'em again with a better camera. I could get one from th' *Whitecap Reader,* I think they use Nikes."

"Nikons," said Roger, not looking up from his work.

"He ought to start over an' run another ad," said Roanoke. "Leave out th' Bronco business, leave out th' Scrabble business, keep in th' fishin' part, axe th' stuff about a serious relationship—"

"He don't want to run another ad," said Ernie. "He don't want to start over, he wants to meet Ava."

"What did he say in his letter to her? Maybe that's the key."

"Beats me. I tried to tell him what to say, but who knows?" Ernie shrugged, looking disconsolate.

For a while, the only sound was Roger's knife against the tupelo wood.

❧

He threw his cup in the wastebasket by the Pepsi machine and fished around in his shorts pocket for fifty-cents, which he gave Ernie for the *Reader*.

Roanoke had pedaled away on his bicycle, Roger was walking Lucas, and Father Tim figured this was as good a chance as he'd get.

"Ernie," he said, "tell me everything you know about Morris Love."

CHAPTER THIRTEEN

Mighty Waters

He was awake ten minutes before the alarm went off, and heard at once the light patter of rain through the open window.

"Timothy?"

"Yes?"

"Is it four o'clock?"

"Ten 'til. Go back to sleep."

"You'll have a great time, I just know you will."

"I'm sure of it. And remember—don't cook dinner. I'm bringing it home."

"Right, darling. I'm excited. . . ."

She was no such thing; she was already snoring again. He kissed her shoulder and crept out of bed.

He was accustomed to rising early, but four o'clock was ridiculous, not to mention he couldn't get pumped up for this jaunt no matter how hard he tried.

He'd entertained every fishing yarn anyone cared to tell, trying to mask his blank stare with a look of genuine interest. Ah, well, surely the whole business would pleasantly surprise him—he'd return home with a

cooler full of tuna, tanned and vigorous from a day on
the water, whistling a sea chantey.

Chances were—and this was not a perk to be taken
lightly—it could even blow a fresh breeze through his
preaching, not to mention make him feel more one-in-
spirit with his parish. After all, he'd been on their turf for
three months and practically the only thing he'd done
that he couldn't have done in Mitford was slap a few
mosquitoes and pick sandspurs from his dog's paws.

He dressed hurriedly in the bathroom, brushed his
teeth, splashed water on his face, and raced to the
kitchen to gulp down a cup of coffee he'd set in the refrigerator last night, figuring cold caffeine to be better
than no caffeine at all.

He packed the canvas bag with his lunch, having entirely dismissed the notion of fried chicken. Where on
earth anybody would find fried chicken at four in the
morning was beyond him. He stuffed in plenty of bottled water and a couple of citrus drinks. No time to eat,
he'd do that on the boat, he was out of here.

His dog followed him along the hall, thumped down
by the front door, and yawned mightily. "Guard the
house, old fellow."

Dark as pitch. He turned the lock, shut the door behind him, and patted his jacket pockets for the rolled-up
canvas hat and bottle of sunscreen. All there.

He stood on the porch and drew in a deep draught of
the cool morning air; it was scented with rain and salt,
with something mysteriously beyond his ken. He didn't
think he'd ever again take the ocean for granted. He
daily sensed the power and presence of it in this new
world in which they were living.

All those years ago when he was a young clergyman
in a little coastal parish, the water had meant nothing to

him; it had hardly entered his mind. He might have lived in the Midwest for all the interest he took in the things of the sea, except for the several bushels of shrimp and clams he'd surely consumed during his curacy. His mind, his heart had been elsewhere, in the clouds, perhaps; but now it was different. Though he wasn't one for swimming in the ocean or broiling on the beach, he was making a connection this time, something he couldn't quite articulate and why bother, anyway?

The light rain cooled his head as he trotted down the front steps, opened the gate, and got into the Mustang parked by the street.

Goin' fishin'! he thought as he buckled the seat belt. The way he'd worried about this excursion had made it seem like a trek to Outer Mongolia, but so far, so good. And just think—there were thousands, probably millions of people out there who'd give anything to be in his shoes.

It was still dark when he found the marina where the charter boats were tied to the dock like horses waiting to be saddled.

He pulled into the nearly full parking lot, took his gear from the trunk and locked up, then stood by the Mustang, peering into the murky light. People were huffing coolers as big as coffins out of vans and cars, muttering, calling to each other, laughing, slamming doors.

More than once, he'd heard charter boats called party boats, and fervently hoped this was not one of those deals.

Raining a little harder now, but nothing serious. He wiped his head with his hat and put it back in his pocket, checking his watch. Five o'clock sharp.

He hefted the cooler and started walking, looking for *Blue Heaven* and trying to get over the feeling he was still asleep and this was a dream.

Someone materialized out of the gray mist, smelling intensely of tobacco and shaving lotion.

"Mornin', Father! Let's go fishin'!"

"Otis? Is that you?"

"Cap'n Willie told me you were on board today. I didn't want you goin' off by yourself and havin' too much fun."

Otis was schlepping a cooler with a fluorescent label that was readable even in the predawn light: *Bragg's for All Your Cement Needs.*

A bronzed, bearded Captain Willie stood on the deck wearing shorts and a T-shirt, booming out a welcome.

"Father Timothy! Good mornin' to you, we're glad to have you!" He found himself shaking a hand as big as a ham and hard as a rock. "Step over lightly, now, let me take that, there you go, welcome to *Blue Heaven.*"

"Good morning, Captain. How's the weather looking?" It seemed the boat was lurching around in the water pretty good, and they hadn't even gone anywhere yet.

"Goin' to fair off and be good fishin'." Captain Willie's genial smile displayed a couple of gold teeth. "Meet my first mate, Pete Brady."

He shook hands with a muscular fellow of about thirty. "Good to see you, Pete."

"Yessir, welcome aboard."

"This your first time?" asked the captain.

"First ever."

"Well, you're fishin' with a pro, here." He pounded Otis on the back. "Go on in th' cabin, set your stuff down, make yourself at home. And Father . . ."

"Yes?"

"Would you favor us with blessin' th' fleet this mornin'?"

"Ah . . . how does that work, exactly?"

"All th' boats'll head out about th' same time, then after the sun rises, you'll come up to th' bridge an' ask th' Lord for safe passage and good fishin'. Th' other boats can hear you over th' radio."

"Consider it done!" he said, feeling a surge of excitement.

"We'll have prayer requests for you, like, the last few days, we've all been prayin' for Cap'n Tucker's daughter, she's got leukemia."

"I'm sorry. I'd feel honored and blessed to do it."

"We thank you. Now go in there and introduce yourselves around, get comfortable."

Father Tim stuck his head in the cabin.

Ernie Fulcher, sitting with a green cooler between his feet, threw up his hand and grinned from ear to ear. "Didn't want you runnin' out th' first time all by your lonesome."

"Right," said Roger, looking shy about butting in. "We didn't think you'd mind a little company."

⊶

Madge Parrott and her friend Sybil Huffman appeared to be dressed for a cruise in the Bahamas. They were clearly proud to announce they were from Rome, Georgia, and this was their first time on a fishing charter. They were out for marlin, would settle for tuna if necessary, but no dolphin, thank you, they'd heard dolphins could sing and had feelings like people.

Both were widows whose husbands had been great fishermen. This trip was about making a connection with the departed, as they'd heard Chuck and Roy talk about deep-sea fishing like it was the best thing since sliced bread. Madge confessed that even though she and Sybil didn't drink beer, they didn't see why they couldn't catch fish like anybody else.

He noted that the group shared a need to explain what they had in their coolers, some even lifting the lids and displaying the contents, and issuing hearty invitations to dip in, at any time, to whatever they'd brought along.

"You run out of drinks, me'n Roger got all you want right here," said Ernie, patting a cooler as big as a Buick. "Got Sun-drop, Mello Yello, Sprite, just help yourself."

"And there's ham and turkey on rye," said Roger. "I made two extra, just in case, plus fried chicken."

Everybody nodded their thanks, as the engines began to throb and hum. Father Tim was mum about the contents of his own cooler—two banana sandwiches on white bread with low-fat mayo.

"Y'all need any sunscreen," said Madge, "we're loaded with sunscreen. It's right here in my jacket pocket." She indicated a blue jacket folded on the seat, so that one and all might note its whereabouts in an emergency.

"And I've got Bonine," said Sybil, "if anybody feels seasick." She held up her package and rattled the contents.

"Have you ever been seasick?" Madge asked Father Tim.

"Never!" he said. Truth was, he'd never been on the sea but a couple of times, and always in sight of shore, so there was no way he could have been seasick. And for today, he'd done what Ernie and Roger so heartily recommended—he'd stayed sober, gotten a good night's sleep, and didn't eat a greasy breakfast.

"Only twelve percent of people get seasick," Roger said, quoting his most encouraging piece of information on the subject.

Ernie lifted the lid of his cooler. "Oh, an' anybody wants Snickers bars, they're right here on top of th' ice. There's nothin' like a Snickers iced down good'n cold."

Madge and Sybil admitted they'd never heard of icing down a Snickers bar, but thought it would be real tasty, especially on a hot day. Sybil pledged to try one before the trip was over.

Otis announced that anybody who wanted to help themselves to his Kentucky Fried, they knew where it was at. He also had cigars, Johnnie Walker Black, and boiled peanuts, for whoever took a notion.

It was the most instant formation of community Father Tim had ever witnessed. He felt momentarily inspired to stand and lead a hymn.

Captain Willie gunned the engines, and the stern of *Blue Heaven* dug low into the water as they moved away from the dock at what seemed like full speed. Father Tim realized he didn't know how he felt about riding backward, not to mention that the water seemed mighty rough.

Very dadgum blasted rough, he thought as they plowed farther out in an unceasing rain. He looked around the hull of the small cabin, where everyone appeared totally sophisticated about being tossed around like dice in a cup. They were all holding on for dear life to whatever they could grab, and yelling over the roar of eight hundred and fifty horses running wide open.

Otis Bragg was clearly tickled pink to have two women on board who didn't know fishing from frog's legs. He'd already begun a seminar on how to keep your thumb on the fishing line, how to hold the rod, how to hold your mouth, and how to position your feet when reeling in a big one. Father Tim listened as attentively as he could, then finally slumped against the back of the padded bench and peered through the door of the cabin.

Out there, it was rain, churning waters, and diesel smoke. In here, it was earsplitting racket and the worst ride he'd had since Tommy Noles had shoved him down a rocky hillside in a red wagon without a tongue.

⟨⟩

The sun was emerging from the water, staining the silver sea with patches of light and color.

Pete Brady came into the cabin, holding a dripping ballyhoo in one hand. "You'll want to go up to the bridge now, sir. Better put your jacket on."

"Right!" he said. He was glad to leave the cabin; only a moment ago, he'd had the odd sensation of smothering. . . .

He stood, holding on to the table that was bolted to the deck, then made his way to the door, praying he wouldn't pitch into Madge Parrott's lap.

"You tell th' Lord we're wantin' 'em to weigh fifty pounds and up, if He don't mind." Otis chewed his cigar and grinned.

Father Tim clung to the doorjamb. "How do I get to the bridge?" he asked Pete.

The first mate, who appeared to be squeezing the guts from a bait fish, jerked his thumb toward the side of the cabin. "Right up the ladder there."

He peered around and saw the ladder. The rungs were immediately over the water, and went straight up. Three, four, five . . .

"*That* ladder?"

"Yessir, be sure'n hold on tight."

He peered into the black and churning sea, and made a couple of quick steps to a chair that was bolted to the cockpit deck. Pete was bustling around without any difficulty in keeping his footing, but Father Tim had the certain feeling that if he let go of the chair, he'd end up at the Currituck Light.

He turned and lunged for the bottom rung of the ladder, but miscalculated and bounced onto the rail. Too startled to grab hold, he reeled against the cabin wall, finally managing to grip the lower rung. Thanks be to God, Pete was baiting a hook and facing seaward, and his cabin mates were oblivious to his afflictions.

Lord Jesus, I've never done this before. You were plenty good around water, and I'm counting on You to help me accomplish this thing.

He reached to an upper rung and got a firm grip.

The spray was flying, the waves were churning, the sun was rising . . . it was now or never. He swung himself onto the ladder and went up, trying in vain to curl his tennis shoes around the rungs like buns around frankfurters.

He hauled himself to the bridge, grabbed the support rail for the hard top, and stood for a moment, awed. The view from the bridge literally took his breath away.

How could anyone doubt the living truth of what the psalmist said? *"The heavens declare the glory of God, the skies proclaim the work of his hands!"* He wanted to shout in unabashed praise.

His shirt whipped against his body like a flag; his knees trembled. This boat was flying, no two ways about it, and beneath their feet, the endless, racking, turbulent sea, and a sunrise advancing up the sky like tongues of fire.

Surely this was the habitation of angels, and life in the cabin a thing to be pitied.

He lurched to the helm, where Captain Willie was holding a microphone, and grabbed the back of the helm chair.

"We're glad to have you with us, Father! Greetings to you from th' whole fleet on this beautiful September day!"

His stomach did an odd turn as he opened his mouth to speak, so he closed it again.

The captain winked. "Got a little chop this mornin'."

He nodded.

"A real sharp head sea."

He felt sweat on his brow as the captain spoke into the microphone.

"We're mighty happy to have Father Tim Kavanagh to lead us in prayer this mornin'. He's from over at Whitecap, where Toby Rider has his boat shop. Anybody with a prayer request, let's hear it now."

The VHF blared. "Father, my little boy fell off a ladder on Sunday, he's, ah, in the hospital, looks like he's goin' to be fine, but . . . his name's Danny. We thank you."

"Please pray for Romaine, he had his leg tore up by a tractor fell on 'im. Thank you."

"Just like to ask for . . . forgiveness for somethin' I done, there's no use to go into what, I'd appreciate it."

Several other requests came in as he bent his head and listened intently, gripping the helm chair for all he was worth.

"That it? Anybody else?"

He fished in his pocket for his hat. Though the rain had stopped, he put it on and pulled it down snugly above his ears. Then he took the microphone, surprised that it felt as heavy as a lug wrench.

"We'd like to pray for th' owner of th' marina and his wife, Angie, too," said Captain Willie. "She's got breast cancer. And Cap'n Tucker's daughter, we don't want to forget her, name's Sarah, then there's Toby Rider, lost his daddy and we feel real bad about it. Course we'd like to ask God's mercy for every family back home and every soul on board. . . ."

Captain Willie turned to the helm, grabbed the red knob, and cranked the engines back to idle.

In the sudden quiet, the waves slammed against the hull, dulling the gurgling sound of the exhaust. They seemed to be wallowing now in the choppy sea; they might have been so much laundry tossing in a washing machine.

His heart was hammering as if he'd run a race. But it wasn't his heart, exactly, that bothered him, it was his stomach. It seemed strangely disoriented, as if it had moved to a new location and he couldn't figure out where.

"Our Father, we thank You mightily for the beauty of the sunrise over this vast sea, and for the awe and wonder in all the gifts of Your creation. We ask Your generous blessings upon every captain and mate aboard every vessel in this fleet, and pray that each of us be made able, by Your grace, to know Your guidance, love, and mercy throughout the day . . ."

The names of the people, and their needs, what were they? His mind seemed desperately blank, as if every shred of thought and reason had been blown away like chaff on the wind.

Lord! Help!

"For Sarah, we ask Your tender mercies, that You would keep her daily in Your healing care, giving wisdom to those attending her, and providing strength and encouragement. . . ."

More than three decades of intercessory prayer experience notwithstanding, he found it miraculous that the names came to him, one by one. He leaned into the prayer with intensity, feeling something of the genuine weight and burden, the urgency, of the needs for which he prayed.

He wiped the sweat from his forehead. "Oh, Lord, who maketh a way in the sea, and a path in the mighty waters, we thank You for hearing our prayers, in the blessed name of Your Son, our Savior, Jesus Christ. Amen."

The captain took the microphone and keyed it, thanking him.

He noted what appeared to be a look of compassion on the captain's face as they shook hands.

"*Blue Heaven, Salty Dog,* come back."

"*Blue Heaven,* go ahead, *Salty Dog.*"

"Just want to say we really appreciate Father Kavanagh's prayers, and sure hope he doesn't succumb to the torments of a rough sea. OK, *Salty Dog* back to eighty."

"*Blue Heaven* standin' by on eighty."

As the captain gunned the engines, Father Tim careened to the rail and leaned over.

The goodwill and fond hope of *Salty Dog* had come too late.

Twice over the rail should nip this thing in the bud. Already his ribs hurt from the retching; it was probably over now and he could go down the ladder and have something to drink, maybe even a bite to eat—that was the problem, going out on rough seas with an empty stomach. . . .

He was amazed at his agility on the ladder, as if by the earlier practice shot he'd become a seasoned sailor. No big deal, he thought, looking down at the waves hammering the boat.

Good grief! He scrambled off the ladder and leaned over the rail, the bile spewing in a flume from his very core, hot, bitter, and fathomless.

$$\backsim$$

It was his head. He seemed to have lost his head the last time over the rail. He reached up feebly and felt around. No, it was his hat he'd lost. It had slithered off and dropped into the sea, and his scalp was parching like a Georgia peanut.

"Let 'im set there, we ain't findin' any fish," he heard Otis say. He opened his eyes and realized he was sitting in the privileged fighting chair. The fighting chair. What a joke.

"Hat," he said. "Hat."

Nobody heard him, because he found he couldn't speak above a whisper. He had no energy to force audible words through cracked lips.

Fine. He'd just sit here until they dumped him overboard, which he wished they'd do sooner rather than later. He'd never known such suffering in his life, not from mayonnaise that had nearly taken him out at a parish picnic, not from the diabetic coma brought on by Esther Bolick's orange marmalade cake, not from the raging fever he had as a child when he saw his mother as a circus performer who made lions jump through hoops.

"What I don't like about th' Baptists," Otis was saying, "is they won't speak to you at th' liquor store."

Laughing, shuffling around, general merriment—

people living their lives as if he weren't there, as if he were invisible, a bump on a log.

"That's th' way it is, some days," said Pete. "You're either a hero or a zero. Yesterday, we were haulin' 'em in faster than I could bait th' hooks; today, I don't know where they are."

"You got to pump 'em," said Ernie. "Like, say you're reelin' in a fifty-pound tuna, you got to raise the rod up real slow, then drop down quick and *crank*."

Conversations came and went; it was all a kind of hive hum, he thought, as when bees returned from working a stand of sourwoods.

"Now, you take tarpon," said Otis. "I was down in th' Keys where they grow too big to mount on your wall. Tarpon you just jump a few times and then break 'em off before you wear 'em out, you wear 'em out too bad, th' sharks eat 'em."

"I never fished any tarpon," said Ernie.

He opened his eyes and shut them fast. Pete was showing Madge and Sybil how he prepped the bait.

"See, you pop th' eyes out like this . . . then you break up th' backbone . . ."

"Ooooh," said Madge.

"Don't make 'er faint," said Otis.

"I have no intention of fainting, thank you!"

"Then you squeeze their guts out, see. . . ."

"Lord help," said Sybil.

"Thing is, th' more they wiggle in th' water, th' better they catch."

"Clever!" said Madge. "That is *really* clever."

Without realizing how he got there, he was at the rail again, on his knees.

"On his knees at th' rail," said Madge. "That is very Episcopalian."

"Or Luth'ran," said Sybil. "Can't that be Luth'ran?"

He didn't know who it was, maybe Otis or Ernie, but someone held his head while he spewed up his insides and watched the vomitus carried away on the lashing water.

"We been out every day for forty-one days straight," said Pete, who was currently varying the bait, trying anything.

"Sometimes you just pray for a nor'easter so you can get a break, but if th' weather's good, you have to go."

The weather today is not *good,* he tried to say, but couldn't. Why in blazes did we go today if you don't go when the weather's not good? *Answer that!* Plus, *plus* . . . he wished he could discuss this with Roger . . . his math told him that, discounting the crew, he represented more than any twelve blasted percent.

He declined the fighting chair in case anyone got a strike, and sat feebly in an adjacent chair.

"What do you think the winds are right now?" asked Roger.

"Oh, fifteen, sixteen miles an hour. This ain't nothin'. I know somebody was out all night last night in forty-mile winds."

General, respectful silence. Diesel fumes.

"We need to think positive," said Madge. "Smoked loin of tuna! That's how *I'm* thinkin'!"

"Must be lunchtime," said Otis. "Believe I'll have me a little shooter. Want one?"

"Maybe later."

"Thank you, you go on, but I wouldn't mind shuckin' a few peanuts with you."

He was baking, he was broiling, he was frying, he

was cooked. Sunscreen. He remembered the sunscreen in his jacket pocket, but he wasn't wearing his jacket. Someone had helped him remove it earlier.

"Look," said Sybil. "Th' poor man needs something."

"What?" said Madge. "Oh, mercy, look at his head, it's red as a poker. Where's his hat?"

"He went to the rail and came back without it."

"Here you go," Otis was patting sunscreen on his head and followed it with a hat.

"Bless you," he managed to whisper.

"What'd he say?"

"He said bless me." He thought Otis sounded touched. "Father, you want some water or Coke? Coke might be good."

"Nossir," said Ernie, "what he needs is ginger ale. Anybody got ginger ale?"

"Fruit juice," said Madge, "that's what I'd give somebody with upset stomach."

"No deal with th' fruit juice," said Pete. "Too much acid."

"How about a piece of ice to just hold in his mouth?"

"I don't know about that. They say when you're real hot you shouldn't swallow somethin' real cold, it can give you a heart attack or maybe a stroke."

"He's moving his lips. What's he saying?"

Otis leaned down and listened. "He's praying," said Otis.

❧

They had veered east, then south, but weren't finding any fish. Neither was the rest of the fleet. Occasionally a boat would get a couple of strikes, radio the news, and everybody would head in that direction. But so far,

Blue Heaven had taken only two dolphins, and thrown back a few catches that were too small to gaff.

They were currently idling the boat several miles south of Virginia, and trolling a spreader bar. The chop was as bad as, or worse than, before; they were wallowing like a bear in cornshucks. He thought of looking at his watch, but why bother? The misery was interminable. There was no hope that anyone would turn back to shore for a sick man, much less send a helicopter. He was in this scrape to the bitter end.

He denied to himself that he had to urinate, as doing that would require going through the cabin where this thing first snared and suffocated him. He wouldn't go back in that cabin if they tried to drag him in with a team of mules.

Occasionally, a kind soul visited his chair and stood for a moment in silent commiseration.

"Sorry, Tim."

"You're going to make it, buddy."

Even the captain came down from the bridge and laid a hand on his shoulder. "Hang in there, Father." Their concern was a comfort, he had to admit, though he was hard-pressed to get over the humiliation he felt.

At one point, someone assured him he wasn't going to die, which he found altogether lacking in comfort, since he didn't much care either way.

"Did you hear about th' guy got dragged off th' boat reelin' in a marlin?"

"No way."

"It was in th' paper, said th' marlin was four hundred pounds, said it pulled th' guy over th' stern."

"He would've been sucked into th' backwash."

"Wadn't. Somebody went in after 'im, saved 'im. But that's not th' half of it. He got th' marlin."

"Bull. That never happened in this lifetime."

"I'm tellin' you it's th' truth, it was in th' paper."

"I've heard of fish takin' first mates over," said Pete.

"There is no way I want to listen to this mess," said Madge.

He was shocked to find himself kneeling at the rail again, with no power over this thing, none at all. He felt completely out of control, which frightened him utterly; he might have been a piece of bait himself, without will or reason to alter his circumstances.

"Number five," somebody said. "That's th' fifth time."

"Seven. He heaved over th' bridge rail twice."

"You ready to eat? I'm half starved."

"I've been thinkin' about what I made last night. Tuna salad. On French bread! Oh, and there's late tomatoes out of my neighbor's garden. Delicious!" said Madge. "I'll cut 'em up so we can all have a bite."

"Tuna out of a *can?*" asked Otis. "That'd be sacrilegious."

"Are we goin' to just leave 'im out here?" wondered Sybil.

"Father? *Father!*"

Why did people think the sick automatically went deaf?

What? He couldn't say it audibly, so he thought it, which should be sufficient.

"Do you want to go inside?"

"Don't take him inside," said the first mate. "You lose th' horizon when you do that. That's usually what makes people seasick, is losin' th' horizon."

"But he's been sittin' out here since it quit rainin'. I think we should at least put sunscreen on his arms. Look at his arms."

He felt several people pawing over him, and tried to express his gratitude.

"Lookit. He doesn't have socks on. Rub some on his ankles."

"Th' back of his neck," said Ernie. "That's a real tender place, slather some on there."

"He's an *awful* color," said Madge.

He realized he should have been more specific in his will; now it was too late to say that he did *not* want an open casket.

⌁

He slept, or thought he might be sleeping. Perhaps he'd slipped into a state of unconsciousness, his mind vacant as a hollow gourd. If there was anything he distrusted, it was an empty mind. He forced himself to open his eyes and saw only glare, a shining that moved and heaved and shuddered and danced and tried to force entry to his stomach. In truth, he'd never been especially aware of his stomach. When it was empty, he put something in it; when it was full, he was happy. Now he felt it as a raw and flaccid thing that swung in him like a sheep's bladder with every swell that tossed the boat.

He wanted his wife. Lacking that consolation, he pulled his jacket around him and squeezed his eyes shut and dreamed a dream as vacant as mist.

⌁

Thank God! He might actually be feeling better.

His eyes seemed clear, some strength was returning; but he didn't want to count his chickens, no, indeed. He rubbed ChapStick on his lips and hunkered down under Otis's hat, wondering about his sugar, which must have dropped straight to the floor of the Gulf Stream. He wished he'd brought his tachometer . . . no, that wasn't it. What was it, anyway? Could he possibly have suffered brain damage from this terrible assault? *Glu*cometer, that's what it was.

Weak . . . terribly weak. He realized he was thinking of Ernie's Snickers bars, iced down cold. A small flicker, a flame of hope rose in his breast. *Thank You, Lord. . . .*

He looked out upon the restless water and saw other boats on the horizon—one there, two there, like family.

"We had the worst nest of yellow jackets in our church wall-l-l!" said Sybil.

"What'd y'all do about it?"

"Swatted 'em with our hymnals and bulletins."

"Why didn't you kill 'em?"

"They only flare up once a year, late April or May, and only on th' side where hardly anybody sits, anyway."

"Yesterday a hero, today a zero," muttered Pete, hauling up bait that looked like a glorified Christmas tree.

Father Tim waved his hand to Ernie, who came over and squatted by the chair.

"What can I do for you, buddy?"

"Snickers," he said, hoarse as a bullfrog.

"Snickers?"

He nodded, feeble but encouraged.

$$\backsim$$

"We got us one!" yelled Ernie. "Otis! Where's Otis?"

"In th' head. You take it!"

Father Tim had heard of total pandemonium, but he'd never seen it 'til now. Six people erupted into a full horde, and swarmed around him like the armies of Solomon.

"We got a fish here! Yee-hah!"

"Got another one right here. Take it, Madge!"

He looked at the throbbing lines crisscrossed over and around the stern like freeways through L.A.

"That's a keeper!" Pete gaffed something and pulled it in.

"Way to go, Roger!"

He saw the rainbow of color that shimmered on the big fish as it went into the box, where it thrashed like a horse kicking a stall. Pete pulled out the gaff and hosed blood from the deck.

The captain was fishing off the bridge; everybody was fishing. He heaved himself from the chair, out of the fray, and huddled against the cabin.

In the fighting chair, Madge was crouched into the labor of hauling in something big.

Otis had his thumb on her line, helping her raise and lower the rod. "You got to pump 'im, now," he said, clenching his cigar in his teeth.

"Oh, law! This must be an eighteen-wheeler I've got on here!"

"Keep crankin'!"

Captain Willie called over the speaker, "Please tend to the left-hand corner, Pete, tend to the left-hand corner, we got a mess over there."

"A fishin' frenzy," muttered Pete, streaking by in a blur.

Madge cranked the reel, blowing like a prizefighter. "This fish is killin' me. Somebody come and take this bloomin' rod!"

"Don't quit!" yelled Sybil, aiming a point-and-shoot at the action. "Keep goin', Chuck would be proud!"

"That ain't nothin' but solid tuna," said Otis. He helped Madge lift the rod as the fish drew closer to the boat.

Father Tim rubberlegged it to the stern and looked over. The black water of the morning had changed to blue-green, and the fish moved beneath the aqua surface, luminous and quick.

He thought it one of the most beautiful sights he'd ever seen.

"Here it comes!"

He stepped back as Pete darted to the right of the fighting chair, lowered the gaff, and hauled the tuna onto the deck.

"Way to go, Madge!"

"Beautiful! *Beautiful!*"

Whistles, cheers, applause.

"That'll weigh in seventy, seventy-five pounds," Otis said, as Madge staggered out of the chair, grinning into Sybil's camera.

The captain was catching fish, Ernie was catching fish, Roger was catching fish.

"Got a fish on th' line!" yelled Pete. "Who'll take it?"

"I'll take it!" As Father Tim thumped into the fighting chair, hoots of encouragement went up from the entire assembly.

He was back from the dead, he was among the living, he was ready to do this thing.

$\backsim$

"How was it, darling?"

"Terrific!" he said, kissing her. "Wonderful fellowship, *great* fellowship—fellows in a ship, get it?"

"Got it. And the weather?"

He shrugged. "A little rough, but not too bad."

"What's for supper?" she asked, eyeing the cooler he was lugging.

"Yellowfin tuna and dolphin! Let's fire up the grill,"

he said, trotting down the hall, "and I'll tell you all about it!" By the time he hit the kitchen, he was whistling.

She hurried after her husband, feeling pleased. He'd come home looking considerably thinner, definitely tanner, and clearly more relaxed. She'd known all along that buying him a chair with Captain Willie was a brilliant idea.

CHAPTER FOURTEEN

Letting Go

"Turn around a minute and don't look," Roger said.

Father Tim turned and faced the book room, where Elmo sat on the windowsill, licking his paws after a meal of thawed finger mullet.

"OK, you can look now."

Roger had positioned the carved head on the body of the green-winged teal; the duck was gazing at him in a way he found positively soulful.

"Aha," he whispered.

"I set the eyes a while back and forgot to show you."

"It'll be as close to th' real thing as you'll ever see in this life!" Ernie Fulcher was grinning as if he were personally responsible for the whole deal. "Fact is, you can compare it to th' real thing right now, if you want to. We got one we keep in th' freezer for when he needs somethin' to go by."

"That's OK," said Father Tim, not eager to see a dead duck in a Ziploc bag.

"Until I set the eyes," said Roger, "it didn't have any character at all, there was no personality. The eyes lying on the worktable are nothing, but set them in place and this piece of wood becomes a duck."

"Amazing! Just amazing."

"I've got to burn all the feathers, now they've been chiseled, then I'll gesso everything and start to paint. See these speculum feathers on the wing? They'll be green, and the under-tail coverts here, they'll be a champagne color."

Roger passed his handiwork to Father Tim, who took it, feeling oddly reverent.

Though he didn't know why, and he certainly didn't know how . . . this was his duck.

He was getting ready to leave when Junior Bryson came in, looking as if he'd lost his last friend.

Lucas's tail thumped the floor in greeting.

"I done it," Junior said.

"Done what?" asked Ernie.

"Talked to Ava's daddy."

"Come and sit down," said Ernie, pulling out a chair. "You want a Pepsi, have a Pepsi! Or get you a root beer."

Junior shook his head at Ernie's offer and thumped down at the table, looking, thought Father Tim, considerably pale around the gills. He changed his mind about leaving and sat down with Junior.

Roger placed the duck in its carry-box.

Roanoke lit a Marlboro.

Silence.

"Well?" said Ernie.

Junior sighed. "Well, I finally worked up th' nerve to

call 'er daddy, so I got th' phone book that has Swan-quarter, and found a Goodnight listed in it."

"Smart!" said Ernie.

"It wadn't too smart," said Junior. "I was thinkin' her daddy's name would be Goodnight, but then, when th' phone started ringin', it hit me that Goodnight was prob'ly her married name an' she might answer th' phone."

"Right!" said Ernie, hoping for the best.

"I was about to hang up, when a man answered. That kind of th'owed me. I thought it might be, like, you know, a boyfriend. But it was her daddy, Mr. Taylor. He lives at Ava's."

Roanoke blew a smoke ring. Lucas's yawn sounded like a squeak from a door hinge.

"Well, I'd practiced what I wanted to say, but when he answered, I forgot everything."

"Right," said Ernie. "It usually works that way."

"So, anyhow, I said, 'This is Junior Bryson from over at Whitecap, Ava might of mentioned me.' "

"That was a good start."

"He said, 'Are you th' fella plays Scrabble and fishes?' " Junior's face brightened momentarily. "I said, 'Yessir.' He said, 'I like a fella says yessir, most people've forgot about sayin' yessir.' "

"And what'd you say?"

"I said, 'Yessir, you're right about that.' "

"Common ground!" exclaimed Ernie. Roger and Father Tim nodded their agreement.

"So I said I was hopin' Ava might go out with me, I do Sound an' ocean fishin' both, an' have a little boat I take crabbin' an' all, I could offer her a variety of fishin' options."

"That should of done it right there!"

"I said I'm pretty sharp at Scrabble and could prob'ly give her a good run for th' money."

"An' what'd he say?"

"He said she beats th' stuffin' out of him all th' time, not to mention beats her sister an' some of th' neighbors."

Ernie whistled through his teeth.

"I told him about my job, how I was Employee of th' Month back in April an' all. . . ."

"What else?"

"I told him I own my own house an' keep my truck washed an' waxed, that I change th' oil myself an' just put on a new set of Michelins." Junior looked exhausted.

"That's all your cards right there," said Ernie. "You laid 'em on th' table, that's all a man can do. So what'd he say?"

Junior looked at his hands. "He said I sounded pretty decent an' responsible."

Ernie beamed. "Then what?"

"So then I told him I hadn't heard back from Ava, an' wondered if he'd be willin' to give his permission for me to take 'er out an' all."

Father Tim glanced around. Roanoke was cleaning his fingernails with a pocketknife. Roger was pondering the situation intently. Ernie looked nervous.

"So he said, 'Well, son, I like what you're sayin', I really do, and I thought those snapshots showed a fine-lookin' fella, but your letter failed to convince Ava that you're a Christian, and that's a requirement of hers as well as mine.' Then he said she wrote me a note a day or two ago and he guessed I hadn't got it yet."

Ernie looked disgusted. "Shoot, maybe you don't want to go out with somebody that could whip your butt at Scrabble. You thought of that?"

"Just because she whips her daddy don't mean she can whip me."

"So, what can we do here to move things along?" asked Roger.

It appeared that Roger's CEO mode was kicking in.

Junior's gaze searched every face for an answer to this probing question, and at last zeroed in on Father Tim, who knew Junior's look very well.

"Would you like to have a talk?"

Junior nodded.

"Anytime, just let me know."

Junior appeared suddenly hopeful. "How about right now? We could go set in my truck."

Roger and Ernie gave the clergy an approving nod.

"Consider it done," he said.

⌒

"If you need air-conditionin', we can roll th' windows up."

Father Tim noticed Junior's hands were trembling. A talk with the clergy sometimes did that to people.

"Not for me. But you might pull over in the shade," he said. *Lord, give me wisdom here. May Your Holy Spirit be with us. . . .* His heart was moved for Junior Bryson.

As Junior started the motor, a shattering blast of country music erupted from speakers the size of drink crates. Junior hit the off button, embarrassed. "I'm really sorry 'bout that."

"No problem," said his passenger, barely able to speak for the adrenaline pumping into his system.

Junior eased the truck under the leafy branches of a nearby tree. "We could ride around if you'd rather do that," said Junior.

"This is fine, we can sit right here. I think we're getting a little breeze."

Junior switched off the ignition and was silent for a moment, looking anguished. "I hate to tell you this, sir."

"What's that?"

"I all of a sudden have to go to th' toilet."

"Go right ahead. I understand."

Junior swung down from the cab and loped across the parking lot.

Juniors uneasiness reminded him, somehow, of himself, as he met with his first bishop all those years ago.

"Why did you decide to become a priest, Timothy?"

"I was called, sir."

"Who called you?"

"God."

The tall, angular Bishop Quayle sat quietly in the leather chair, holding his hands upright before him with all his fingertips touching. Father Tim remembered noting that his fingers formed a sort of steeple, which he thought becoming to a bishop.

"You will have times of doubt."

"Yes, sir."

"Which you can't imagine now, of course."

"No, sir."

"Do you genuinely love Christ with all your heart?"

"Yes, sir, I do."

"What is the chief reason you love Him?"

"Because He loves me."

Their visit had been short, but rewarding. Bishop Quayle prayed with him and made the sign of the cross on his forehead. "I think you'll do, Timothy," he said, smiling. The young priest marked the extraordinary light shining in the bishop's eyes; it was this light that had encouraged him most.

Junior opened the door and slid into the seat looking contrite but refreshed. "I'm sorry, Father. I'm . . . kind of nervous."

"I understand."

"Well," said Junior. "I was hopin' you could help me with what to do about Ava."

"Aha."

"I've got 'er picture right here . . ."—Junior fished it from his shirt pocket, looking proud—"so you could remember what she looks like." He balanced it in a standing position on the volume knob of the radio.

"Here's what I told her in th' letter. I said I went to church when my mama was livin' an' got baptized when I was fourteen. I reckon that makes me a Christian."

He smiled. "*Did* it make you a Christian?"

"I don't know. I mean, seem like bein' baptized was a big deal, th' way I remember it."

"It is a big deal. A very big deal. But it's what happens in our hearts, in our spirits, that's a much bigger deal. What was going on in your heart when you were baptized, do you remember?"

"Nothin' much. Me'n some other people went out to th' creek, th' preacher laid us back in th' water, I come up and dried off, and we all went an' ate catfish at Cap'n Willie's."

"When we ask Jesus to come into our hearts and save us—and if we really mean it—something always happens. Something powerful. Sometimes we sense it the moment we ask, sometimes later. But it never fails to happen."

Junior shrugged and shifted in the seat, which caused his elbow to hit the horn. They both jumped. " 'Scuse me," he said. A few drops of perspiration appeared on his forehead.

"I don't know what Ava's thinking," said Father Tim, indicating the photograph. "Maybe you'll learn more from her letter. But she may be looking for someone who has a personal relationship with Christ."

"I don't see how'n th' world you can have a *personal* relationship with 'im. That don't seem possible to me. That don't seem . . . *possible.*"

"That's a hard one to understand, how a God so powerful can be so personal. Yet, when you ask the Son of God to come into your heart, something incredible happens."

"What?"

"He actually comes in."

Junior looked blank.

"He comes in and quickens our spirits so that we're truly alive for the first time. We see with new eyes, we hear with new ears, we're able to receive His love." He thought it was moments like this that he lived for. "The relationship becomes deeply personal, one-on-one."

"I'm sorry, sir, but . . . I just don't get it."

"That's OK. I'll pray for you to get it."

Junior sighed. "What am I goin' to do about Ava?"

"Keep being honest, just as she will be, I'm sure. Whatever happens, honesty is always the best policy."

Junior stared into the vacant lot next door.

"God certainly loves our honesty. You can tell Him anything Junior, anything!"

"I wouldn't want t' tell 'im *anything.*"

He grinned. "Might as well. He knows it anyway."

Junior blushed.

"He not only wants to be your Savior and Lord, He wants to be your best friend. Pretty hard to imagine, but true. Anyway, I think that because you and Ava both admire honesty, everything's going to turn out just fine."

"You think so?"

"I do."

"Thank you, Father. I really thank you."

"Anytime you have questions, anytime you want to just sit and talk, call me or drop by St. John's."

"Yessir, I will. Can I carry you down to church?"

"I'd appreciate it."

Junior removed the photograph from the knob, gave it a furtive glance, and put it back in his pocket. As they wheeled out of the lot, Father Tim couldn't help but see Roger and Ernie peering through the window.

Mother hens! he thought, waving.

—❦—

The phone on his desk rang twice.

"St. John's in the Grove! Father Kavanagh speaking."

"Hey!" said Dooley.

"Hey, yourself, buddy!" He loved hearing the boy's voice, he could even hear the grin in it. "What's up?"

"I've got . . . like, you know, like a girlfriend."

Whoa. "A girlfriend? Tell me everything."

"Her name's Caroline."

His heart sank. But what business was it of his? "Where did you meet her?"

"I met her at a dance at her school, and we've been writing. You know. Calling each other."

"Aha. What school?"

"It doesn't matter, I mean . . ."

"No, I'd like to know. What school?"

Dooley sounded a little ticked at having it gouged out of him. "Mrs. Hemingway's."

That school where all the girls are geeks, and wear weird shoes and funny glasses? *That* school? "Smart, I suppose . . ."

"Totally smart, straight A's. And really . . . like, you know . . ."

He knew. "Great-looking? Beautiful?"

"Umm, yeah. Yessir. Totally."

He was thrilled that Dooley could confide in him. Who wouldn't be? That pleasure, however, was considerably diminished by wondering what Lace Turner would think of this.

He'd never ask, of course; no, indeed, not for anything.

⊖

"Father?" It was Janette's doctor, speaking in his low-country drawl. "I've got a little slip of paper around here somewhere. Janette asked me to give you a message. Let's see, I can't read my own handwriting, I suppose that's no news. . . ."

Father Tim laughed.

"Here it is. Let's see. 'The cactus is beginning to bloom.' "

Tears misted his eyes. "She's coming along, then?"

"Improving. Yes, definitely."

"When do you think she might be coming home?"

"Ten days, maybe two weeks. We want to be absolutely certain the suicidal stuff is behind us."

"Will she be able to care for the children?"

"Yes, we think so. It might help to give her a day or two to settle in, if possible. I understand her cousin is having a time of it, four children in a one-bedroom apartment. . . ."

"We'll do whatever it takes on our end."

"Excellent. Let's just say two weeks, maximum."

"Thanks be to God!" He felt a weight move off his heart. "Thank you, Doctor. Well done!"

❧

"Father Tim?"

"Speaking. Is that you, Rodney?"

"All we could turn up on th' back door an' th' knob was Puny's prints. Then we dusted your mantel and your desk and so on, but didn't find anything. She's rubbed a good bit of lemon oil around in there."

"Right."

"Course we found some of your prints on th' desk drawers, you remember we took your prints a few years ago."

"I do."

"Sorry to be so long gettin' back to you."

Ah, well. He'd done his duty, they'd done theirs, and that was that.

❧

Had Emma Newland vanished from the face of the earth? Whenever she called, he fervently wished she hadn't. When she didn't, he wished she would. Go figure.

Maybe they were still in Atlanta. Maybe Harold had seen the phone bill and laid down the law. Maybe she didn't care anymore what happened to her old boss— out of sight, out of mind.

He dialed her number and charged the call to Dove Cottage.

"Hello!"

"Emma?"

"Is that *you?*"

"It's me, all right. What's up in Mitford? Tell me everything, it's my nickel."

"After we went to Atlanta and saw Jean, we went to New Orleans, Harold had three weeks piled up with th' post office. The food in New Orleans was great, it was unbelievable, you'd never in a hundred *years* believe how much we ate, I think I have gout."

"Gout?"

"From eating all that French food, they say it'll give you gout."

"Does your big toe hurt?"

"My big toe? What does that have to do with anything?"

"With gout, that's usually what's affected. Very painful."

"My toe is fine and dandy, so it must be somethin' else."

"Where did you eat?"

"Sometimes we got carry-out Cajun and ate in th' RV, th' rest of th' time we ate in th' restaurant in th' motel. Meals came with the room, and all for only eighty-eight dollars a day. For *two!*"

"You definitely don't have gout," he said.

"Have they gotten you any help yet? Even *Harold* has help."

"Everybody pitches in." He wondered why on earth he'd called.

"I haven't checked Ed Sikes in Oregon, if that's why you called. We just got in a few days ago, and I'm up to my ears in laundry, plus Snickers has fleas and they're so bad they're jumpin' on th' counter, I thought I'd spilled pepper. Th' termite man is on his way right now, you wouldn't *believe* what it's goin' to cost and I have to be out of th' house for three hours while they do it, and then come home and *vacuum* for five straight *days*, it's all that rain we had, I'm sure Barnabas is *covered* with fleas. . . ."

"Not that I've seen."

"Well, I don't know why he *doesn't* have fleas, the way th' weather's been, fleas *breed* in weather like we've had."

His erstwhile secretary was positively hopping mad that his dog didn't have fleas.

"Speakin' of fleas, did you hear what Rodney Underwood just got to hunt criminals, you'd never guess."

"True. I wouldn't."

"A rockwilder! You should see people scatterin' when it trots down th' street, Adele Hogan walks it every morning and it drags Joe Joe Guthrie around every evening, I'd hate to be a criminal in this town! Speakin' of criminal, have you heard what Miss Pattie's done now?"

Miss Pattie was a Hope House resident whose mind had been lost some years ago and was found only on the rarest of occasions. Her antics had long been of particular interest to Emma.

"Miss Pattie's too old to get into mischief, I should think."

"Well, think again, she steals everything she can get her hands on in Mr. Berman's room, then goes and throws it out her window."

"No!"

"His money, his bedroom shoes, his good leather belt, you name it. He got undressed the other night and looked around for his pajamas and they weren't there, so he draped himself in a blanket like a red Indian and called the nurse and told her if Miss Pattie didn't stop this mess, his son will sue for a million dollars."

"Can't the staff *do* something?"

"They locked her window, that's the best they can do, they say she's going through a phase."

"What does Mr. Berman say?"

"He says she has a terrible crush on him."

"That makes sense," he said, recalling that Mr. Berman was a very handsome old man.

"Speakin' of crazy people, Coot Hendrick actually believes he's going to win th' election. Can you *imagine* havin' a mayor who's two san'wiches short of a full picnic?"

He suddenly realized that Emma's sluice gate had opened and he was being swept along as if by a raging torrent.

"So, Emma, glad to hear you had a great time in New Orleans. Let me know what you find out about Ed Sikes."

He hung up and wiped his face with his handkerchief.

The search committee was meeting regularly, chatting each other up in the churchyard, whispering among themselves in the parish hall, polling the congregation for general opinion, and basically going about the task of replacement as if eager to unload their interim.

When he laughed with Sam Fieldwalker about their apparent urgency, his senior warden insisted that quite the opposite was true. The committee was hastening to do their job, yes, but in fact, several parishioners had expressed a desire to have their interim remain full-time. Besides, Father Tim was too young to retire. Hadn't Father Grace served St. John's until he was eighty-seven?

Not every interim was urged by the parish to stay on. In fact, many were viewed with suspicion and some with utter disregard. He remembered what one of his early bishops was fond of saying—that the interim who didn't make enemies was a man who wasn't doing his job. The job, it was popularly supposed, was to stir things up, to throw out the old and make way for the new.

Who could, after all, forget Father Harry?

Father Harry, who was seventy-one when his life as an interim began, thoroughly relished the task of disrupting the comfort level of a parish. His style was to barge in and take command before they knew what hit them.

If the congregation was attached to Rite Two, he celebrated Rite One. If they were stubbornly fond of traditional music, he switched them to praise songs. If they venerated their choir and organ, he had them sing a cappella for weeks on end. If they believed children should be seen and not heard, he invited the small fry to take up collection and read simpler Epistles. If their former priest had avoided the very mention of mammon, Father Harry talked about it at considerable length, with special emphasis on tithing. Further, he enjoyed reinstituting the observance of Morning Prayer, which, if not entirely forgotten by most parishes, was thought to be quaintly antique.

When the incoming priest was finally in place, the congregants were so relieved to be done with the old troublemaker, they went for almost anything the newcomer cooked up.

Father Harry could get the job done, all right. As for himself, Father Tim leaned rather more to what C. S. Lewis had said about worship procedures in *Letters to Malcolm*.

"A good shoe is a shoe you don't notice. . . . The perfect church service would be one we were almost unaware of; our attention would have been on God. But every novelty prevents this. It fixes our attention on the service itself, and thinking about worship is a different thing from worshipping."

He relished a note left on his desk by nine-year-old Margaret Wheeler.

> *Deer Father Tim when we get a new priest I hope he is just like you.*
>
> *Love, Margaret   PS But I hope he has kids!!!*

∽

Mayoral Candidate Agrees with Opponent

Andrew Gregory, one of two mayoral candidates for the election on November 3, says he agrees with his opponent, local native Coot Hendrick.

"Mr. Hendrick is absolutely right to fight for the preservation of early Mitford history, though the hope of winning this particular battle appears lost. If elected, I shall do everything in my power to preserve what is good and positive about Mitford. One of my first projects will be to encourage owners of several local buildings to seek listings on our National Register, and receive federal funding assistance for much-needed restoration.

"For nearly two decades, our incumbent mayor, Esther Cunningham, has set an example of community service that raised the standard of this office for all time. It will be a privilege to try and carry on her remarkable vision."

Gregory said that, if elected, he would also work to bring "sensitive, balanced growth to Mitford, which includes increased lodging, food and retail opportunities."

Gregory, his wife, Anna, and his brother-in-law, Anthony Nocelli, are owners of the popular Lucera Restaurant, located in their private residence known to one and all as Fernbank. Mr. Gregory is also the owner/proprietor of Oxford Antique Shop, a Main Street landmark.

Town Council Meeting Turns Musical

Mrs. Beulah Mae Hendrick, 92-year-old mother of Mitford mayoral candidate, Coot Hendrick, was a surprise visitor at last Monday's meeting of the town council.

Mrs. Hendrick was allowed to open the meeting with a song learned from her grandfather, who was the son of Mitford's founder, Hezikiah Hendrick. Local legend has it that Hezikiah Hendrick shot five Union soldiers running from their regiment, and buried them on what is now property belonging to Ms. Edith Mallory.

State law rules that property containing grave sights can not be disturbed or developed. Ms. Mallory contends there is no proof or evidence that such graves exist on her 90-acre property. Ms. Mallory is currently beginning construction on a 3,000 sq. ft. extension of her home, Clear Day, near or on the sight of the stone foundations of the old Hendrick cabin.

Mrs. Hendrick, who stood beside her wheelchair to sing the song, said afterward, "It will prove we're right!" A written copy of the lyrics was sent to Ms. Mallory by certified mail last Tuesday morning.

Shot five Yankees
a-runnin' from th' war
Caught 'em in a cornfield
Sleepin' by afar

Now they'll not run no more, oh
They'll not run no more!

Dug five graves
With a mattock and a hoe
Buried 'em in th' ground
Before th' first snow
Now they'll not run no more, oh
They'll not run no more!

Mr. Coot Hendrick said, "Mama has known and sung this song all her life, which right there ought to be proof the graves exist."

At press time, a spokesman reported that the town council has received a letter from Ms. Mallory's lawyer in Florida, stating that no proof of graves exists, and the matter is officially closed. He also said nobody could dig five graves with a mattock and a hoe, and that folk songs do not document real life.

A town council spokesman said, "I think it's a low-down shame to shoot people in their sleep, even if they are Yankees."

Ms. Mallory has issued a firm restriction against any digging or trespassing on her property, and has posted signs to that effect.

—⊖—

New Name, Location For Hair House

Ms. Fancy Skinner, proprietor of Mitford's popular Hair House, is moving her beauty Salon uptown and changing its name.

Ms. Skinner, who currently operates Hair House in her basement off Lilac Road, stated, "It's time to go Main Street!!

"I and my customers agree this calls for a more up-town name. The new name will be A Cut Above."

Ms. Skinner is moving in over the Sweet Stuff Bakery, which means that all hair work in Mitford will now be concentrated in one building, as Joe Ivey barbers on the street level behind the Sweet Stuff Bakery kitchen.

A Cut Above will feature all hair services for both sexes, with cuts starting at $12 and up. Fancy's Face Food, a specialty skincare line with organic ingredients, will be available. "But don't even think about using it," says Ms. Skinner, "unless you want to look and feel ten to fifteen years younger and make an all-around better showing for yourself."

A grand opening will held on Tuesday, beginning at nine a.m. with sugar-free gum for all, and a door prize of acrylic nails.

Congratulations to A Cut Above!!!!

Local Laughs
—by Anonymous

Seen the new sign in Percy Mosely's window?

"Shoes are required to eat in the Main Street Grill. Socks can eat anyplace they want to."

Then there's the sign on the door of the labor room at Mitford Hospital:

"Push, push, push."

I guess by now everybody's heard about Evie Adams's midnight snail hunt. Seems she was out with a salt shaker and flashlight hunting down snails in her flowerbed, when one of Chief Rodney Underwood's officers rode by her house on South Main and saw this light bobbing around in her yard. The officer who shall be nameless parked up the street and tip-toed down to Evie's with his pistol cocked. He said

the moon was out and he thought it was pretty odd
that the burglar was wearing a chenille robe and hair
curlers.

After he nearly scared the daylights out of her,
Evie handed him an extra salt shaker and made him
help finish the flower bed, all of which is to say Evie
got the last laugh.

Well, that's it for now!! See you back here next
week and don't take any wooden nickels.

———— ⟲ ————

Displaying her skills with the ability to fax directly
from her computer, he found Emma's note at the office.

<To: Father Tim
<From: Emma Newland
<Date: Monday
<Memo: There is no Ed Sikes in Oregon.
<See you at the wedding. Do you want me to bake a ham
so you don't have to?
<Love to all.

———— ⟲ ————

He couldn't believe this was happening.

As he approached Morris Love's place on an afternoon walk, his dog suddenly lurched forward with all
the power and muscle of a horse. The leash jerked from
his unsuspecting hand and Barnabas dove under the
gate in a flash. Déjà vu!

His anger erupted with such violence, he was astounded.

"Barnabas!" he thundered.

Was he so dim-witted he couldn't have prepared for
this, anticipated it, *expected* it to happen? He would
never walk this way again, Barnabas was confined to

the yard and the back porch 'til doomsday. He'd been treated like a king for years and was now exercising royal privileges. Father Tim couldn't believe the stubborn, willful, selfish disobedience of a dog he'd done everything for. . . .

"Barnabas! *Come now!*" He hardly recognized his own voice; it gave him a positive chill. If he were a dog, he'd either flee the county at the sound of it or slink back to face the music and get it over with.

Hearing the booming bark fade deeper into the Love jungle, he scaled the wall and dropped down on the other side, breathing hard. He didn't want to go through this nonsense again, he really didn't. He certainly didn't want his churlish neighbor ranting at him as if he were some rum-nosed chicken poacher. So what if Morris Love had had a hard time of it? Hadn't plenty of other people, and was that any excuse for refusing to exercise at least a modicum of human kindness toward a neighbor?

He was huffing and blowing as if he'd done the Nags Head Wood Run instead of a mile-long lap through the neighborhood.

He hadn't, for some time, been forced to use Holy Scripture on his dog, a ploy that worked best to keep Barnabas from leaping into the arms of the unsuspecting, or giving their ears and noses a good licking. Though he had no precedent for the current circumstances, it was worth a try.

" 'I delight to do thy will, O my God, *yea,* thy law is within my *heart*!' " He fairly bellowed the line from the psalmist; he thought he'd made the leaves tremble on a bush.

Silence. He felt like a maniac.

Ah, well.

What if he simply gave up and went home? Barnabas would follow eventually; he'd be lying outside their front door in no time flat, looking doleful. But what would that solve? It would only give his dog the dumb notion he could do it again anytime he liked. No, indeed, he was going in after his dog and dragging him home by the collar, and no treats for a week, maybe a *month.* . . .

He stormed down the driveway as if going to a fire, whistling and calling right and left. There was an occasional thrashing in the bushes. Birds started up and flew above him, chattering. A squirrel dashed across his path as he came upon the house.

Beside the drive as it curved toward the front door was something he hadn't noticed before. It was an antiquated verdigris plaque set into a concrete slab and nearly taken by ivy. A house marker, he supposed. He stooped and squinted at the engraving: *Nouvelle Chanson, 1947.*

He wasn't eager to disturb his neighbor, no, indeed, but what could he do? He stood up and let it fly. *"Barnabas!"*

"Is that you again?" Morris Love shouted from an upstairs window.

"Yes, dadgummit, Mr. Love, it is."

"Out! *Out!*"

Please, no more of that drivel. "I can't go out 'til I find my dog. My *dog,* Mr. Love! I'm sorry, for heaven's sake." He stomped through the undergrowth at the side of the house, where he thought he heard a commotion.

"Barnabas! *Come!*" Now there was furious barking at what could be the rear of the house. He suddenly felt the insects chewing on his legs, and if that weren't enough, it was steaming in here. Until he came over the wall, he hadn't noticed the humidity, nor had he realized his desperate thirst.

"Your dog has treed a squirrel off the west side!" Morris Love's hoarse announcement was matter-of-fact.

Father Tim darted into grass that grew to his waist; Lord only knows what was lurking on the ground. He needed a machete, a sling, a hay baler, to get through this stuff. Slogging to the rear of the house, he stumbled over a pile of bricks that had toppled from a chimney and lay hidden in the grass. He fell onto a jagged piece of mortar and hauled himself up. Stubbed toes, skinned knees, cut hands, chewed legs . . . he was biting his tongue.

He forged along the endless rear of the house and rounded the corner, dripping with sweat. Aha, by George, there he was, the impudent beast, sitting on his rear end at the foot of a tree and gazing heavenward as if in prayer.

His dog turned his head and gave him the sort of look that precedes the guillotine.

Speechless, his master pointed to his feet, shod in running shoes. Barnabas thoughtfully considered this gesture for some moments, then arose slowly and, head down, walked toward his master and sat a couple of yards away. Father Tim made the pointing gesture again. Barnabas arose, plodded over, and sat by his master's right foot.

He reached down and plucked the leash from the grass.

"Forgiveness," he said aloud to his dog, "is giving up my right to hurt you because you have hurt me." He didn't know where that particular wisdom had come from, but there it was.

Barnabas sat, looking stoic.

He put his hand through the loop and wrapped the leash around his arm twice. Then, giving his eaten legs a vigorous, overall slapping, he turned to get the heck out of here.

He heard Morris Love laughing behind one of the many shuttered windows on the second floor. It was an odd laughter, to say the least, composed of short explosions of sound.

"Mr. Love," he yelled. "I hope we're entertaining you sufficiently."

"More than sufficiently." Morris Love quit laughing, and the coldness in his voice returned. "You know the way out, Father."

"Yes, indeed, it's becoming all too familiar." His own tone of voice wasn't exactly the one used in greeting people at the church door.

Blast. That high wall ahead must be the back of another wing, though there were no windows. Or perhaps it was the rear of the loggia he'd glimpsed earlier. From the look of things, this meant a longer distance to the front, through a deeper, yet denser thicket.

He had stumbled into some kind of brier patch, or tangle of vines that scratched like a cat. Extracting himself from the snare of this blasted stuff was no easy job. Maybe he shouldn't forge ahead, but retrace his steps. This was maddening, alarming. He felt a moment of panic.

"Go back the way you came." Morris Love was speaking directly above his head.

He tore himself from the vines that snarled about his clothes and stomped back the way he'd come.

Fleas. Emma's suspicion was being confirmed. He yanked up his pants legs and was relieved to find they weren't fleas after all, though something probably worse. He went at a trot, trying to avoid the pile of rubble, and finally made it to the driveway, where he stood and wiped his dripping face with the tail of his T-shirt.

"There's water in the faucet behind you."

Water! He turned and saw the spigot attached to a pipe standing about knee level. He cranked open the tap, letting the sediment flow out, then washed the cut on his hand and splashed his face and head. Cupping his hands, he drank deeply and let Barnabas drink, then drew off his shirt and dried himself and slipped it on again. Good Lord, what a refreshment. He was revived, restored; holy water, indeed!

"God bless you!" he shouted, spontaneous and thankful.

"I don't believe in God." Morris Love's voice contained a positive snarl.

"God believes in you!"

"Then why did He give me such a body?"

"Why did He give you such musical genius?"

"I assure you I think very little of answering a question with a question."

"Sometimes a question is the only answer I have, Mr. Love!"

He saw a rusted ornamental lawn chair a few feet to his right, just below the upstairs window where he presumed Morris Love to be standing. He hadn't noticed the chair on his previous safari, nor had he been aware, until now, of his extreme weariness.

He walked to the chair and sat, glad for the chance to catch his breath. What could the lord of the manor do to him anyway—dump a flowerpot on his head?

"I'm sitting down for a moment," he announced, too spent to shout. "I hope you don't object."

He gazed at the view before him, the way the light slanted into the dense tangle of trees and was lost in the foliage. A jungle, indeed. Yet this place had surely been beautiful once, a tropical island within an island, so exotic and unfamiliar that the thought of busy lives just over the wall seemed preposterous.

"Let me ask you, Father, how do you find the conscience to go about practicing the sham of belief?"

He was stunned by the question.

"I don't get your meaning," he said, and he didn't.

"The meaning seems clear enough. You wear a collar, you recite a creed, you speak of God, and yet, as a man whom I presume to be more than nominally intelligent, you cannot possibly believe there is a loving God, or any God at all."

"Quite the contrary, Mr. Love. I find it impossible not to believe in a loving God."

"I see it is useless to discuss a high truth with you."

"Then you see blindly." Though he didn't wish to be harsh; he had every desire to be plain.

"Blindness, you may be certain, has never been one of my handicaps."

"Do you consider your physical condition a handicap?"

"You speak as a fool. Of course I do."

"Many do not, Mr. Love. For example, there are currently several practicing and highly successful physicians with your precise physical condition."

"Not my precise condition at all. You deceive yourself grossly, Father, by presuming to know me. You do not know me now, nor will you ever."

"We're both being presumptuous, Mr. Love. You

presume me to be covertly faithless, I presume you to be more physically proficient than you think you're able to be. Tit for tat, as my grandmother used to say. Now let's be done with it, shall we?"

"Out! *Out!*" bellowed Morris Love.

"Yes, indeed, and thank you for your hospitality." He set off at a trot down the driveway, his dog loping ahead on the leash.

The shouting continued in his wake. "Out! *Out!*"

"Out and away, and never to return!" he muttered, breaking into a run as he neared the gate.

$\sim$

In the last couple of days, the air had been miraculously devoid of humidity, and was instead filled with snap and sparkle. Light slanted, sound intensified, clouds vanished from a sky so cerulean it appeared enameled.

He was on his knees, weeding and adding fresh pine straw to the beds, glad to feel his hands in the dirt.

He couldn't, however, ignore the sense of conflict in his spirit—of loving the new season and at the same time feeling the sorrow it brought. It had taken years to name the sorrow and, at last, to face it down.

His father had died on October twelfth, more than forty years ago, and every autumn the heaviness surfaced again. During that dark time in the cave, he'd been able to forgive his father once and for all, which had worked wonders in his spirit, in his whole outlook. Yet something of the suffering remained, like a tea stain on linen, and returned each autumn in the changing light, to remind him.

The conflicting feelings experienced at his father's death were so intricately entwined that he'd never been able to disentangle them, and saw no useful purpose in trying again.

Indeed, perhaps it was time to forgive himself—for having felt relief at his father's passing, for anguishing, even now, over never having pleased him, for continuing to wonder, when he could not know, about his father's soul. Oh, how he'd longed to lead Matthew Kavanagh to Christ, to see the hellish torment of his father's spirit transformed by peace and certainty. But it hadn't happened; it was as if his father, in a last effort to thwart his son, had determined to hold himself away from God for all eternity.

Yes! he thought, thrusting the trowel into the dirt. It's time to let go of it, all of it. . . .

He would surrender this thing right now, completely, though he may be tempted again and again to snatch it back.

He sat in the grass like a child, his legs in a V in front of him, and prayed.

When he lifted his head, he knew at once that he was being watched. He looked through the pickets to Morris Love's hedge and, without thinking, threw up his hand and waved.

He'd broken a few lacy tendrils from the sweet autumn clematis, and was coming into the kitchen to wash up and find a vase when he saw Cynthia in the window seat. She was joggling Jonathan on her knee, as the boy laughed and clapped his hands. Seeing the look on her face, he felt a stab of something he couldn't name.

"Hello, darling!" said his wife.

CHAPTER FIFTEEN

Lock and Key

On his way home from a visit with Janette, he stopped by Ernie's.

Roger looked up and nodded, absorbed in burning the speculum feathers of his duck. Roanoke hoisted a forefinger.

"Junior's got good news!" said Ernie. "He got that letter said she wouldn't go out with 'im, but said she was comin' with her sister to see a girlfriend that lives here, an' she's goin' to drop by and say hello. October twenty-second!" Ernie announced the date as if it were right up there with the day the English landed on Whitecap.

"Said she'n her sister would meet Junior for coffee somewhere, so he wrote back and said Mona's, nine-thirty!"

"Bingo!" Father Tim exclaimed, pulling up a chair. "I'm glad to hear it." He liked the smell of

Roger's burning wood, it made the place seem positively cozy.

"Junior's goin' to quit drinkin' beer til then, see if he can drop ten pounds."

"Aha."

"Yeah, an' goin' to massage his scalp, try to grow some hair," said Roanoke. "But there ain't no way that's goin' to happen."

"If it works, let me know," said Father Tim.

"Plus," said Ernie, "*plus* I sold Elmo's bed—lock, stock, and barrel."

"The Zane Greys?"

"Th' whole shootin' match. Man come in yesterday, bought a couple sinkers, wandered off in there, come back with th' box in his hands. He said how much, I said fifty bucks, he said I'll take it."

"Where did Elmo wind up sleeping last night?" he asked.

"A box of mixed westerns is where I found 'im this mornin'."

Roger didn't look up from his work. "Tell him about *The Last of the Plainsmen*."

"Fella gave me cash, sat down right over yonder, went through th' whole box one by one, an' found it— a signed hardback first edition! Didn't even know it was there. Worth a fortune, prob'ly two hundred, easy. He said I ain't payin' any more for this, I said I ain't askin' any more, a deal is a deal. But I got to tell you, it broke my heart. Two hundred *bucks!*"

"It'd bring a tear to a glass eye," said Roanoke, tapping a Marlboro from the pack.

Elmo appeared at the door of the book room, looking frazzled and disgusted.

"So, Elmo," said Father Tim, "how are you liking mixed westerns?"

⟶ꝏ⟵

He didn't go home from the office; he went to the beach.

At the bottom of the dune, he took off his socks and stuffed them into his shoes, then rolled up his pants legs and started to walk. No wife, no toddler, no dog, no nothing.

There was a fierceness in him that he didn't completely understand. Maybe he could walk it off, walk it out; maybe it would vaporize over the ocean and descend on Argentina as a minor typhoon. He felt angry at a lot of people for a lot of reasons—at Jeffrey Tolson for being cruel, at Janette Tolson for being passive, at Cynthia Kavanagh for losing her heart to someone else's child, at Morris Love for being imprisoned when he might be free. He was even angry with himself, but for what?

A gull started up from a tidal pool and circled above him, crying. He realized, then, that he was running, running for the way it felt to his bones, his beating heart. He heard the sand churning away from his feet, *chuff, chuff, chuff,* and realized he was the only soul on the beach.

All this vast world, all this great ocean, all this infinite sky, he thought—and Morris Love imprisoned behind a wall in a body he hated.

But, thought Father Tim, hadn't he, too, lived in a prison of his own for years on end, alternately fearing and despising and secretly rebuking his father? As a believer, his freedom in Christ had been severely handicapped for wont of letting go of the old bondage; of the old Adamic bitterness he'd unwittingly nurtured. Chances are, Morris Love's father had been much like Matthew Kavanagh—disappointed and indignant, betrayed by the issue from his own flesh.

And who was praying for Morris Love? Who remembered him at all, except in island legend? Instead of a living, breathing, feeling soul, he'd become apocryphal in the minds of everyone but a housekeeper, an organ tuner, and a retired clergyman who, but for the grace of the living God, would himself be a soul under the Enemy's lock and key.

And another thing—if Morris Love so renounced God, why did he play so much of His music?

Chuff, chuff, chuff . . .

He wondered why he hadn't been praying for Morris Love. How could he continue shirking a mission that had, literally, been dumped in his own backyard?

He muttered aloud as he ran, panting and huffing in a chill breeze coming off the water. That was precisely why he was feeling aggravated with himself: God had found him out for a shirker.

⟿

He looked up from the kitchen sink where he was washing tomatoes. His wife, on an errand to pick the last of the basil from the herb bed, suddenly hooted, threw her basket into the air, and began hopping on one foot.

"Ow! Ow! Rats, darn! Hoo! Hoo! *Ha!*"

His wife was a veritable rain dancer, complete with tribal language. What in the world . . . ?

"Timothy! Timothy! *Help!* Oh, ow, ow, *ugh!*"

"Cynthia?" He flew out the back door. *Please, God, not a snake or a terrible cut from broken glass.* . . .

"Yellow jackets!" she shouted, still hopping.

"Here," he said, taking her arm, "I'll help you in."

"I can't put my foot down, Timothy, it's dreadful, it's excruciating, I can't walk!"

"Climb on, then," he said, bending his knees. She threw her arms around his neck and clambered onto his back and he hauled her to the kitchen and thumped her in the window seat like a sack of onions.

"Let's have a look," he said, squatting down. "Aha, two stings, and right between the toes."

"Do something, Timothy, you can't *imagine* how it hurts!" His wife was not a complainer, he knew she meant business.

"Tobacco!" he said. He'd heard that tobacco draws the sting out. He'd seen a cigar butt just the other day. Where was it? "I'll be back!"

Exactly where Otis had thrown it into the bushes when he came by last Tuesday. . . .

He shredded the short stub and mixed it into a paste with water. "Here!" he said, rushing to present it in one of his grandmother's soup bowls. "Put your foot in this."

She did as she was told, shutting her eyes and grimacing. "Ugh! My toes feel exactly like they're being amputated with a handsaw by a doctor in the wilds of Montana, sometime around 1864."

"Really, now." His wife could go a tad over the top.

"It's true, Timothy, that's *exactly* the way it feels."

Jonathan, fully awake from a nap, was pounding him on the back as he squatted by the soup bowl. "You stop!" he shouted. "You stop makin' her cry!"

Truth be told, he was a mite weary of surrogate parenting.

"Look," said his stricken wife, "my toes are swelling up and turning red. How hideous."

"Give it time," he said of his home remedy. "I'll get you a couple of aspirin, then I'll call Marion and see what she recommends."

She drew her breath in sharply and winced. "Have you ever been stung?"

"Not once," he said. "Not a single time."

Even in her suffering, his wife was able to summon an imperious look. "What kind of American boyhood could you possibly have *had,* Timothy?"

⟡

He always enjoyed that moment when he could gaze out to his congregation and, as it were, take its pulse. Did it appear eager? Resigned? Grumpy?

Every Sunday, he discovered a different climate of affections, a brand-new meshing of personalities and spiritual longings, all of which assisted in the feeling that what he did was never the same old thing.

There was his buddy, Stanley Harmon, on vacation from the Baptists and seeing what the Anglicans were up to. Stanley would supply St. John's on the twenty-seventh while Father Tim married Pauline and Buck in Mitford.

His wife was beaming at him from the second row of the gospel side, where she sat with Sam and Marion . . .

. . . and there were the Duncans, with their children lined up like so many goslings. Once a month, according to family tradition, the whole lot skipped Sunday School and joined in the service. One, two, three, four hair bows bobbed on dark curls, as the two boys busily colored pew bulletins.

He was dropping his eyes to the opening hymn when he glanced to the rear of the church and saw a face as coldly immobile as if it were carved in stone.

His heart pounded as his gaze locked briefly with Jeffrey Tolson's, in whose countenance he saw anger and arrogance and, yes, defiance.

—◯—

" 'Ye who do truly and earnestly repent you of your sins, and are in love and charity with your neighbors . . .' "

Because he had long ago committed these words to memory, he wasn't looking at the prayer book, but at his congregation. He noted that some swiveled in their pews and glared at the man in the back row.

" '. . . and intend to lead a new life, following the commandments of God, and walking from henceforth in his holy ways, draw near with faith, and make your humble confession to Almighty God, devoutly kneeling.' "

The parishioners sank to their knees as one, producing a corporate sound of rushing water. Jeffrey Tolson stood and looked for a moment toward the altar, then turned and walked quickly from the nave.

—◯—

He dreaded his time in the churchyard today, as people poured out into the sunshine. Oliver Hughes withheld his hand, muttering, ". . . to let him come back in here, ransackin' th' church, takin' th' women out one by one like a fox in a henhouse . . ."

". . . carryin' 'em off to his den!" said Millie Hughes, stomping away in disgust.

Marion Fieldwalker gave him a wordless hug. Sam murmured, "My goodness gracious," and laid his hand on his priest's shoulder.

Otis stopped and looked him in the eye, saying only, "We want you to fix this."

Jean Ballenger shook his hand, as usual, but said nothing. Her mouth, which was set in a distinct grimace, said it all.

His wife, who was walking with a temporary limp, came to him and slipped her hand in his.

There were more eloquent ways to express it, but his grandmother's way covered it sufficiently:

When it rains, it pours.

They were leaving for Mitford in a matter of days, and in the meantime, he must find and talk with Jeffrey Tolson, speak with Stanley Harmon and inform him of the circumstances, and confirm Father Jack as the celebrant when Stanley preached. He also needed to oversee loose ends for the Fall Fair on November ninth, and meet with the indomitable Busy Fingers group who were going hammer and tong to complete nearly a thousand dollars' worth of items for the fair, including aprons, embroidered pillowcases, oven mitts, and an ambitious needlepoint of the Last Supper. Most important, he must get up to Dorchester, with the Eucharist for the captain and his visit with Ella.

Possibly the Dorchester trip could wait, but no, his heart exhorted him otherwise. The old captain had waited long enough no more excuses, this must be done. And how was he to find Jeffrey Tolson, who, some said, was living on the island, but was as elusive as a trout in a pool?

Worse, what would his parishioners think about their priest vanishing to Mitford in the face of a highly disturbing situation?

He dreaded still more a final thing he must do. Before baring his concerns, however, he imagined their conversation. Perhaps he'd bring it up as they lay in bed.

"Cynthia," he might say.

"Yes?"

"You're growing . . . attached to Jonathan." A simple observation, not a criticism.

"Really? Am I?"

"Yes."

He'd considered the whole issue very carefully and knew it wasn't jealousy. It was fear, fear for her feelings, which ran as deep as the ledges of the continental shelf.

"What is your point, exactly?"

"I see how much you care for him. And you know he'll be going home soon."

"Well, yes, Timothy. Of course. Is there some reason I shouldn't care for him?"

What might he say, then? That he thought it best for her to start letting go, to prepare herself in some way he couldn't fully suggest or understand? Though Jonathan had come to them only weeks ago, his wife had bonded with the boy as if he were her own. But then, hadn't he grown to love Dooley in the very same way? He remembered his dark fears that someone would snatch the boy from him. . . .

In the end, he decided to say nothing at all. Jonathan would be going home, and that would be the end of it.

He was relieved, terribly relieved, that he hadn't brought it up; that he would even think of doing such a thing seemed strange and insensitive.

⚬

"Banana bread!" crowed his wife, dumping a panful onto the counter.

"My mommy, my mommy, she makes bread," said Jonathan, nodding in the affirmative.

"One loaf for us, one loaf for the neighbors," she announced. "But wait, I forgot—we don't know the neighbors."

It was true. A couple of times, they'd waved to the people in the gray house, who seemed to come and go randomly, and the family next door hadn't shown up for the summer at all; one of the shutters on the side facing Dove Cottage had banged in the wind for a month.

Neighbors, he mused. It was an odd thought, one that made his brain feel like it had eaten a pickle.

He heard the music as he stepped off the porch into the backyard.

No idea what it might be. But one thing was certain: it was strong stuff. . . .

He listened intently as he trotted to his good deed. The steady advance of the brooding pedal tones appeared to form the basis of a harmonic progress that he found strangely disturbing. Above this, an elusive melody wove its way through a scattering of high-pitched notes that evoked images of birds agitated by an impending storm.

The effect, he thought as he heaved himself up and over the wall, was confused, almost disjointed, yet the music seemed to produce an essential unity. . . .

Clutching the bread in a Ziploc bag, he stood at the foot of the window from which his neighbor usually conducted his audiences, and listened as the music moved toward its climax.

He might be one crazy preacher, but he didn't think so. In fact, he'd come over the wall as if it were the most natural way in the world to go visiting. He was feeling pretty upbeat about his impetuous mission—after all, this was his neighbor for whom he was now praying, and besides, who could refuse a loaf of bread still warm from the oven?

When the music ended, he shouted, "Well done! Well done, Mr. Love!"

Floorboards creaked in the room above. "Father Kavanagh . . ."

"One and the same!"

"Your dog isn't here," snapped Morris Love.

"Yes, and what a relief! I brought you some banana bread. My wife baked it, it's still warm from the oven, I think you'll like it."

Silence.

If his neighbor didn't go for the bread, he'd just eat the whole thing on the way home.

"She said to tell you it's a token of our appreciation for your music."

Silence.

"What was that piece, anyway? It was very interesting. I don't think I've heard it before." He was a regular chatterbox.

Silence.

He began to as feel as irritable as a child. He'd come over here with a smile on his face and bread in his hand, and what did he get for his trouble? Exactly what he should have expected.

"Mr. Love, for Pete's sake, what shall I do with your *bread?*"

"Leave it in the chair," said Morris Love.

"Do what?"

"Leave it in the chair!" he roared.

He considered this for a moment, then determinedly walked over and sat down. He was tired of darting away from his irate neighbor like a hare before the hound.

Wasn't the trip over worth a moment of small talk, of mere civility? He'd give it a quick go, then he'd be gone.

"Mr. Love, I couldn't help but notice the sign, *Nouvelle Chanson*. How did the house come by that name?"

"My grandmother gave the house its name. She sang with the Met, and counted Rose Bampton and Lily Pons among her friends. Melchior was my grandfather's close acquaintance."

"Aha."

"When my grandparents built this house in 1947 as a summer home, she hoped for a new beginning for their marriage—a new song, if you will." Morris Love's manner was impatient, though decidedly less hostile. "But it didn't work that way."

Father Tim waited a moment. "How *did* it work?"

"My grandparents could only live the old song."

"The old song . . ."

"Little acts of unspoken violence, Father, and bitter hatred towards one another."

Morris Love was actually talking with him. He realized he'd been holding his breath, and released it carefully. "Who taught you to play the organ?"

"My grandfather. Once he had made his fortune, he began to study the organ. In the forties and fifties, several great organ masters spent summers here, instructing him. By the time I came along, he was respectably accomplished and began to teach me at an early age."

"Someone said he had an organ built especially for you. . . ."

"Yes. When I was six years old."

"Is that the organ you play today?"

"That was a toy, Father, a mere toy. I play my grandfather's custom-built Casavant, which was further customized for me."

"I've never seen a Casavant, though I may have heard one without knowing it. It's among the finest in the world, of course."

"More accurately, it is the most magnificent of instruments. Casavant came here to do an acoustical analysis, and worked with the architect to complete this room. My grandfather was a man of exacting preferences."

"I suppose the key covers are of an exotic wood?" It was a small thing, but he'd always been interested in the key covers on old keyboard instruments.

"Only the sharps, which are ebony. The naturals are purest ivory, and of exceeding beauty in their age."

This was pretty heady stuff; he could imagine the splendid hulk of it reigning over the room above. He dove in headfirst. "I'd like very much to see it sometime, and hear you play . . . without walls between us."

He listened to the beating of his heart in the long pause that followed. He'd stepped in it now, he'd pushed too far, and just when he was getting started.

"That would be . . . inappropriate." There was something wistful in Morris Love's voice, he was sure of it. *Lord, speak to his heart.*

"Mr. Love, may I call you Morris? And please—call me Tim."

"I have never addressed a priest by his first name. I find it a repugnant modern custom."

"You've known priests, then? You went to St. John's?"

"Only for baptism. The priests at St. John's often came here, some to pray over me, others to drink my grandfather's French wines. The only joy I ever found in those visits was their occasional gifts of sheet music purloined from the church."

"Your mother and father . . . were they—"

"Out! *Out!*"

He jumped. The shock of hearing the inevitable made his scalp prickle. The tone and repetition of that furious decree were nearly more than he could tolerate. Feeling an invasive weariness in his spirit, and not knowing what else to say or do, he stood to leave.

"Father . . ."

"Yes?"

"You may call me Morris."

"Morris," he said, suddenly hoarse with feeling. "Please don't let the squirrels get your bread. I hope you like it. Try warming it in the oven for breakfast, that's what we do."

He examined an odd intuition, then addressed a question to the window. "Tourette's?"

"Yes. A mild form."

"I'll come again," he said. But there was no reply.

<hr>

Marion Fieldwalker looked up from the checkout desk. "Why, Father Tim! We're tickled to see you!"

"I'm looking for a medical encyclopedia, Marion. Something comprehensive." Given the cost per pound for shipping, he'd decided against dispatching his own to Whitecap.

"You've come to the right place. One of our retirees studied at Harvard Medical School, and gave us a wonderful one. It takes a crane to lift it!"

"Bingo!" he said.

<hr>

While he was here, he wanted to take a look at Dostoyevsky's *Notes from the Underground,* the memory of which resonated profoundly with what he was learning about his neighbor.

It was a work that made him squirm for its dark despair, yet he flipped through it diligently, sneezing from the dust and mold. Out of curiosity, he turned to the card at the back. Aha! One other reader had visited these pages before him, twelve years ago.

Amused, he inscribed his name on the card, *Timothy A. Kavanagh.* For posterity!

"I am a sick man," wrote Dostoyevsky's fictional diarist. "I am a spiteful man. I am an unattractive man. . . .

"The more conscious I was of goodness and of all that was sublime and beautiful, the more deeply I sank into my mire and the more ready I was to sink in it altogether . . . in despair there are the most intense enjoyments, especially when one is very acutely conscious of the hopelessness of one's position. . . .

"I was rude and took pleasure in being so. . . .

"I might . . . be genuinely touched, though probably I should grind my teeth at myself afterward and lie awake at night with shame for months. . . .

"Now I am living out my life in my corner, taunting myself with the spiteful and useless consolation that an intelligent man cannot become anything seriously, and it is only the fool who becomes anything."

Not light summertime reading. He closed the musty book, relieved to look through the window to the bright and cloudless day.

━━◦◦━━

Seated at the antiquated library table, he ran his finger quickly along the text.

". . . characterized by rapid, repetitive, involuntary

muscular movements called 'tics,' and involuntary vo-
calizations . . .

"Phonic tics are diverse and consist of syllables,
words (e.g., 'okay'), short phrases (e.g., 'shut up', 'no,
no'), and full sentences. Tics are sudden, involuntary,
repetitive. . . .

"Tics intensify during periods of stress and anxiety and are frequently misinterpreted as 'nervous
habits.' . . .

"Many suffer depression . . . often become with-
drawn and even suicidal . . .

". . . evidence that Tourette's syndrome is not an
emotional or psychological problem, but a chronic,
hereditary neurological disorder."

"I'd like to check this out," he said, toting the large
tome to the desk.

"Oh, my goodness, that doesn't check out. It's ref-
erence."

Marion must have noted the disappointed look on
his face.

"But we'll make a special exception for clergy," she
said, smiling. "Would you like a wheelbarrow to help
you carry it to the car?"

$$\backsim$$

He didn't have to go looking for Jeffrey Tolson.
Shortly after he unlocked the church on Tuesday morning, Jeffrey Tolson came looking for him.

It wasn't stone from which his face had been carved,
thought Father Tim, it was ice. He noted that Jeffrey
wore the open-necked white shirt with full sleeves that
he'd worn on his earlier visit.

He felt the towering wall between them as they sat in

the office. He had no sermon to preach. He'd let Jeffrey Tolson do the talking he'd come to do, then he'd lay his cards on the table, plain and simple.

"I intend to come back to my church," said Jeffrey Tolson. A muscle twitched in his jaw.

"Your church?"

"My grandfather's church, my father's church, and my church. Yes."

"Being born into this church body confers no special distinctions or ownership. You've hurt a great many people here, Jeffrey."

"There is such a thing as forgiveness, Father."

"Are you asking forgiveness from the people of St. John's?"

Jeffrey crossed his legs and moved his left foot rapidly back and forth. "If that's what it takes."

"Then you're admitting you sinned?"

"No. I'm admitting I made a mistake."

Father Tim looked carefully at the man before him. "There's a bottom line to asking forgiveness. And it's something I don't see or sense in you in the least."

"A bottom line?"

"Repentance. Forgiveness isn't some cheap thing to be gotten on a whim. It's purchased with a deep desire to please God. It's about renouncing. . . ."

"I have renounced. We aren't living together anymore."

"You're speaking of the flesh; I'm speaking of the heart."

Jeffrey Tolson's face blanched. "As choirmaster here for fourteen years, I've heard a good deal of Scripture. You aren't the only one equipped with the so-called truth. I seem to recall that St. Paul said, 'Forgive one another as God in Christ forgave you.' "

"Do you believe Christ is the divine Son of God?"

Jeffrey Tolson shrugged. "I suppose so. Not necessarily."

"We're told that everyone who believes in and relies on Him receives forgiveness of sins through His name. It's not really about asking me or the vestry or anyone at St. John's; it's about hammering it out with Him."

Jeffrey drummed the desktop with the fingers of his right hand.

"To repent means to turn, to turn from whatever binds or enslaves you. What, for example, do you intend to do about your family?"

"Janette has the house and the car, she has a successful sewing business, and as soon I get work on the island, I'll see that she gets a check every week."

"As soon as you get work?"

"You're not from Whitecap, so it probably never occurred to you that getting work on the island is either difficult or impossible."

He heard the sneer in his visitor's voice, and made every effort to keep his own voice even as he spoke. "You could go across to work, like half the population here."

"I'd prefer to work on the island. Commuting is expensive and inconvenient."

"Let's see if I have this right, Jeffrey. You abandoned your wife and children to enter into an adulterous relationship with a married woman, left the island for several months during which your contribution to your family was a grand total of one hundred dollars; you grieved everyone in the church and your choir in particular, and now you state that you don't necessarily believe Christ to be the Son of God, yet you wish His forgiveness."

Jeffrey Tolson opened his mouth to speak, but Father

Tim raised his hand. "In addition, you wish to wait 'til you find work that's convenient, while your wife, currently hospitalized and without income, soldiers on with the fallout as you trot back to God's house, whistling Dixie." He was livid. "When you can return to this place with a humble spirit, confessing your sins and longing for His gift of forgiveness, you'll find a willing heart to hear you." He stood from his desk, shaken.

Jeffrey Tolson stood also, his face white with anger. "I'll come for my son tonight. Have his things ready."

"You'll come for your son? I don't think so. Jonathan was given into our care by Janette. It is Janette who directs his coming and going, and that, you may rest assured, will hold up in a court of law." While he didn't know for certain that it would, it certainly seemed that it should.

He thought he might be punched out on the spot, but didn't care; he felt reckless, invincible.

"You can't stop me from attending St. John's."

"You're absolutely correct, I cannot. But I don't advise it."

Jeffrey Tolson uttered an oath. "Father Morgan, unlike yourself, was a peacemaker. You're no Father Morgan."

"Thanks be to God!" he said, holding his office door open.

"Father, before you take your days off, wouldn't you like to put in your order for a new sport coat?"

He looked at Jean Ballenger's newly trimmed bangs, which were curling upward like the lashes of a film star. "A new sport coat?"

"For Janette, to help her get started back in business when she comes home. I'm going to order a paisley shirtwaist; Marion's ordering a red dress, she says she wears too much navy; and we thought you might like to order a sport coat."

"Well . . ."

"Something blue would be good on you."

He had three blue sport coats, but he didn't say anything.

"Penny Duncan is ordering a wrap skirt, even though she doesn't have gobs of money to throw around and sews like a dream herself! Don't you think that's sacrificial?"

"I do."

"And Cynthia could order a suit in linen or piqué, maybe something with a nice peplum, I think she'd look stunning in a peplum."

"How much is a sport coat?"

"I don't have any idea."

"Why don't you get back to me on that?"

"Oh, I will!" she said, making a note on her pad. "I just think it would be the Christian thing to do, don't you?"

He grinned at the earnest Jean Ballenger trotting down the hall to solicit orders from the Busy Fingers group, which was currently living up to their name, bigtime.

It was rather a nice thought, actually, that he'd soon be looking into the nave and seeing his entire congregation turned out in new duds, whether they needed them or not.

———⟡———

The encounter with Jeffrey Tolson had shaken him badly. He sat in the study at Dove Cottage with his head in his hand for longer than his wife liked.

"Timothy, dear, what *is* it?" she demanded on a third inquiry.

"Ahhh," he said, lacking the energy to tell the sordid thing. Besides, did this mean Jeffrey Tolson might be hanging about to forcibly take Jonathan while Cynthia and the boy were alone? He despised even thinking this.

$$\sim\hspace{-0.5em}\circ\hspace{-0.5em}\sim$$

He was just getting into bed when he heard the knock.

What time was it, anyway? He peered at the clock on the nightstand. Past ten.

Through the glass panels in the front door, he saw what appeared to be a flashlight bobbing on the porch. He switched on the porch light and threw open the door.

It was someone in uniform, and someone plenty big, to boot.

"Would you identify yourself, sir?"

"Tim Kavanagh. Why do you ask?"

"I have a civil paper to serve you. You're being sued."

"I beg your pardon?"

"Are you the Reverend Timothy *A.* Kavanagh?"

"I am, yes." His heart was hammering.

"I'm Bill Deal, th' sheriff of this county." Bill Deal pocketed his flashlight and brought out his wallet to display a badge. "I hate to do this to you, I believe you fish with Cap'n Willie."

Speechless, he opened the screen door, took an envelope from the man, and gazed at it, dumbfounded. The sheriff cleared his throat and stepped to the edge of the porch, looking at the sky.

"Prob'ly goin' to get us some rain before long. Well, you take it easy, Reverend." The sheriff lumbered down the steps, walked to the front gate, and got in the car.

He stood there in the chill October air as if mesmerized.

Cynthia called from the hallway. "Timothy, what's going on?"

"I have no idea, I don't know."

Nor did he want to know.

CHAPTER SIXTEEN

Dorchester Island

It wasn't that he couldn't understand the general intent of the papers he'd been served—he could. It was that he wasn't able to make it all come together in any sensible order; each time he read them, it was as if his mind split like an atom. He knew only one thing for certain—he was deeply alarmed.

He went to the study and took his quote book from the shelf, the quote book he'd made entries in for fifteen years. He wanted something St. Francis de Sales had said; he'd copied it into the book just the other day. . . .

Do not look forward to what may happen tomorrow; the same everlasting Father who cares for you today will take care of you tomorrow and every day. Either He will shield you from suffering, or He will give you unfailing strength to bear it. Be at peace, then, put aside all anxious thoughts and imaginations, and say continually: "The Lord is my strength and my shield; my heart has trusted in Him and I am helped. He is not only with me but in me and I in Him."

It was after eleven o'clock when he dressed and drove to St. John's, went down the cement steps by the light of the moon, and faxed the papers to his cousin's home in New Jersey. The fax machine was located in Walter's study where he'd be sure to find the papers the following morning, before he left for his law office in Manhattan.

Father Tim scribbled a cover sheet with St. John's phone number and a brief message:

Please call me the moment you look this over. I'll be at the church office by six a.m.

He didn't want to have the conversation with his attorney cousin at home, where his wife was already in a state of trepidation over this ghastly turn of events.

$\sim$

He left Dove Cottage at five forty-five, bundled into a sweater and jacket.

"Layspeak, Walter, layspeak."

He sat at his desk in the chill basement office, drinking a tepid cup of coffee from home and scribbling on a legal pad. "Start at the beginning. I'm writing everything down." *Put aside all anxious thoughts and imaginations. . . .*

"Hélène Pringle is suing you, as trustee, for one-third of the escrow funds of Hope House."

"Right." His voice sounded like the croaking of a

frog, and he realized he was again holding his head in his hand.

"She claims to be the illegitimate daughter of Josiah Baxter. . . ."

Miss Sadie's father. This claim seemed so bizarre and extraordinary, his mind couldn't contain it; the whole notion kept flying out of his head, even as he tried to poke it back in.

"But why now, after all these years . . . ?"

"I've no idea. Apparently they're basing the suit on Baxter's holographic will, in which he decreed that a third of his estate would go to Hélène Pringle's mother, Françoise, upon his death. When did Baxter die, anyway?"

He'd tried to work this out in his mind last night. The date was on the urn in the columbarium at Lord's Chapel. He'd seen it numerous times, but couldn't remember exactly. "Sometime in the late forties."

"How old was he at the time of death?"

"Miss Sadie told me once . . . in his seventies, I think. In fact, I believe she said he died soon after an extended trip to France." He knew Miss Sadie's mother had died in 1942, so Josiah Baxter must have been a widower when . . .

"Of course, the domestic statute of limitations has run out by several decades," said Walter.

"Then they don't really have a case?"

"Unfortunately, the suit is based on French law, involving an obscure treaty between France and the U.S., which was adopted at the end of World War II. I don't know much about it, probably something that spun off the problem of occupation troops and paternity issues."

He thought the whole thing a veritable hash of mystery and confusion.

"Looks like Pringle's attorney is French—Louis d'Anjou of d'Anjou and Pichot—and both Pringle and her mother are French citizens. Let me look into it; I know almost nothing about French law. You've got thirty days to file a written response to the allegations."

He shook his head as if to wake himself from a bad dream.

"I'll call her attorney and see what's what, and get back to you in a couple of days—right now, I'm in court on a big one."

"Anything," he said. "Anything you can do . . ."

He hung up, as winded as if he'd run a mile on the beach.

Ava Goodnight was coming day after tomorrow, the day of the Dorchester trip. He'd have breakfast at Mona's, let Roanoke give him a trim around seven-thirty, tend to a couple of things at St. John's, then go back to Ernie's no later than nine-thirty to meet Ava and her sister. So . . . if he and Cynthia and Jonathan left shortly before eleven, they'd arrive at Ella's around noon. They'd visit with Ella, then he'd administer the sacraments to Captain Larkin and they'd head home. Considering all they had to do before Mitford, he'd suggest they tromp through the graveyard another day; heaven knows, the dead weren't going anywhere.

"Our trek to Dorchester is coming up day after tomorrow," he said over the last of their lunch. "We'll try to keep it short. I know you have plenty to do."

"Jonathan may not be able to go," she said. "He has a miserable cough and his nose is dripping like a faucet."

"Allergies?"

"I don't think so, and besides, Timothy, I hear there's a storm front moving in."

"If we had to drop everything each time a storm came our way, we'd get absolutely nothing done around here!"

She looked bleak. "A lawsuit, a sick boy, a ten-hour drive, and a storm front . . ."

"When it rains, it pours," he said. "No pun intended."

Jonathan ran into the kitchen and clambered onto Cynthia's lap. *"Heavens!"* she exclaimed, wiping his nose with the lunch napkin. "Now, *blow!*"

"We're looking forward to seeing you, buddy."

"Me, too. Mama said Buck came in the other day, he's bunkin' with Harley, she says he lost weight an' all for th' wedding. Poo's wearin' a suit, I can't believe Poo in a suit."

"What are you wearing?"

"Umm," said Dooley. "A suit."

"Don't forget your shirt and tie—or, you could borrow one of my ties."

"Your ties are too . . ."

"Too what?"

"Boring."

For someone who was usually in a collar, he'd never thought much about ties. Maybe he needed to buy something . . . upbeat! Something Italian! "What time are you rolling into Mitford?"

" 'Bout eleven Friday morning."

"How are you feeling about the appearance before the judge?"

"Not too good."

"It'll go well, don't worry. And how are you feeling about Caroline?"

Dooley was shrugging; he could practically hear it. The boy was blushing; he could sense it.

"Ah . . ."

"Pretty good?"

"Well, yeah, she's really neat, really interesting. She does these great watercolors, like Cynthia. You should see the one she did of the mountains behind her school, it was exactly like real life, except better."

"I'll be darned."

"She's got this cool laugh, too, sort of like . . . like this." Dooley made an odd sound, something between a snort and a cackle. "That's not right, it's more like . . . I don't know!"

"I can kind of guess."

"Plus she's really funny."

Dooley Barlowe was a goner, as far as he could tell.

～ⓔ～

"We can't go, dearest, he's burning with fever. I hope it's only the flu. Nearly everyone in story group was croupy and sick on Wednesday; I'd never have taken him if I'd known. I have a call in to his doctor."

He felt the boy's head, he looked at his red eyes and runny nose, he listened to his labored breathing. Convinced that hauling Jonathan to Dorchester would only make things worse, he finally told her. "Jeffrey Tolson may be hanging about. I don't think he's dangerous, but there's no telling what he might do."

"He can do nothing here!" she said, looking fierce. "We'll keep the doors locked and you'll only be away in broad daylight, so there's no use at all to worry. I'll send Ella the lasagna I froze the other day. Single women almost never make lasagna!"

His wife could convince him of anything. Feeling mildly relieved, he went to the study and closed the door and sat in the chair and prayed about it. He had written Captain Larkin the other day to say he was coming, and the last thing he wanted to do was disappoint. Should he go, or move the trip to a later date?

After he prayed, he listened.

God would have him go. He felt certain of it.

The sky was gunmetal from horizon to horizon; it seemed as if a leaden weight had been clamped over Whitecap like a lid on a turkey roaster.

He paced the front porch, unable to think clearly, anxious about leaving tomorrow. Maybe he should skip the Ava business and leave early, but Ernie was as excited about this little gathering as any parent, a fact he didn't feel like treating lightly. Besides, he wanted to see Ava Goodnight, who, let's face it, had accumulated some pretty heavy mystique without even trying.

Cynthia would be fine, she'd insisted on it, and he'd call her from Ella's house at least once, maybe twice.

While he was thinking of it, why didn't he have a car phone? Everyone else seemed to be zooming around at top speed, yammering into one as if their lives depended on it. Yet there was nothing in the thought of a car phone that attracted him. Wouldn't people break into his car and steal it, or did they steal phones anymore? Maybe car phones were now so cheap and run-of-the-mill that no one wanted the hassle of smashing a window. Anyway, if he had one, wouldn't he have to keep the top up on the Mustang? Otherwise, they could just reach in and yank it off its hinge or whatever.

Why was he thinking such nonsense? He was thinking nonsense because he dreaded thinking the real thing; he was trying desperately to hide from the reality of the lawsuit.

He zipped his jacket and sat in his favorite rocker, looking into the gathering dusk.

The lawsuit dogged him like a dark cloud. What on earth could be the possible meaning behind it all? Thank God, Walter was more than a cousin who happened to practice law. Walter was a tough, no-nonsense attorney with a decent reputation and several heavyweight clients; surely he could help him hammer this thing through.

He realized he was wringing his hands, something he'd hardly ever caught himself doing, and stopped it at once.

Yet, even more than the fret and worry of being slammed with a lawsuit was the possibility of losing a third of the escrow, which included part of what Andrew Gregory had paid for Miss Sadie's antiques, and a third of what the money had earned in mutual funds, making Hélène Pringle the possible recipient of around a hundred and fifty thousand dollars. Miss Sadie had trusted him to be a good steward of all she left behind, and he'd never begrudged this enormous responsibility, not for a moment. Now he felt the full weight of it squarely on his shoulders, with no one to turn to but someone he'd known since childhood as Potato Head.

God hadn't given him much family, but God *had* given him Walter; perhaps, just as Mordecai said in the Book of Esther, for such a time as this.

So—he had excellent legal counsel, and he and Cynthia were praying the prayer that never fails. What more could be done, after all?

Aha! His neighbor was at it again, though he didn't recognize the music.

He walked to the north side of the porch and cupped his hands to his ears. Interesting. Very interesting.

He squatted, then sat on the end of the porch, swinging his legs over the side.

Yes! That's it, Morris! What you're doing with the bass, keep it up, great, beautiful, have at it. . . .

He slipped off the porch, trotted to the rear gate and unlatched it, then went into the twilit street, where he stood for a moment, listening.

─◈─

His wife would not like him pulling a disappearing act, no, indeed, but he'd be gone only five, maybe ten minutes, she'd never miss him; his dog, however, was another matter. If Barnabas knew he'd gone on a joyride without him . . .

He dropped to the ground on the other side of the wall, and found himself jogging along the driveway.

When he reached the house, he thumped into his chair under the window, and listened.

He alternately nodded enthusiastically and wagged his head. He wagged his head at the foreboding passages in the music, though he knew they gave greater light to the passages of illumination.

Man alive, that Casavant was blowing the roof off.

When the music ended, he felt tears on his cheeks. He waited a few moments.

"Morris?" he shouted.

"It's you, Father."

"Yes."

There was a long, oddly comfortable silence.

"I'm going away for a few days and I came to say . . ." There was a sudden lump in his throat. "I came to say I think the music is . . ." The music is what? Moving? Powerful? How did critics manage to make a living with a language that must often fail them?

"Wonderful!" he shouted. Full of wonder! That was the best he could do for the moment.

"Perhaps you'd like to come in . . . and see the Casavant."

Had he heard right? He wiped his eyes on his shirt-sleeve. "Why, yes, thank you, I'd like that." His wife would be frantic, but this was an extraordinary invitation. He was stunned. . . .

"The door is open. Take the stairs. I'll meet you on the landing."

He bolted from the chair, careful not to stumble over the uprooted bricks that once paved the entranceway.

The heavy front door opened easily, and he stepped into a dimly lit foyer. The light appeared to come from a single bulb in a wall sconce, though a large chandelier loomed above his head.

There was definitely a musty smell, but everything looked clean and orderly. Ornately carved armchairs stood on either side of a heavy mirror in which he was startled to see himself. On the floor, a pattern of black and white tiles, and to the right, a curving stairwell and a vast, lighted oil painting on the high wall. The painting was of rolling countryside, somewhere in Europe, perhaps, with a church spire and a procession of people in a lane.

"Father."

He looked toward the landing and saw Morris standing at the rail.

"Morris!"

"Come up."

He went up, as if in a dream. There was absolutely no sense of reality about where he suddenly found himself. He knew only that he needed to be here, was supposed to be here. . . .

Morris held his hands behind his back, apparently declining a handshake, as Father Tim looked directly into his eyes. He noted Morris's prominent forehead and the deep, vertical furrow between his heavy brows.

"You are not surprised," Morris said flatly.

"No, not at all."

"Come with me," said his host.

He was surprised, however, to see that Morris walked with such difficulty. As if sensing his curiosity, Morris turned and said, "Spinal stenosis, aggravated by arthritis. It is not uncommon to my condition. We're in here." Morris stood aside so that he might enter first.

As he stepped over the threshold, he drew in his breath. There, in a room illumined by lamplight, stood the Casavant, regal beneath the rank of elaborately stenciled facade pipes. With its ornamented mahogany casework, he thought the organ possessed the aura of a great throne.

He might have gaped interminably, but turned his gaze to the room itself, which was paneled with walnut. His eyes moved along the intricately detailed dentil moldings and carved inlays, to the open window where Morris must stand when talking with him; it was free of draperies, with only a simple pelmet above, perhaps to enhance the acoustics of the room.

Floor-to-ceiling bookcases, a bare, polished floor, velvet-covered chairs sagging with use, a love seat in a far corner . . .

"Beautiful!" he said, gawking unashamedly. Yet, a prison, nonetheless. He felt the awful weight of the room on his spirit, as if the only thing that ever stirred the air might be the music.

He sensed Morris's eyes on him. "Thank you for asking me in. I'm grateful to be here."

"My housekeeper comes every other day—Mamie has been with me since childhood—and my organ tuner comes as needed. I'm not completely without social intercourse."

"I'm glad. It's one of the things that keeps us soldiering on in this life."

"We strive to keep up appearances in this part of the house, but the grounds are without hope. My grandfather planted a jungle. It cannot be beaten back, and we long ago gave up trying."

Morris's head suddenly wrenched toward his right shoulder, jerking in a manner that seemed uncontrollable. "Out!" he growled. *"Out!"*

Father Tim walked to the organ, making a conscious effort to appear oblivious to what he'd just seen. "The pedals . . ."

"Yes," said Morris, as the tic passed. "Casavant provided a second pedal board for me, elevated one position above the standard pedal board.

"I've considered what I might play for you . . . the Widor Toccata, perhaps. You may know that the Casavant is designed for French voicing. The company founders spent a great deal of time in France, and scaled the pipes to play French repertoire especially well."

Morris slid stiffly onto the bench and pulled the chain of a green-shaded lamp over the keyboards. "You'll find this piece quite vibrant. It demonstrates all the tonal colors of the instrument. Listen to the reed stops, if you will. They're very distinctive, and altogether different from the more mellow English reed stops."

Father Tim stood by the organ, enthralled.

"Please sit," said Morris.

Father Tim hurried to a slipcovered armchair and sat, closing his eyes as the music began. Flashy and flamboyant, upbeat and positive, Widor made the hair stand up along his right arm and leg. Ah, the difference in being in the room with the music rather than sitting outside as a lowly trespasser!

The music so filled him with a nervous and exuberant energy that it flowed out at the climax as laughter.

"Wonderful!" Couldn't he come up with something less tiresome, for heaven's sake? "Marvelous! Bravo!"

Morris reflected for a moment. "And now, perhaps Bach's Great Prelude and Fugue in G Minor. . . ."

As the fugue subject unfolded, he wondered, as he always did when he heard this favorite composition, how a theme in a minor key could express such confident joy and abiding faith. The music soared around the room like a bird set loose from its cage, causing his scalp to prickle.

"Thank you," he said afterward, supremely happy.

Morris labored to rise from the bench, and stood by his instrument. "Thank you for listening, Father. You have an attentive and sympathetic ear."

Father Tim rose from the chair, which gave off the faint odor of old tobacco. "How I wish you might share your gift with . . ." It was hardly out of his mouth before he knew he'd said the wrong thing.

Morris's face grew hard. "Never speak of that again."

"I'm sorry," he said. "You have my word, I'll never speak of it again."

"The wine cellars were depleted years ago. I have nothing to offer you."

"You've given me more than I could possibly wish. Thank you, Morris, thank you. I'll go along, now. My dog will be furious that I've come without him."

Morris did not smile. "I'll walk you to the landing."

At the landing, he had a sudden urge to throw his arms around the man, shake his hand, make the sign of the cross over him—something, anything, to express his deep feeling. "You're faithfully in my prayers," he said.

His host's head jerked toward his shoulder. "Out! Out!"

Father Tim's heart pounded as he moved quickly down the stairs, angry with himself for failing to say the right thing, for the terrible alarm those words always ignited in his breast.

In the foyer, he turned briefly to look at Morris, then opened the door of Nouvelle Chanson and stepped into the October night.

─◦─

He went at a trot—down the dark driveway under a hidden moon, over the wall, across the street, through the gate, up the steps to the back porch, and into the kitchen, panting. She probably had that sheriff out searching for him. He dreaded facing her. How could he have been so thoughtless and insensitive?

"Is that you, dearest?" Cynthia came into the kitchen, rubbing her eyes. "I hope you weren't waiting for me on the porch all this time. I started a new illustration and, well, you know how it is, I forgot." She looked at the kitchen clock. "Good heavens! Eight-thirty! I hope you haven't felt neglected."

"Oh, no, no! Don't even mention it," he said.

⟶⟵

Jonathan was on antibiotics delivered from the pharmacy, and Cynthia would spend the day doctoring him for tomorrow's journey to Mitford.

He rose at six a.m., dressed more warmly than usual, and set off for Mona's.

It had definitely been a while since he'd had breakfast like he used to have at the Grill. It gave him a positive thrill to place his order.

"Two medium poached, whole wheat toast, hold the butter, and a side of grits."

"Do you want coffee?" asked the shy waitress, whom he hadn't seen before.

"The hard stuff, no cream, no sugar. Are you new?"

"Yessir, this is my first day. I'm kind of . . . nervous."

"I certainly didn't notice! I'm Father Kavanagh, glad to see you."

"I'm Misty Summers. My name tag says Missy, they got it wrong and have to do it over. Glad to meet you."

"Misty Summers! Now, there's a name for you. Very pretty name."

"Thank you," she said, blushing. "Would you like water? I can get you filtered, Mona serves filtered to special customers, I'm sure you must be special."

"Why on earth would you think so?"

"Your . . ." She indicated his neck. "You know."

"Ah. My collar."

"I've hardly ever met any Catholics."

"I'm Episcopalian."

"Oh," she said. "Well, I'll be right out with your water and your coffee."

"Thank you," he said, pleased to be here with a newspaper and the respite to read it. He really didn't want to make the Dorchester trek, but intended to get this day behind him, no matter what. Besides, when he called last night to say Cynthia and the boy weren't coming, Ella told him she was breaking out the damask tablecloth, which she hadn't used since her mother died and all the neighbors brought food and sat with her.

"There you go!" said Misty, setting a steaming mug before him. She looked like a milkmaid from a storybook, he thought. No makeup, long, chestnut hair caught in a ponytail, and a simple skirt and blouse under the café's signature green apron.

"Where are you from, Misty? Whitecap?"

"Oh, no, sir, Ocracoke. I just moved here two days ago, and was real blessed to get this job right off."

"I'm sure you'll do well. I believe you'll like Whitecap."

"Yessir," she said, pouring his coffee. He couldn't help but notice that her hand shook slightly.

"Try not to worry about getting everything right today," he said

She lifted her gaze and he noticed her eyes for the first time. Warm. Trusting.

"I'll pray for you."

"Thank you, I really appreciate it. We'll have your order right out. Did you want ketchup?"

"Ketchup?"

"For your hash browns."

"Hash browns?"

She clapped her hand to her mouth. "Oh, gosh, I forgot, you're having grits!"

She fled to the kitchen, flustered.

As relaxed as if he had the whole day in which to do nothing, he opened his newspaper to the editorial page and settled happily into the green vinyl-covered seat of Mona's rear booth.

"Look here!" said Roanoke.

"Look here what?"

"Your hair's growed a good bit more'n I'd expect."

"Olive oil," said Father Tim, propped on the stool like a schoolboy.

"You rub olive oil on your head? I never heard of that one."

"Eat a lot of it on salads."

"Seems like God would've let a man have some say in where 'is hair grows, don't it? I mean, here you got all this hangin' down in back, an' not that much on top."

"Tell me about it."

Snip, snip.

"They say we'll prob'ly get a bad storm tonight," said Roanoke.

"I'm running up to Dor'ster. I hope it holds off 'til I get back."

"Temperature's droppin' pretty steady, too."

There was Elmo, sitting in the doorway to the book room and scowling at him as if he were a mangy hound. "Yo, Elmo!" he said.

At 9:25, according to the clock over Ernie's cash register, the entire room erupted into a bedlam of laughter, fish stories, and adrenaline-driven babble. He figured they wanted Ava and her sister to think this was a busy, prosperous enterprise, not some pokey little deal on a backwater island. Adding to the general vibration was the fact that Roger was nearly through burning, and would soon begin painting.

Father Tim had to admit that Junior was looking good. Instead of washing or ironing anything, however, he'd run across and bought new jeans, a shirt and jacket, and a new cap that read *Go, Bulls.*

"I'd take that off," said Roanoke.

"Why? She's seen my pictures, she knows my hair's a little . . . you know."

"That's not what I mean. I mean she might not like th' Bulls."

Junior looked stubborn. "I don't want to take it off," he said. "It's brand-new."

"Yeah, but what if she likes Carolina? You'd sure wish you was wearin' one that says *Go, Heels.*"

Glowering, Junior snatched the hat off his head and threw it in the corner.

"Now, don't go upsettin' him!" said Ernie, picking up the hat. "If you feel good wearin' th' thing, put it back on."

Junior crammed the hat back on his head and sat stiffly, looking miserable.

"Tim, you ought to tell Junior how you caught that big yellowfin tuna, take everybody's mind off—"

The screen door slammed as Ava Goodnight walked in and stared anxiously at the roomful of men.

The silence was sudden, complete, and absolute.

Ernie appeared turned to stone, Roanoke's hand froze at his shirt pocket where he was reaching for a Marlboro, and Junior's mouth was hanging open.

"You must be Ava!" said Father Tim, walking over and shaking her hand.

"And you must be Father Tim," she said, smiling. "Betty will be here in a minute, Betty's my sister, she's next door in the ladies' room." Ava caught her breath and looked as if she might change her mind and run out the way she'd come in.

"And this is Junior. Junior Bryson." As the only one still able to function around here, he guessed the social stuff was up to him.

Junior rose slowly from the table and walked toward Ava as if in a trance. Father Tim wished to heaven that Junior would close his mouth.

"How're you?" asked Junior.

Ava extended her hand. "I'm just fine. How're you?"

"Just fine, an' how 'bout you?"

"And this," he said, pushing on, "is Roanoke Clark. He's a friend of Junior's."

Roanoke grinned and touched his forehead, a remnant gesture, Father Tim supposed, from the days men tipped their hats to women. "Pleasure."

"That's Roger Templeton. . . ."

"How do you do?" said Roger, standing respectfully.

"And I'm Ernie," said Ernie, recovering his speech and bounding over to shake Ava's hand. "We're glad to have you, nice to see you, come and sit down! We know you're goin' next door for coffee, but I could pour you a little somethin' in a cup, like a Cheerwine or a Dr Pepper, but you probably drink Coke, I could open you a Coke, how's that? On th' house!" Ernie was still shaking Ava's hand.

"Oh, no," said Ava, "I don't need a thing. But thanks a lot."

Father Tim figured somebody better make a move or

Ava was out of here. "Ava, we're sorry we're a roomful of men. My wife would have come to meet you this morning, but we have a sick boy at home."

"I'm sorry," she said, appearing to mean it.

"Come and sit with us a minute," he said. "Roger, show Ava your duck."

Roger shyly held up his green-winged teal.

"Isn't that a marvel?" asked Father Tim, who was beginning to feel like the Perle Mesta of the Outer Banks.

Ava glanced at the door, looking for Betty. "Really nice! Really pretty!"

"We'd like you to feel welcome on Whitecap," said Father Tim. "Have you been here before?"

"No, sir, I never have. But my friend who lives on Tern Avenue—we've been meaning to get together for a long time."

Junior was currently grinning from ear to ear. He expanded his chest and adjusted his jacket sleeves, which Father Tim judged to be a mite on the short side.

"Oh, law!" said Betty, barging through the screen door. "Are we runnin' late, my watch has stopped, hey, y'all, I'm Ava's sister, her much *old*er sister, who're you?"

"I'm Tim Kavanagh. Glad to see you, Betty." The Lord had sent an icebreaker, and not a moment too soon.

"Hey, Tim, how're you, I hope I don't have lipstick on my teeth, do I have lipstick on my teeth? I dropped my compact in th' ladies room and busted my mirror, but since I already *had* seven years of bad luck, I hope I'm off th' hook!"

She fastened her gaze on Ernie. "An' you must be th' bigwig of this place, you *look* like you're th' bigwig."

"Why, yes, ma'am, I'm Ernie Fulcher, one an' the same. Have a seat and meet everybody. We're glad to have you."

"I don't suppose ya'll'd have a little drop of Diet Pepsi or somethin,' I'm dry as a *bone*! I did th' drivin,' since Ava was busy doin' her nails and takin' her rollers out, an' drivin' always makes me thirsty, does it *you*?"

"Oh, yes, ma'am," said Roanoke, glad to be asked. "When I was haulin' lumber, I sometimes drank a whole case of Cheerwine between Asheville an' Wilmington."

"And you're Junior! I declare, you're better-lookin' than your pictures, don't you think so, Ava? A *whole* lot better-lookin' if you ask me, which nobody did!" Betty whooped with laughter and thumped down at a table, hanging the strap of a large shoulder bag over the chair back.

Betty patted the tabletop. "Come on, honey," she said to her sister, "sit down a minute and meet all these nice fellas who've been dyin' to see you, then we'll go next door and have a bite to eat, right, Junior?"

⸺◦⸺

"Now, that's what I call a good-lookin' woman . . . ," said Ernie, dazed and staring at the door.

Without glancing up from his duck, Roger nodded in agreement.

"But seems like she might be too much for Junior."

Roanoke ground his cigarette out in a bottle cap. "You ain't tellin' us nothin' we don't know."

Roger burned a feather. Lucas yawned. The Dr Pepper clock ticked over the cash register.

"Well," said Father Tim, pushing back from the table, "you all can sit here 'til Judgment Day, but I've got fish to fry."

Ernie looked at him, anxious. "D'you think Junior stands a chance?"

"God only knows," he said, meaning it.

⟡

The lowering overcast continued—across the bridge, up the coast, and over the causeway to Dorchester. As he hit the island, the rain began.

He turned the heater on, pondering the fact that he could never think rationally when Morris yelled, but at last he understood that the harsh, repetitive command had little to do with him; in his opinion, it meant something else entirely—out of this body, out of this prison, out of this terrible exile. . . .

There . . . a stop sign, and Little Shell Beach Road. He looked at his watch, checked his odometer, and turned right. One and a half miles to Old Cemetery Road . . .

The lawsuit. It swam into his mind relentlessly. *The Lord is my strength and my shield. . . .*

He'd hold off on saying anything to the Hope House Board of Trustees until he talked again with Walter. The irony, he thought, of a stranger moving into his own house to set up shop to sue him. And why had she moved to Mitford to sue, when she might have done it just as well from Boston? It was the most mind-boggling turn of events imaginable.

He prayed as he slowly moved south on the small island of Dorchester—for Junior, Misty Summers, Cynthia, Jonathan, Janette, Morris Love, Buck and Pauline . . .

Old Cemetery Road. He hooked a right, hearing his tires crunch on gravel.

. . . for Dooley's missing brothers, Dooley's appearance before the judge, Busy Fingers' ability to complete the Lord's Supper needlepoint on time . . .

. . . and Jeffrey Tolson. He didn't want to pray for Jeffrey Tolson, but drew a deep breath and did it anyway. Could he personally forgive Janette's husband, even if the man wasn't repentant for the pain he'd caused?

He wanted to, he was required to, and, yes, he would keep trying to—with God's help.

〜

Ella was looking for him. The moment he hit the porch, she opened the door and he blew into her living room with a gust of rain.

"Oh, mercy," she said, shaking his hand, "you're soaked! But come and stand by the piano. I've got the hair dryer ready."

"The hair dryer?"

"To dry you off!" she said, pleased to be helpful.

〜

He had heard of time warps, and was utterly delighted to be in one. Ella Bridgewater's cottage was as pleasant as anything he'd seen in years. He felt instantly at home. In truth, it appeared as if his own mother might have placed Ella's turn-of-the-century furniture and the numerous family photographs in polished silver frames.

Small flames licked up from a single log in the fireplace, and a stack of wood lay by the hearth, ready for anything.

He inhaled deeply of the glorious aroma in the house, which seemed largely composed of salt air, wood smoke, and sea bass with lemon butter. Sitting by the fire as Ella prepared lunch, the clock ticking on the mantel, he felt as contented as a country squire.

This, he presumed, was the place where antimacassars went when they died—they were in evidence everywhere, and starched to beat the band. His mother had used sugar water to starch her own; as a child he'd had an awful desire to eat the one on the piecrust table; it made his mouth fairly water to see it.

Ella brought a small etched glass and a decanter. "There you are!" she said, clearly delighted to have his company. "That's my plum wine, I hope you like it, it won a blue ribbon in 1978! Lunch in ten minutes. And now you're settled, I'll send Louise in."

She went briskly to an adjoining room, out of which a canary momentarily flew. It made a beeline for the piano, where it perched on the bench and cocked its head at him.

"Louise, do sing for Father Timothy, he's come all the way from Whitecap."

To his astonishment, Louise began to warble with great charm and enthusiasm, and finished her rendition perched on an antimacassar atop the piano.

"Amazing!" he said. "Bring her to St. John's for a solo!" They could do worse than sit and listen to one of God's creatures sing from the depths of an unfettered heart.

~

The rain increased to gusting, wind-driven sheets that made the small house shudder as they sat at the table.

"Minor and I made plans to marry, and then, two weeks before the ceremony was to take place in our little church down the road, he was ballooning over Nova Scotia, and . . . well . . ."

"I'm sorry," he said.

Ella lifted her glass in a salute, and soldiered on as

hostess. "Plums are very hard to find nowadays, unless you buy them in a store, and I'm hardly ever tempted to do that. You know what the problem is?"

"I confess I don't."

"Everyone works away from home these days, they don't keep their fruit trees sprayed or pruned, and the poor things simply fall down in the pasture or the yard or wherever, and that's the end of it."

" 'The world is too much with us; late and soon,' " he said, quoting Wordsworth. " 'Getting and spending, we lay waste our powers;/ little we see in Nature that is ours;/ we have given our hearts away, a sordid boon!' "

"Exactly," she agreed. "Amen!"

He was feeling anxious as they finished their dessert. "Do you have a TV we could watch for weather news?"

Ella sighed. "There hasn't been a TV in this house for years! Do you remember when the Dallas Cowboys beat the Denver Broncos in the Super Bowl?"

"I don't believe I do," he said.

"Mother and I were watching the game, sitting right over there, when the screen went black as pitch. I remember to this day what Mother said, she said, 'Ella, do you think this happened because I bet two dollars on the Cowboys with Joe?' Joe was our postmaster. We tried to have it fixed, but it was dead as a doornail, and we never replaced it."

A clap of thunder broke above them so loudly that he started from his chair. "Just . . . looking for a phone!" he said.

He dialed Dove Cottage as Ella stood by, peering at him anxiously. Her mother had taught her never to use a phone in a storm. She was, in fact, eager to unplug everything electrical, including the lamps, though she supposed that wouldn't be proper during a visit by clergy.

Cynthia reported that things were fine at home, and she was praying for him. While his wife implored him to do nothing reckless in such bad weather, he should, nonetheless, hurry home.

He was wanting out of here fast, though he felt compelled by common courtesy to look at a couple of photographs before leaving. There was Minor standing by a hot-air balloon, quite fit and handsome in a flight suit. Glaring from an oval frame, Mrs. Bridgewater appeared sufficiently formidable to wither the hollyhocks that served as background.

"I just hate this storm. I walked down to church last night and raked Mother's grave and dusted the pews . . . but you'll see it all another day." Ella's rouge was two perfectly circular spots. "And I wanted to show you our live oak. It's the oldest on the island as far as anybody knows. Maybe you can get a peep at it as you leave. It's just a few yards from that side of the porch."

"We'll do the full tour another day. I look forward to it."

"Well, then," she said, slipping a parcel into his hand. "This is a smidgen of my plum wine, and a few morsels of sea bass for your Violet. I'd so love to have a c-a-t, but I *can't* have a c-a-t, you know, as long as Louise is with me."

"Aha. Well, I'm off, and can't thank you enough. I've been happy in your home, Ella, and very much like your idea for next Sunday's anthem."

"Thank you for coming, Father, it was an honor. Now, left out of the driveway and two blocks on the right in the old white two-story, that's Captain Larkin.

Remember to look for the blue truck in front and beware the dog, they say he bites."

She opened the door and was struck forcibly by a blast of cold wind and rain.

"I'll pray for you!" she called, as he dashed into the deluge.

***

He'd been out in a few storms, but this one worried him. As soon as they got back from Mitford, he'd have the blasted car radio fixed so he could find a little weather news when he needed it.

Driving at ten miles an hour, he managed to spot what he presumed to be the captain's house, and pulled up behind the blue truck. Any dog that would take the trouble to bite in weather like this was welcome to try, he thought, as he grabbed the wet umbrella and a leather box containing the home communion set.

He slogged to the concrete steps in a driving wind that threatened to invert the umbrella, and opened the screen door to the porch. A scowling face peered through the glass panels of the front door and quickly vanished.

Lord, bless this time, he prayed as he knocked, *and keep us safe from any harm in this storm. . . .*

He nearly leaped from his sodden loafers as a violent clap of thunder rolled overhead and the door opened. An elderly man with the countenance of an angel peered out.

"Hurry in, Father, hurry in!" said Captain Larkin.

CHAPTER SEVENTEEN

Bread and Wine

He stepped into a large parlor that smelled of fireplace ashes and stale bacon, like country houses he remembered from his Mississippi childhood.

His glance took in an afghan-covered sofa, two worn reclining chairs, a television set on a rolling stand, and a bevy of family portraits lining the white beadboard walls. To his right, a stairway with a curved banister, and closed double doors to what was probably a dining room. The house had once been rather fine, if unpretentious, and he was glad for its refuge.

"Where's your oilskins at, Father?" The captain spoke in a loud voice over the din of rain on the tin roof.

"I'm afraid I'm a mountain man, Captain, with nary an oilskin to my name." He shucked out of his damp jacket and hung it on a peg by the door.

"Brother!" shouted his host. "Bring Father a dishrag, if ye don't object."

He thought Captain Larkin was as lively and quick as any Santa Claus, though he walked with a cane and had a distinct limp. The captain also possessed a combination of the pinkest cheeks and bluest eyes he had ever seen.

The old man hobbled to the sofa and straightened the afghan. "Come sit an' make yourself to home. We'll have ye dried off here in a little."

The man who shuffled into the room looked exactly like the captain, yet his countenance was remarkably different; a scowl appeared permanently etched into his face as if by steel engraving. Light and darkness, observed Father Tim—fire and ice, north pole and south!

"This is Twin Brother," said Captain Larkin. "Brother, this is th' Father from down at St. John's."

" 'Bout time you come," said the old man, glowering at him. "We been lookin' out for you since Brother fell four year ago, he could've killed hisself an' it wouldn've mattered to you none."

"I'm sorry I wasn't around then. I came to St. John's in early July."

"Four months ago," said Brother, glaring at him through filmy eyes. He handed over a rag and Father Tim took it, mopping his head, face, and hands. He felt a chill go along his spine as the thunder crashed again, directly over the roof.

"Bad 'un," said Captain Larkin, shaking his head.

◦━◦

"Will you join us, Brother Larkin?"

"No, sir, I'll not!" snapped Brother, leaving the room. Opening one of the double doors, he turned and shouted, "I don't abide with such foolishness."

Father Tim closed his eyes, took a deep breath, and

kept a moment of silence that amplified the sound of the lashing wind and rain. A single light bulb, hanging by a long cord from the ceiling, swayed slightly, causing shadows to dance across the pictures on the wall.

"Peace be to this house and to all who dwell in it. Graciously hear us, O Lord, Holy Father Almighty, everlasting God, and send thy holy angel from heaven to guard, cherish, protect, visit, and defend all who dwell here."

Father Tim saw Brother peering at them from behind the door, as he poured wine from a small cruet into an equally small chalice.

Though he knew he might have stood, the captain chose to kneel. Grasping the arm of his recliner and going to his knees with considerable difficulty, he joined Father Tim in the Lord's Prayer, then cupped his hands to receive the wafer.

"Lord," the captain prayed from memory, "I'm not worthy that Thou should come under my roof, but speak th' word only and my soul shall be healed."

"The Body of our Lord Jesus Christ, which was given for you, my brother."

Tears flowed down the pink cheeks of Captain Larkin as he raised his hands to his mouth and took the wafer.

"The Blood of our Lord Jesus Christ, which was given for you, my brother."

The captain drank and wiped his eyes on his shirt-sleeve.

Laying his hands on the captain's head, Father Tim prayed, "The blessing of God Almighty, the Father, the Son, and the Holy Spirit, be upon you and remain with you forever, amen."

"Amen," said the old captain.

Father Tim helped him to his feet and they embraced warmly. The tender spirit of this good man flowed out to him with the smell of liniment and unwashed scalp, of shaving talcum and clothes hung too long in a forgotten closet.

"The Lord be with you, Captain."

"And with thy spirit," replied the supplicant, beaming through his tears.

The wind suddenly roared down the chimney and huffed a shower of ashes into the room. He was in too deep with this storm. It didn't appear to be passing over and seemed to be growing worse, moment by moment. Only a lunatic would go out in . . .

"Captain, may I use your phone?"

"We've not had one in a good while. Too much money for too little talkin' is what Brother calls it."

"Ahh." He went to the front door and stood looking out, agonized. He couldn't see his car or the truck parked in front of the porch, only a gray film as if a heavy curtain had been lowered. He shivered in his knit shirt.

The captain reached up and pulled the chain on the light bulb. "B'lieve I'll just switch this off."

In the odd twilight of the storm-darkened room, the old man eased himself into his recliner and sighed.

"Blowin' a gale," he said.

Father Tim thumped onto the sofa.

He'd wait for a letup—every storm had a letup once in a while—then he'd run for it and drive as far as he could go. One way or another, he'd make it home. . . .

"My great-grandaddy come over from Englan' in a little ship called *Rose of Sharon*. It broke up in a bad storm 'bout this time of year, and him an' five other men was warshed up on Dor'ster. We speculate it was about where this road ends at, down past th' church. Back in those days, th' beaches was littered with shipwreck of ever' stripe an' color, an' so they went to work and knocked together a little shack where they could look out for another ship an' git picked up."

What was this stubborn streak that had made him so all-fired determined to come to Dorchester today as if it were some life-or-death, do-or-die endeavor? Worse, how could he have left his wife saddled with a sick boy and a storm warning? Had he bothered to listen to a weather report and check out the particulars? No, he'd shrugged it all off as if it were nothing. . . .

"They wadn't hardly nobody livin' on these little islands back then 'cept Indians, there's some as thinks it was part of Wanchese's crowd. Story goes, my great-grandaddy wadn't more'n twenty year old when he married a Indian woman off of Whitecap, had a head of hair down to her ankles. I been tol' me'n Brother has th' cheekbones and nose of a Indian, but I don't know, I couldn't say."

Please, God, don't let this storm hit Whitecap and take the bridge out, keep the bridge in good-working order, the bridge, that's the crux of the matter. . . .

"I built this house for my wife, Dora, back when I was runnin' trawlers. Dora was nineteen year old when we moved in, an' cheery as any angel out of heaven Then, when we went down to Whitecap to keep th' light, Brother moved in an' managed things for me. When I quit keepin th' light, I stayed on in Whitecap 'til Dora died, then come back to Dor'ster where I was born an' raised at."

Two thirty-five. An hour's drive in a storm like this would surely double, maybe triple the driving time, so he'd be home by five-thirty, maybe six o'clock, max. . . .

"I've been foolin' with Canada geese a good while, now, ever' fall I pay a neighbor to sow wheat an' winter rye 'round my pond out yonder. This spring, we seen nests as had four to eight eggs apiece. . . ."

He recognized a growing sense of foreboding . . . something that pressed on his chest and worried his breathing. Maybe he wouldn't wait for a break, he'd take his chances. . . .

He bolted off the sofa. "Captain, I've got a wife and boy to get home to, I'm going to run on, it's been a pleasure meeting you, I know how much they care for you at St. John's, God bless you and keep you, I'll be back before Christmas."

The old man looked at him, dumbfounded. "You ain't goin' out in this, are ye?"

"Yes, sir, I am," he said, running to snatch his damp jacket from the hook.

"Brother!" yelled the Captain. "Come an' say good-bye to th' Father, if ye don't object."

The dining room door opened, and Brother peered out, holding a jar of peanut butter with a spoon in it.

"The Lord bless you, Brother Larkin."

The old man scowled at him. "Goin' out in that, you'd do better to bless y'rself."

As he tossed the drenched umbrella into the backseat and slammed the door, he spied the lasagna sitting on the floor behind the passenger seat. Dadgummit, he'd forgotten to give Ella her present. Cynthia had even tied a bow around the foil-covered dish.

He sat for a moment and considered running it in to the twins. Then, feeling the chill of his sodden clothes, he squelched the notion.

He passed what he thought was Ella's house, but didn't see a light. No, indeed, St. John's organist was snug in her cottage with every plug pulled, as disconnected from civilization as any soul on the Arctic tundra.

A mile and a half to the highway . . .

With no yellow line to guide him, he kept his eyes strictly on the right side of the road, but there were long moments when the wipers were of no effect on the streaming windshield and he lost visibility entirely.

At the end of the gravel lane, he had a moment of sheer panic about pulling out to the highway. Pummeled by gusting sheets of wind and rain, he searched for headlights moving toward him from either direction, but saw nothing.

He eased onto the asphalt, praying.

Was this a hurricane? Surely not, or by now he'd be sitting upside down on the mainland in somebody's tobacco field. Besides, he would have heard if a hurricane was predicted; this was merely a heavy storm with high winds, of which they'd seen more than a few since moving to these parts. The thought consoled him, but a subsequent thought of the sea, roiling and churning not far from the highway, gave his stomach a wrench.

In truth, he had no clue about what he should be doing. To cling on in Dorchester seemed wasteful of precious time, but to push ahead seemed potentially hazardous and plain stupid.

He would push ahead.

Twice, he was tempted to pull into what he thought was a service station, but he seemed to be developing a kind of sixth sense for driving in these conditions, a sense that he didn't want to abandon too hastily.

He remembered what Louella said during their last visit. Something like, "You git in any trouble down there, jus' remember Louella's up here prayin' for you."

"Pray for me, Louella!" he shouted, finding comfort in the sound of his own voice.

On either side of the highway, trucks hunkered down like great beasts, waiting out the storm.

Easing south on what he estimated to be the last half of the coastal highway, the Mustang slammed into something unseen. It was a hard hit, and the motor died instantly.

His heart thundering, he leaped from the car and saw a tree limb fallen across both lanes. He pushed against the wind to get back in the car and switch on the emergency lights—he was a sitting duck out here—then, head down, he dived back into the squall to try to move the limb. Blast. The car had rolled over the limb before the motor died.

In the driver's seat, he turned the key in the ignition. Nothing. Again. Nothing. Flooded.

He tried to think calmly. If he could lift the front of the car backward over the limb, he could then push the Mustang onto the side of the road, out of harms way. He had never lifted a car. . . .

He got out and walked to the right, checking the shoulder. But there was no shoulder; it was a drop-off to a creek, which was quickly rising to the roadway.

His glasses slid off his nose and he caught them and

put them in his pocket, half blind. He was a desperate fool, the worst of fools. The rain was hammering him into the asphalt like a nail.

He saw it as he turned from the creek.

It was the lights of a truck bearing down in his lane.

His heart racing, he ran to the rear of the car and threw up both arms, waving frantically. *Dear Jesus, let him see my lights. . . .*

But what if the driver didn't see his lights? He could be chopped liver between the grille of a tractor-trailer and the bumper of his own car.

"Please!" he shouted over the roar and din of the rain. *"Please!"*

He jumped out of the way as he heard the air brakes applied. The massive vehicle rolled to a stop only inches from the Mustang.

His legs were cooked macaroni, warm Jell-O, sponge cake as he walked to the driver's side of the cab and looked up in utter despair.

The window eased down. "What's your trouble?"

"Limb on the road, motor's flooded."

The driver climbed out of the cab in a flash, wearing an Indiana Jones hat with a chin strap, and a brim that instantly shed water like a downspout.

"I'll take a look." The driver bent into the rain and walked to the front of the car, squatted and peered underneath. "Goin' to need a chain. Get in your car, I'm goin' to haul you over th' limb, then we'll roll it off in Judd's Creek."

Sitting in the car, he heard the chain being attached to his rear bumper, and soon after felt the jerk as the big rig reversed its gears and rolled him backward over the limb. He pulled on the emergency brake and returned to the fray.

Together, they heaved, pushed, and rolled the sodden limb off the road and into the creek.

"Where you headed?" the driver shouted.

"Whitecap!"

"I'm runnin' by Whitecap. Come on an' follow me, but not too close or th' spray'll blind you. Just keep your eyes on my taillights and marker lights."

"Done!"

"I'll pull into that vacant lot by th' Whitecap bridge."

"God be with you!" he shouted.

He followed the truck for roughly half an hour in steadily decreasing rain. About four miles north of Whitecap, the storm had blown over, and he turned his wipers off.

In the vacant lot, rainwater stood in deep pools, and he saw a metal sign blown from Jake's Used Cars leaning against the entrance to the bridge.

But, *hallelujah,* there was no sign claiming the bridge was out.

Dodging the pools, the driver pulled the refrigerated rig into the lot, and Father Tim parked alongside.

Leaving the motor running, the driver swung down and shook his hand with an iron grip.

"Tim Kavanagh. I can't thank you enough."

"Loretta Burgess," said the driver. "Glad to help."

"Loretta?" he said, stunned. "I mean . . ." Well, well. Holy smoke.

Loretta Burgess laughed and removed her sodden hat. A considerable amount of salt-and-pepper hair fell around her broad shoulders. "I don't care what they say, Padre, it ain't totally a man's world."

"You're right about that!"

"I'd show you th' pictures of my grandkids if we had time, but I'm runnin' behind th' clock. You take it easy, now."

As Loretta Burgess pulled onto the highway, he turned to get back in the car. He was standing with his hand on the door handle when he sensed something odd and troubling:

The air was strangely, eerily quiet.

And then he heard the siren.

CHAPTER EIGHTEEN

Simple Graces

Three army trucks blew past the vacant lot, tailed by a mainland ambulance with a wide-open siren.

He scratched onto the slick pavement and followed the procession across the bridge without any memory of doing it.

As he came off the bridge, he was clocking seventy, but had no intention of slowing down. Wherever the rescue squad was needed, he could be needed. Instantly he prayed for the need, whatever it might be, and realized he'd been praying, almost without ceasing, since six o'clock this morning. Surely, days on end had been packed into this single half day.

Water rushed across parts of Tern like bold creeks, carving out sections of asphalt. Whatever the vehicles ahead of him plowed through, he plowed through.

As the cavalcade turned left on Hastings, he saw the tree hanging, as if in a sling, on the sagging power lines. Across from the fallen tree was the gray house on the corner, the one Cynthia always admired—another tree had slammed across the roof, caving it in, and scattering bricks from the chimney into the yard. Next door, a section of picket fence dangled in a tree, and over there, a limb had smashed straight down, like an arrow from above, into the hood of a car.

In the rearview mirror, he saw two more troop trucks behind him and, farther back, another ambulance.

A chilling fear was spreading through him like a virus.

In the sullen afterlight of the storm, he had returned to a place he hardly recognized.

Several houses this side of Dove Cottage appeared to have taken a beating, but without any serious damage.

As his house came into view, his heart was squeezed by a kind of terror he'd never known.

Dove Cottage had no porch.

Its facade was oddly blank, like a staring face. He saw that the porch had been blown into the neighbor's yard, partially intact, the rest in smithereens. Pickets from the fence were scattered everywhere. A few had landed on the roof.

The need he'd prayed for only moments ago was partly his own.

He parked at what had been his front gate, as the stream of vehicles behind him blew past. He fled toward the house and stood looking up to the front door, wondering how to get in.

"Cynthia!"

The back porch . . .

He raced around the house and into the kitchen, where he stepped on fragments of china that crunched like bubble wrap under his feet.

"Cynthia! Barnabas!"

He skidded down the hall, and halted at the living

room door, where the entire floor had caved in at the middle, in a deep and perfect V.

Their furnishings lay neatly piled along the crotch of the V, and on top of the pile was his mother's Limoges vase; it appeared unharmed, as if it had rolled down one side of the collapsed flooring and, at the last moment, landed conveniently on a chair cushion.

"Cynthia! *Please!*" He tore along the hall to the bedrooms, which looked as if nothing more than a strong wind had ruffled the bedcovers, as if the porch had not been blown to kingdom come, nor the living room destroyed.

But what if she and Jonathan had been in the living room when . . . ?

He raced out the back door and into the street, thinking he would flag down an ambulance, a neighbor, anybody. But there was no help in sight. Many in the neighborhood worked across, and only a lone pickup truck roared past, the driver refusing to make eye contact.

What had happened? Was it, in fact, a hurricane? Did tornadoes hit the coast? He'd never asked. All his life, he had ignored weather as much as he could, for what could one do about it, anyway?

He would burrow through the furniture like a mole, through the chairs and tables and books and magazines. . . .

Somewhere at the bottom was the rug. If he got to the bottom and found the rug, he'd know she was nowhere in the house. . . .

He called her name unceasingly as he clawed his way through the detritus of their everyday life, terrified that he might find her.

But there was no one, nothing.

And how in heaven's name was he to crawl up the slick, polished floor, from the hole he'd lowered himself into?

～

"Father! You down there?"

White-faced, Junior Bryson squatted over the threshold of the living room and looked into the pit.

"I'm here, Junior. Have you seen my wife?"

"No, sir, I just drove up from th' Toe an' seen your porch was blowed off. I was goin' to Ernie's. I hear he took a bad hit."

"Can you pull me up?" He'd never been so glad to see a face. He was trembling with feeling and with cold.

"I'm pretty much out of shape, I don't know, but I'll lay down and hook my feet on either side of th' doorway. . . ."

Junior positioned himself and, huffing, reached toward Father Tim.

"OK, you hang on, now, just kind of climb up my arms or whatever."

"This room was built pretty high off the ground, so it's a stretch."

"But don't be pullin' me down in there with you," said Junior, "or we'll both be in a good bit of trouble."

"I can't seem to get any traction with these loafers," he said, breathing hard.

Blast loafers into the next century, he was over loafers.

～

"It just happened," Junior said, as Father Tim hurriedly changed into dry clothes and pulled warm socks onto his numb feet. "About thirty, forty minutes ago, looks like it tore up th' north end and blew on out to sea, th' rain an' wind just stopped all of a sudden. But we didn't have no damage at th' Toe, not a'tall. Far as I know, 'lectricity's down all over th' island, an' Mr. Bragg's phones went out. How's th' bridge?"

"Still working."

"That's a blessin'," said Junior.

On his way out the back door, he turned and did a final search for Violet, looking under the beds, and hoping she wasn't stranded under the study sofa, which he couldn't get to because of the collapsed living room.

They walked at a trot to the truck and the car.

"Good luck findin' your wife and th' boy. I'm sure they're fine, prob'ly at th' grocery store or post office when it hit."

"Thank you, buddy."

But his wife couldn't have been at the grocery store or the post office; she had no car. She was, he decided, at the church with Jonathan, where she'd gone to work on the Fall Fair. He felt so certain of it, he wanted to shout.

As he drove away from Dove Cottage, he wondered—where was her bicycle? She usually hauled it up the steps and left it on the front porch. Surely she wouldn't have been out on her bicycle. . . .

More cars were on the street now, people coming from across or from the Toe; there was a veritable snake of solid traffic along Hastings, and not a little horn-blowing.

He hated seeing Ernie's. The right wall had crumbled, leaving the framing and a pile of bricks. Glass from the front window was missing as well, and books lay scattered around the parking lot and into the street.

All that unrefrigerated bait, all those books open to the elements, they'd better get a tarp over it, and fast.

But he couldn't think about Ernie's right now.

A camera unit from a mainland TV station blew around him as he wheeled the Mustang into the empty parking lot next to Ernie's, and set off running to St. John's.

$\backsim\!\!\!\!\!\multimap$

"She's leanin' to th' side of my politics, is what it is." Ray Gaskill, who lived in the house closest to St. John's, removed a toothpick from his mouth and surveyed the damage.

Roughly one-third of a live oak had split off and collapsed across the roof of the church, knocking the building askew.

"It's racked to the right," said Leonard Lamb, looking ashen.

"Who was in it?" asked Father Tim.

"Nobody. Sometime after you left for Dor'ster, the women packed up and went over to the Fieldwalkers' to work."

"The organ?"

"It's OK, if we can get a tarp on before it rains again. We can't find Sam, and the phones are down so we can't call Larry to bring a tarp from the ferry docks. Looks like I'll have to go across if th' bridge is working."

"No problem with the bridge."

"Or we could maybe get a tarp from up Dor'ster, maybe at the boat repair."

He felt ridiculously guilty that he hadn't picked up a tarp.

"Trouble is, the plaster's cracked pretty bad and when we set her straight, that'll crack it even worse."

"This ain't nothin' to the' Ash Wednesday storm," said Ray, chewing the toothpick. "Now, that was a storm. This wadn't but prob'ly seventy-five-, maybe eighty-mile-an-hour winds."

He thought St. John's neighbor seemed personally proud of the catastrophe that struck in '62. Though it spared lives, its fury had pretty much battered everything else along five hundred miles of shoreline.

"I've got to find Cynthia," he said. "Do you have any idea . . . ?"

"I don't," said Leonard. "Marjorie's at the Fieldwalkers'. She'd probably be able to say."

Come to think of it, why would Cynthia have taken Jonathan out in a terrible storm, when he was burning with fever and on medication? And she wouldn't have taken Barnabas and Violet to the soiree at the Fieldwalkers'. . . .

His heart was in his throat.

"Looks like some of th' sidin's popped off. That'll expose your studs to water," said Ray.

"What about the basement?" he asked Leonard.

"You don't want to know."

And he didn't. Not until he found Cynthia.

"I'll be back," he said.

~ø~

When he picked up the Mustang, he spoke with a young police officer in the crowd milling around Ernie's.

"Why is the army in here?" he asked, afraid of the answer.

"They're not any army in here. We use army surplus trucks in storms 'cause saltwater eats up th' brake linin's on our patrol cars. These babies stand way up off th' road."

"Was anyone hurt at Ernie's?"

"No, sir. They think it was all that water in th' ground that did somethin' to part of his foundation, made his wall fall in. Then a big trash can blowed into his front window, an' the' wind scattered books from here to Hatt'ras."

"What about Mona's?"

"One of th' waitresses got her arm burned pretty bad, a deep fryer come off th' stove, fella in a pickup just ran 'er across to ER."

"I've lost my wife," he blurted.

The young man removed his hat. "Gosh," he said.

"I mean, I can't find her," he explained, feeling foolish. Why was he standing here?

Not knowing what else to do, he shook the officer's hand and ran to his car.

Close to tears, he turned the car around in the parking lot and headed onto Hastings, which was covered with water.

He suddenly recalled the time on the beach, only days ago, when she had reached up and stroked his cheek and said she wanted to remember him like this always. Had that been some terrible omen?

With the Whitecap police directing traffic, he made his way back the way he'd come.

⟲

The door was not only unlocked at the old Love Cottage, it had been blown open, and most of the furniture overturned. The wind had heaved a rocking chair through a front window; shattered glass was strewn on the sodden floor.

"Cynthia!" There was a basement here, Otis had said so; maybe when the porch had been ripped off their house, she'd come here, fearing worse.

Shaking as with palsy, he searched for the door to the basement, opening closets, finding the water heater, listening for the booming bark of his dog. . . .

"Cynthia! *Please!*"

There! Hidden in the bedroom they'd slept in all those eons ago . . .

He threw open the basement door and peered down into a dark void, unable to switch on a light.

"Cynthia!" he bawled.

Silence.

He turned from the mildewed odor that fumed up at him, and closed the door and put his head in his hands and did what he'd been doing all day.

"Lord," he entreated from the depths of his being, "hear my prayer. . . ."

Maybe there was a note at Dove Cottage.

Maybe there was something on the kitchen counter telling him where they'd gone. If not, he'd drive to the Fieldwalkers' if there were no power lines across the roads. He'd heard that was a problem in some parts of the north end, but so what, he had two feet, and besides, they couldn't have just vanished off the face of the earth. They had to be somewhere. . . .

He parked at the side of Dove Cottage and sprinted across a yard that felt like marsh beneath the soles of his running shoes.

"Father!"

Morris Love . . .

He turned and looked across to the wall. Something odd over there, a blank spot in the sky where a tree had stood. . . .

"They're over here!"

Again, his cognition lapsed, and he wouldn't recall racing from his yard and across the street and through the iron gate, which Morris Love had unlocked and swung back as he dashed onto the familiar turf of Nouvelle Chanson.

"Timothy!"

There had been times of absolute, unfettered joy in his life—his ordination, his wedding, and the day he and Walter stood on a hill in Ireland and looked across to the site of the Kavanagh family castle.

With his wife in his arms, his dog jumping up to lick his face, and Jonathan tugging on his pants leg, he experienced a moment of supreme joy that he felt he may never know again.

"Violet?" he said.

"In the kitchen, having a tin of Mr. Love's sardines."

He regretted that both he and his wife were tearful with happiness, but what could he do?

They saw Morris turn from the reunion in the foyer and stand by the window. There was suffering on his face in profile, something that snatched away the joy in their hearts.

"A nail," said his wife, explaining the bandage on her hand. "Right in the palm."

They sat in the cavernous kitchen lighted by candles in a silver stand, and waited for the teakettle to boil over a can of Sterno. Not seeming to know his kitchen, Morris had been unable to provide anything more than the Sterno and a kettle already filled with water. Cynthia had helped herself to his cabinets and found tea, along with a bag of Fig Newtons, which Morris said belonged to Mamie, but urged them to help themselves. Seeing their reluctance, he ate one himself, out of courtesy.

They all fell to.

"Milk!" said Jonathan. "My mommy, she gives me *milk* and cookies."

"No milk, dear," said Cynthia, hauling the boy onto her lap with one hand. "And no water in the taps, just what we have in the kettle."

"There's apple juice," said Morris.

"I'll get it!" said Father Tim.

"*No.* I'll get it." Morris rose stiffly and went to the refrigerator; he removed a container and poured juice into a glass.

"Say thank you," urged Cynthia.

"Thank you," said Jonathan, gulping it down.

"When the winds became so terrible," she said, "I remembered my bicycle and was afraid it would be blown off the porch like our rockers were last August. So I went out to bring it in the house and it wasn't there, and you know how I love my bicycle. I mean, I could never replace it, it's old as the hills."

"More," said Jonathan.

"More, *please,*" counseled his wife.

"More, more, more, please, please, *please!*"

Morris took the glass and got up again, obviously with considerable difficulty, and refilled the glass.

"Thank you," said Jonathan.

Cynthia beamed with pride, and continued her report. "And so, I peered off the porch and saw that my bike had been blown into the side street. I ran down to get it, and all of a sudden, things were flying around in the air, and I realized it was pickets off our fence, they were just showering down, and I raised my hand in front of my face and a picket with a nail in it . . ."

"I'm sorry," he said, taking her bandaged hand.

"Just boom. Nailed. Ugh. Now you finish, Mr. Love."

"Please call me Morris."

"Morris!"

"I had looked out from the music room and seen the tree go over. Fortunately, it fell away from the house, and I had a view of the street. The rain was very heavy and visibility wasn't the best, but I thought I saw your wife, and she appeared to be in distress. I remember you said you were leaving town and I thought she may need . . . help."

"And so he came out to me," said Cynthia, "and at just that moment we saw the porch break off the front of the house. It was awful. I thought—"

Jonathan nodded energetically. "I was, I was *in* th' house!"

"Yes, you were, and so Morris ran to the house with me and we got Jonathan and Violet and Barnabas and he brought us all over here and we stood in his music room, sopping wet, to see if the rest of the house was going, but it didn't, and then Morris saw that I was dripping blood on his carpet. I'm terribly sorry about that, your housekeeper won't be a bit happy—"

"It's a dark Oriental, no one will ever know."

"And he washed my wound and put antibiotic cream on it and bandaged me up." His wife beamed at Morris Love, who visibly blanched at the warmth and directness of her feeling.

Father Tim cleared his throat. "Thank you, my friend."

"I was scared," said Jonathan, whose nose was running like a tap. "I was *cryin'*."

He wiped Jonathan's nose and smoothed his hair, feeling a rush of affection. "And what about the bicycle?" he asked his wife.

"Mr. Love—I mean Morris—went back out into that awful storm and retrieved it. It's under his stairwell."

Morris shifted in the chair, looking uneasy.

"There goes the kettle!" said Cynthia. "Now please sit still, Morris, this is my job."

⟜⟀

"I'm hungry," said Jonathan.

"I'm starved," said Cynthia.

His own stomach was growling. "We must get home and see what's up, anyway. What do we have in the refrigerator?"

"Nothing. Zip. A salami, a tomato. We're going to Mitford, and so I didn't want to leave anything."

"A salami and a tomato. It's a start," he said, cheerful.

"You're welcome to look here. I don't know, Mamie brings everything. . . ." Morris lifted his hands as if bereft of a solution.

"Bingo!" cried Father Tim.

"Bingo!" repeated Jonathan, slapping the table.

"It just occurred to me, I have just the ticket. Homemade lasagna! Velvety blankets of pasta layered with fresh spinach, fresh ricotta, mozzarella, a thick tomato sauce sweetened with chopped onions, and veal ground from the shank. Precooked, freshly thawed, and ready to roll."

"Mercy!" said his wife. "That sounds like my recipe. Where on earth did it come from?"

"The floor of my car," he replied, feeling as if he'd just hung the moon. "Morris, will you break bread with us?"

—⊙—

"Be thankful for the smallest blessing," Thomas à Kempis had written, "and you will deserve to receive greater. Value the least gifts no less than the greatest, and simple graces as especial favors. If you remember the dignity of the Giver, no gift will seem small or mean, for nothing can be valueless that is given by the most high God."

Father Tim remembered what the old brother had said as he ate his portion of the lasagna with gusto, and set some on the floor for Barnabas.

He thought it was the best thing he ever put in his mouth. His wife, who had always possessed a considerable appetite, was hammering down like a stevedore. Even Morris Love appeared to enjoy her handiwork, and Jonathan ate without prejudice or complaint.

Further, Ella Bridgewater had saved the day. In the packet with the sea bass, which Violet devoured, was the small jar of plum wine, which, to conserve water and washing up, they poured into their empty tea cups and drank with enthusiasm.

—⊙—

They went across the street with Morris Love's flashlight, and into the cold kitchen of Dove Cottage. He thought their house felt as if all life had gone out of it, as if the terrible assault had wounded it in some way that was palpable.

He was walking into the hall when the floorboards

creaked and he saw a shadowy figure coming toward him.

"Good heavens, who's there?"

Jonathan let out a howl.

"It's Otis!" said his landlord, beaming his flashlight up. "You're in a bad fix here."

"Tell me about it."

"Looks like that sorry porch wadn't nailed onto th' house for shoot. I can't tell what all's goin' on 'til I get some daylight and a couple of men out here, but I want you and th' family to come stay at my motel. We'll fix you up with a choice room and king-size bed."

"Oh, no, that's fine, we'll just set up camp right here."

"No water here, no power, no heat, an' I don't know what's under these floors that might go next. When th' porch tore off, looks like a rotted floor joist or somethin' gave way in your front room."

Cynthia looked at him. "Otis is right, dear. Jonathan is sick, and the house is a terrible mess. Besides, we need our rest for tomorrow's trip."

"We won't be going to Mitford," he said.

His parish needed him here. God would work out the details.

—⊖—

Holding the sleeping boy in his arms, he stood on the back steps with Otis while Cynthia did some hurried packing with the aid of a flashlight.

"Not a scratch on my place," said Otis, "save for somebody's deck furniture bobbin' around in th' pool. When I heard what was goin' on up here, I run home lookin' for Marlene and couldn't find her. It like to give me a nervous breakdown, she was supposed to be home.

Well, in two or three hours, here she comes, paradin' in like th' Queen of Sheba, complainin' of th' rain ruinin' her hair. She'd been across havin' her roots touched up."

"Aha."

"Where trees blow down, they sometimes take out th' water lines, and course, th' water lines is takin' out th' roads. Thank th' Lord she was drivin' th' four-wheel."

Jonathan stirred in his arms and put the warm palm of his hand on Father Tim's cheek. "What about power?" he asked Otis. "How long to get everything back up?"

"Th' whole island's lost power. That'll prob'ly take four to five days to get goin' again. Water, I don't know, maybe two days. And it'll take a week of hard haulin' to get th' roads graded and asphalted."

He thought the whole thing seemed a dream. "How long 'til we can hold services?"

"The church looks pretty bad. Shingles are poppin' off like corn. But we got tarps on 'er, three of 'em. I had one, Larry brought one, Sam scrounged one. I've got people comin' tomorrow to look it over, see what it's goin' to take, an' how long." Otis heaved a deep sigh. "Th' water runnin' in turns plaster to mush, then when it dries, it turns to powder."

The tenant echoed his landlord's sigh.

"But this'll bring us together," said Otis, adopting a positive view of what lay ahead for the body of St. John's.

Father Tim felt a drop of rain on his cheek. "Oh, boy," he said, stepping onto the back porch.

He heard his parishioner draw a cigar from his pocket and remove the cellophane. There was a moment of silent consideration.

"Dadgum if I ain't goin' to *smoke* this sucker!"

In the flame of a monogrammed lighter, Father Tim saw the face of a happy man.

———⌒———

Cynthia stood inside the door of Number Fourteen at Bragg's Mid-Way Motel and peered at their room, which was lighted by a kerosene lantern.

"Ugh!" she said vehemently. "Shag carpet!"

CHAPTER NINETEEN

Jericho

His wife looked utterly downcast as he dressed the following morning. She sat on the side of the bed in her nightgown, shod in his leather bedroom shoes, refusing to make any direct contact with the carpet.

"You could take me to church and keep the car," he said, desperate to be helpful.

"I can't be dragging Jonathan around in this rain."

They had eaten a breakfast of cheese sandwiches, which Otis had made himself and delivered at six a.m. with scorching coffee in a thermos. The paper sack included a side of bananas, apples, raisins, and oranges, juice and crackers for Jonathan, and packaged brownies from the convenience store.

"I hate to leave you. You can go to the Braggs', you know. Otis invited us."

"Not in a hundred years," she said, setting her mouth in a profoundly straight line. "Make that a thousand!" Marlene Bragg had suggested his wife stop highlighting her own hair and see a professional; further, she proclaimed that fuchsia wasn't becoming to Cynthia's skin color, and recommended another shade of blusher to bring out the blue of her eyes. This had not set well.

"Marjorie and Sam begged us to come." Sam had shown up at the motel last night at eleven, hoping to rescue them.

"But their guest room has a leak in the ceiling and there's no water. Sam says they're using his grandmother's chamber pot."

"There are worse things than chamber pots," he said, trying to console.

"I can't imagine what."

He didn't want to say it, but how about being trapped in a motel room with no power, no phone, and a three-year-old?

He buttoned his shirt, surveying the scene. The kerosene lantern glowed against the dusk of the rainy morning; the oil-fired heater hissed in the corner; Jonathan slept soundly, clutching a pillow; Barnabas snored in the vinyl armchair; Violet snoozed on a mat in the bathroom. Cozy as it all appeared, he would not want to spend the day here. No, indeed.

"How's your hand?"

"Throbbing."

"Do you think you need to see a doctor?"

"I don't think so. Morris poured something on it that was absolutely scalding before he put on the cream. I think it's fine, dearest, don't worry. I'll have a look under the bandage before you come home with lunch. Ugh! Did I say *home?*"

"Home is anywhere you are, Kavanagh."

She fell against the pillows, sighing.

"What do you think of our neighbor?" he asked, putting on his shoes.

"The strangest, yet loveliest sort of man. I feel that underneath his pain is the deepest tenderness. Then again, is it pain, Timothy? I don't know, perhaps it's something more like anger, a terrible, corrosive anger."

"Odd that he would be so adept at home doctoring."

"He said he learned from Mamie."

"Aha. Well. I'll be back around twelve. Maybe the rain will let up and you can drop me at church and take the car."

"Where would I go?" she asked.

"I don't know. The library?"

"The library isn't open today."

"The grocery store?"

"And watch mold grow in the dairy case?"

He had a great idea. "I could bring you some pot holders to finish up for the Fall Fair." There! Just the ticket to keep her mind occupied.

"Pot holders?"

She looked at him as if he were something that had crawled through the pipes and into the kitchen sink.

⏤‿⏤

As phone service was up in other parts of the village, he drove two blocks and stood in a queue to make calls from a pay booth at the rear of Whitecap Drugs.

When the Hope House switchboard answered, he asked for the dining room.

"Pauline . . ."

"Father! We saw on the news you had a bad storm last night."

"Yes. And Pauline . . ." He'd rather be shot than say it. "I . . . can't come. I can't come for the wedding on

Sunday. I'm calling to ask if you can . . . cancel, that is, postpone it for two weeks until we get cleaned up here."

There was a moment of silence. The disappointment on the other end was palpable.

"Or," he said, and he really despised hearing these words out of his mouth, "you could get someone else to officiate, someone else to—"

"Well, no, Father, I mean that's fine, we don't want anybody else, you know we were goin' to keep it really simple, anyway, so it's . . . not much trouble to postpone it."

"I'm sorry, I can't tell you how sorry . . ." He was literally nauseous over the whole thing, especially hating that Jessie's, Poo's, and Dooley's glad excitement would have to be put on hold.

"Well, but don't worry," she said. "We'll set another date. We didn't even run it in th' newspaper, but I did tell everybody in the dinin' room, and Miss Louella, she was goin' to come, but . . . they'll all understand."

"What about Buck? How will this affect his plans?"

"Oh, he's not goin' back to Alaska. He's finished up his part. He's goin' to try an' set up his own business in Mitford."

"Hallelujah!"

"So, I understand," said Dooley's mother, "really I do."

But he could hear the sadness in her voice. He was good at hearing sadness in people's voices. . . .

"Two weeks," he said. "No matter what, we'll be there. And we'll talk again in a few days, all right?"

"Yes, sir. How bad is it down there?"

"No lives lost, as far as we know, but power out, and phones down in places, and no water on the north end. The church has taken a hard hit, part of a big tree fell across the roof and . . ."—he felt suddenly close to tears—"and our cottage had some damage."

"I'm sorry," she said, her voice husky with feeling. He knew that she, too, was good at hearing sadness in others.

———⊖———

He was able to reach Buck in Harley's basement apartment; Buck would go with Dooley to court on Monday, and Harley would return Dooley to school, as planned. They would reschedule the wedding for mid-November.

He took a deep breath and went through yet more telephone rigmarole—access code, the number he was calling, his calling card number, his PIN number, then through the switchboard, where, it was declared, there was no answer in the room, and so up to the fourth-floor nurses' station, and down the hall to the sitting room with the cordless. . . .

"Hello?"

"Janette . . ."

"Oh, Father, I'm so glad to hear your voice, I saw about the storm on TV. Is Jonathan . . . ?"

"He's doing great! A bit of a cold, that's all. Our house is torn up for a few days, but everyone's safe. We're at Otis Bragg's motel in the village."

"Thank heaven! And Father, I'm so happy about coming home."

"We'll be over to get you on Tuesday as we discussed. Around two o'clock. Is that still good?"

"Oh, yes. Perfect! I'll be ready."

"If you'd like to call, we're in Room Fourteen at Bragg's Mid-Way Motel. Uh-oh, I forgot. Phones are out over there, but should be up and humming in a day or two."

"I'll be so happy to see my baby. Has he been . . . good?"

"Better than good!"

Her laughter was music to his ears.

"We'll take you home and get you settled in with something hot for your supper. We can bring Jonathan on Thursday," he said, following the doctor's advice. "That will give you a chance to—"

"Oh, no, Father, please bring him Tuesday. I've missed my children so much. I can't wait to have my children home."

"Consider it done, then. And when are Babette and Jason coming?"

"They'll be home Wednesday."

"Good, wonderful," he said.

"Have you . . . seen Jeffrey?"

"Not in some time." Taken by surprise, he chose to be vague without being untruthful.

"Jean Ballenger says there's a pile of work waiting for me."

"Including a blazer for yours truly. I haven't had a blazer in years. Cynthia talked me into it and picked out the buttons."

There was a pause. "I'm . . . so very grateful, Father Timothy. For everything."

"So am I," he said. "So am I."

❧

"Emma," he yelled through a lousy connection, "don't bake a ham!"

"What?"

"Don't bake a ham!"

"Spam? What *about* Spam?"

Rats. "I'll call you back!"

When he called back, the line was busy.

⎯⎯⚬⎯⎯

He rang Pauline's small house in the laurels, reluctant to wake Dooley, who had arrived late last night from school.

"Dooley . . ."

"Hey!" Dooley said, hoarse with sleep.

"Hey, yourself, buddy. We've got a problem down here."

⎯⎯⚬⎯⎯

He went out into the rain and stood beside his car for a moment, dazed and heartsick, finding that everything was finally sinking in—all at once.

⎯⎯⚬⎯⎯

On the way to St. John's, he wheeled into Ernie's, which was swaddled front and side with tarps.

Though Books, Bait & Tackle was down for the count, Mona's half of the building was going full throttle, thanks to a serious stash of bottled water, and a generator that had seen the café through the after-effects of several storms and a hurricane. He stepped into the warmth of Mona's, smelling dripping coffee and frying bacon, and loving the refuge of it.

Every booth was full. "Over here, Tim!" called Roger Templeton.

"Squeeze in," said Roger, moving over to make room.

"Roanoke, Junior, how's it goin'? How's Ernie?"

"Haulin' books to th' Dumpster," said Junior. "We're

just gettin' a bite to eat before we pitch in. I took a day's vacation to help."

"Is there any way he can dry the books out?"

"Nope," said Roanoke. "Dead inventory."

"What about Elmo?"

"Seems fine," said Roger, "but he won't come out from under the cash register."

"Junior, I heard you took somebody to ER yesterday. How'd that go?"

"Good mornin', Reverend, what can I get for you this mornin'?" It was Misty Summers, smiling at him and looking prettier, he thought, than the first time he saw her.

"Why, Misty! Did you break your arm?"

"No, sir, it got burned. Hot grease flew off the stove when Ernie's wall fell down."

"Aha." He glanced at Junior, who was lit up like a Christmas tree. "Well, I'm sorry to hear it and hope it heals soon."

"Thank you. It hurts really bad, but the doctor said it's going to be fine. Let's see, now, that was . . . umm, what did you order, sir? I forgot." For some unknown reason, Misty Summers was blushing like a schoolgirl.

"Coffee, no cream, and orange juice," said Father Tim.

"I'll be right back," she said.

"How bad is it at St. John's?" asked Roger.

"Pretty bad. The force of the tree across the roof racked the building to one side. Otis has a crew coming in. Did a good bit of damage."

"When we get Ernie straightened out," said Roanoke, "we'll be down an' give you a hand."

"Why, thanks," he said, touched by the offer.

Walking across the hall to Ernie's, he asked Roger, "By the way, what happened with Ava?"

"Darned if I know. Just out of the picture, it seems. Junior didn't have much to say about her."

"Well, well."

"Looked like a pretty uneven match, anyway."

"Right," said Father Tim, ducking into Ernie's and not liking what he saw.

In the book room, shelves that weren't anchored to the walls had been knocked sprawling, literally scattering books to the wind. The shelves on the fallen wall had crashed with the bricks, piling books among the debris. The smell of wet paper pulp filled the cold, drafty room, which was only loosely protected by the tarp.

Several of Ernie's fishing buddies were stacking ruined books in wheelbarrows.

He embraced the man who, from the beginning, had taken him in like family. "Sorry, my friend."

Ernie tried hard to produce a characteristic smile, but couldn't.

⊙—

He was standing under the tent Sam had erected in the churchyard, drinking coffee with Leonard and Otis, peering at the endless rain and waiting for the contractor to arrive.

"You th' Rev'ren' Kavanagh?" An elderly man in a cap and slicker stepped under the tent.

"I am, sir."

"Albert Gragg."

Albert Gragg tipped his cap and shyly extended his hand. "I'm from up Dor'ster, Miss Ella sent me."

"I hope there's no trouble. . . ."

"She couldn't get you on th' phone. She's fell and broke her hip."

"No!" he said, stricken by the news. He hated to hear this. He didn't like this at all.

"A fracture or a break?"

"Clean break. She's in th' hospital and can't play y'r organ a'tall, said she'd call soon as she can get through."

"What happened?"

"In th' storm, said she heard somethin' hit her porch real hard, thought it was a limb offa that tree she thinks so much of, but it was th' neighbor's doghouse that was out there blowin' around. Said when she went runnin' out to check, th' rain had made 'er porch slippery as hog grease an' down she went. She got to th' phone, called me, an I carried 'er to th' hospital."

"I hate to hear this. You're an old friend, Mr. Gragg?"

"Oh, forty years or more I been lookin' out for Miss Ella and 'er mama, doin' whatnot."

"God bless you for it. Who's her doctor?"

"I don't know, she didn't say."

"Tell her I'll be up as soon as I can, we've got a mess on our hands. Tell her she's in our prayers, and she can count on it."

"Yes, sir," said Albert Gragg, tipping his cap.

"And how's the captain and his brother, do you know?"

"What cap'n?"

"Captain Larkin."

"I can't say. I ain't seen him, he don't get out much. His boy carries his groceries in ever' week or two."

"Well, then," he said, feeling helpless. How many times had he wished there were two of him?

Stanley Harmon stepped under the tent, wiping his bare, bald head with a handkerchief.

"Sorry about this, Tim. Awful sorry."

"Thank you, Stanley. It was a hard hit, all right. Any damage at your place?"

"A few limbs down is all. Y'all are welcome to worship with us on Sunday at eleven, or you could hold your service ahead of ours, at ten o'clock. How'd that be?"

"Terrific. That would be great. Thank you!"

"They say we'll have water by then, so th' commodes'll flush, but far as power goes, bring some candles."

"We'll do it."

"Looks like we won't have power 'til Wednesday. Mildred and I are cookin' on a Coleman stove. Y'all doin all right over at Mid-Way?"

"Oh, fine, just fine."

"You can come stay with us, and I mean it. Mildred said she'd love to have you. Now the kids are off at school you'd have th' whole basement to yourselves, just y'all and our two dogs, Paul and Silas, they wouldn't hurt a fly."

"Thanks, Stanley, we'll hunker down at Mid-Way for a little while, shouldn't be long."

"What else'll you folks need Sunday?"

"I just learned our organist broke her hip."

"Uh-oh. Well, no problem, we've got a crackerjack organist, and come to think of it, he's played a few Anglican services here and there. I'll talk to him and let you know tomorrow. Run by First Baptist in the morning around eight. I'll show you the ropes, give you a key an' all."

"You'll get a crown for this, Stanley!" he called as his colleague dashed into the rain.

Coleman stove! That was the ticket.

Stanley ducked back under the tent. "Oh, shoot, I forgot we can't have organ music without power."

"True enough. How quickly we forget."

"Well, see you in th' morning."

A cappella, then, and no two ways about it.

Less than half the expected crew had shown up at Dove Cottage and, after hauling furniture out of the pit and stuffing it into the study, were tearing out the living room flooring.

According to Otis, the maverick porch had pulled the front wall away, causing the floor joists to collapse. The wall would have to be winched back before they could replace the flooring, and when that was done a crew would come in to do the refinishing. Bottom line, they were looking at a minimum of two or three weeks to complete the job, and the crew couldn't get to the porch before spring.

Hearing this exceedingly unwelcome news, he thought of Earlene Ferguson, who, lacking a porch at the retirement home, simply "dropped off in the yard like a heathen" when exiting her front door.

"Don't worry," said Otis, "I'll have some of my boys from th' Toe put your porch back on. I ain't scared of drivin' a few nails myself."

Shivering in the raw October air, Sam, Leonard, Otis, and Father Tim waited for the contractor, and surveyed the fallen limbs and debris littering the churchyard.

"We ought to stack th' limbs," said Leonard, impatient to get moving.

"No use stackin' limbs in this weather," said Otis.

Rain drummed on the tent roof.

Sam sighed. "Goodness knows, it's sad to see that old tree half ruined."

"It was probably two hundred years old, maybe more. Marjorie and I've seen any number of people married under that tree." Leonard poured coffee from a thermos. "Did you know there are trees still living since before the time of Christ?"

"Where at?" asked Otis.

Leonard blew on his coffee. "I don't know, I forgot. It was in a magazine."

"I ain't believin' it," said Otis.

When the contractor still hadn't arrived at eleven o'clock, Otis bit the end off a cigar, lit it, and, fuming, blew the smoke out his nostrils.

"I'm goin' to be kickin' some butt from here to Chincoteague," he declared, stomping from the tent.

                          ⊖

"How'll we let everybody know where we're holding the service?" Marshall Duncan asked Father Tim. "And how will they know it's at ten, not eleven?"

Ray Gaskill hammered down on his toothpick. "Put a sign at th' post office today, so word gets around. Then put one in th' churchyard, people'll be comin' by to see th' damage."

The road crew roared past St. John's in a parade of heavy equipment, waving at the assembly under the tent.

"You want to see the basement?" Leonard asked Father Tim.

"Is it safe?"

"I wouldn't go down there," said Ray. "No, sir, not me."

"I believe I'll pass. Besides, I've got to run to the motel and take lunch to my wife."

"Where you goin' to get lunch?" asked Ray.

"Mona's."

"Not unless you want to stand in line in th' rain. I just come by there, it ain't a pretty sight. You could go to the grocery store, get you some Vienna sausages in a can, tuna in a can, all kinds of things in a can, and a loaf of bread, some mayonnaise . . ."

"Aha."

"And if I was you," said Ray, "I'd keep th' underside of your Mustang hosed off, you're gonna be eat up with rust."

⟨⟩

He said nothing to Cynthia about the predicted duration of the job at Dove Cottage. If the thought of three weeks at the Mid-Way was enough to make him crazy, there was no telling what it might do to his wife.

⟨⟩

"There's no way to patch it," said Sewell Joiner. "We're talkin' shore up, tear out, strip off, an' set straight—it's goin' to look a lot worse before it looks better."

"Whatever it takes," said Father Tim.

"We'll have to excavate part of th' basement and tear out and rebuild th' wall. You got a bad crack in th' bed joints of th' masonry—"

"We're more in'erested in th' sanctuary right now," said Otis. "What's it goin' to take to get us back in business?"

"First thing we'll do is get some rollin' scaffold inside and tear off th' plaster that's not already fallen off th' ceilin' joists and studs. We'll be tearin' off some sheathin' an' shingles and replacin' that busted roof joist, then we'll use a come-along to straighten th' whole thing up again an' put on a new roof."

"I'd like you to get your boys started in th' mornin," said Otis.

"Tomorrow's Saturday," said the contractor.

"Go on and get 'em over here, we want to move on this thing. It's depressin' to ever'body not to see some action."

"Fine," said Sewell Joiner. "I can do that."

Otis unwrapped a cigar. "How long to get th' job done?"

"Two, three months if we got th' weather on our side. That'll include gettin' replastered and repainted."

Two or three months? Father Tim's heart sank like a stone.

At three o'clock, a crowd of parishioners had assembled under the tent, looking for a report on the damage, volunteering to help, offering consolation, and fervently commiserating. The rain drew on, shrouding the churchyard in a dusky gloom.

"I've got these little bitty mushrooms growin' between my toes," said Orville Hood, who kept St. John's oil tank filled.

"Let me *see!*" squealed Penny Duncan's youngest.

"I was sittin' in th' livin room workin' a crossword when I thought th' world was comin' to an end." Maude Proffitt was swaddled in a yellow slicker and rain hat, with only her eyes visible. "Boom, somethin' hit right above my head. Honey, it was the *ceiling,* it just cracked open like a hen egg. Well, don't you know I jumped across th' room, my feet never touched th' floor! Thank th' Lord I didn't stay in that recliner another minute, or I'd've been pushin' up daisies right over yonder."

"Have a brownie," said Marjorie Lamb. "I baked these yesterday before the power went off."

"Law, what I wouldn't give for a cup of coffee to go with this," said Maude, eating the brownie in two bites.

Sue Blankenship's glasses kept trying to slide off her wet nose. "Did you hear th' Father's poor wife was hit by a picket fence?" she asked a baritone in the choir.

"No way! A whole fence?"

"Well, maybe just a picket."

Ann Hartsell, newly arrived from her nursing job across, saw the church and burst into tears. This caused her two youngsters, just fetched from day care, to erupt in a storm of sympathetic weeping.

"Have a brownie!" implored Marjorie, stooping to their level with the plastic tray.

"Th' trouble with this storm," said Ray Gaskill, "is mainly th' trees. It's *trees* that's done th' damage."

" 'Til I moved here, I never knew islands *had* trees," said Edith Johnson, who was an ECW bigwig.

Jean Ballenger shivered in her winter coat. "We nearly got the Last Supper finished, we're just working on the tablecloth. That much white seems to take forever. If you ask me, I don't believe all those men would have *used* a tablecloth."

"Do you think we should still try to have th' Fall Fair?" asked Mildred Harmon, handing around a plate of ham biscuits.

Father Tim turned aside from talking with the contractor. "Yes, *indeed*," he said. "Rain or shine!"

Jean patted her bangs in place. "What a relief! I

couldn't bear the thought of all that work lying in a drawer 'til next year."

Early the following morning, the rain stopped.

He drove Cynthia, Jonathan, and Violet to Marion's, popped by First Baptist, and arrived at St. John's at eight-thirty as the five-man work crew blew in, on time and ready to roll.

By eleven o'clock, the sun came out, the temperature rose seven degrees, and a third of the north end regained running water.

"Hallelujah!" shouted Father Tim, tossing his rain hat in the air.

Otis stubbed out his cigar and pocketed the butt. "OK, boys, let's stack limbs."

Father Tim popped into the nave now and again to check the crew's progress. He was over the sick feeling, wanting only to see the work move ahead quickly.

Though pews and pulpit were under tarps, and plaster dust covered everything, the stained-glass window at the rear of the sanctuary was unharmed, with only minor cracking and pulling around the frame. The strong early light illumined the image sharply, casting color onto the white tarps. *Come unto me. . . .* That was sermon enough for this storm, he thought, or for any storm.

Each time he went inside, he glanced nervously at the choir loft, anxious for the safety and protection of the organ.

"No problem," said Sewell, who, Father Tim learned, was known to constituents as Sew, pronounced *Sue*.

He decided to stop worrying. If he couldn't trust a

two-hundred-and-fifty-pound man who could kick in the remaining portion of a concrete-block basement wall, who could he trust?

He'd seen smaller crowds show up for Sunday worship.

By noon, more than half the parish had arrived, many with lunch bags from Mona's, some with family picnics. As the ground was too wet to sit on, they sat in parked cars, doors open, calling to one another, ambling through the tent where Sam had set up a folding table and a forty-two-cup coffeepot powered by a portable generator.

"Doughnut holes!" Jean Ballenger plunked down a box from the shop next door to her mainland hairdresser.

"Lookit!" said Ray Gaskill, who didn't want to miss out on the action. He lifted the lid of a bakery box, exposing half a cake, inscribed *HDAY TO RAY* in lime-green icing. "I was sixty-seven last July . . . that's August, September, October, it ain't but four months old and been in th' freezer th' whole time, help yourself."

Penny Duncan arrived with a gallon of sun tea, made before the rains began, and a freezer bag of thawed oatmeal cookies. Mona Fulcher dispatched Junior Bryson with a vast container of hot soup, a pot of chili, and a sack of cups and plastic spoons. Stanley Harmon dropped by with two thawed loaves of homemade bread from the freezer at First Baptist, along with a quart of apple juice he'd nabbed from the Sunday School.

Not knowing that his priest had already asked a blessing, and feeling his own heart so inclined, Sam Fieldwalker offered a fervent psalm of praise and petition.

"A double shot!" remarked someone who had happily bowed for both prayers.

Leonard Lamb popped a doughnut hole in his mouth. "We need a double shot," he said.

⟁

At two o'clock, his adrenaline still pumping, he drove to the motel to fetch Barnabas for a run along the beach.

The heater had raised the temperature of the room to that of a blast furnace. He turned the heater off, snapped on the leash, and was out of there with a dog so relieved to be rescued that he slammed his forepaws against Father Tim's chest and gave his glasses a proper fogging.

⟁

The beach was more littered than usual, but nothing compared to the pictures he'd seen of Whitecap beaches in the aftermath of worse storms.

His brain felt petrified; he could scarcely think. For a man who'd been accused of thinking too much, it was an odd feeling, as if he were living his life in a dream, reacting to, rather than initiating, the circumstances that came his way.

He did know one thing for certain—he had to get his crowd out of the Mid-Way Motel, pronto.

Dodging the detritus of the storm, he ran easily, chuffing south toward the lighthouse and glancing at a sky so blue it might have been fired onto porcelain. The sea beneath was azure and calm, the water lapping gently at the sand.

He saw it, but thought nothing of it. Then, several yards down the beach, he stopped and looked again.

It was a little plane, bright red against the cloudless

sky. He thought of his two jaunts into the wild blue yonder with Omer Cunningham, and the time Omer flew him to Virginia so he could attend Dooley's school concert. Blast, he missed the boy terribly. It had been four months since he saw him vanishing around the corner of Wisteria and Main on his bicycle. " *'Bye, Dad . . .*"

Barnabas skidded to a stop and barked furiously as the plane dipped toward the wide beach, then veered out over the water.

Father Tim stood and watched as it gained altitude and headed south. Did he see someone waving at him from the cockpit?

Probably not, but he waved back, just in case.

He was sitting on the bottom step of the walkway through the dunes, tying a shoelace, when he heard it.

Holy smoke, that plane was not only coming this way again, it was coming in low. Very low.

In fact, it was *landing. . . .*

It blew past him, contacted the sand, and bounced lightly along the beach. As it slowed, farther along the strand, the tail came up, then settled again.

He might have been plugged into an electrical outlet the way his scalp was tingling. It couldn't be, he thought, as he saw the doors open. . . .

But it was.

Barking wildly, Barnabas jerked the leash from under his foot and bounded toward the red plane and the people clambering out of it.

"Omer! Dooley!"

No, indeed, he would not bawl like a baby. He wiped his eyes on the sleeve of his jacket as he sprinted behind his dog. Amazing grace! Hallelujah! Unbelievable!

And it wasn't just Omer and Dooley.

"Pauline!" he yelled to the woman running toward him. *"Buck!"*

Dooley reached him first. "Hey," he said, throwing his arms around Father Tim, who hugged back for all he was worth.

"Hey, yourself, buddy, hey, yourself!"

Dooley cackled. "You're breakin' my ribs! Hey, ol' dog, ol' Barn, ol' buddy." Dooley fell onto the sand with Barnabas, as Pauline shyly gave Father Tim a hug, and Buck and Omer pounded him on the back to a fare-thee-well.

"This is my little Stinson Voyager," said Omer. His proud smile revealed teeth large enough to replace the ivories on an upright. "What d'you think?"

"Beautiful! Handsome! A sight for sore eyes!" said Father Tim.

Buck grinned at him, looking pounds lighter and years younger. "We buzzed over here a little bit ago, checkin' out th' beach. We thought it was you we saw."

"Yeah," said Dooley, "how did you know we were coming?"

"I didn't!"

"Cool."

Omer gave the Voyager's rear tire a swift kick. "Tundra tires. Got those special, since I knew I'd be comin' down on a soft field. By th' way, I had my buddy in Raleigh check it out, he said this end of th' beach was church property, so we could land here, no problem.

"Lookit!" Omer dragged him to the open door and pointed to a storage box behind the backseat. Father Tim smelled something wonderful.

"We're carryin' beef stew, we got fried chicken, we

got bottled water, an' . . . what else we got?" he asked Pauline.

"The ham Emma baked for tomorrow!" said Pauline, flushed with excitement. "And Miz Bolick's orange marmalade cake."

"Yeah!" said Dooley. "Three layers! Plus stuff that Tony and Mr. Gregory and Anna sent, but it all smells like garlic."

Omer was busy pulling cargo from behind the seat. "Couldn't haul but forty pounds, what with icin' down th' food and carryin' three passengers, but we got more comin' next trip."

"Let me get a wheelbarrow," said Father Tim. "We're covered up with wheelbarrows at church."

Out of the corner of his eye, Father Tim saw several onlookers gathering.

"You probably don't want to leave it here long. Whitecap is full of nice people, but . . ."

"Oh, I ain't goin' to leave it here long a'tall. I'm makin' a run back to Mitford here in a little bit."

"Back to Mitford?"

"See, tomorrow mornin', I'm haulin' young 'uns."

"Poo and Jessie," said Dooley. "They're comin'."

"Ah," he said, trying to understand.

Dooley adjusted his ball cap. "You better tell 'im, Mama."

"Well," said Pauline. She looked suddenly shy. "Well . . ."

"We tried to call," said Buck, "but we couldn't get through."

"See, what it is," said Dooley, "is Mama and Buck want you to marry 'em tomorrow."

Buck Leeper, who had probably never blushed in his life, turned beet red. "If you don't mind."

"When I heard what was goin' on," said Omer, "I offered to fly 'em down here."

More hand-shaking, back-slapping, and riotous barking, as his delirious dog dashed around them in circles.

———— ⟡ ————

Hauling a trunk full of food and water, he drove Dooley to the Fieldwalkers', where he let his wife weep the tears he was holding back. That was just one of the many conveniences of marriage, he thought, as Cynthia bawled and clung to Dooley like moss to a log.

———— ⟡ ————

On the way to St. John's, he figured Stanley would let him use the sanctuary for the wedding tomorrow afternoon. If that didn't work, surely they'd loan their basement hall. Then, if worse came to worst, there was always the Town Hall—not a pretty sight, but he'd heard of couples getting married there.

Whatever happened would have to happen fast.

Lord, he prayed . . .

———— ⟡ ————

They said goodbye to Omer, who was leaving with half the crowd trailing along to see the takeoff.

"What it is," Omer explained as they headed down the lane, "is a complete fabric aircraft. You've got your steel-tube fuselage with a fabric cover . . ."

"Could I go in th' church and look around?" asked Buck.

"Sure, grab a hard hat, I'll go in with you. The crew's packing up to leave. They'll be back on Monday and things will start to get serious around here."

Pauline beamed. "Buck don't have to go far to find a hard hat," she said. "May I come in, too?"

"Come on!" he said. "But watch your step. There's plaster lying forty ways from Sunday."

⟡

He called Sew Joiner aside. "Before your men leave, there's something I'd like them to do, if possible. We've just had a very . . . unusual request."

⟡

During the impromptu and elaborate meal at the Fieldwalkers', which Marion called a rehearsal dinner, Father Tim proposed a toast to Buck and Pauline. Buck, who was unaccustomed to much society, bobbed his head with awkward appreciation. Pauline smiled and held his hand, saying little, owing to the fullness of a heart overcome with wonder, and what she supposed might even be joy.

Before Tony's tiramisu was passed around, Cynthia and Pauline trundled off to the bedroom with a kerosene lamp to view the wedding frock. Father Tim loved hearing peals of his wife's laughter issuing from the room, as such frivolity had recently been as scarce as hen's teeth.

He put his arm around Dooley, noting that the boy was now a couple of inches taller than himself. He also checked the look on Dooley's face. Was he happy about his mother marrying Buck Leeper? As far as Father Tim could tell, the answer was yes, definitely.

⟡

Following an evening made more festive by candles and a crackling fire, Buck and Dooley were dispatched

to Room Twenty-two at the Mid-Way. Pauline was invited to bunk in with the Fieldwalkers, who noted that
the guest room leak had stopped and another chamber
pot had been improvised.

Otis announced that the Kavanaghs would be moving on Tuesday afternoon into the million-dollar home
of Martha Talbot, a seasonal resident from Canada who
hadn't been in Whitecap for two seasons, due to a series
of family weddings from Brazil to Portugal, not to mention Bar Harbor, Maine.

It was all quite breathtaking, thought Father Tim,
as he climbed into his pajamas and fell, deeply weary
and as deeply grateful, onto the lumpy bed of Room
Fourteen.

—·—

But he couldn't sleep.

He lay listening to the hiss of the heater and his
wife's whiffling snore. Jonathan thrashed and turned,
kicking him in the ribs once, then twice.

Numb with exhaustion, he got up and put on his robe
and slippers, lit the kerosene lantern, and sat in the worn
armchair by the window. A ten o'clock service followed
by a one-thirty wedding tomorrow, and here he was at
half-past midnight, his eyes as big as the headlights on
Loretta Burgess's eighteen-wheeler.

He went to the bathroom and did a glucometer
check. Ah, well, no more tiramisu for him for a while;
he'd be chopped liver tomorrow.

He took his Bible from the windowsill, opened it in
the low light, and closed his eyes and prayed. *Thank
you, Lord. . . .*

Let's face it, he could have been fished up from the
bottom of Judd's Creek. The nail in the picket could

have pierced Cynthia's eye instead of her hand. If Maude Proffitt hadn't jumped when she did, her ceiling would have landed on her head instead of her recliner. The list was endless. St. John's might have been completely demolished, the whole tree could have come down . . .

He jerked awake, realizing he'd dozed off. Out of the blue, a word had come upon his heart.

He saw the word in his mind as if it were inscribed on a blackboard with white chalk, *J E R I C H O*.

"Jericho," he whispered, puzzled. Barnabas stirred at his feet.

Lord, is this of You? Are you telling me something?

He examined his heart, and realized he felt the peace he always required in order to know whether God was in a particular circumstance.

Intrigued, he turned in his Bible to the Old Testament, to the sixth chapter of Joshua, and began to read:

"Now Jericho was securely shut up . . ."

～⊙～

Out of curiosity, Ray Gaskill opened the door of St. John's on Sunday around noon, and gaped at what he saw.

The shattered plaster had been hauled to either side of the nave and covered with tarps. The floor in the middle had been swept perfectly clean, the broken windows covered, and the rolling scaffolds parked neatly at the rear of the nave.

The pulpit had come out from under its tarp and shone with a lustrous coat of lemon wax, as did two pews that were aligned to face the pulpit. Oil-fired heaters, hissing warmth, flanked the pews on either side.

On a table before the altar, which was laid with an embroidered fair cloth and a silver chalice, paten, and candelabra, stood a vase displaying stems of gold leaves and red berries.

Above the wooden cross, the bright autumn noon gave its light through the window where He stood, arms outstretched, waiting.

CHAPTER TWENTY

Dearly Beloved

"Dearly beloved: We have come together in the presence of God, to witness and bless the joining together of this man and this woman in Holy Matrimony."

He knew most of the service by heart, never liking to see a priest's eyes glued to the prayer book instead of the congregation. He spoke the words today with unusually tender feeling.

"The bond and covenant of marriage was established by God in creation, and our Lord Jesus Christ adorned this manner of life by His presence and first miracle at a wedding in Cana of Galilee. It signifies to us the mystery of the union between Christ and His Church, and Holy Scripture commends it to be honored among all people.

"The union of husband and wife in heart, body, and mind is intended by God for their mutual joy; for the help and comfort given one another in prosperity and adversity . . ."

In the front row, Jessie played with the ruffle on her new dress, Poo gave the proceedings his absorbed attention, Dooley looked oddly proud and moved. Cynthia was beaming.

". . . therefore, marriage is not to be entered into unadvisedly or lightly, but reverently, deliberately, and in accordance with the purposes for which it was instituted by God.

"Into this holy union, Pauline Barlowe and Bernard Leeper now come to be joined."

There were enough teeth showing in Omer Cunningham's grin to play the Wedding March.

"Pauline, will you have this man to be your husband; to live together in the covenant of marriage? Will you love him, comfort him, honor and keep him, in sickness and in health; and, forsaking all others, be faithful to him as long as you both shall live?"

Pauline's response was a fervent whisper. "I will!"

Otis Bragg pulled a handkerchief from his plaid sport coat and blew his nose. Marion Fieldwalker dabbed at her eyes; Sam appeared personally pleased, as if the whole lot of Barlowes were, at the very least, first cousins.

"Bernard, will you have this woman to be your wife; to live together in the covenant of marriage? Will you love her, comfort her, honor and keep her, in sickness and in health; and, forsaking all others, be faithful to her as long as you both shall live?"

He saw Buck's eyes mist with tears. Then Buck cleared his throat and spoke in a voice that could be heard to the ceiling joists.

"I will!"

"Will all of you witnessing these promises do all in your power to uphold these two persons in their marriage?"

Dooley spontaneously stood, then sat again, as those assembled chorused in unison, "We *will*!"

He was choking up himself. He touched his ear, a signal to his wife to pray for him, and step on it.

"Who gives this woman to be married to this man?"

Dooley rose from the pew and came forward, white-faced. Though his heart hammered with anxiety at the responsibility he was about to bear, he felt powerfully certain that this was a good thing; his mother would have someone to care for her, and for the first time ever, his brother and sister would have a real family.

—————— ⌖ ——————

The wedding feast was laid in the basement fellowship hall of First Baptist, where a motley collection of portable generators helped create the welcome aromas of garlic, coffee, hot rolls, and other comestibles, lightly dressed with the scent of gasoline from the generators.

The feast tables were covered with blue paper cloths, and decorated with boughs of red berries purloined from a stand of nandina behind the Sunday School. Votives glimmered on the tables, and along the top of the spinet by the kitchen door.

"Here they come!" someone shouted.

Laughing and excited, St. John's choir, joined by a baritone and soprano from First Baptist, assembled breathlessly in the middle of the room.

As the bride and groom entered, a cheer went up from all who had attended Stanley Harmon's morning service and were thus invited to the feast; then followed the exultant voices of the choir.

> *"Praise, my soul, the King of heaven*
> *to his feet thy tribute bring;*
> *ransomed, healed, restored, forgiven,*
> *evermore his praises sing:*
> *Alleluia, alleluia!*
> *Praise the everlasting King!"*

Pauline Leeper put both hands over her face like an unbelieving schoolgirl, and felt the arm of her husband go around her shoulders. Then she heard the oohs and aahs of her children, who stood beside her. She thought she might never again see, or be blessed with, anything so wondrous.

⟋

Following the blessing and subsequent hymn, Father Tim had a moment's thought of Jeffrey Tolson and the earnest choir he had abandoned. His heart felt suddenly moved toward the man; he wondered where he might be, whether he'd escaped harm during the storm, and if he ever longed for his children. Father Tim watched with both sadness and delight as Jeffrey's son made a beeline toward him with an Oreo cookie in each hand, eager to share one. He squatted and proffered the palm of his own hand, eager to receive it.

⟋

"Law, where'd this cake *come* from?"

"I don't know, plus, who could bake a cake without electricity? Does anybody know who brought it?"

"I heard it was flown in special."

"I declare, this is th' best cake I ever put in my *mouth*."

"I'd give an arm an' a leg for th' recipe, wouldn't you?"

"If nobody minds, I'm goin' to just scrape off these crumbs that're left and give 'em to Mama—then somebody, meanin' me, can lick th' plate it came on."

⟋

He had reserved a piece of the cake, which he wrapped in foil.

He also retrieved a large chunk of lasagna, the drumstick of a baked chicken, four slices of ham, and two biscuits, which he loaded onto a heavy-duty paper plate with a border of irises. He went to the cupboards and found a deluxe-size plastic cup, and stuffed it with potato salad.

Morris Love had been on his mind, and he couldn't shake the thought. He was alone in that dark, rambling house with only candles to light his way, and apparently no clue how to feed himself, unless Mamie was there to do it for him. Even so, she wouldn't have power for cooking, and no Stinson Voyager hauling in victuals.

Aha. A maverick deviled egg. He was tempted to eat it himself, being inordinately fond of deviled eggs, but popped it into a Ziploc sandwich bag. Oh, the infinite resources of a church kitchen . . .

He rummaged around until he found a large, empty jar, took the lid off, and sniffed it. Pickles. He rinsed it out with water from a plastic jug, and filled it with sweet tea.

"I'll be right back," he told his wife. "Looks like this will go on for at least another hour."

"Where on earth . . . ?" she asked, wondering at the bulging plastic grocery bag.

"I'll tell you later." He gave her a jovial kiss, square on the mouth.

～

Things were different now that the weather had turned cooler. There was no open window to shout to.

At the door, he stood on one foot and then the other, and scratched his head.

Why not ring the bell? That was an original thought!

He pressed the bell, but heard no results from inside. Maybe the bell had a quirk, like most doorbells, and had to be pressed in a certain way. He pressed again. Nothing. What Morris Love needed was a *dog*, for Pete's sake.

When he carved out the chunk of lasagna at church, it was still warm. If he kept standing here, it would be cold.

Hardly believing his audacity, he opened the door and stuck his head into the dim foyer.

"Morris!" he yelled, loudly enough to be heard upstairs. "Morris, it's me, Tim Kavanagh! I've brought your *supper*!"

There, that ought to get a rise out of a man who was, for all he knew, subsisting on Fig Newtons.

"Father . . ."

He nearly jumped out of his skin. Morris Love appeared from behind the stairwell, a ghostly apparition if he'd ever seen one.

"Holy smoke, Morris, sorry I was yelling when you were standing right there."

"Come in," Morris said, not appearing to mean it.

⟨⟩

He followed Morris into the cold and cavernous kitchen, illumined only by two small windows above the sink, and set the bag on the table.

"The lasagna is still warm," he said. "I hope you'll eat it soon."

He felt like a mother coaxing a child, and stood back from the table, suddenly awkward.

"Thank you," said Morris, standing with his hands in the pockets of a burgundy bathrobe.

Thank you? A mere *thank you*? He wanted to see the man tear open the bag and dive in!

Father Tim opened the bag and pulled out the heavy plate and set it on the table. "It's on a plate," he said, feeling progressively uneasy. "You can just peel off the aluminum foil. And here's some tea, I put lemon in it. . . ."

Somewhere in the house, a clock chimed three o'clock.

"Well . . . ," he said, not knowing what else to say.

"Your neighborly kindness will, I'm sure, guarantee your place in heaven," said Morris.

Father Tim found his scowling countenance formidable in the dusky light. "Ah, well, it's not kindness that gets us into heaven," he said, feeling himself in quagmire to his knees.

Morris narrowed his eyes. "I would ask you to consider that I have lived alone without the sap of neighborly interaction for most of my life. And yet, over and over again, you would intrude upon the privacy and solitude I find agreeable. This behavior, which I fail entirely to understand, exhibits the most careless disrespect."

"But . . ."

"I am not a novelty, Father, some bizarre experiment to satisfy your prejudices about the essential spirituality of the human heart. I do not need your kindness, nor do I want your salvation."

"It is not my salvation."

"In addition, I do not desire your friendship, nor do I crave your admiration of my pathetic musical skills."

Father Tim felt an alarming weakness in his legs.

"One further thing. Save your breath, Father, and stop praying for me."

He found his ground, and stood it. "Save your own

breath, Morris. I shall pray for you until . . ." His mind raced. *Until the Lord comes with his hosts? Until it suits me to stop?*

". . . until the cows come home!" He delivered this fervent declamation straight up and straight out, meaning it from the depths of his being.

He turned from the kitchen and walked quickly across the foyer, hearing the chilling and inevitable words that cut like knives.

"Out! *Out!*"

Closing the front door behind him, he trotted up the driveway in the late afternoon light that slanted through the canopy of trees.

———⌐———

They were crammed into Room Fourteen like sardines in a tin, seven of them, including Violet and Barnabas.

He thought the least they could do was give the Fieldwalkers and Lambs a break. Not only had their good friends pulled off a feast for more than forty people, they'd come in behind the work crew's cleanup and readied the altar and nave for the wedding.

Though a small and certainly impromptu wedding, he noted it was kicking up a considerable swirl of activity.

Buck had reserved a couple of additional rooms, which were in the process of being cleaned, for Omer and the kids, all of which occasioned the hauling of various sacks, pokes, and grips from Room Fourteen into adjacent quarters, with much trailing of vagrant socks and sweaters, and leaving open of the door—a feature his dog particularly relished.

As Omer rambled in the village, and the newlyweds

inspected the island in one of Otis's pickup trucks, he and Cynthia put their heads together about dinner. Should they even have dinner, since they'd eaten at two-thirty? Children were always hungry, weren't they? Of course.

But then, Mona's was shut tight as a clam on Sunday, which occasioned searching the yellow pages for what was open across, reminding them of Cap'n Willies, which seemed the perfect solution; further, he learned that Pauline, Buck, and Jessie were flying home first thing in the morning with Omer, and Harley was arriving this evening to fetch Dooley and Poo back to Mitford early tomorrow, as Omer couldn't do another double airlift, given his need to attend a huge going-away party for his sister-in-law and outgoing mayor, Esther Cunningham, imminently headed west with her husband in the RV.

Breathless, Father Tim reserved a room for Harley, whose reason for an early departure tomorrow morning, according to Dooley, was the emergency overhaul he was doing on the motor in Lew Boyd's wrecker.

The crowd from next door returned, vibrating with energy.

He hated to bring up the unwelcome subject. "I thought you had to be in court tomorrow morning."

"Oh," said Dooley. "I forgot."

"Forgot what?"

"Buster Austin went bawlin' to Chief Underwood and said he was th' one that done it . . . did it . . . not me. He was scared out of his mind about goin' in front of a judge, so they ain't . . . isn't . . . any court. Not for me, anyway. Sorry I forgot to tell you. There was so much goin' on. . . ."

Father Tim sank onto the foot of the bed, feeling as if a great weight had rolled off his shoulders.

"Oh, somethin' else I forgot, Harley said your cousin Walter called, said he couldn't get in touch with you down here, said he had somethin' to tell you about a lawsuit, somethin' really important, said to call him."

The lawsuit!

The weight that had just rolled off, rolled back on and dug in.

"Ahh," he said, wanting nothing more than to seek the opiate of sleep, to put the lawsuit, the storm, the sickening confrontation with Morris Love, out of his mind.

He stood and put on his jacket. "Let's go for a ride," he said to Dooley. "I'll show you around the island."

"Cool," said Dooley. "I'll drive!"

"We want to go, *too!*" shouted Jessie.

Barnabas trotted to the door and sat, looking hopeful.

Poo raced from the bathroom. "Can we go see the lighthouse?"

"I could, I could go, too," said Jonathan, pulling on his hat and grabbing his coat.

Father Tim turned to his wife, who looked decidedly pale around the gills. "Hallelujah," she murmured.

$$\backsim$$

"When we get back to that place we're stayin' at, you can be it," said Jessie.

"It what?" asked Poo.

"Th' husband."

"I don't want to be no husband."

"See, you can marry Jonathan, and I'll say th' words, 'cause I like them words."

"I ain't marryin' no baby," said Poo.

"I'm *not* a baby!" exclaimed Jonathan.

"Well, so Jonathan can be Buck, I can be Mama, and _you_ can say th' words, then."

"Say what words?" asked Poo.

"Dearly belove-ud."

"I ain't sayin' that."

Dooley looked into the rearview mirror. "Don't say ain't!" he told his brother.

———

He lay curled in the fetal position, his back to his wife and Jonathan, feeling a kind of numb pain he couldn't explain or understand. Life was a roller coaster, that simple. Joy and healing here, desperation and demolition there.

With all his heart, he'd desired healing for Morris Love's brokenness, and who was he to think he might give a leg up to such a miracle? There were times when he didn't like being a priest, always on the front line for justice and mercy and forgiveness and redemption; trying to figure out the mind of God; giving the Lord his personal agenda, then standing around waiting for it to be fulfilled. He didn't have an agenda for Morris Love, anymore; he was giving up the entire self-seeking, willful notion. His desperate neighbor belonged to God; it was His responsibility to get the job done. He had schlepped in a paltry sack of victuals when what the man needed was the awesome, thunderstriking power of the Almighty to move in his heart and soul and spirit like a great and consuming fire. . . .

He wiped his eyes on his pajama sleeve.

"So, Lord," he whispered, "just do it."

———

Though he managed to spend a full half hour with Buck, he had almost no time with Dooley. On Monday morning, he insisted on making the breakfast run to Mona's, and let Dooley drive. They arrived at Mona's as she opened the doors, and waited in the front booth while the kitchen pulled together sacks of sausage biscuits, ham biscuits, fries, Danish, coffee, milk, and Coke for the crowd at Mid-Way.

"How are things with Caroline?" He already knew about Dooley's grades, which were excellent and worthy of all praise. Now he was going for the nitty-gritty.

Dooley reached into the neck of his sweatshirt. Grinning, he pulled forth a small gold ring, set with a single pearl and attached to a chain he was wearing around his neck.

"What does that mean . . . umm, exactly?"

Dooley shrugged. "Just . . . you know."

"Right. Ever see Lace?"

"I ran into her at the drugstore one Saturday. She was in White Chapel with a bunch of girls."

"Did you talk?"

Dooley shrugged again. "Not exactly."

Oh, well. Time would tell.

The boy was becoming handsome, that simple. Father Tim observed sinew gathering on his bones, and noted that his long, slender fingers would be well suited, indeed, to his calling. "Any more thoughts on whether to vet small animals or large?"

"Both," Dooley said with feeling. "I want to vet both."

"Good!" he said. "Good."

"Harley, thanks for making such a long trip. Sorry Omer's plane won't hold but four."

"Don't even think about it, Rev'rend. Hit was good t' git on th' road."

"What do you see of our tenant?"

"Seen 'er twice. She looked kind of hunkered down, like she's scared of 'er own shadow. Somebody said she was lettin' 'er piana students go, an' headin' back up north. She ain't tryin' to run out on th' rent, is she?"

"Oh, no, she's paid up. Well, God be with you, Harley, Poo, Dooley."

" 'Bye, Dad."

" 'Bye, buddy. See you down here for Christmas, OK?"

"OK!"

"Harley, we want you to come, too."

"Yes, sir, Rev'rend, we'll be here."

"All right, hold her between the ditches."

Feeling a kind of emptiness, he watched the red truck pull out of the motel parking lot and head left on the highway toward Mitford.

$\backsim$

"Fella down th' beach said he was sittin' on his deck, said he'd just pulled out his glasses to read th' paper when a book fell in his lap, *whop*."

"No kidding." He had to get out of here fast; he'd only popped by to see how Ernie's reconstruction was coming.

"I'm tellin' you!" said Ernie, who appeared to be more like his old self. "*Th' Mustangs* by Frank Dobie is what it was. That book come right offa my shelf."

"Amazing," he said, wanting to be respectful.

"Bull," said Roanoke.

"Th' storm was Thursday, th' book dropped in 'is lap Sunday. Must've blowed somewhere to dry off, then was picked up by a stiff wind and sent south."

Roanoke fired a match head under the tabletop and lit a Marlboro. "I ain't believin' that."

"Told me he liked th' book all right, but wouldn't give two cents for th' endin'."

"That's gratitude for you," said Roanoke.

———⊙———

He didn't want to do this, not at all.

"Walter Kavanagh here."

"Walter . . ."

"Timothy! What in blazes happened down there?"

"Storm. Bad. Busy." Sheer dread had reduced his speech to primitive monosyllables.

"Well," said Walter, "I'm afraid you're not going to like this."

"It never once occurred to me that I might like it."

"D'Anjou says a love letter accompanies the holographic will, which makes the old man's personal feelings and legal intentions perfectly clear and in accordance with the will."

"How do we know it's Josiah's Baxter's handwriting and not some forgery?"

"D'Anjou seems to believe that matter is sufficiently demonstrable in court, he didn't say how. Frankly, I think d'Anjou is behind this thing and pushing hard. He's been minding the family's affairs for years. I get a sense of personal greed here. If it were my case, I wouldn't feel so confident—I mean, no one coming forward for fifty years? But he thinks he can convince the jury."

"What about the money Miss Sadie left to Dooley?"

Walter and Cynthia were the only other living souls who knew that Miss Sadie had left Dooley more than a million dollars in trust. "That was her mother's money. Surely this legal action couldn't—"

"No, I don't think so. Don't get ahead of things, Timothy. In any case, it looks like we have to go through with this. I'll work with you on the response to the court; we've got three weeks to pull it together. Can you call me Wednesday night? I have some ideas."

Though he knew full well there was no sorrow in heaven, he hoped, nonetheless, that Miss Sadie wouldn't get wind of this deplorable mess. Shortly before her death, she'd learned of an illegitimate half-sister, born to her mother before she married Josiah Baxter. This dark secret, however, had an exceedingly bright side—Miss Sadie ended up with Olivia Harper as her beloved grandniece, which had been, of course, an inarguable benediction.

But another illegitimate half-sister? It seemed like pure fiction; he hated to think what this lawsuit might have done to his old friend and parishioner if she were still living.

In ways he couldn't yet fully understand, he sensed his life would be entwined with Sadie Baxter for the rest of his days.

At one o'clock on Tuesday, he drove to the Mid-Way from a couple of home visits, and helped Cynthia load Jonathan's things into the car. Jonathan talked endlessly.

"I'm goin' home, Cyn'dy."

"I know, dear."

"Will you come an' see me?"

"Of course."

"An' you can see Babette an' Jason, too."

"Will you come and see us?"

"Maybe I could sometime." Jonathan put on his hat.

"We'll bring your movies later. They're at our house that fell down in the front."

"You could, you could watch 'em again before you bring 'em to my house. That would be OK if you want to."

He glanced at his wife as they piled into the car, and felt her suffering as his own.

~~~

He was fairly stunned when he saw Martha Talbot's house, sitting quite alone at the end of an oyster-shell lane. A million smackers rising off the undeveloped bank of the Sound was a pretty impressive sight.

"Wow," Cynthia whispered.

"You must be living right, Kavanagh."

They parked in the two-car garage, simply because it was a luxury to have one, and went up the stairs to the front door.

"Here," he said, giving her the key. "You do the honors."

As the door swung open, they stood looking across the sunlit living room and through the wall of windows to the Sound. The water lay as smooth as a lake, glinting in the sun.

His wife gave a small gasp of wonder and delight.

"Now we're talking!" she said.

~~~

They prowled through the spacious house like a couple of kids, amazed at their discoveries. Central vacuum system, enormous fireplace in both living room and master suite, glorious views all around, a room with the right light and location for her work, a room with a comfortable and easy spirit for his study, an intercom system, a large kitchen in which they felt decidedly lost, and a media room that, thanks to its dumbfounding technology and wall-size television screen, caused them to shut the door hastily.

They thumped onto one of two sofas in the living room, thinking to build a fire against the chill.

"Well," he said.

"Well," she said.

He wouldn't have mentioned it for the world, but he wished they had Jonathan to put some life in this place.

"Let's unload the car, then. I'll bring Barnabas and Violet up."

"Wouldn't it be marvelous if we had power?" she mused.

"Just in case, try the lamp."

Sixty watts sprang to life at her touch. "Thanks be to God!" they shouted in spontaneous unison.

They leaped up and dashed to the kitchen and turned on the faucet, which spat and chugged and released a brackish stream of water into the sink.

"Try the phone!" she crowed.

A dial tone!

"The heat . . ." They trotted in tandem, searching for a thermostat.

Having located it at the end of the hallway, they grabbed each other and exchanged a fervent hug as the furnace roared into action.

"Priest and deacon die and go to heaven!" he whooped.

Ah, but no million-dollar house on the Sound could ease the sorrow of his wife's heart.

He lay in the strange bed and held her as she wept.

⎯⊖⎯

Maybe the bright, three-quarter moon was keeping him awake. . . .

He got up and looked through the French doors that gave onto the upstairs deck. A ribbon of platinum cascaded across the water. Only a mile and a half from Dove Cottage and they were in another world. A miraculous thing.

He closed the draperies over the doors, patted his sleeping dog at the foot of the bed, and lay down again.

He remembered the sleepless exhaustion that had helped crank his diabetes into high gear.

Hadn't Hoppy advised him to find a good doctor when he arrived? Of course. But had he done it? No way.

No more excuses, he promised himself. He would inquire around first thing tomorrow morning. And he must rid his mind of the lawsuit. It was useless to worry and fret about this alarming thing. He and Walter would do what they could; beyond that, he was dependent upon grace alone.

Be anxious for nothing . . .

He began to mentally recite one of the verses he'd tried to live by for a very long time.

. . . but in everything, with prayer and supplication, with thanksgiving, make your requests known unto God, and the peace that passes all understanding will fill your heart and mind through Christ Jesus.

"Ahhh," he sighed.

Jericho.

Not that again.

Lord, I'm no mind-reader. Reveal to me, please, what You're talking about here.

He tried to open his heart and mind to the answer, but dozed off and fell, at last, into a peaceful slumber.

⟨—◦—⟩

As twilight drew over the Sound, he heard the front bell ring and trotted to the door, wondering who'd be poking around out here.

He saw a car parked in the circle, and a woman standing at the foot of the steps. Before him on the stoop were two small persons in pirate costumes, and a very much smaller person clad in a sheet and extending a plastic pumpkin in his direction.

"Trick or treat!" said Jonathan Tolson.

⟨—◦—⟩

Feeling oddly distant from one another as they sat in the chairs that flanked the fireplace, they piled onto a sofa. "You know what I'm craving?" she asked.

"I can't begin to know."

"Your mother's pork roast with those lovely angel biscuits."

"My dear Kavanagh, who was it who refused to tote the Dutch oven on our journey into the unknown?"

"I was wrong and I admit it. Can't you make her roast without it?"

"I never have."

"Does that mean you never will?"

"A pork roast in that oven is a guaranteed, hands-down success. Why should I be tempted to veer off on some reckless tangent, like wrapping it in foil or roasting it on a pizza pan or whatever?"

"You're using your pulpit voice," she remonstrated.

"A thousand pardons," he said, getting up to fiddle with the dials on the home entertainment system and trying to make something, *anything,* happen.

"Julia Child didn't require a Dutch oven to make a pork roast," she said, arching one eyebrow.

"And how did you come by this arcane knowledge?"

"I looked it up in her cookbooks in our new kitchen."

"Well," he said, not knowing what else to say.

"Five pounds of flour . . . ," she murmured, making a list. Cynthia Kavanagh was bound and determined to have biscuits on her dinner plate, whate'er betide.

"Do we really want to buy flour, only to haul it back to Dove Cottage?"

"How long do you expect we'll be here?"

"They said the job will probably take three weeks, four at the most."

"Right. Now, double that prediction, thanks to lumber that doesn't arrive on time or is out of stock altogether, and for the crew who decides to go to another job for a whole week, and the rainy weather that makes the floor too tacky for us to move in for ten days, and . . . you get the idea."

"Two months," he said. "Buy the flour."

Cynthia saluted him with her glass. "Here's to Martha Talbot!"

"And here's to Miss Child, bless her heart!"

He wouldn't admit it, of course, but this was as toothsome a pork roast as a man could want, not to mention their first square meal at Sound Doctrine, the name they found engraved on a plaque at the door.

⟨⦵⟩

"Three guesses!" said Emma, munching what sounded like popcorn.

"Andrew won by a landslide!"

"Well, he won, all right, but not by a *landslide,* a lot of people who were born in Mitford voted for Coot. Anyway, guess what else."

"Just tell me and get it over with."

"No, you have to guess. Guess what's going to happen to Coot as soon as Andrew's sworn in."

"He'll be the envoy to our sister village of Mitford, England?"

"No, but I love the idea of a sister village! Somebody ought to recommend that to Andrew, he'd pick right up on it. Guess again."

"I give up." After one guess, she usually let him off the hook.

"Andrew's goin' to appoint him to chair a historical committee!"

What he'd always feared might be true, he now knew for a fact—in appointing Coot Hendrick to chair any committee at all, Andrew Gregory had proved to be a man of far greater largesse than himself.

⟨⦵⟩

He'd done his utmost to sever the umbilical cord that typically united a parish to a long-term priest, and felt it was at last a done deal. Indeed, he hadn't heard a word from Esther Bolick or anybody else at Lord's Chapel in a month of Sundays. So, the heck with his interim bishop and two-for-a-penny wisdom, he was calling the Bolicks.

"Esther?"

"Who's this?"

"How quickly you forget. It's your old priest."

"Father Hammond?"

"Esther!"

"Just kidding. How in th' world are you? We hadn't heard from you in a coon's age."

"Lots to do in a new parish, but I think about you and Gene and pray for you faithfully. How is he?"

"Better. I've tried to stop worryin' myself sick."

"I'm very glad to hear it. And you may be glad to hear that your fame now extends to Whitecap. In truth, I'm calling with a total of eleven requests for your marmalade cake recipe. I know you don't give it out, but they implored me to ask."

"Eleven?" He didn't know whether she was pleased with the number or disappointed.

"I'm sure as many more are interested, but I've personally received the names of eleven, including that of the Baptist preacher who's renowned for his lemon meringue pie."

"Oh, all right," she said, "I don't see why not. That recipe's been bootlegged forty ways for Sunday, anyhow."

"They'll be thrilled, and not only that, I'll be a hero."

"Cynthia has a copy I told her she could use. She can pass that around."

"Yes, but it's in Mitford. Do you think you could mail me a copy?"

"I declare, that recipe will pester me to my grave. But I'll do it. What's your address?"

"Just send it to St. John's, post office box fourteen." He gave her the zip code. "Bless you, Esther."

"Father Talbot moved into that big house up th'

street from the Harpers. He's th' handsomest thing you'd ever want to see, an' th' whitest teeth, oh, mercy. . . ."

He seemed to recall hearing this before.

"We think he bleaches, you know, wears what they call bleach trays, like people on TV."

"So, I'm glad to know Gene is—"

"And *nice*? You wouldn't want to *see* nicer! Crosses th' street to talk to you, waves at you from his car . . . not to mention has been to visit Gene on a house call, and he was just *installed* two days ago!"

"My goodness," he said, quoting Sam.

"And his children—why, they're meek as lambs and smart as whips, plus you should see his wife, she's a regular movie star. And *preach*? Up a *storm*! Why, he brings th' house down! We're goin' to tie his leg to the altar, is what Gene says. This one's too good to let get away."

"Ahhh," he said, exhaling.

～⊙～

He and Walter had talked for more than an hour, but he felt precious little consolation.

What should he do, if anything, about the rumor she was moving back to Boston? Didn't she owe him the courtesy of telling him she was leaving? On the other hand, what did courtesy have to do with anything—under the circumstances?

Walter suggested he lie low on that one, but go ahead and inform the Hope House board of the lawsuit.

He dreaded this like the plague, for more reasons than one. He would wait until after the weekend, when things were . . . calmer. At the moment, St. John's was under exterior scaffolding front to back, a Bobcat was digging out part of the basement, and a backhoe was on the job, doing God knows what. As anyone in their right mind could see, this was no time to call a board and relay bad news.

⟶⊙⟵

As he and Cynthia offered their nighttime prayers, he exhorted the Lord with something from "St. Patrick's Hymn at Evening."

" 'May our sleep be deep and soft,' " he whispered, " 'so our work be fresh and hard.' "

His wife, who was again going at her book hammer and tong, liked St. Patrick's way of putting it.

⟶⊙⟵

Nonetheless, he still wasn't sleeping soundly.

And he could scarcely believe what he felt God was writing upon his heart.

"You're sure about this?" he asked aloud, standing on the upstairs deck at sunset. A snowy egret flew over the roof and settled into the tall grasses at water's edge.

"I'd hate to get this wrong," he said.

Then again, if he got it wrong, what did he have to lose?

Nothing.

Nothing to lose, and everything to gain.

He spent much of Monday morning speaking with Hoppy Harper and other members of the board. They were shocked, of course. But he was glad he made the calls, because they were rallying together, and he felt the encouragement of it.

They agreed that it was a blow, but if the suit succeeded, they felt they could replace the money via other avenues.

He felt the encouragement, yes, but in the very pit of his stomach was a sick feeling that appeared to be lodged in for the long haul.

"Barnabas and I are going to walk around the old neighborhood, see what's what." Nine o'clock, now, and a meeting at ten with Sewell Joiner at the church. Perfect timing.

"And please do something about cleaning up the car," said Cynthia. "It looks like a farm wagon."

"Consider it done."

"I don't know what you *do* to cars," she muttered.

"We had a storm, remember?"

"But that was days ago, and the rust is going to leap onto the fenders any minute, mark my words."

"Rust . . ."

"It's a living thing, you know. It *grows.* Have you noticed the cars and trucks running around down here? There's hardly anything left but chassis and steering wheel."

"Surely you exaggerate."

"Surely I do, but please—washed and waxed and whatever else it needs; I must have it tomorrow to go up hill and down dale."

"Tomorrow's supposed to be a beautiful day, you could ride your Schwinn."

"Not if it's under Morris Love's stairwell."

"Good point," he said. "See you for lunch."

After checking the progress at Dove Cottage, he began his first march around the wall of Nouvelle

Chanson by walking east from the iron gate, hooking a left on Hastings, and praying as he went.

Staying hard by the wall, he trotted north on Hastings and rounded the corner into the lane that dead-ended in front of Ernie's.

He saw the figure up ahead, crossing the lane toward the Love wall. It was someone tall and slender, dark in color, and, though carrying what appeared to be a grocery bag in either arm, moving gracefully.

"Easy," he said to his dog, who was always curious about who and what crossed their path.

Though trying not to stare, he witnessed the sudden collapse of a paper bag, and saw items go spilling onto the sandy lane. Grapefruits rolled hither and yon.

He sprinted ahead.

"Here, let me help!" he said to the woman. "Barnabas, sit!"

Barnabas didn't sit; he reared on his hind legs so he might greet the stranger who stood looking at him with alarm. Grabbing his dog, Father Tim trotted to a small tree growing outside the wall and fastened the leash around it.

"There. I'm sorry. He's harmless." He went to his knees and began collecting grapefruits and bananas, sticks of butter that had burst loose from their package. . . .

"At least there were no eggs," he said, looking up at the elegant, dark-skinned woman who looked down upon him.

"Thank you kindly." Her voice was soft and lilting—genteel, he thought. "That's a big dog," she said simply.

"He is that. Well, now, what shall we put all this in?"

"I'll go back to the house and get my basket," she

said. "I almost never carry groceries without my basket, but this mornin' . . . if you'd watch this for me, I'd thank you."

"Be glad to," he said, taking the other bag from her arm.

She walked toward the house at the opposite side of the lane, a house he'd often noticed and admired for its tidy appearance and large, well-tended garden. He'd exchanged greetings with a man working the garden one summer evening, and had occasionally seen a wash hanging on the clothesline. In a world that seldom displayed its wash on a line, the sight always, and happily, took him back to his boyhood.

He stood guarding the small pile of groceries, organized neatly in the middle of the lane, as she left the house and came toward him carrying a large basket. He thought she moved regally for her age, though he couldn't really determine her age.

"Always, always, I use this basket," she said pleasantly, "and this mornin', wouldn't you know . . ."

Together, they stooped down and loaded the basket.

"May I carry it for you?" he asked.

"No, sir," she said, standing. "I'm just goin' right through there." She pointed to an opening in the thick hedge that camouflaged the wall.

"Ah. Morris Love's place."

"Yes, sir."

"You're Mamie," he said, noting her carefully braided hair and the printed scarf tied round like a headband.

"Yes, sir, I'm Mamie. And you're the preacher whose wife sent Mr. Love that nice banana bread."

"I am!" He was as excited as a child. "So pleased to meet you, Miss, Mrs. . . ."

"Just Mamie is all," she said.

"Sure I can't carry that for you? I'd be happy to."

"Thank you, I've been carrying this basket through there for more years than I care to reckon. Well, I hope you'll tell your wife that Mr. Love enjoyed the taste of lemon in her bread."

"Oh, I will. And thank you. Thank you!" A woman with a strong and lively spirit. . . .

Feeling strangely moved and oddly blessed he watched her disappear along a well-worn path through the opening in the wall.

⌖

He looked eagerly for her when he circled the wall on the second day, which was Wednesday, but she didn't appear. What he did see was a small wash, neatly arranged on the clothesline and flapping smartly in the November wind.

He received the welcome sight as a sign, a confirmation, and walked on, praying.

⌖

He timed his walk around the wall on Thursday for nine-fifteen, which was when they had met, but Mamie was nowhere to be seen. The sight of smoke puffing from her chimney gave him a curious delight, and he wondered why he had such a strong desire to see her again.

He trotted to the end of the lane and then, as he turned left around the wall, the answer came.

It was as if he'd found someone who'd been lost to him for many years.

⌖

"Timothy, ring Harley, he's at Lew Boyd's. I wrote the number by the phone."

"How's the book coming?" he called as he popped into his study at Sound Doctrine.

"Great! I've something to show you after dinner!"

It had taken his wife, who was surprisingly shy about her work, a good two years to open up and really share her work with him. So he was always pleased when . . .

"Lew! Tim Kavanagh here. How's it going?"

"Pretty good, soon as we git this wrecker rollin' again."

"Harley's the one for the job, all right. Is he around?"

"Hold on, and come see us, hear?"

He heard the cash register ring; Lew shouted for Harley; someone asked directions to the restroom.

"Harley speakin'."

"Harley! You called?"

"Yes, sir, I did. Let me get on Lew's cordless."

Static, shuffling around, a horn blowing.

"OK, I'm out at th' grease pit, cain't nobody hear."

He didn't want any bad news, no way. . . .

"Hit looks like I've found y'r angel that was stole."

CHAPTER TWENTY-ONE

True Confessions

"An' you'll not believe where at," said Harley.

"Where?"

"You know that ol' car of Miss Pringle's? Well, she brought it in to git th' fluids changed an' said she'd be travelin' in it pretty soon an' was wantin' it to be safe an' whatnot. Lew was up to th' post office so I said, fine, I'll look after it."

"Right, right."

"She walked up th' street an' I got t' checkin' it out, an' seen 'er tars needed rotatin'. See, I had 'er keys an' all, an' a little time t' do it, an' looked like she'd want me to, so I opened up 'er trunk and lifted that panel in there to see if I could find 'er wheel key. Well, see, they's this deep pocket, you might say, on either side under th' panel. I looked in one side an' th' key wadn't in there, an' they was what looked like a sheet stuffed in th' other side."

He was on the edge of his chair.

"So I pulled th' sheet out to look an' Lord help, there was that angel you had on y'r mantelpiece."

He would not jump to conclusions. "About twenty inches high?"

"Yes, sir. An' kind of a dirty gold."

Bronze. "What sort of base?"

"Marble, looked like."

"What color was the marble?"

"Green. An' since she hadn't asked me direct t' do anything but change th' fluids, I didn't do nothin' to 'er tars, or she might figure I found somethin'. When she come back, I jis' said, Miz Pringle, y'r tars need rotatin'."

He sat back in the chair and felt the beating of his heart.

⟐

He preferred acting to reacting.

If Hélène Pringle was leaving for Boston, he needed to act fast.

Certainly, he didn't want to focus on this nasty piece of news as he made his fourth trip around the wall. He wanted to keep his mind and heart free of personal anxiety, so he could pray with an unfettered spirit.

God help me, he thought, as he parked the Mustang at the side of Dove Cottage and set off for Hastings with his dog.

⟐

Ernie was standing in the parking lot with a couple of fishermen, and hailed him to come in. Without breaking stride, he raised his hand and waved. "I'll be back!" he called.

The glass had been replaced, the side wall was up, and except for some old bricks that hadn't been hauled away, Books, Bait & Tackle was looking fairly normal.

He was only a few yards this side of the passage in the wall when Mamie came through the front door of her house, carrying an empty wicker laundry basket.

"Good morning, Mamie!"

"Good mornin', Father. How do you like this weather?"

"Oh, I like it. Crisp!"

"My husband built us a good fire again this mornin'. They're calling for frost tomorrow."

As she stepped into the lane with him, he couldn't contain his question another moment. "May I ask where you were educated?"

"Virginia," she said softly. "Mr. Redmon sent me off to a school for young ladies of color. I was sixteen when I left Whitecap, and came home again when I was twenty."

"Ah," he said. Her gentle elegance was balm to his soul.

"Mr. Redmon had his enemies, but he wasn't a bad man, Father, not at all. He gave my mother this house."

"I like your house!" he said, meaning it.

"I remember when Mr. Morris was born, the year before I went to Virginia. I hated to leave him. He couldn't hold his head up 'til he was several months old and couldn't walk 'til he was two and a half. He was . . . special, something told me that."

"His mother . . . ?"

"His mother ran away from her baby. She could never bear to be with him. He had middle-ear infections for the first few years, and used to cry and cry with the pain. Mr. Redmon had all kind of doctors come here, and then Mr. Morris got the base of his skull operated on. There was no end to the suffering, it seemed. No, his mother ran away and stayed most of her life in Europe. Her and Mr. Redmon's other son died in a bad house fire. It was my own mother who took care of Mr. Morris 'til I came home and helped out."

"I see."

"I don't have any idea why I'm standing here talking to you like this, Father, except I believe you to be a kind man. I wouldn't want Mr. Morris to know we talked about such things."

"No, it's between us."

"I've spent many a year trying to help heal the hurt, but there's only One who can heal."

"Yes." He gazed directly into her eyes, finding a kind of refuge he couldn't name. "Morris is blessed to have you."

"I'm blessed to have him. I never dreamed I'd stay on in Whitecap after I saw a little of the world, but I came home and married a good man, and then, when the Lord took Mother . . ."

"Yes?"

". . . I began treading the path through the hedge, just as she'd done for so long."

"Are there any regrets, Mamie?"

"No regrets. Noah and I raised a fine son. He's a doctor in Philadelphia. He looks in on Mr. Morris every time he comes home."

He was happy to hear everything this unusual woman had to tell him, feeling honored, somehow, that she would talk with him at all.

"I see in your face that you understand Mr. Morris, how he's suffered."

He didn't reply. How could he understand?

"He's known a lot of cruelty in this life. Mr. Redmon demanded an awful lot of him. Yet, look at the gift he's been given. Mother was proud of that, and so am I."

"I hope to meet your husband one day. We said hello this summer. And if you ever take a notion to visit St. John's, we'd love to have you."

"Noah and I go across to church. There were never many people of color on Whitecap. Big Daddy Johnson used to take us across in a little fishing boat, then the ferry came, and then the bridge."

"Were you born here?"

"My people washed up on shore like timbers from the old ships. We think our wreck happened sometime around 1860."

"I've kept you far too long, Mamie, forgive me. You're an interesting and gracious lady, and it's a privilege to have this time together."

"I hated that Mr. Morris had nothing to offer when you and your family visited. The next day was grocery day, and what we had on hand, he couldn't heat in the oven."

"By His grace, we had a feast, and food for the soul, as well!"

"I hope we'll meet again," she said, stepping onto the path with her laundry basket.

"The Lord be with you!" he called after her.

She turned and looked back. " 'And with thy spirit!' " she said, quoting the prayer book. "That school I went to in Virginia was an Episcopal school." She smiled, then turned again and vanished along the path.

⌇

"You don't know when she's leaving?"

"No."

"Issue a search warrant for her arrest," said his cousin.

"*What?*"

"Immediately."

"But . . ." Hélène Pringle in *jail*? That meek little woman whose feet didn't touch the floor when she sat down?

"Call your local police chief, that guy you're such buddies with, and describe the angel. Tell him to search her car trunk. If it's not in the car, they'll search the house. You told me the angel has some value?"

"I'm guessing three, maybe even four thousand dollars."

"You can have her arrested for felonious larceny, not to mention felonious breaking and entering. That's a Class H on both counts. If she's convicted, we're talking up to ten years each count. Chances are, she'd get off with three years for each Class H, but for a piano teacher, that's a very long time."

He hung up, stricken over this sordid turn of events.

He and Cynthia would talk and pray about it tonight, and make the decision regarding a search warrant in the morning. He'd never had anyone arrested, and certainly not a woman, but was that the issue here? Wasn't the issue about money being wrongfully gouged out of the Hope House coffers? If it hadn't been for Miss Sadie's meticulous thrift and careful investing, there may not have been any money there at all. Didn't that count for something?

He realized he was once again sitting with his head in his hands.

Whatever the morning's outcome, he could not, would not, miss his fifth walk around the wall.

He called Rodney Underwood at home at eight a.m.

"Rodney, I have a disagreeable piece of business for you."

"I don't guess it's anything as big as th' man in th' attic; prob'ly won't ever get another deal like that." Rodney was talking about the jewel thief who lived in the attic at Lord's Chapel until he turned himself in to local authorities during a Sunday morning worship service.

"I'd like you to take a search warrant to the rectory. I have reason to believe my tenant stole the angel."

The spoken words chilled his blood. He was saying things that couldn't be taken back.

"Unknown to her, Harley Welch found the angel in the trunk of her car while it was at Lew Boyd's."

"You sure it's th' same one? Did he give you a good description?"

"Yes. About twenty inches high, bronze, green marble base."

"You lookin' to search just th' car or you think we ought to have a warrant for the house, too?"

"Both, to be safe."

"It takes a little while to process a search warrant, but I'll personally get right on it."

"What happens if you find the statue?"

"We'll take 'er into custody, take 'er over to th' magistrate in Wesley. He'll prob'ly put an investigative hold on 'er for about twelve hours 'til we get th' statute fingerprinted, get photographs an' all."

"The statue . . ."

"Right, th' statute."

He called Walter. "I didn't like doing it, but it's done."

"Good. When they have the angel in hand, let me know and I'll call her attorney."

In truth, he was only doing what was within the law, but he was literally nauseous over it. So was Cynthia. Oddly, taking legal steps against an unlawful act had made them both feel like criminals.

─── ᴐ ───

He didn't want to see Mamie or anyone else this morning. He put his head down and walked quickly, focusing his mind and spirit entirely upon Morris Love and the look on Morris's face as he was ordered from Nouvelle Chanson for what may have been the final time.

He would not exhort God this morning to heal, to bind up, or to transform. He would exhort Him only to bless.

He prayed silently.

Bless the gift You have given him, Lord, to be used to Your glory, bless his spirit which craves You and yet bids You not enter, bless the laughter that is surely there, laughter that has dwelled in him all these years, yearning to be released, longing to spring forth and be a blessing to others. . . .

The laughter of Morris Love—that would be a miracle, he thought, and remembered how he had prayed to hear Dooley Barlowe laugh. That prayer had been answered; he smiled to think of Dooley's riotous cackle.

Thank You for blessing Morris with a quick and lively mind, an inquisitive intellect, and a soul able to form majestic music which ardently glorifies the Giver. Thank You for blessing Morris with Mamie, who, out of all those offered the glad opportunity of loving him, was the only one who came forth to love and serve on Your behalf.

The tears were cold on his face.

Lord, bless him today as he sits at his keyboards, as he breaks bread with Mamie, as he looks out his window onto a world which betrayed him, and which he now betrays. As he lies down to sleep, bless him with Your holy peace. As he rises, bless him with hope. As he thinks, bless him with Your own high thoughts.

Now, Father, I bless You—and praise You and thank You for hearing my prayer, through Christ our Lord who was given to us that we might have new life, Amen.

He walked on.

"It's a done deal," said Rodney, not sounding quite like himself.

"How . . . did it go?"

"We found y'r angel in th' car, like you said, but your tenant broke down pretty bad. . . ." Rodney cleared his throat.

"Broke down?"

"Bawled like I never seen, wrung 'er hands. Me an' th' boys hated to do what we did."

"What did you do?"

"Took her over to th' magistrate an' they're holdin' her 'til everything's nailed down, fingerprints, reports, an' all."

"Then what?" he asked.

"Looks like th' charge'll be felonious breakin' an' enterin', felonious larceny, and felonious possession of stolen property."

He shook his head, hoping to clear it.

"Based on th' evidence, th' magistrate'll issue a warrant for her arrest, an' she'll have to post bond. In two, three weeks, she'll have to show up before a district judge, an' dependin' on how that goes, a grand jury will hear state's evidence which could land 'er in Superior Court."

"What if she leaves and goes to Boston?"

"She can go anywhere she wants to, long as she comes back to court."

"What if she doesn't?" He might as well know the worst-case scenario.

"They'll issue an order for 'er arrest, plus an order of forfeiture on th' bond."

"In other words, she wouldn't want to do that."
Hélène Pringle hunted and pursued . . .

"Nobody with a lick of sense would want to do that."

Enough. He couldn't go on with this, he was a basket case, let Walter deal with it.

$\backsim$

Before services at ten o'clock, he would walk around the wall for the sixth time, and on Monday, seven times consecutively. Then he would have accomplished the thing God had asked him to do.

"I'm a fool for Christ!" he said with St. Paul. Thank heaven nobody had a clue what he was doing; to the world, he was walking his dog, he was getting his exercise, he was increasing his heart rate.

$\backsim$

Sunday night on the Sound.

Not a bad life, he thought, sitting on the sofa and holding his wife's hand. He had at last figured out how to work the TV and which of the several remotes it required, and they were watching the Discovery Channel.

"Ugh," said his wife, as a lion bored its head into a carcass, "they're always eating each other."

"That's life," he said as the phone rang.

He muted the sounds of the African plain. "Hello!"

"Father Kavanagh?"

Hélène Pringle. "I am desperate to talk with you."

He thought his hand shook, holding the receiver. "I'd be eager to talk with you, as well, Miss Pringle."

"I cannot go on this way, with so much to confess, so much to make known, it is . . ." She paused. "It is agony."

He heard the great strain in her voice.

"I would give anything to speak with you face-to-face," she said, "but—"

"Just a moment, Miss Pringle." He put his hand over the mouthpiece, as his mind raced over the schedule here—a vestry meeting with Sewell Joiner, Sam would handle it, they could run to Mitford and get back home the morning of the Fall Fair. . . .

"Want to go to Mitford?" he asked his wife.

"Consider us packed!" she said, beaming.

He would walk seven times around the wall tomorrow, first thing—they could be in the car by ten o'clock, and in Mitford by eight on Monday evening. "Miss Pringle, we'll see you at the rectory Tuesday morning at eleven. Will that be convenient?"

Miss Pringle was weeping quietly and, he assumed, unable to speak.

"Take your time," he said. "My time is yours."

⟳

He was on his fourth lap when Mamie appeared suddenly on the path from Nouvelle Chanson, startling him.

"Ah, Mamie!"

She laughed easily, her breath making vapor on the air. "I'm just going over home to get mayonnaise. Mr.

Morris hardly ever touches it, but this mornin' he has a taste for a little mayonnaise on his grilled cheese."

This seemed to please her very much.

"Mamie, I wonder if I might get my wife's bicycle one day soon. I don't think Morris wants me to come fetch it personally."

Her eyes told him she understood. "I'll roll it down here for you anytime."

"I'll be back around this way in, say . . ."—three and a half laps to go—"twenty, thirty minutes? Would that be good?"

"Fine," she said. "Just fine."

"You could leave it there on the path, where no one can see it. I'd be grateful."

"I used to ride a bicycle—it was a pretty green color with a little bell. I loved my old bicycle."

"Borrow this one anytime," he said.

$\diagdown\!\!\!\!\!\bigcirc\!\!\!\!\!-$

As they drove into Mitford at eight-fifteen, he felt he was seeing it anew. Though cloaked in fog, the sights he expected to be so familiar seemed fresh and original, almost exotic to his eyes. Lights sparkled in shop windows, street lamps glowed in the heavy mist, the display window of Dora Pugh's Hardware was dressed with pumpkins and shocks of corn stalks.

"I love our town," said his wife, peering out like a kid. Barnabas had his nose flattened against the rear window; even Violet, standing in Cynthia's lap with her paws against the glass, was gazing intently at Main Street.

He realized he was grinning from ear to ear, but when he saw Fancy Skinner's pink neon sign above the Sweet Stuff Bakery, he laughed out loud.

⟋◯⟍

Once they got into the yellow house and turned on the lights and Harley delivered a pan of fudge brownies, it was too late to go visiting in Mitford. Puny, warned of their homecoming, had put roast chicken, potato salad, and tomato aspic in the refrigerator. They fell upon the meal like dock hands.

Afterward, they changed into what he'd been raised to call "nightclothes," and wandered around the house, seeing it all over again, claiming it with their eyes.

"Timothy!" exclaimed his wife. "Doesn't that picture look perfect over the sage-green vase?"

"You must have thought so when you put it there," he said, amused.

"I love our home, Timothy."

"As do I." He thumped down at his desk and idly looked through the drawers.

"What do you think she's going to say tomorrow?"

"I can't imagine, I don't know. I don't think she would have called if she didn't want to make peace. And she spoke of confession. . . ."

"I feel so sorry for Miss Pringle."

He glanced out the study window toward the rectory, where, through the hedge, he saw a light dimly burning in the kitchen.

"As do I," he repeated. "As do I."

⟋◯⟍

Lessons for the Piano, he read on the black and white sign placed in the grass by the front walk, *Inquire Within.*

⟋◯⟍

Hélène Pringle stood in the middle of the rectory living room and looked at him, red-eyed and plaintive. She was dressed simply in a longish dress and worn gray cardigan, and bereft of jewelry or any fanciful adornment. Her hair was swept back severely, as if she'd just dipped her comb in water, and pinned into a chignon.

"I can't tell you how sorry I am . . . and I beg your forgiveness."

He hated that she wrung her hands as she said this. "You are forgiven," he said, meaning it.

"Please sit, Father. I have a long story to relate to you. I pray you aren't in a hurry."

"I'm in no hurry at all." If he did nothing else on this trip, it would be fine with him. Looking around for Barbizon, but failing to spy the outsize mop, he sat in the chair, glad for the ease of it.

"I suppose I should offer you coffee or tea," she said, still standing.

"No, please, Miss Pringle, I have no want of anything. Thank you."

It hurt him, somehow, to witness her terrible anxiety. "Please," he said, smiling.

She sat on the sofa and gazed at her hands in her lap.

"Let me begin, then," she said, "at the beginning."

He was puzzled to realize he scarcely recognized this room, which had been part of his life for more than sixteen years.

"I have two very strong memories of my early childhood," she said, barely speaking above a whisper. "No one ever believed it possible for me to remember the first, for I was still an infant, lying in a pram. I had been rolled outside to the lawn and parked under a tree, and I remember so vividly the color of the leaves above me, almost . . . chartreuse, a delicate and tender shade of green

I've seen only once or twice since. I shall never forget the intricate lacework of the leaves, and the sparkle of that wondrous color as they danced in the breeze."

She looked up from gazing at her hands, and he suddenly recognized something vaguely familiar about Hélène Pringle, but he couldn't have said what it was.

"The other early impression that shall remain with me always was when *ma grandmère* looked down upon me as I lay in my little bed in her country home outside Barbizon. I was very sick, and later, as an adult, I thought the whole dreadful episode might have been a feverish dream, but it was not.

"I was perhaps three years old then. She was wearing her lace cap, and the points of the lace appeared to me like the jagged edges of broken glass. I saw every wrinkle in her face; she was suddenly terribly, terribly frightening to me, but I was mesmerized and could not look away. 'You,' she said, 'have no father. I hope you like that piece of news, *ma petite chère.*' Then she poked me in the chest with her finger, which had a long and hurtful nail, and I wept for the enormous fear I suddenly had of my grandmother, Hélène."

He'd never wanted the ability to feel the pain of others so keenly, but he had it, he had always had it, and there was no help for it. Perhaps it was just as well, for into this empathetic endowment had been lumped the ability to experience his own pain.

"I understand," he said.

She looked at him now with a certain steadiness in her gaze. "At the age of nineteen, my mother, Françoise, went up to Paris to live with her Tante Brigitte. Tante Brigitte was my grandfather's sister, and not a careful person in the least. She was altogether the wrong guardian for my beautiful and innocent mother.

"I think, Father, that aunts and uncles don't always take their roles as seriously as they might."

He saw traces of an old bitterness in her face as she spoke.

"I have always believed that Tante Brigitte conspired to introduce my mother to . . . to . . ." She looked at her hands again.

"Josiah Baxter?"

"Yes. He was a man of wealth, and old enough to be my mother's grandfather."

"Ah," he said.

"It grieves me more than you can know to tell you these things that have lain on my heart for so many years without being spoken."

She wept quietly, placing a handkerchief against her eyes and holding it there.

"*Pardon, j'en suis désolée!*" she said, at last. "I'm sorry to break down like this."

"Please don't be."

"Mr. Baxter . . . brought many expensive things to the apartment in Paris—paintings, sculpture, beautiful objects . . . my mother has memory of a little hand-carved chair with a needlepoint cushion . . ."

He had seen such a chair in Miss Sadie's bedroom; at the last minute of their negotiations at Fernbank, Andrew Gregory had bought it, along with numerous other pieces of furniture and table linens.

". . . and all those lovely things were shipped to his home in America. The men would come and crate them up, and away they would go across the water, to a place my mother would never know or see.

"I don't mean to imply that he never gave gifts to my mother. He gave her several fine pieces of jewelry which are long vanished, sold to help further my education. And he regularly gave money to Tante Brigitte for the household."

Something about her . . . so familiar . . .

"One day, Mr. Baxter . . ."

He noted that she spoke this name with difficulty, drawing a short breath before she said it.

". . . brought the angel to my mother. She told me that he said, 'Here, my dove, is something to watch over you in my absence.'

"Then he pulled a small key from his waistcoat and gave it to her. 'Unlock the little hiding place in the base of the angel,' he said. My mother examined the base very carefully, but could not find a way to insert a key. He took the key from her then, and turned the angel on its side . . ."

Hélène Pringle sat for a moment as if made of stone. He sensed that she had heard this story many times; her gaze did not take him in at all, but replayed before her eyes the movie she had made of her mother's memories.

". . . and slid out the bottom, which had appeared to be only a piece of felt to keep the statue from marring the furniture. Just inside the lip of the marble base was a very tiny keyhole."

"Ahh," he said.

"Mr. Baxter turned the little key in the hole and the bottom of the base, a thin slab of marble, was released into his hand. 'Now,' he told my mother, 'look inside.'

"She looked inside and found two pieces of paper, folded many times. 'Open this one first,' he told her, and she did. It was his will, written in his own hand and in French, though he spoke and wrote hardly any French at all. He had asked a Paris attorney to translate the wording into the language of my mother, and he had copied it in a very awkward and labored hand. It stated that upon his death he was bequeathing a third of his assets to my mother."

Hélène Pringle drew a deep breath and went on.

"In English, he wrote at the bottom, 'This is a codicil to my final will and testament, which is in the keeping of my solicitor, William Perry, of Philadelphia, Pennsylvania.' It was signed in his handwriting, and dated April 14, 1947. He told her he was traveling back to America with a copy for his solicitor.

"My mother said she felt a strange sort of joy and wonder, yet at the same time a fearful sense of dread. She then withdrew the other folded paper. It was . . . a love letter. I hope you might read it one day."

She sat with the handkerchief pressed to her eyes again, making no sound.

"Afterward," she continued, looking at him, "everything was placed back in the marble base, the key was turned in the lock, and the little slab with the felt bottom was put into place.

"Then Mr. Baxter slipped the key into the pocket of my mother's frock and said goodbye until his next visit, which he supposed would be in the summer, in July.

"That afternoon, the men came to crate the pieces he had bought for his home in America, and Tante Brigitte told them what was to be packed and what was to be untouched. Somehow, the angel was packed and taken away and put on the ship to America. . . ."

He saw the stricken look on her face, as if it happened only yesterday, or last week, and was as near to her in reality as this room in which she was sitting.

"Tante Brigitte sent a man to the docks to look for the crate, but the boat had gone."

She rose from the sofa and walked around the room, anxious and alarmed, then stood in front of the windows and drew the sheer panels apart and looked into the street.

He waited, sick with the weight of her distress.

She turned and came again to the sofa and sat down. "He never returned to Paris. You recall that the will was dated the day of his leave-taking, April 14, 1947. I was born December 12, 1947."

The room might have been contained in a timeless, noiseless bubble. He couldn't hear the ticking of a clock or a car moving in the street; he heard only the beating of his heart.

"When he did not come in July, my mother dispatched a letter to his lumberyard near Mitford, and heard nothing in reply. Several weeks after I was born, a letter was sent again. Two months later, it was returned to us unopened, and stamped *Addressee Deceased.*

"Tante Brigitte wrote a letter to the manager of Baxter Lumber Company, believing she could extort money somehow, and it, also, was returned, with *Out of Business* written on the envelope in longhand. Years later, I would pore over those returned envelopes, pondering the words *deceased* and *out of business,* and their tormenting finality.

"My family had lost all hope of any connection with my . . . with the American visitor to the little apartment in Paris.

"My aunt was not entirely poor, Father, but her means were limited, and there was no family friend or legal counsel to fall back upon. She sent my mother home to Barbizon with a seven-month-old child, to live with *ma grandmère.*"

There was a prolonged silence during which Hélène Pringle stared at the piano, as if it might contain an answer long sought.

"Perhaps to compensate for this terrible strait in the family affairs, Grandmère Hélène created a legacy of bitterness and hatred that I hope never to witness again in this life. Bitterness and hatred, Father, are contagious, did you know?"

"I know," he said.

"She infected my mother with this virulent acrimony, and I, too, became horribly contaminated by it. It was as if . . . as if a venomous liturgy were composed among us, and we recited it, day after day, religiously. It became to us larger than the real world. Our entire focus was upon the bitterness and anger felt toward my father and his money and his fine American home named Fernbank and his deceased wife whom he had called beautiful, and his much-adored Sadie and the fact that she had someone called China Mae to serve her and do her laundry and braid her hair.

"My grandmother would begin the recitation with the arrival of her breakfast tray, telling me how my mother never had *le courage, le cran, le culot,* to pursue the matter to its utmost and final outcome, to claim her portion, no matter what the effort, even if it meant going to America and seeking the thing that contained all our future prospects.

"My mother was once a very beautiful woman, but she sacrificed her beauty to bitterness and sorrow. Do you understand?"

"Yes," he said. "I've seen it happen that way."

"I was never . . . beautiful. I wonder how I could have been born to someone so lovely when I was . . ." She looked away.

"When you were what?" he asked.

"Short and plain, like my father."

Just plain Sadie . . . the thought came to him out of

the blue. It was the way Miss Sadie had often referred to herself. Just plain Sadie, whose feet, when she sat on the love seat at Fernbank, had never touched the floor. Of course. That was the familiar thing he had recognized in this lost and lonely woman who had come seeking what she believed to be her brightest hope.

"I developed an image of my father over the years, based upon my grandmother's view of his wicked and profligate conduct, his willful neglect of duty, and his great and selfish wealth. He became monstrous to me, yet I can't tell you how I longed to love him a little, if only a little, but I could not."

He didn't like the ashen look on her face.

"Would you care for some water, Miss Pringle?"

"*Non, merci.* But then, yes, that would be ——"

"I know just where it is," he said, sprinting toward the kitchen.

He realized he was shaking his head again, as if to clear it and make some sense of all he was hearing. His kitchen seemed strange to him, as if he'd never stepped foot in it before. *Lord,* he prayed, *may Your peace be upon this house. . . .*

He took a glass from the cabinet and ran the spigot for a moment and filled the glass and went along the hall to the rectory parlor. *And bless this woman in ways I can't think to ask. . . .*

"There," he said, as she drank it down. He took the glass from her as if he were a nursemaid and returned to his chair and sat again, holding it.

"Before my grandmother died fourteen years ago, she contended that a trip to Mitford would be a completely sensible thing to do. She believed the angel would be found sitting on someone's mantel, ripe for the picking."

"And so it was," he said gently.

"I determined that I would do this thing for my mother, who, by the way, married Albert Pringle and went to live in Boston about the time I finished college. They were married for seven years before he died of pneumonia. He was a lovely man. I took his name out of gratitude for his kindness. I think he helped relieve my mother of some of the anger. She became almost . . . almost kind again, and every so often, with Albert, I heard her laugh."

"Ahh."

"I always loved my mother, even when her malice removed her from me over and over again. A year ago, when our finances became so . . . strained, I promised her I would come to Mitford. I didn't tell her I would look for the angel, Father, I told her I would come to Mitford and find it."

"I admire confidence, Miss Pringle."

"I could not believe my good fortune when I discovered that you and Miss Sadie had been dear friends, and that your old rectory was for lease, right next door to your home. I believed then with all my heart that I'd been sent on a mission that would . . . would redeem all the hurt, somehow." She looked at her hands again.

"A mission?"

"Yes. I don't know much about God, Father, that is your forte, but I felt somehow that God had a hand in my coming here. I hope you don't think it's impertinent of me."

"No, Miss Pringle, not impertinent in the least."

"I suppose you wondered why I would bring my furnishings and set up a piano practice with only a six-month lease."

"That did cross my mind."

"I wanted . . . let me say that all my life since I was a young child, I've felt the need of a fresh start, a new beginning. I came here to find the angel, but very deep down, I also hoped I wouldn't find it. I came thinking that perhaps Mitford could be . . ." She sighed and shook her head slowly.

"But then, I've spent my life devoted to the desire for retribution—perhaps there are no new beginnings for someone like me."

"New beginnings are always possible," he said. "What of your mother? What are her circumstances?"

"My mother is in a nursing home outside Boston. Her mental faculties are keener than my own, but a series of health problems causes her to require care I cannot give. Albert left us a bit of money and I've gotten on rather well with my piano lessons, but . . ."

He saw the toll this was taking on her, that it would take on almost anyone to recite a legacy of suffering and loss.

"I'm sorry," she said, "I lost my point, somehow."

"Take a deep breath," he said. "Let's rest for a moment, shall we?"

"Rest?"

There! For one fragile instant, he thought he saw Miss Sadie in Hélène Pringle's face.

"Oh, no, Father, I can't rest until I've told you everything."

He nodded.

"I was very bold that day to look into your window. I stacked one cement block on top of another. Can you imagine my great joy and consternation when I peered into your lovely, sunlit room and spied the angel?"

He nodded.

"It was precisely where my grandmother contended

it would be found. I was dumbstruck. I hadn't realized I might have to . . . to thieve something that in a sense didn't belong to me, but which, in quite another sense altogether, was mine."

"Yes," he said. A conundrum if ever there was one.

"Perhaps I deceived myself that if I located it, I could buy it, or . . . I suppose I never thought it through. And so, I began to watch your housekeeper come and go, and one afternoon I saw that she failed to lock the door when she departed. At dusk, I slipped to your house and let myself in. I was as quiet as a breath, and it was all done very quickly.

"My good fortune was alarming, Father; to want something so terribly for so many years, and then . . . it was unthinkable! I began to believe that circumstances had been formed just for me, just for this moment, it was a sign that all I was doing was destined. I brought the angel here."

Relief flooded her face. She seemed immediately stronger as she openly confessed the theft to him.

"I drew all the shades and draperies, and placed it on my bed, where I used the little key to unlock the base, and there . . . there were the papers, never once disturbed for more than a half century. I wept like I had never wept before, to hold something of my father's in my hands. I read the letter, and in it, I found a tenderness of feeling which I'd never hoped he might possess. The letter opened its secrets before me like the petals of a flower, and I discovered my father's true affection—and his humanity. I know that his behavior was very wrong, but you see, for all his wrongdoing, I was able at last to love him a little."

Now he heard a clock ticking somewhere, perhaps in the hallway, as if the bubble had been pierced and life was flowing into them again.

"I sent the papers to my mother's attorney in Boston. I was fearful to have them copied, fearful of being seen using the Xerox machine at the post office, and knowing no other way to proceed, I sent the papers by registered mail to Monsieur d'Anjou. He encouraged me in this thing which others might deem merely a bizarre and frivolous gamble.

"After I sent the papers, I became frightened that the angel would be found here, and so I hid it in the trunk of my car.

"I express to you again my sorrow at having done something that grieved you and the trustees at Hope House."

"It is a cloud," he said, "with a silver lining."

"Do you really believe so?" she asked, anxious again.

"I can't know so, but I do believe so."

"Thank you," she said, looking at him directly. "I went up to Hope House before Monsieur d'Anjou served the lawsuit, and looked around. It is. . . . a wonderful place, the sort of place I wish for my mother."

"It was all Sadie Baxter's idea," he told her, "every bit of it, from the rooms overlooking the valley to the Scriptures over each doorway . . . the atrium, the fine medical help, the chaplain, all."

"I know the consequences of my actions, Father. I know that I can go to prison for what I have done. Nonetheless, I must tell you that I'm glad I did it. Very, very glad. I took something from you, yet I gained far more than the temporary possession of an angel on a marble base. There's a surprising sense, now, of owning something deeply precious—I don't yet understand what it is. But I know . . . it is in here." She placed her hand over her heart.

"I've grown to feel almost at home in Mitford. I've never known what it is to feel completely at home anywhere, but here, there's a solace I never found before. And so, I have gained even that."

Now it was he who got up and walked to the window and stood with his hands behind his back, peering without seeing through the sheer panels. It was hard to take it all in, to know what to do with all he had heard, but he knew this:

Something must be done with it. For Hélène Pringle; for Sadie Baxter, who, in heaven, would not be judging wrongdoing on anyone's part; and for himself; for his own peace of mind; and certainly for God, who may, indeed, have brought this woman to a crisis of renewal.

"Miss Pringle," he said, turning around, "I'm prepared to drop all charges against you. That may take some doing. I understand I'll have to meet with the district attorney, who may not take kindly to dropping the charges. But that is what I intend to do."

"Father," she said, standing. "I withdraw the lawsuit."

"Thank you," he said. "And the angel is yours."

"*Non! Ce ne serait pas juste!* That would not be fair. . . ."

"It is completely fair. It was the rightful and intended home for the letter and the will. They are all pieces of God's puzzle, and I believe the pieces must be kept together."

She stood by the sofa, awkward and moved; he wanted to go to her and give her a hug, but clergy had been historically advised to avoid such intimate contact, with no one looking on to approve.

"Well," he said, swallowing hard.

"Thank you, thank you, Father. *Mon Dieu, encore*

des larmes!" She retrieved the handkerchief from her cardigan pocket and pressed it again to her eyes.

"Miss Pringle," he said, taking a handkerchief from his own pocket, "we are a pair."

$\sim$

He walked across to the rectory before they left for Whitecap, and knocked on the door. He hardly recognized Hélène Pringle. She was holding her shoulders erect; she was looking him in the eye.

"May I have a moment?"

"Please!" she said, opening the door wide.

Aha. There was that blasted cat, curled on the sofa and staring him down. "I won't come in; I just wanted to give you something."

He handed her an ivory envelope.

"Whatever you find inside, please receive it in the spirit in which it is given. Promise me that."

She looked dubious for a moment, then smiled. "Well, then. I shall do it, Father!"

"Good. And Miss Pringle?"

"Yes?"

"We hope you'll stay on in Mitford."

"But . . ."

"I know it's too soon to say, but we trust you'll think about it."

Tears swam in her eyes. *"Oui,"* she said. *"Oui. J'y penserai."*

Passing from the rectory into the bright midday of Mitford, he looked again at the sign in the yard.

He thought it might as easily have read, *Lessons for the Heart, Inquire Within.*

CHAPTER TWENTY-TWO

A New Song

On the morning of the second Sunday of Easter, seven wild ponies trotted through the open gate of the corral near the lighthouse. Cropping grass with seeming contentment, they were spied by a jogger, who managed to close the rusting gate and then ran on, shouting the news along his route to whoever was up and stirring.

The marvelous sight drew Whitecappers of every age and disposition, all gleeful that the ponies from up Dorchester had escaped the government fence that ran into the Sound and, swimming around it, had struck out for Whitecap.

Penny and Marshall Duncan packed up their brood and drove the derelict Subaru to the corral, where they proffered a thank offering of hay and a large scoop of oats purloined from their lean-to barn. On Monday, the *Whitecap Reader* announced that the government would be coming to cart the ponies back where they belonged, so if anybody wanted to observe their brief homecoming, they'd better hop to it.

In the village, merchants prepared for the wave of

tourists that would wash over them only two or three weeks hence. They were eager to see an economy that had slowed to a trickle once again surge like the incoming tide: quite a few prices were discreetly raised and the annual flurry of stocking nearly empty shelves began.

The dress shop reordered Whitecap T-shirts printed variously with images of the lighthouse, the historic one-room schoolhouse moved from the Toe to the village green, and the much-photographed St. John's in the Grove; the grocery store manager decided to dramatically expand his usual volume of hush puppy mix, much favored by tourists renting units featuring a kitchen; and Whitecap Flix, the sixty-two-seat theater rehabbed from a bankrupt auto parts store and open from May 15 through October 1, voted to open with *Babe,* convinced it was old enough to bill as a classic. To demonstrate their confidence in the coming season, Flix scheduled a half-page ad to hit on May 15, and included a ten-percent-off coupon for people who could prove it was their birthday.

Hearing of the advertising boom coursing through the business community, Mona elected to run a quarter-page menu once a month for three months, something she'd never done before in her entire career. Plus, she was changing her menu, which always thrilled a paltry few and made the rest hopping mad. She figured to put a damper on any complaints by offering a Friday night all-you-can-eat dinner special of fried catfish for seven ninety-five, sure to pacify everybody. Due to space too small to cuss a cat, she had resisted all-you-can-eat deals ever since she opened in this location, since any all-you-can-eat, especially fried, was bad to back up a kitchen. All-you-can-eat was a two-edged sword, according to Ernie—who could not keep his trap shut about her business, no matter what—because while you could draw a crowd with it, in the end you were bound to lose money on it since people around here chowed down like mules. In the end, all-you-can-eat was what some outfits called a loss leader. Mona did not like the word "loss," it was not in her vocabulary, but she would try the catfish and see how it worked, mainly to draw attention from the fact there was no liver and onions on her new menu, nor would there ever be again in her lifetime, not to mention skillet cornbread which crowded up the oven, cooked cabbage which smelled to high heaven, and pinto beans. Lord knows, she couldn't do everything, this was not New York City, it was Whitecap, and though she'd been born and raised here, it was not where she cared to spend the rest of her life, she was investing money in a condo in Florida, even if Ernie had expressed the hope of retiring to Tennessee. Tennessee! The very thought gave her the shivers. All those log cabins, all those grizzlies stumbling around in the dark, plus moonshine out the kazoo . . . no way.

Sometime in April, a sign appeared in the window of Ernie's Books, Bait & Tackle:

> Buy Five Westerns
> Any Title, Get a
> Free Zane Grey
> or Louis L'Amour,
> Take Your Pick.

Hardly anyone going in and out of Mona's had ever read Zane Grey, though several had heard of him, and a breakfast regular seemed to remember L'Amour as a prizefighter from Kansas City. Two days after the sign went up, a potato chip rep dropped a hundred and eighty-seven bucks on the special offer and posted Ernie's phone number and address in a chat room devoted to the subject of Old West literature. In the space of eight working days, the book end of the business had blown the bait end in the ditch, and Ernie hired on a couple of high school kids to handle mail orders.

Roanoke Clark was painting one of the big summer houses, and had hired on a helper who, he was surprised to learn, stayed sober as a judge and worked like a horse. He pondered making this a permanent deal, if only for his partner's nearly new pair of telescoping ladders, not to mention late-model Ford truck, an arrangement that would prevent the necessity of renting Chess Doyle's rattletrap Chevy with a homemade flatbed, for which Chess dunned him a flat forty bucks a week.

In the Toc, Bragg's was busy pumping diesel and dispatching tons of gravel and cement to construction sites as far away as Williamston, not to mention an industrial park in Tyrrell County.

At the north end of the small island shaped like a Christmas stocking, St. John's in the Grove was at last divested of its scaffolding. The heavy equipment had vanished, the piles of scrap lumber and roofing had been hauled away, and the errant flapping of loose tarps was heard no more.

Behind this effort had come a parish-wide cleanup. Brooms, rakes, hoes, mattocks and shovels were toted in, along with fresh nursery stock to replace what had been damaged in the general upheaval.

During the windy, day-long workfest, someone discovered that the coreopsis was beginning to bloom, and Father Tim was heard to say that their little church looked ready to withstand another century with dignity and grace.

⎯⦿⎯

For months on end, winter weather had delayed work on the reconstruction. He was up to here with plaster dust, drilling, sanding, and sawing. No wonder some of his colleagues resisted the role of "building priest." It probably wasn't the fund-raising they detested, it was the actual putting up and hammering down.

Fortunately, they'd been able to save the old oak, and he was glad for the bonus of increased light that now shone on St. John's.

On a bitterly cold, but bright May morning, he unlocked the front door and stepped across the threshold into a new nave, yet with its old spirit still intact. He sat midway on the gospel side and looked around paternally.

A church, like any other home, had its own singular and individual spirit, and he'd grown to love the unique spirit of St. John's. At Lord's Chapel, he'd felt the bulk and weight of the river stone as a mighty fortress, a sure defense. St. John's, on the other hand, gave him the distinct sense of vulnerability and innocence; it seemed fragile, somehow, as indeed it had been.

Two Sundays hence, the parish would celebrate this glad rebirth with a dinner on the grounds and the first homecoming in more than thirty years. They wouldn't take the long tearing out and putting back for granted, not at all; they would observe it for what it was—a benediction of a high and precious order.

⎯⦿⎯

"St. John's in the Grove, Father Kavanagh here."

"Hey, Dad."

"Hey, yourself, buddy!"

"Me and Caroline broke up."

"Ahh. Too bad."

"I'm glad, though. You know what she did?"

"What?"

"Just ran up to me at th' dance and grabbed th' chain around my neck and yanked it so hard, it came apart, and she took her ring back."

"Good grief!" That sounded exactly like something Peggy Cramer might have done.

"Next time, I'm goin' out with somebody more like . . . like . . ."

"Like who?" *Lace Turner!*

"Like, you know, maybe Cynthia."

He could practically feel his chest expand. "Now you're talking!" he said.

"I really liked it down there at Christmas."

"It was great, and we're looking forward to spending the summer together."

"Me, too, and when are we goin' to talk about my Wrangler?"

"I've got Harley checking around for the best deal. We'll get back to you as soon as we find something."

"Not too old," said Dooley, meaning it.

"Right. Not too old. We're looking for mint condition, low mileage, so don't worry about it."

He wasn't going to worry about it, either. This summer, Dooley would be living at the beach with a sharp little ride and a job at Mona's. Father Tim felt the excitement of it as his own.

"So, tell me, why did Caroline do . . . what she did?" Dooley Barlowe seemed to bring out mighty strong feelings in the opposite sex. He remembered the time Lace Turner had nearly knocked Dooley's head off for stealing her hat.

"I don't know, it was weird. Somebody said I was supposed to be dancin' with Caroline, and that I forgot and talked the whole time to Lace, but that's not true, I hardly talked to Lace more than five minutes—I don't know, maybe fifteen."

"Aha. Well." *Well, well, well.*

$\sim$

He sat in his office, mildly addled by the persistent smell of fresh paint and new carpet, and struggled without success to keep his mind on his sermon outline.

Finding Jessie Barlowe had been a fluke, but finding Sammy and Kenny would take a miracle.

There was no way he could trace Kenny via the clues of "thinning hair" and "headed for Oregon."

As for Sammy, Buck had called to say that someone saw Sammy with the road crew who worked on the highway from Holding to New Hampton more than six years ago. The boy's father had once worked on that road crew; maybe Sammy had been taken by his father. It disturbed him that he might one day have to confront Dooley's father; it wasn't a pleasant thought at all, yet he couldn't shut it out of his mind. When they returned to Mitford, he would have to pursue this fragile thread, this vapor upon the air.

$\sim$

Before lunch, he went down his list of calls.

"If I was going to pass from a broken hip, I'd already have passed," said Ella Bridgewater.

"Absolutely!"

"I'm not ready to be carried down the road in a box just yet!"

"Amen!"

"I am going to the graveyard, though, to plant a little something on Mother's grave. We'll see how this hateful contraption works on gravel."

Ella Bridgewater hobbling down an isolated gravel lane on an aluminum walker? Wearing a long, black dress and toting a spade and a bush?

"I'll come up next week and go with you."

"Now, Father," she said, obviously pleased, "you don't have to do that!"

"I know I don't *have* to, which is another reason I'm happy to."

"You beat all!"

"Worse has been said," he told her.

⏤⚬⏤

"Louella!"

"Who that talkin'?"

"Father Kavanagh."

"Honey, how you doin'?"

"I can't complain. But how about you, how's the hip?"

"That hip ain't keepin' me down. This mornin' I rolled to th' kitchen an' made a pan of biscuits."

"Buttermilk?"

"Thass all I use."

"Wish I could have one." He sounded positively wistful. "With plenty of butter and . . . what kind of jam, do you think?"

"Huckleberry!" said Louella.

"Bingo!"

"When you an' Miss Cynthia comin' home?"

"I don't know. Maybe by the end of the year. Soon!"

"Not soon enough. We miss you aroun' here. I go an' pray with Miss Pattie, poor soul. Law, law, that Miss Pattie . . ."

"What's Miss Pattie done now?"

Louella gave forth with her rich, mezzo laughter.

"Miss Pattie have eyes for Mr. Berman, you know he's a mighty handsome man. Now she quit throwin' 'is clothes out th' window, she likes to wear 'is shoes,"

"How on earth does she get around in his shoes?"

"Oh, she in a chair, you know, like me; she can't walk a step. She put those shoes on, climb up in that buggy, an' off she go, pleased as punch."

"Aha."

"Mr. Berman is *sweet,* honey, he gave her a pair of alligator loafers, said to Nurse Lola, let 'er have 'em, a man can't wear but one pair of shoes, anyway. Ain't that nice?"

"I'll say!"

She sighed. "Not a soul to sing with up here."

He sighed. "Not a soul to sing with down here."

"You hit one and I'll join in," she said, chuckling.

He didn't think he'd ever sung four verses of anything over the phone before, but when he finished, he was definitely in improved spirits.

His wife set freshly made chicken salad before him, with a hot roll and steaming mug of tea. She stood holding his hand as he asked the blessing.

"What do you think of me coming home for lunch?" he asked. "I've known some who don't take kindly to husbands falling in to be fed." Might as well learn the truth, which his wife seemed generally enthusiastic to deliver.

"I love that you come home for lunch, Timothy, you're my main social contact now that I'm working so hard to finish the book." She set her own plate on the table and kissed the top of his head.

"How's it coming?"

"Peaks, valleys, highs, lows," she said, sitting down.

"Life," he said.

"Oh, gosh, that reminds me, I need the car this afternoon. I'm running over to the Sound to sketch a blue heron."

His wife needed live fodder, flesh and blood; no Polaroids for her, thank you—she was *plein air* all the way. Except for an occasional beach umbrella or background bush that might be lifted from memory, she went looking for the real thing. Violet, who was certainly the real thing, was the fourth or fifth white cat in an unbroken chain of actual Violets adopted by his wife over the years. He had, himself, been recruited to appear as a wise man in her book *The Mouse in the Manger.* He didn't think he'd looked very wise in her watercolor— more idiotic, truth be told—but she'd been pleased.

They'd once gone to the woods together, where he tried to enter her world of absorption as she fixed her gaze on lichen—but his mind had wandered like a free-range chicken, and he ended up thinking through a sermon based on Philippians four-thirteen.

"Oh, and after the Sound, I'm running by Janette's and taking the children out for ice cream."

"Good deal." He thought her eyes were as blue as wild chicory.

"By the way, just before you came in, Roger Templeton called. He said he didn't reach you at church."

"Aha."

"Wants you to give him a ring."

"Will do."

They ate quietly, the clock ticking over the stove.

"Timothy . . ."

"Yes?"

"Don't ever leave me."

Every so often, quite out of nowhere, she asked this plaintive thing, which shook and moved him. He put his fork down and took her hand. "I would never leave you. Never."

"Even when I'm old and covered with crow's-feet?"

"I love your crow's-feet, Kavanagh."

"I thought you once said I didn't have any crow's-feet." He was relieved to see her veer away from the fleeting sadness, and laugh.

"You've nailed me," he said, grinning.

He lifted her hand and kissed her palm and held it to his cheek. "You mean everything to me. How could I ever thank you for what you are, day and night, a gift, a gift. . . ."

She looked at him, smiling. "I love it when you talk like that, dearest. You may come home for lunch whenever you wish."

⎯⊙⎯

Roger met him at the church office on Wednesday morning, carrying a paper bag closed with a twist-tie, and looking bashful.

"Face your desk and close your eyes," said Roger.

Father Tim did as he was told, hearing the rustle of the paper bag being opened.

"Okay, you can turn around now."

The green-winged teal in Roger's outstretched hands looked him dead in the eye.

Newly painted in all its subtle and vibrant colors, he

found it beautiful, breathtaking, alive. He opened his mouth to speak, but found no words.

"It's yours," said Roger.

"You can't mean that."

"It's yours. It's been yours all along. I saw the look on your face when you watched what I was doing. I know that look; it's yours."

He took it reverently, moved and amazed.

"Turn it over," said Roger, flushing with pleasure.

He turned it over. On the flat bottom was burned the name of the island, today's date, and a message:

> *Green Winged Teal*
> *For Tim Kavanagh*
> *From Roger Templeton*
> *Fellows in a ship*

Clutching the prized possession in his left hand, he embraced Roger Templeton and pounded him on the back.

"Thank you," he said, just this side of croaking.

"I've only given away a few. Ernie has one, and my son and his wife, and . . ." Roger shrugged, awkward and self-conscious.

"I can't thank you enough, my friend. I'll treasure it more than you know."

He set it on his desk and gazed at it again, marveling.

A few months ago, he'd relinquished an angel; today, he'd been given a duck. He'd come out on the long end of the stick, and no two ways about it.

He stood in the sacristy, vested and waiting with the anxious choir, and the eager procession that extended all the way down the steps to the basement.

There was new music this morning, composed by the organist, something wondrous and not so easy to sing, and choir adrenaline was pumping like an oil derrick. Adding voltage to the electricity bouncing off the walls was the fact that the music required congregational response, always capable of injecting an element of surprise, if not downright dismay.

He peered through the glass panels of the sacristy door into the nave, able to see only the gospel side from this vantage point. He spied quite a few faces he'd never laid eyes on, given that today was Homecoming.

Some of the faithful remnant had been beaten to their pews by the homecomers, so he had to search for Otis and Marlene and the Duncan lineup, on the far right. Down front was Janette with Jonathan on her lap, flanked by Babette and Jason, *thank You, Lord.* And two rows back was Sew Joiner, gazing at the work on the walls and ceiling, and generally looking like he'd hung the moon.

At the sound of the steeple bell, the crucifer burst through the door and into the nave with her procession, the organ played its mighty opening notes, and the choir streamed forth as a rolling clap of thunder.

Carried along by the mighty roar and proclamation of the organ, the choir processed up the aisle with vigor.

> "*Sing to the Lord a new song*
> *And His praise from the ends of the earth*
> *Alleluia! Alleluia!*
> *You who go down to the sea, and all that is in it*
> *Alleluia! Alleluia!*"

The congregation joined in the first two alleluias as if waking from a long sleep; at the second pair, they

hunkered down and cranked into high gear, swept along
by the mighty lead of the choir.

> *"Let them give glory to the Lord*
> *And declare His praise in the coastlands*
> *Alleluia! Alleluia!"*

As the choir passed up the creaking steps to the loft,
the organ music soared in the little nave, enlarging it,
expanding it, until it might have been o'ercrossed by the
fan vaulting of an English cathedral.

Quickly taking their places by the organ, the choir
entered again into the fervent acclamations of Isaiah
and the psalmist.

> *"Sing to Him a new song*
> *Play skillfully with a loud and joyful sound*
> *Alleluia!*
> *For the work of the Lord is right*
> *Alleluia!*
> *And all His work is done in faithfulness!*
> *Alleluia!"*

A full minute of organ music concluded the first part
of the new work, celebrating God's grace to the people
of St. John's, and the joyful first homecoming in three
decades. Many of the congregants, marveling at the
music that poured forth from the loft, turned around in
their pews and looked up in wonderment.

> *"Alleluia! Alleluia!"*

In the ascending finale, which was sung a cappella, the soprano reached for the moon and, to the

priest's great joy and relief, claimed it for the kingdom.

~⊙~

"When trees and power lines crashed around you, when the very roof gave way above you, when light turned to darkness and water turned to dust, did you call on Him?

"When you called on Him, was He somewhere up there, or was He as near as your very breath?"

He stood in front of the pulpit this morning, looking into the faces of those whom God had given into his hand for this fleeting moment in time.

"What some believers still can't believe is that it is God's passion to be as near to us as our very breath.

"Far more than I want us to have a bigger crowd or a larger parish hall or a more ambitious budget . . . more than anything as your priest, I pray for each and every one of you to sense and know God's presence . . . as near as your breath.

"In short, it has been my prayer since we came here for you to have a personal, one-on-one, day-to-day relationship with Christ.

"I'm talking about something that goes beyond every Sunday service ever created or ever to be created, something you can depend on for the rest of your life, and then forever. I'm talking about the times you cry out in the storm that prevails against you, times when your heart and your flesh fail and you see no way out and no way in, when any prayer you utter to a God you may view as distant and disinterested seems to vanish into thin air.

"There are legions who believe in the existence of a cold and distant God, and on the occasions when they cry out to Him in utter despair and hear nothing in reply, must get up and stumble on, alone.

"Then there are those who know Him personally, who have found that when they cry out, there He is, as near as their breath—one-on-one, heart-to-heart, savior, Lord, partner, friend.

"Some have been in church all their lives and have never known this mighty, marvelous, and yet simple personal relationship. Others believe that while such a relationship may be possible, it's not for them—why would God want to bother with them, except from a very great distance? In reality, it is no bother to God at all. He wants this relationship far, far more than you and I want it, and I pray that you will ponder that marvelous truth.

"But who among us could ever deserve to have such a wondrous and altogether unimaginable thing as a close, personal, day-to-day relationship with Almighty God, creator of the universe?

"It seems unthinkable, and so . . . we are afraid to think it.

"For this fragile time in history, this tender and fleeting moment of our lives, I am your priest; God has called me to lead this flock. As I look out this morning, my heart has a wish list for you. For healed marriages, good jobs, the well-being and safety of your children; for Eleanor, knees that work; for Toby, ears that hear; for Jessie, good news from her son; for Phillip, good news from his doctor. On and on, there are fervent desires upon my heart for you. But chief among the hopes, the prayers, the petitions is this: *Lord . . . let my people know.* Let them know that the unthinkable is not only real, but available and possible and can be entered into, now, today—though we are, indeed, completely undeserving.

"It can be entered into today, with only a simple prayer that some think not sophisticated enough to bring them into the presence of God, not fancy enough to turn His face to theirs, not long enough, not high enough, not deep enough. . . .

"Yet, this simple prayer makes it possible for you to know Him not only as Savior and Lord, but as a friend. 'No longer do I call you servants,' He said to His followers in the Gospel of John, 'but friends.'

"In the storms of your life, do you long for the consolation of His nearness and His friendship? You can't imagine how He longs for the consolation of yours. It is unimaginable, isn't it, that He would want to be near us—frail as we are, weak as we are, and hopeless as we so often feel. God wants to be *with us*. That, in fact, is His name: Immanuel, God with us. And why is that so hard to imagine, when indeed, He made us for Himself? Please hear that this morning. The One who made us . . . made us for Himself.

"We're reminded in the Book of Revelation that He created all things—for His pleasure. Many of us believe that He created all things, but we forget the very best part—that He created us . . . *for His pleasure.*

"There are some of you who want to be done with seeking Him once a week, and crave, instead, to be with Him day after day, telling him everything, letting it all hang out, just thankful to have such a blessing in your life as a friend who will never, under any circumstances, leave you, and never remove His love from you. Amazing? Yes, it is. It is amazing.

"God knows who is longing to utter that simple prayer this morning. It is a matter between you and Him, and it is a prayer which will usher you into His presence, into life everlasting, and into the intimacy of a friendship in which He is as near . . . as your breath.

"Here's the way this wondrous prayer works—as you ask Him into your heart, He receives you into His. The heart of God! What a place to be, to reside for all eternity.

"As we bow our heads to pray under this new roof and inside these new walls, I ask that He graciously bless each and every one of us today . . . with new hearts."

He bowed his head and clasped his hands together and heard the beating of the blood in his temples. Ella Bridgewater, sitting next to the aisle with her walker handy, looked on approvingly. Captain Larkin, seated to her right, bowed his head in his hands.

"Sense, feel God's presence among us this morning . . ."

He waited.

". . . as those of you who are moved to do so, silently repeat this simple prayer:

"Thank You, God, for loving me . . .

". . . and for sending Your Son to die for my sins.

"I sincerely repent of my sins . . .

". . . and receive Jesus Christ as my personal savior.

"Now, as Your child . . .

". . . I turn my entire life over to You.

"Amen."

He raised his head, but didn't hurry on. Such a prayer was mighty, and, as in music, a rest stop was needed.

The recitation of the Nicene Creed was next in the order of service, and he opened his mouth to say so, but closed it again.

He looked to the epistle side and saw Mamie and

Noah; Mamie was smiling and nodding her head. Behind them were Junior Bryson and Misty Summers; he thought Junior's grin was appreciably wider than his tie.

"If you prayed that prayer and would join me at the altar, please come." He hadn't known he would say this; he had utterly surprised himself.

Some would be too shy to come, but that was God's business; he hoped he wouldn't forget and leave out the Creed altogether.

"If you'd like to renew your baptism vows in your heart, please come. If you'd like to express thanksgiving for all that God has fulfilled in your life, please come. If you'd like to make a new beginning, to surrender your life utterly into His care, please come."

Though this part of the service was entirely unplanned, he thought it might be a good time for a little music. His choir, however, was stricken as dumb as wash on a line.

From the epistle side, four people rose and left their pews and walked down the aisle.

On the gospel side, five parishioners and a homecomer stood from the various pews and, excusing themselves, stepped over the feet of several who were furiously embarrassed and looking for the door.

Father Tim opened a vial of oil, knelt for a moment on the sanctuary side of the rail, and prayed silently. One by one, the congregants dropped humbly to their knees, at least two looking stern but determined, others appearing glad of the opportunity to do this reckless thing, to surrender their hearts in an act of wild and holy abandon and begin again.

He dipped his right thumb in the oil and touched the forehead of the first at the rail, making the sign of the cross and saying, "I anoint you, Phillip, in the name of the Father, and of the Son, and of the Holy Spirit . . ."

In the choir loft, the organist rose from the bench, and walked stiffly down the stairs and along the center aisle with the aid of a cane.

Madeleine Duncan scrambled to her knees in the pew and whispered in her mother's ear, "Look, Mommy, it's a little tiny man with a big head."

Observing the penitent who now approached the altar, Leonard Lamb didn't realize he was staring with his mouth open, nor that tears suddenly sprang to his eyes.

Marion Fieldwalker poked Sam in the ribs. "Who's that?"

"Good gracious alive!" Sam whispered, as if to himself.

As Father Tim touched the forehead of the man kneeling before him, it seemed that an electric shock was born from the convergence of their flesh, it arced and flashed along his arm like a bolt.

"I anoint you, Morris, in the name of the Father, and of the Son, and of the Holy Spirit, and beseech the mercy of our Lord Jesus Christ to seal forever what is genuine in your heart. May God be with you always, my brother."

———

"The Lord drew me up
out of an horrible pit,
out of the miry clay,
Alleluia!
and set my feet upon a rock,
Alleluia!
steadying my steps and

> *establishing my goings,*
> *Alleluia!*
> *And he has put a new song*
> *in my mouth, a song of praise*
> *to our God!*
> *Alleluia! Alleluia! Amen!"*

***

" 'No one,' " he told Barnabas as they walked down the lane to the beach, " 'appreciates the very special genius of your conversation as the dog does.' "

His dog did not reply.

"Christopher Morley said that."

Barnabas plodded ahead.

"Don't you think there's a certain truth in it?"

What if someone heard him out here talking to his dog? Then again, why couldn't a man talk to his dog whenever he took the notion?

"Ah, my friend, what a sunset this is going to be." He felt positively jaunty, as if spring were luring something out of him that hadn't emerged in a very long while.

He'd asked his wife to come along, but she had a far more important and monumental thing to do than watch a spectacular sunset on a glorious evening; indeed, she was washing her hair.

He'd experienced this feeling of lightness only once before since coming here. It was the day he walked to Ernie's for the first time, free as a bird. Whole hours of freedom had lain before him in a strange new place with secrets yet to be revealed. Why couldn't all of life give one that feeling, the feeling of being on the brink of discovery? Wasn't every moment a revelation? Who ever knew, after all, what lay around the bend?

Ah, well, he'd probably be moping around like the rest of the common horde in a day or two. He'd better sop up this carefree business while he could.

He found himself whistling the organ piece from yesterday's service; difficult though it was, it contained an inner melodic line that he found thoroughly fascinating. What a miracle it had all been; he shook his head with the wonder of it, remembering the stunned delight of his congregation, and Mamie's soulful joy. Indeed, there had been enough gladness in the day to make memories for a month of Sundays.

They left the pavement and went along the boardwalk through the dunes. "Sit," he said, standing on the walk before they trotted down the steps. Watching the color begin to wash over the water, it suddenly occurred to him that St. John's should haul some chairs out here for an early Sunday service.

What a nave, what a sanctuary! And the ceiling beat any fan vaulting he'd ever laid eyes on, hands down. Why on earth they hadn't held this year's sunrise service right here was beyond him; he must be as dumb as a rock.

Well, then, maybe next year. If there was a next year. Very likely, St. John's would call their priest by winter.

They went down the steps and along the beach, not running, not jogging, but strolling. About a quarter of a mile into the walk, he let Barnabas off the leash.

That sunset is smokin', he thought, sitting on the sand to take off his shoes and socks. He remained sitting, looking, wondering.

It had been a joy to see Janette Tolson in church with her children yesterday, her life restored and settled. But it wasn't a joy to see the toll it was taking on her to go it alone, sewing until two in the morning, and rising early to get the children ready for school and Jonathan off to day care.

He dropped by to see her more often than he should, perhaps, but generally stayed only long enough to assure her of his prayers and encourage her in her work. Single parents were a dime a dozen in today's world. Such a thing rolled off the back of modern society like water off a duck; it had become the common run of so-called civilized life.

But it hadn't become common to him, not in the least. It always hurt him to see the damage and confusion and, too often, the utter desperation of those forced to go it alone. In short, it was a hard row to hoe, and fraught with unique assaults by the Enemy.

The last time he visited, she mustered the courage to ask again, "Have you seen him?" He hadn't, nor had anyone else, as far as he knew. "He could be dead," she said, looking across her sewing machine and out the window. "The storm . . ."

It was true. Nobody knew where he was living on the island, or in what sort of circumstances. If the ceiling plaster had narrowly missed Maude Proffitt, who was to say whether the storm had left its fatal mark elsewhere?

But hold on. He was doing the thing he had a made a resolution only yesterday to try to consciously avoid—he was thinking too much. "That young Timothy," an elder in his mother's church once said, "he thinks too much."

He never forgot that offhand remark, though he couldn't have been more than seven or eight years old. How much thinking was too much, he had wondered, and who was to say? Should he quit thinking anything at all once in a while, and go around with an empty mind? He tried to empty his mind and found it completely impossible to do. Or maybe other people could empty their minds and he was the only one who could not. This was disturbing. On the other hand, were there people who thought too little? As an adult, he occasionally considered that he might know a few. . . .

He whistled for his dog, who bounded out of the surf and stood before him, shaking salt water forty ways from Sunday.

"Sit," he said. Barnabas sat.

He remembered the time when the only thing he could get his dog to do was eat. It was years before he sat when asked, or came when called. Old age, that's what it was. Old age and wisdom! If Barnabas had been, say, two years old when he came to the rectory—and that was seven years ago—then in dog years he was . . . sixty-three. About the same age as his master. OK, then, it wasn't old age at all, no indeed, it was merely wisdom.

So thinking, he got up and ran down the beach, his dog loping beside him.

⌀

They had turned into the lane when Barnabas stopped and growled low in his throat.

It was dark now; a single street lamp burned just up the road. He saw that someone approached them, thrown into silhouette by the light.

"Who is it?" he asked. "Who's there?"

"Father Kavanagh?"

He recognized the voice at once. "Yes."

"I'm sorry to startle you." Though the figure walked closer, Barnabas stopped growling. In fact, his tail was wagging.

The white shirt gleamed like a pearl. "I've been hoping we could talk."

"I've been hoping that, too."

"If you have time."

Father Tim reached out, extending his hand into the darkness. "My time," he said, "is yours.

Visit America's favorite small town—
one book at a time

Welcome to the next book,

In This Mountain

CHAPTER ONE

Go and Tell

Moles again!

Father Tim Kavanagh stood on the front steps of the yellow house and looked with dismay at the mounds of raw earth disgorged upon his frozen March grass.

Holes pocked the lawn, causing it to resemble a lunar surface; berms of dirt crisscrossed the yard like stone walls viewed from an Irish hilltop.

He glanced across the driveway to the rectory, once his home and now his rental property, where the pesky *Talpidae* were entertaining themselves in precisely the same fashion. Indeed, they had nearly uprooted Hélène Pringle's modest sign, *Lessons for the Piano, Inquire Within;* it slanted drunkenly to the right.

Year after year, he'd tried his hand at mole-removal remedies, but the varmints had one-upped him repeatedly; in truth, they appeared to relish coming back for more, and in greater numbers.

He walked into the yard and gave the nearest mound a swift kick. Blast moles to the other side of the moon, and leave it to him to have a wife who wanted them caught in traps and carted to the country where they might frolic in a meadow among buttercups and blue-bells.

And who was to do the catching and carting? Yours truly.

He went inside to his study and called the Hard to Beat Hardware in Wesley, believing since childhood that hardware stores somehow had the answers to life's more vexing problems.

"Voles!" exclaimed the hardware man. "What most people've got is voles, they just think they're moles!"

"Aha."

"What voles do is eat th' roots of your plants, chow down on your bulbs an' all. Have your bulbs bloomed th' last few years?"

"Why, yes. Yes, they have."

The hardware man sighed. "So maybe it is moles. Well, they're in there for the grubs, you know, what you have to do is kill th' grubs."

"I was thinking more about ah, taking out the moles."

"Cain't do that n'more, state law."

Even the government had jumped on the bandwagon for moles, demonstrating yet again what government had come to in this country. "So. How do you get rid of grubs?"

"Poison."

"I see."

" 'Course, some say don't use it if you got dogs and cats. You got dogs and cats?"

"We do."

He called Dora Pugh at the hardware on Main Street.

"Whirligigs," said Dora. "You know, those little

wooden propellerlike things on a stick, Ol' Man Mueller used to make 'em? They come painted an' all, to look like ducks an' geese an' whatnot. When th' wind blows, their wings fly around, that's th' propellers, and th' commotion sends sound waves down their tunnels and chases 'em out. But you have to use a good many whirligigs."

He didn't think his wife would like their lawn studded with whirligigs.

"Plus, there's somethin' that works on batt'ries, that you stick in th' ground. Only thing is, I'd have to order it special, which takes six weeks, an' by then . . ."

". . . they'd probably be gone, anyway."

"Right," said Dora, clamping the phone between her left ear and shoulder while bagging seed corn.

He queried Percy Mosely, longtime proprietor of the Main Street Grill. "What can you do to get rid of moles?"

Percy labeled this a dumb question. "Catch 'em by th' tail an bite their heads off is what I do."

On his way to the post office, he met Gene Bolick leaving the annual sale on boiled wool items at the Irish Woolen Shop. Gene's brain tumor, inoperable because of its location near the brain stem, had caused him to teeter as he walked, a sight Father Tim did not relish seeing in his old friend and parishioner.

"Look here!" Gene held up a parcel. "Cardigan sweater with leather buttons, fifty percent off, and another twenty percent today only. Better get in there while th' gettin's good."

"No, thanks, the Busy Fingers crowd in Whitecap knitted me a cardigan that will outlast the Sphinx. Tell me, buddy—do you know anything about getting rid of moles?"

"Moles? My daddy always hollered in their holes and they took off every whichaway."

"What did he say when he hollered?"

Gene cleared his throat, tilted toward Father Tim's right ear, and repeated the short, but fervent, litany.

"My goodness!" said the earnest gardener, blushing to the very roots of what hair he had left.

&

He heard the receiver being crushed against the capacious bosom of his bishop's secretary, and a muffled conversation. He thought it appealingly quaint not to be put on hold and have his ear blasted with music he didn't want to hear in the first place.

"Timothy! A blessed Easter to you!"

"And to you, Stuart!"

"I was thinking of you only this morning."

"Whatever for? Some interim pulpit assignment in outer Mongolia?"

"No, just thinking that we haven't had a really decent chinwag in, good heavens, since before you went down to Whitecap."

"An eon, to be precise." Well, a couple of years, anyway.

"Come and have lunch with me," suggested his bishop, sounding . . . sounding what? Pensive? Wistful?

"I'll do it!" he said, decidedly spontaneous after last Sunday's Easter celebration. "I've been meaning to come for a visit, there's something I'd like us to talk over. I may have a crate of moles that must be taken to the country. I can release them on my way to you."

"A crate of . . . moles."

"Yes." He didn't want to discuss it further.

But he couldn't catch the blasted things. He prodded their tunnels with sticks, a burlap sack at the ready; he shouted into their burrows, repeating what Gene had recommended, though in a low voice; he blew his honorary Mitford Reds coach's whistle; he stomped on the ground like thunder.

"I give up," he told his wife, teeth chattering from the cold.

He noted the streak of blue watercolor on her chin, a sure sign she was working on her current children's book starring Violet, the real-life white cat who usually resided atop their refrigerator.

"But you just started!"

"Started? I've been working at it a full half hour."

"Ten minutes max," Cynthia said. "I watched you, and I must say I never heard of getting rid of moles by shouting down their tunnels."

He pulled his gloves off his frozen hands and sat on a kitchen stool, disgusted. His dog sprawled at his feet and yawned.

"I mean, what were you *saying* when you shouted?"

He had no intention of telling her. "If you still want them caught and crated up, you do the catching and crating, and I'll haul them to the country. A fair division of labor." He was sick of the whole business.

Cynthia glared at him as if she were his fifth-grade teacher and he a dunce on the stool. "Why don't you just stop fretting over it, Timothy? Let them have their day!"

Have their day! That was the artistic temperament for you. "But they're ruining the lawn I've slaved over for years, the lawn you dreamed of, longed for, indeed craved, so that you might walk on it barefoot—and I quote—'as upon a bolt of unfurled velvet.' "

"Oh, for heaven's sake, did I say such a silly thing?" He rolled his eyes.

"Timothy, you know that if you simply turn your head for a while, the humps will go down, the holes will fill in, and by May or June, the lawn will be just fine."

She was right, of course, but that wasn't the point.

"I love you bunches," she said cheerily, trotting down the hall to her studio.

❦

He pulled on his running clothes with the eagerness of a kid yanked from bed on the day of a test he hadn't studied for.

Exercise was good medicine for diabetes, but he didn't have to like it. In truth, he wondered why he didn't enjoy running anymore. He'd once enjoyed it immensely.

"Peaks and valleys," he muttered. His biannual checkup was just around the bend, and he was going to walk into Hoppy Harper's office looking good.

❦

As the Lord's Chapel bells tolled noon, he was high-tailing it to the Main Street Grill, where a birthday lunch for J. C. Hogan would be held in the rear booth.

Flying out the door of Happy Endings Bookstore, he hooked a left and crashed into someone, full force.

Edith Mallory staggered backward, regained her balance, and gave him a look that made his blood run cold.

"Edith! I'm terribly sorry."

"Why don't you watch where you're going?" She jerked the broad collar of a dark mink coat more securely around her face. "Clergy," she said with evident distaste. "They're always preoccupied with lofty thoughts, aren't they?"

Not waiting for an answer, she swept past him into Happy Endings, where the bell jingled wildly on the door.

～

" 'Er High Muckety Muck traipsed by a minute ago," said Percy Mosely, wiping off the table of the rear booth.

Father Tim noted that the slur of her perfume had been left on his clothes. "I just ran into her."

"I'd like t' run into 'er . . . ," said the Grill owner, "with a eighteen-wheeler."

If there was anyone in town who disliked Edith Mallory more than himself, it was Percy Mosely, who, a few years ago, had nearly lost his business to Edith's underhanded landlord tactics. It was clergy, namely yours truly, who had brought her nefarious ambitions to utter ruin. Thus, if there was anyone in town whom Edith Mallory could be presumed to despise more than Tim Kavanagh, he didn't have a clue who it might be.

"Ever' time I think I've seen th' last of that witch on a broom, back she comes like a dog to 'is vomit."

"Cool it, Percy, your blood pressure . . ."

"An' Ed Coffey still drivin' 'er around in that Lincoln like th' Queen of England, he ought t' be ashamed of his sorry self, he's brought disgrace on th' whole Coffey line."

J. C. Hogan, *Muse* editor and Grill regular, slammed his overstuffed briefcase into the booth and slid in. "You'll never guess what's hit Main Street."

Percy looked fierce. "Don't even mention 'er name in my place."

"Joe Ivey and Fancy Skinner are locked in a price war." J.C. pulled a large handkerchief from his hip pocket and wiped his face.

"A price war?" asked Father Tim.

"Head to head, you might say. Fancy had this big sign painted and put in her window upstairs, said, *Haircuts Twelve Dollars, All Welcome.* First thing you know, Joe puts a sign downstairs, says, *Haircuts Eleven Dollars.*"

Joe Ivey's one-chair barbershop was located in a former storage room behind the kitchen of his sister's Sweet Stuff Bakery. The only other game in town was Fancy Skinner's unisex hair salon, A Cut Above, which rented the upstairs area over the bakery. "Poetic irony," is what one Grill customer called the arrangement.

"So Fancy cranks her price down to ten bucks and has her sign repainted. Then Joe drops his price, changes his sign, and gives me an ad that says, 'Haircuts nine-fifty. Free chocolate chip cookie to every customer.'"

"Cutthroat," said Percy.

"I don't know where this'll end," said J.C., "but if you need a haircut, now's the time."

"Happy birthday!" Father Tim thought they should get to the point.

"Right. Happy birthday!" said Percy. "You can be one of th' first to order offa my new menu."

J.C. scowled. "I was used to the old menu."

"This is my an' Velma's last year in this hole-in-th'-wall, I wanted to go out with a bang." Percy stepped to the counter and proudly removed three menus on which the ink was scarcely dry and handed them around. He thought the Wesley printer had come up with a great idea for this new batch—the cover showed the Grill motto set in green letters that were sort of swirling up, like steam, from a coffee mug: *Eat here once and you'll be a regular.*

"Where's Mule at?" asked Percy.

"Beats me," said Father Tim. "Probably getting a haircut."

"So how old are you?" Percy wanted to know.

J.C. grinned. "Fourteen goin' on fifteen is what Adele says."

"Gag me with a forklift," said Mule, skidding into the booth. "He's fifty-six big ones, I know because I saw his driver's license when he wrote a check at Shoe Barn."

"OK, give me your order and hop to it, Velma's havin' a perm down at Fancy's and I'm shorthanded. Free coffee in this booth, today only."

"I don't want coffee," said Mule. "I was thinkin' more like sweet ice tea."

"Coffee's free, tea's another deal."

J.C. opened his menu, looking grim. "You spelled *potato* wrong!" he announced.

"Where at?" asked Percy.

"Right here where it says 'tuna croissant with potatoe chips.' There's no *e* in *potato*."

"Since when?"

"Since ever."

Look who's talking, thought Father Tim.

"I'll be darned," said Mule. "Taco salad! Can you sell taco salad in this town?"

"Taco salad," muttered Percy, writing on his order pad.

"Wait a minute, I didn't say I *wanted* taco salad, I was just discussin' it."

"I don't have time for discussin'," said Percy. "I got a lunch crowd comin' in."

Father Tim noticed Percy's face was turning beet-red. Blood pressure, the stress of a new menu . . .

"So what is a taco salad, anyway?" asked Mule.

The *Muse* editor looked up in amazement. "Have you been livin' under a *rock?* Taco salad is salad in a taco, for Pete's sake."

"No, it ain't," said Percy. "It's salad in a bowl with taco chips scattered on top."

Mule sank back in the booth, looking depressed. "I'll have what I been havin' before th' new menu, a grilled pimiento cheese on white bread, hold th' mayo."

"Do you see anything on this menu sayin' pimiento cheese? On this menu, we don't *have* pimiento cheese, we ain't goin' to *get* pimiento cheese, and that's th' *end* of it." The proprietor stomped away, looking disgusted.

"You made him mad," said J.C., wiping his face with his handkerchief.

"How can a man make a livin' without pimiento cheese on his menu?" Mule asked.

" 'Less you want to run down to th' tea shop and sit with th' women, there's nowhere else to eat lunch in this town . . ."—J.C. poked the menu—"so you better pick something offa here. How about a fish burger? Lookit, 'four ounces breaded and deep-fried haddock filet served on a grilled bun with lettuce, tomato, and tartar sauce.' "

"I don't like tartar sauce."

Father Tim thought he might slide to the floor and lie prostrate. "I'm having the chef's salad!" he announced, hoping to set an example.

Mule looked relieved. "Fine, that's what I'll have." He drummed his fingers on the table. "On the other hand, you never know what's in a chef's salad when you deal with this chef."

"I'm havin' th' tuna melt," said J.C., "plus th' fish burger and potato skins!"

"Help yourself," said Mule. "Have whatever you want, it's on us." He peered intently at the menu. "'Chili crowned with tortilla chips and cheese,' that might be good."

"Here he comes, make up your mind," snapped J.C.

"I'll have th' chili deal," said Mule, declining eye contact with Percy. "But only if it comes without beans."

Percy gave him a stony look. "How can you have chili without beans? That's like a cheeseburger without cheese."

"Right," said J.C. "Or a BLT without bacon."

Father Tim closed his eyes as if in prayer, feeling his blood sugar plummet into his loafers.

❧

So what are you doing these days?

It was a casual and altogether harmless question, the sort of thing anyone might inquire of the retired. But he hated it. And now, on the heels of the very same question asked only yesterday by a former parishioner . . .

"So what'n th' dickens do you do all day?"

Mule had left to show a house, J.C. had trudged upstairs to work on Monday's layout, and Percy stood beside the rear booth, squinting at him as if he were a beetle on a pin.

After nearly four years of retirement, why hadn't he been able to formulate a pat answer? He usually reported that he supplied various churches here and there, which was true, of course, but it sounded lame. Indeed, he once said, without thinking, "Oh, nothing much." Upon hearing such foolishness out of his mouth, he felt covered with shame.

In his opinion, God hadn't put anyone on earth to do "nothing much." Thus, in the first year following his interim at Whitecap, he'd given endless hours to the Wesley Children's Hospital, second only to the church as his favorite charitable institution. He had even agreed to do something he roundly despised: raise funds. To his amazement, he had actually raised some.

He'd also worked on the lawns of the rectory and the yellow house until people had been known to slow their cars and stare. Occasionally, a total stranger would park at the curb and ask if they could take a picture.

During the second year, he'd given a hand to their new mayor, Andrew Gregory, and supplied pulpits in Wesley, Holding, Charlotte, Asheville, Morganton, Johnson City, and, for a span of several months, Hickory. Somehow, it had been enough. Almost.

He was never unaware that something was gnawing at him, he couldn't say what. Perhaps it was nothing more or less than his masculine ego needing a good-size feeding; in any case, there was a certain restlessness in his spirit, something of feeling unworthy and not quite up to things anymore.

His wife suggested they go to the Dordogne, or even Africa, and he tried to get excited about traveling to faraway places, but couldn't.

In the end, why beat around the bush? A church! That's what he needed. He was homesick for his own flock to feed, to herd around. Occasionally he even missed typing a pew bulletin, though he would never have confided such a peculiarity to another living soul.

Why had he retired, anyway? He might have stayed on at Lord's Chapel 'til the cows came home. When he finally severed that comfortable connection, he was hugely up for freedom and adventure, yet now he wondered what he could have been thinking.

Sometime during the winter, a compelling thought had occurred to him, something for which he and Cynthia had since been seeking God's wisdom. Not knowing exactly how to press forward with such a notion, he decided to discuss it with Stuart. That would help settle things.

In the meantime, he'd begun doing what any self-respecting retired clergyman ought to do: He was writing a book, notably a book of essays that he'd begun on the first day of the new year.

The only problem with this was, he couldn't tell anyone about it.

Percy leaned into the booth and squinted down at him, knitting his brows. Father Tim could practically feel his hot breath. "So do you lay up in th' bed of a mornin'—or *what*?"

Percy wouldn't know an essay if he met it on the street; thus he found himself reporting a list of activities so monumental in length that Percy yawned in his face. Later, he wished he hadn't included the part about cleaning mildew off his old shoes and organizing his socks by color. He also felt that his confession of cooking *and* washing up most evenings was a little over the top—in fact, certain to be fodder for idle gossip from one end of Main Street to the other.

Another thing that dogged him was the uneasy suspicion that writing essays was an indulgent and egocentric thing to do. For that reason, he considered changing horses in midstream and writing his memoirs.

Didn't memoirs have a certain cachet these days? In some circles, they were a positive rage. However, he couldn't imagine saying to anyone, *I'm writing my memoirs.* Writing about one's life presumed that one had a life worth writing about. And, of course, he did, but only since marrying his next-door neighbor at the age of sixty-two. Now, *that* was memoir.

But no, he wasn't a memoir man; when push came to shove, he was an essay man. He had longed, rather childishly, to reveal his secret to someone; after all, he was more than ninety pages along and very much liking the momentum he'd gained.

When Mule didn't show up for breakfast the following morning due to a treadmill test at the hospital, Father Tim impulsively decided to reveal his personal tidbit to J. C. Hogan, who was as close to literati as Mitford was likely to produce in this lifetime.

"Say that again," said J.C., cupping his ear as if he'd misunderstood.

"Essays!" he repeated, suddenly feeling like a perfect idiot. "I'm . . . ah, writing a book of essays."

The *Muse* editor had a blank look as he forked a sausage link. "I've read a couple of essays," he said, shoving the sausage into his mouth and following it with half a buttered biscuit. "Doo fimmity glogalong. Doo muss ahtoo."

Father Tim sighed. "That's one way of looking at it."

"So," said J.C., "what kind of business do you think Edith Mallory will bring in here when Percy retires?"

"Heaven only knows. It's anybody's guess."

"I could go for a shoe repair," said J.C., coaxing the last of the grape jam from the container. "Or a dry cleaner. I'm over goin' all th' way to Wesley to get my pants pressed."

"You wouldn't have to get 'em pressed if you'd quit hangin' 'em on th' floor," said Percy. Percy had visited the editor's bachelor quarters prior to his marriage to Adele and had been thunderstruck.

No matter how hard he tried, Father Tim couldn't imagine meeting J.C. and Mule at the tea shop. It just wouldn't be the same. Besides, Percy had declared he wouldn't be caught dead in the place, which was wallpapered in lavender forget-me-nots with matching ruffled curtains.

"Percy!" J.C. yelled in the direction of the grill, "who d'you think Godzilla will move in here when you retire?"

Percy looked disgusted. "A pet shop is what Ron Malcolm said was comin'." The very *thought* of that smell blasting out onto Main Street was enough to make a man throw up his gizzard.

"No way!" said J.C. "People in Mitford don't get pets at a pet shop. They wait 'til somethin' shows up at their back door. Idn't that right?" he asked Father Tim, who, after all, should know.

～

" 'O Lord, You are my portion and my cup . . . ,' " he recited in unison with Cynthia and the other congregants at St. Paul's in Wesley. " 'It is You who uphold my lot. My boundaries enclose a pleasant land; indeed, I have a goodly heritage. I will bless the Lord Who gives me counsel; my heart teaches me, night after night. I have set the Lord always before me; because He is at my right hand I shall not fall.' "

Cynthia slipped her arm around him as they shared the Psalter. " 'My heart, therefore, is glad, and my spirit rejoices; my body also shall rest in hope. For You will not abandon me to the grave, nor let Your holy one see the Pit.'

" 'You will show me the path of life; in Your presence there is fullness of joy, and in Your right hand are pleasures for evermore.' "

His heart felt warmed by the familiar words, words he had memorized—when? How long ago? Had he been ten years old, or twelve?

He looked upon his wife and was moved by a great tenderness in his breast. The boy who had recited those words before a hushed Sunday School class in Holly Springs, Mississippi—what a miracle that he was standing now in this place in Wesley, North Carolina, more than half a century later, feeling the arm of his wife about his waist and knowing a fullness of joy he'd never believed he might experience.

~

Stuart Cullen didn't appear to be a venerable and much-esteemed bishop. Indeed, at the age of seventy-one, he looked like a man who had just come in from tossing around a football on a back lot.

Father Tim felt oddly proud that his bishop and best friend from seminary looked young and vigorous and entirely without airs; it was a sight to make a man puff out his chest, hold in his stomach, and step smartly into the room where Stuart looked up from the antique walnut desk and smiled.

"My friend!" Stuart exclaimed.

They met in the middle of the room and embraced, the bishop feeling fond of his longtime favorite priest, the priest feeling glad he'd never had the ambition to rise to the top, though he knew perfectly well that's where the cream resided in the jug. In truth, he was glad someone else was willing to shoulder the staggering weight of higher church life and leave him in peace.

"You look terrific!" said Father Tim, meaning it.

"And old," Stuart said.

"Old? What is old? Old is a matter of—"

Stuart chuckled. "Now, Timothy, don't preach me a sermon. Have a seat."

He had one, amused to see that he and Stuart were dressed almost identically, both of them wearing khakis, a sport shirt, and a collar. "Gold Dust twins," he said, indicating their gear.

"Except you're not old, Timothy."

"What is this business about being old? I'm creaking in the joints like a hay wagon."

"I always liked your rustic imagery," said Stuart.

"Too much Wordsworth at an early age," replied Father Tim.

"Speaking of rustic, did you drop your moles off in the country?"

"A failed mission," he admitted. "We never caught any to drop off."

"I despise moles. Or is it voles? And what's the difference, anyway?"

"You don't need to know," said Father Tim. "Now tell me what's up. You're looking quizzical. Or perhaps philosophical."

Stuart sat in a leather wing chair opposite his retired priest and gazed out the window to the garden that his wife cultivated and he puttered in. A pink dogwood in early bloom trembled in a gusting wind. He turned his gaze on his visitor.

"I want to build a cathedral."

"Ahhh." Father Tim reflected a moment on this striking pronouncement. "Building cathedrals isn't a job for the aged."

"Thinking about it has made me face my mortality;

it strikes me that I may never live to see it finished. In truth, considering the funds we'll need to raise and the time it will take to raise them, I may not be around for the groundbreaking, much less the dedication. We're not going to borrow a cent, you see."

"Well, then, we may both be dead and gone."

"I'll be seventy-two in eleven months, at which time, as you know, they'll chase me off with a broom. I've always regretted our strict retirement policy. I've never felt better in my life. Why should I be forced to retire at seventy-two?"

"Beats me," said Father Tim.

"In any case, I'm getting a very late start on a cathedral!"

"If you don't mind the platitude, it's never too late."

"I also wonder whether this notion is merely a self-serving desire for immortality, some . . . strut of the flesh."

They pondered this together, quietly. The clock on the mantel ticked. "Do you think," asked Father Tim, "that the desire for immortality was the driving force behind Michelangelo's *David* or da Vinci's *Mona Lisa*?"

The bishop crossed his legs and appeared to gaze at the toe of his shoe.

"Or behind, shall we say, Handel's *Messiah*?"

"I don't pretend to know what's behind much of anything we humans do. There are days when it seems that everything we do is for unutterably selfish reasons, then come the days on the mountaintop when we're able to know the galvanizing truth all over again, which is that we earnestly seek to do it all to the glory of God."

"What has God said to you about this thing?"

"Quite a lot. Actually, I think it's His notion entirely. I'm clever enough, I suppose, but not quite so clever to drum up the . . . particulars of this idea. I must confess that when it all came to me, I wept."

"Then it has nothing to do with seeing your name chiseled over the door? St. Stuart's on the Hill?"

Stuart laughed. Ah, but Father Tim liked hearing his bishop laugh!

Stuart's secretary opened the door and poked her head into the room. "I'm off to lunch. I don't suppose the two of you need anything?"

"Only a bit of humility, seasoned with patience and fortitude," said the bishop.

"On whole wheat or rye?" asked his secretary, closing the door.

"Some of us," said Stuart, "are interested in initiating only what we'll see come to fruition, but I've always looked beyond the present, beyond the day, a propensity that's both a blessing and a curse."

"Niebuhr spoke to that," said Father Tim.

"Indeed. He said, 'Nothing that is worth doing can be achieved in our lifetime; therefore we must be saved by hope. Nothing which is true or beautiful or good makes complete sense in any immediate context of history; therefore we must be saved by faith.' "

" 'Nothing we do, however virtuous,' " quoted Father Tim, " 'can be accomplished alone; therefore, we must be saved by love.' "

Stuart leaned forward slightly in the chair. "I have enemies, you know."

Father Tim didn't say it, but he did know, of course.

"As you're aware, ours is the poorest of the southeastern dioceses. So far, the idea of a cathedral has been largely dismissed as flamboyant, self-seeking, a display of spiritual pride, and a flagrant waste of money which could be used for higher purposes."

"And that's just for openers, I'm sure."

"The diocese exists in a culture in which a cathedral smacks of European decadence, though the Baptists down the road just built a church to seat two thousand and nothing was thought of it, nothing at all."

"Where will the cathedral be built?" asked Father Tim, looking on the bright side.

Stuart rose from the chair, grinning, and buttoned his jacket. "Come. I'll show you on our way to lunch."

"This is a cow pasture, Stuart!" He knew for a fact that he'd just stepped in something.

"Ah, Timothy, open your eyes! A cow pasture, yes, but one that slopes down to a magnificent view of the city! Look where we're standing, for heaven's sake! It's a habitation for angels!"

The wind swept words from their mouths; their coats billowed and flapped like sails.

". . . transept," yelled Stuart, pointing toward the brow of the hill. ". . . cruciform!" he shouted, waving with outstretched arms. Though it was nearly impossible to distinguish what Stuart was saying, his bishop's countenance spoke volumes; he was as radiant as the youth Father Tim remembered all those years ago in seminary.

They hurried back to the car, swept along by the chill wind at their backs.

"So here are the particulars," said Stuart, forgetting to put the key in the ignition. "We'll build our cathedral of logs."

"Logs."

"Yes! Honest materials straight from our own highland forests, with scissor trusses of southern yellow pine, a roof of hand-split shakes, oak pews constructed by local artisans. . . . I can't tell you how this excites me, Timothy! *Plus* . . ."

His bishop had a positive gleam in his eye.

"Plus, such materials are exceedingly cost-wise!"

"Aha."

"We think we can do it for six million," said Stuart. "A pittance, all things considered. At last we'll have what we've needed for so many years—a common meeting place for our scattered diocese, a center of learning, and one day, I trust, a great choir school."

The bishop started the car and they rolled slowly down the hill along the tree-lined street. "Pray for me in this," he said quietly.

"I've been praying for you more than forty years, my friend."

"Don't stop now. You know, of course, that you are faithfully in my prayers, and ever will be."

"Yes," said Father Tim. "And I'm grateful."

"But I've talked too much about my own interests. Forgive me, Timothy. Tell me what brought you today, what's on your heart."

The discussion of a great cathedral was a tough act to follow, but there was hardly a beat between the question and his answer.

"The mission field."

Stuart winced visibly. "You're not keeping busy enough, retirement generally gives too much time to think."

"Don't talk down to me, Stuart." He hadn't treated Stuart's dream lightly, and he didn't take kindly to having his own casually dismissed.

"You're right, of course."

"This is important to me, and to Cynthia. Besides, the commission is to go and tell, not sit home and fossilize."

"I reacted that way because you're diabetic. You don't need to be stumbling around in some bleak outpost with no medical assistance."

"I take two insulin shots a day, monitor my sugar closely, eat at regular intervals, exercise twice a week—it's no big deal. Actually, my doctor would forbid a bleak outpost; we won't go far from home."

"Any idea where?"

"Somewhere in Appalachia," he said. "It's where the Dooley Barlowes and Lace Harpers come from."

"Who is Lace Harper?"

"An exceptional young woman who's the adopted daughter of my doctor and his wife, off to her first year of college this fall. It wasn't long ago that she was living in the dirt under her house."

"Whatever for?"

"To escape a drunken father who beat her senseless."

"Dear Lord."

"Until the Harpers took her in, she was almost completely self-educated, thanks to the county bookmobile. Now she's one of the brightest stars her private school has ever seen. We're exceedingly fond of Lace, we cherish the notion that someday she and Dooley might . . . well, you understand."

"I see. And your boy, Dooley, he's doing well, isn't he?"

"A freshman at the University of Georgia, where he'll study veterinary medicine. If you recall, Dooley's the son of an abusive father he scarcely knew, and of a formerly alcoholic mother who gave her children away.

Pauline has since come to know Christ and has married a believer; the transformation is wondrous. All this is to say I've seen what a difference it can make for kids like Dooley and Lace to be given a break, to be loved. In truth, it makes all the difference!"

Stuart braked, waiting to turn left, and looked at his old friend. "An English missionary said, 'Some want to live within the sound of Church and Chapel bell; I want to run a rescue shop within a yard of hell.' You have my blessing." Of all his clergy, Timothy Kavanagh had been the one he could depend on completely, the one whose theology never wavered and whose friendship genuinely counted.

"I'll need your help, Stuart, your input about the ministries we should consider."

The bishop wheeled into the restaurant parking lot and switched off the ignition. He looked at Father Tim and nodded his assent. "You'll have that, too," he promised.

The last book in the
Mitford Series is coming
from Viking in Fall 2005

Light from
Heaven

ISBN 0-670-03453-3

Want more Father Tim?
Consider it done.

THE FATHER TIM NOVELS
A new series by Jan Karon
Coming 2007

VIKING